Seven Score and Four

By

Dave Spiering

This book is a work of fiction. Places, events, and situations in this story are purely fictional. Any resemblance to actual persons, living or dead, is coincidental.

© 2003 by Dave Spiering. All rights reserved.

No part of this book may be reproduced, stored in a retrieval system, or transmitted by any means, electronic, mechanical, photocopying, recording, or otherwise, without written permission from the author.

ISBN: 1-4107-4588-0 (e-book)
ISBN: 1-4107-4586-4 (Paperback)
ISBN: 1-4107-4587-2 (Dust Jacket)

Library of Congress Control Number: 2003094486

This book is printed on acid free paper.

Printed in the United States of America
Bloomington, IN

About the Book

Seven score and four years ago our nation was gripped in a titanic debate over rights, liberties, and national destiny. The rights of one class or race of people to deprive another of liberty and exploit or enslave them was the most noteworthy of these. Other issues that came to bear in the struggle were state rights, private endeavors and public concerns, economics, tariffs and regional rivalries. All together, they would result in the most traumatic war in American history. The guiding light on both sides was a moral and legal Judeo-Christian foundation.

This war resulted in a balance between liberty and rights that set the course of American freedom for most of a century. This balance has now been redefined, as also the moral and legal foundation rewritten. The Judeo-Christian standard was banished to the trash heap of history to be replaced by secular humanism.

Rights and liberty now are freed from a standard of fixed absolutes. Truth today is defined on a sliding scale of popular opinion based on situations and not set standards of right and wrong. And this new standard permeates every corner of American life. A redefined right of atheism abridges Christian liberty and expression. The removal of religions display from schools and public cites is only one example of this.

A woman's liberty to reproductive freedom usurps the unborn's right to life. But her freedom of action is restricted in the rights of government to dictate everything from seat belts to tobacco. Property ownership is the right of all, but again, the government restricts liberty on its usage. The list is endless.

But this redefinition extends to history as well. The past is being rewritten to fit this modern standard. If truth is relative, so history itself is not exempt from revision. In fairness, this book gives the modernist a fair opportunity to do so.

iv

Chapter 1

That the ground moved on Thursday, January 20, 2005 was an understatement of incredible magnitude. That its aftershocks would be felt spanning more than a century was a stunning reality. Or maybe it is reality itself that was shaken, as our human perceptions of past, present, and future were at the epicenter of upheaval.

At 1:30 AM Pacific Time, an earthquake registering 9.1 on the Richter scale devastated Seattle. The last one of such magnitude was believed by many to have occurred on January 26, 1700, long before cities and civilization existed as we know it. This one not only hit a civilized world, it also confronted a failed government policy. More directly, it underlined the ineptitude of the Bush Administration.

For years, scientists had been working on earthquake prediction. In the years since 2000, technology gave hopes of profound breakthroughs, but budget restraints prevented greater progress. But even so, scientists had been able to give a 10 per cent chance of an earthquake during the decade. Bush's efforts to upgrade civil defense, building codes, and infrastructure improvements had been feeble at best. The result was nearly 850 deaths, and devastation of unprecedented dimensions.

Psychics had also been busy over the year before this day. This was the year of the second moon cycle since the 1967 Age of Aquarius had begun. Those who read what the spirits told them had predicted this to be an earth shattering day. They just didn't know that part of this would be literal. But they had seen images of the demise of their greatest nemesis, the Christians.

And the second great event of the day did nothing to dampen those predictions. Tom Daschle was inaugurated as America's 44th President, culminating a picture perfect campaign. He had been drafted by his party after no other candidate seemed able to break the convention deadlock. His heroic strategy to stifle Bush policies and put two additional moderates on the Supreme Court made him a party super star. That he was from the small state of South Dakota was not an issue. He had been greatly aided by the gay community, women's groups, and proponents of genetic and cloning research. Environmentalists, minority activists, and the non-Christian religions provided massive financial and volunteer support. But his greatest assistance was from the news media. All the major TV networks, CBS, ABC, NBC, and CNN actively promoted him as the progressive moderate with the answers to our problems. Associated Press, United Press International, and other organizations played their part as well. Because of the wisdom of the Shays-Meehan campaign finance reform, opponents were effectively silenced. Anyone foolish enough to break the law and address his stand on the issues in the two months before the election was already in prison. The same rules gave him 302 of 435 in the House of Representatives and a total of 58 Democrat Senators. His running mate, Dianne Feinstein became the first woman Vice President. Even her California Senate seat had been saved for the party.

But both these events could not match the significance of an announcement by UCLA scientists. That day they had successfully tested a time machine. Journeying back to 2001, a computer and several animals had returned unharmed after a three hour visit.

Worm hole travel had been theorized by physicists for years, but now was a reality. There were limits. Travel could only be done into the past. There were, also, some yet unexplained features as well. Objects traveling through time had to stay in a narrow 200,000 mile distance in relation to the sun. It also made the object arrive at the same time of day. Leaving at Noon on January 20, 2005 it had arrived at Noon on January 20, 2001. Leaving 2001 at 3:00 PM, it arrived at 3:00 PM in 2005.

But it was not immediately affected by our travel through the galaxy. Investigations could not explain why. Later experiments would show, though, that travel beyond 200 years was affected by this, and become impossible. Small details, though to elated scientists and ambitious social engineers who now could go where only science fiction had ever tried before. And the failed, feeble voices of the obsolete past, George Bush Jr. could not stop it from happening. A score of far sighted corporate donors had made it happen.

Earthquake survivors were among the first to see the benefits of time travel. For nearly 3,000 fractured and thousands of other wounded families, it could provide immediate healing. To go back and leave town before it hit, or even to have never lived there, now such choices were becoming reality. In the months ahead, the potential for rewriting history would become legion. Preventing disasters, assassinations, or even wars was possible.

Lewis Pasteur once said that "chance favor only a prepared mind". In the 21st Century, America had blossomed into the glorious liberty of a post Christian civilization. No longer did the moral shackles it imposed bind her. Humankind now redefined the family, human values, even life itself to meet the needs of an enlightened and brave new age. No outmoded scruples would prevent the prudent use of this incredible advancement.

Politically, all of the pieces were in place to make theory into policy. The Supreme Court now had seven moderates and only two right wing reactionaries from a bygone era, Clarence Thomas and Sandra O'Connor. David Souter was now Chief Justice, and Ruth Beder-Ginsburg and Stephen Breyer were his two closest associates. Virtually every regional circuit court of appeals judge now was moderate as well. Thanks to eight years of Bill Clinton's Presidency, and four years of Daschle's Senate heroics in blocking Bush's radical right-wingers this was reality. Right wing judges that still remained were being challenged, and often impeached.

The Democratic control of the White House and Congress also mirrored the new values system of the people. For the first time in history, a major political party viewed Christianity as a social evil and a threat to the nation. George Bush Jr. was a "Don Quixote" attacking windmills of social and moral reform while the countrie's security and economy were imperiled.

Security concerns were paramount. After a decade of domestic terrorism, from Timothy McVeigh and Terry Nichols in Oklahoma to the refinery attack in October of 2004, it was the national priority. Everyone had concluded that much of it, including the 9-11 attack on the World Trade Center was preventable. All that would have been needed was a little more surveillance, a little more monitoring of personal lives, a little more governmental control. America was more than ready to trade a little liberty for security, something those of a Christian persuasion could not understand or accept. Bush's anemic homeland security was expanded.

The Democrats and news media did fully understand this issue. To rely upon God or a god for security was an archaic concept from a superstitious past. The government must take responsibility for the health, security, and welfare of the people. House Leader Nancy Pelosi and Senate Leader Barbara Boxer promised quick action in all areas.

By March, 2005, bills were sent to Daschle to provide for even greater security. All weapon owners were required to submit to a background check that included association with potential radical groups. This included fundamentalist Christians. Firearms, regardless of age, would be profiled by ballistics fingerprinting. Owning more than three would require a special annual license. In addition, any chemical or materials that could be used to make bombs, ammunition, or other weapons were monitored. To get around the 42 Republicans in the Senate, the vote was taken in an emergency meeting room at the Pentagon and only 22 of the Republican Senators cleared security for that meeting. Daschle immediately signed this into law.

A month later loopholes were discovered and tightened. To prevent driver's license fraud, genetic fingerprinting of all drivers became law. License plates were fitted with a location device to enable the tracking of any vehicle at any time. Within 18 months all vehicles would be required to have a genetic I.D. ignition lock to prevent anyone but authorized drivers from operating them.

Campaign finance was also further reformed. In one senate race, Kit Bond, Republican from Missouri, private individuals had worked together to circumvent the law. Each one, in time and money, had "individually" gotten the word out on him and his opponent's record in such a way to get Bond re-elected. This was now made illegal. Also, victims of prior discrimination and abuse, gays, minority advocacy, environmental, women's issues should be allowed to be excluded from the law. Again, Daschle signed this into law.

As the year progressed, a number of social issues were also addressed and past injustices corrected. The Gay community was given full civil rights. This included marriage, insurance, and Social Security survival benefits. Most importantly it ended religious discrimination. No longer could churches bar gays and lesbians from membership or leadership positions based on their orientation. This also was true for practicing alcoholics, adulterers, drug addicts, or any other group. No church doctrine could condemn these groups, or speak against their lifestyles. It was time for the church to learn and practice a little tolerance and love. Churches and ministers would also be required to be licensed and accept governmental approval of their functions.

Other laws addressed the family. Spanking and other acts of violence or coercion of children were prohibited. Child health and education were protected. Home schooling was now illegal. Proper diet and physical activity were mandated. Parents of overweight children could face stiff penalties and loss of their liberties. Smoking in any place children frequented, or lived, was prohibited. So was compelling a child to attend religious services or training.

As 2006 dawned, even more far reaching civil rights policies were enacted. All victims of past abuse, either as a race or class, or as individuals were entitled to reparations for their injuries. Blacks, Indians, and other minority groups would receive a negotiated cash settlement for past discrimination. Churches, gun groups and owners, and anti-abortion groups were subject to lawsuits. They also were subject to a tax to help pay for their past sins. Even individuals who were in leadership positions of those groups could be sued by victims of past crime, abuse, or discrimination.

By 2006 the earthquake survivors had been able to put their lives pretty much back together. Many had relocated, others were rebuilding in Seattle. Both U.S. Senators, Patty Murray and Maria Contwell were grateful for the way Washington DC had responded to the emergency. But the tragic memory of the event could not be erased from much of the Northwest.

While the "Time Machine" technology was still both, top secret and in its experimental stage, Seattle was raising tremendous pressure for its use. If a team of credible leaders could be sent back to Seattle, 850 lives and, at least, some property could be saved. The only drawback was that "travelers" would have to go back to January of 2002. Unfortunately, the worm hole had to line up exactly with past positions of the earth in orbit, as occurred once every four years. This would send the economy in the Northwest plummeting. It also could provide security risks to the nation if a rapid mass exodus took place. And at this point it could jeopardize the existence of the time travel device itself. Seattle, Tacoma, and in Oregon, Portland, had provided much of the technology and hardware necessary to develop it. To save Seattle, either the effort would have to wait until very late 2008, or the warning would have to be given many years sooner. The plan was put on hold.

The time travel program was exceeding all expectations. Paleontology Professor Paul Blake had successfully visited a grandfather in March 1949, a year before the professor's birth. In April of 2005, he then began a series of travels (in the four year increments) all the way back to 1905. Later, other scientists went back as far as 1810, but they were almost lost in travel at that point.

Technology also had opened the "travel window" to within 300,000 miles for extremely small objects by August, fueling hopes of freer travel.

Also, objects as large as a dump truck were transported that month. In September, hovercrafts were successfully transported while in flight. From April efforts were made to conduct all tests in unpopulated regions. The occasional "stray" probably fueled UFO legends, but both the scientists and the military on the whole, performed extremely well. In early 2006, the debate on its potential was intensifying.

Everyone had relatives or friends who had died in accidents or of disease. Even more of concern was the growing toll of preventable afflictions in an aging population. Not only was this an emotional drain, it was a financial one as well. Smoking alone had provided a terrible burden on the health care system. Substance abuse, especially alcohol, had added its toll. But a silent epidemic of poor diet and exercise habits threatened to sink the whole system.

The present government had taken steps to correct these concerns for the future. Following the bold leadership of California, junk food and beverages were removed from the nation's schools in March, 2006. Foods determined to be junk foods were assessed with a health tax. As a step to reduce the obesity crisis, all Americans were now under Federal monitoring for weight and cholesterol levels. A high cholesterol level or body fat levels above 30 per cent resulted in a monitored diet program.

To protect both the environment and health, the emissions of green house gases would be punitively taxed as well. Once again, following the lead of California, emissions of carbon dioxide headed the list. Drivers of cars not meeting the new standard were also subject to stiff annual vehicle taxes. By years end, the Daschle administration had preserved, even strengthened, America's heritage of rights. He also had laid the foundation for a safer, healthier, and more prosperous future.

But not everyone seemed pleased with his accomplishments. In every region of the nation Christianity was on the upsurge. What was even worse, all the growth was in the fundamentalist groups. No longer meeting in public centers, a majority was meeting in private homes or businesses. Nearly one in four Americans now were associated with these fringe groups. There were not enough government agents to police these small groups, and their total disregard for civil rights impeded progress.

Unfortunately, they also could vote. Some states, like California, had found ways to stem the tide. With a comprehensive voter identification system, that state had cancelled the voting rights of suspected fundamentalist subversives. What had made the program so successful was an in-house surveillance policy. Anyone suspected of extremist activities was subject to monitoring, and if found guilty, denied the right to vote.

Even so, in the fall of 2006, Republicans scored significant gains. In the House of Representatives they gained 78 seats, just 3 short of a majority. In the Senate they picked up 4 seats. The Socialists, Greens, and Oxygen (women's) parties caused much of the House gains due to a bleeding off of votes. But the impediment was just as real for Daschle's policies.

Calling a lame duck session, he was able to get approval for a nation wide program after the California model. And to prevent the repeat of small parties affecting so many elections, all politicians were required to obtain a license through the Federal government. Only the top two prospects would be given approval. While this upset some of his own allies, all could see the need for this policy, at least those of his party. It also passed, and as with all his policies, the Supreme Court refused to overturn it. Fear of a return to the era of institutionalized Christian bigotry outweighed lesser concerns.

During 2006 the developments in time travel capability were so numerous that sometimes they failed to grab front-page attention. In June, the aircraft carrier Eisenhower made a historic journey. Embarking to a lonely and rarely traveled spot in the Denmark Straits she was locked into the wormhole field. On June 17, she was transported back to June 17, 1974. For 12 hours she recorded every radio and television frequency her sensitive gear could pick up before returning to 2006. By years end the movement of a whole fleet battle group was achieved.

What had yet to be determined was its mission. Any intervention into the past would alter the present. This was made apparent on December 13th. In an experiment to test a theory of tapping the sun as an energy source, a power surge was mirrored back at the sun. The surface of the sun was bruised as the device hit the year 1862. A mass of plasma energy was deflected preventing a display of the Northern Lights on the night of the battle of Chancellorsville. While the unalterable records in UCLA's science vaults showed lights on that date in history no historical accounts elsewhere mentioned their existence. While this change did not alter the course of the Civil War, it did prove a warning of what could happen. The device was also lost as it ricocheted into history unknown.

Several ideas had been floated. The idea of going back to 1947 and averting the Cold War was offered. Another date was 1939, prior to the outbreak of World War II, or 1911 prior to World War I. Each time objections were raised over potential advantages to the wrong parties, Stalin, Hitler, Kaiser Wilhelm. So were the issues of technological security, economic or social disruption, or more importantly, the neglect of an earlier, preventable atrocity.

One thing was certain. Any trip to the past would involve a military presence of significant size. Daschle had secured adequate funding to pull a number of old Navy ships out of mothballs and restore them to mission capability. Available aircraft, including every usable transporter also were pulled out of retirement and refitted for action. Crews were being trained for operation. Old armored vehicles, trucks, and transport units were overhauled. The list of needs even included the construction of 30 portable runways capable of handling any aircraft.

That a mission into the past to rewrite and correct history was needed had already been established. "When" was the issue. The politically popular, but largely frivolous call for a trip to pre-earthquake Seattle soon gave way to the need for social reform. The educational community was the steadiest and loudest voice for a redress of past injustices. There were the massacres and forced relocation of the Indians and the issue of women's rights and children's rights, which came up frequently. Persecution of the non-Christian community, from Wicca to Moslem, was an outrage. So was the mistreatment of alcoholics, adulterers, and alternate lifestyles by the legalistic Christian establishment.

But more and more the issue of greatest interest was slavery. For decades the educated elite had focused on national guilt for the past sins of prejudice and discrimination. Many lines of evil and the growing forces that eventually stopped them seemed to form a junction in the Civil War years. In Europe, also, the time was right. Darwin was winning the intellectual world. The forces of democracy and socialism were on the rise. In 1862 Russia had freed all serfs from slavery. And nationalism (particularly German) could be halted before it led to world war.

As early as February 20, 2005, Susan Santag for The New York Times had raised the question of "what if" in reference to the Civil War. Only a smattering of attention in other publications until September followed it. A team of Southern leaders headed by Earnest Hollings, whose state, South Carolina, had led the Rebel charge, began to push the idea of rewriting history in the 1860's. This prompted a series of articles in November and

December by the Times, only this time, other papers began to pick up on the idea.

In April 2006, the Brookings Institute addressed the issue of a Civil War era intervention in depth. If social engineering and nation building could work in the 21st Century, why not in the 19th as well? A time for the probability of greatest success was also established. Since the Emancipation Proclamation took full effect at the beginning of 1863, America was becoming focused on a moral cause. But to wait until 1864 would have allowed the radical Republicans and the religious right to take center stage in American politics. Also, if the dreadful carnage of Gettysburg or Sherman's March to the Sea were averted, there would be a much kinder and gentler history.

By mid 2006 a significant following had arisen nation wide. Still, many felt that three other times might be better. One group called for intervention in the 1820's. It hoped to avert many of the scourges against the Indians, protect the environment during the advance of the Industrial Revolution, and check European Imperialism. Another wanted to wait until time travel technology could take them back to the time of the American Revolution. Others wanted to go back to the birth of Jesus and end Christianity before it could begin.

It was not until after the Lame Duck session ended that the issue could be fully decided. While many would have wanted to go back farther than 1800, the technology was not able to safely provide this option. With the resurgence of radical fundamentalism, to wait for this technology to become reality was potentially risky. Already nearly a dozen plots to destroy the worm hole device had been discovered and thwarted. As for the 1820's, the infrastructure and transport systems were too primitive to enable easy conversion for modern usage. Even the developments by the 1860's were lacking, but adaptations could be made. The year 1863 would fit the four-year cycle, and would hit a pivotal point in history. While small objects could safely be transported to 1862 or 1864, risks outweighed the probability of success. The mission goal was 1863, definitely before Gettysburg, and, if possible, before May 1st.

But standing firmly in the path of the plan was the powerful minority party in Congress. Buoyed by their election gains, they had power to block Daschle's agenda. The 46 Republicans in the Senate could filibuster indefinitely. In the House, their narrow minority could often find at least 4 Democrats who could be "bribed" into their camp on various votes. Daschle would have to go above Congress if he had any hopes of achieving his mission. The War Power's Act that his own party had enacted in the 1970's was also a snare.

In a move that sacrificed a degree of American sovereignty, he presented his agenda to the United Nations for approval. On February 1st, in a speed unknown in U.N. history, both the Security and General Council gave approval to his project. In exchange, Daschle agreed to the request of U.N. sponsorship of it. A U.N. Coalition under the command of a high-ranking head of state would rewrite history. At least 17 nations would send some contingency to join the predominantly United States based force. The U.N. would have the ultimate responsibility to over-ride U.S. authority. But within the bounds of American history, Daschle had virtually free rein.

Daschle also irrevocably opened the United States territories to U.N. authority. All U.S. law and policies were now subject to international authority, and the U.S. Military now swore allegiance to the U.N., as well as, the U.S. For American forces abroad, this was nothing new. In Bosnia, under Clinton, American service personnel were required to swear allegiance to the U.N. Those radical few who refused upon the claim of their sovereignty as Americans were court martialed. Most Americans realized the frivolity of the issue and ignored it. Now, the needs of the hour took it one step further.

This time a few more voices were raised, namely the 46 closed minded Republicans in the U.S. Senate. For this, the U.N. authorities had conferred on Daschle a significant new power. Under U.N. law, that now applied to the U.S., any governmental power or representative suspected of terrorist sympathies could be removed from their position. With this new authority Daschle now had the power to tame Congress.

On Friday, February 2, 2007, Daschle presented his package to the U.S. Senate. In a surprise move, Feinstein allowed, on Daschle's request, each Senator to speak for 15 minutes prior to casting his or her vote. Christopher Bond of Missouri had the distinct honor of being the first Republican called to vote. After voicing his deep misgivings, he voted 'no', and was summarily impeached as a terrorist sympathizer and a proxy voter was given his place.

Orrin Hatch of Utah, Senate Minority Leader rose to take his 15 minutes, on Party approval, out of turn. He spoke of a day in history, in 83 B.C. In Rome, Consul Sulla had forced the Senate to declare him to be their

Supreme (dictator). While addressing the Senate, some were distracted by a tumult in the streets. It was the death cries of thousands of his opponents. So, now was Daschle, as the Supreme in what was once the greatest Republic on earth. In his zeal to rewrite the past he would destroy the future. But before Hatch could continue he was arrested. As he was removed he cried out "I was born free, I will die free, also".

But Americans were not interested in the issues of sovereignty or separation of powers. They had become enchanted with greater things, of rights for all, protecting the environment, bringing peace and harmony with the least loss of life possible. Outside of Christians and other extremists groups, public support was overwhelming for Daschle's actions. Dan Rather and Ted Turner most eloquently used their power as media icons to lock this support into a summons for volunteer support. To show theirs, they and Sontag offered their services in the rewriting of the American vision.

By late March, operation plans had been completed. On Tuesday, April 24, 2007, the first units of the military support would begin arriving in obscure locations, such as Bonneville in Utah. By the 26th key locations near large cities would be occupied. Air units would begin action against Southern targets by Friday, the 27th, or Monday in 1863 time, Lincoln would be contacted. By the 29th the entire force of nearly 560,000 U.N. Coalition personnel, and equipment, would arrive, 15,000 of them non-Americans in origin.

To achieve this, Daschle relied heavily on units taken out of reserve and weapons out of retirement. But many state of the art ones were included, the USS Donahue Surveillance vessel, and three B-2 bombers. At sea 110 ships were built around five aircraft carriers, the Constellation, Forestall, Enterprise, Coral Sea, and Kennedy. All retired nuclear surface ships had been activated as the cruisers, Bainbridge and Long Beach. Over 2,500 aircraft, heavy emphasis on helicopter and cargo transport and roughly six combat divisions would be used. Airports, portable harbors and bridges, electric generators, storage tanks, and mountains of other materials were also headed back in time. Nearly 450,00 of the travelers were military or past military personnel.

It was hoped that the South would capitulate by May 1. Lincoln would be expected to welcome the Coalition as liberators. A quick consolidation of power should keep Europe, especially France and Britain, out of war. Diplomacy, economic opportunity, and technological potential should then persuade the governments in North America and Europe to accept Coalition guidance. By years end, most, if not all, Coalition mission would be completed.

The domestic scene in America was becoming serious, however. Much of it was senseless violence and vandalism, and most of that by those under age 20. The failed policies of the Bush Administration were clearly to blame. The failure to adequately finance education, to meet the needs of one-parent families, to fund security and law enforcement programs all contributed. Bush had been more interested in faith based initiatives, abstinence programs, and promoting individual responsibility than in facing reality. Now America was paying for it in aimless youth, without a purpose in life, bent on venting their frustrations on an unprepared nation.

Another Bush failure, neglect of the economy, had led to recession that began early in 2006. Many had tried to falsely blame the Daschle agenda of health, security, environmental, and civil rights reform. To this the news media had risen eloquently in defense of the administration and the righteousness of its goals. Unfortunately, though, many of the new unemployed had lost sight of these causes and were contributing to the social problems now so evident. While the youth were without purpose, these older Americans were without opportunities. As many lost homes and other possessions, even despite liberal bankruptcy laws, they turned to crimes of theft. Security resources were being stretched thin, and that almost led to disaster.

The increasing militancy of the Reactionary Right had already led to several attempts to destroy the time travel system, as well as many other targets. The ample supply of illegal firearms had done much to fuel their efforts, as well as those of hardened criminals. In their ingenuity, they had found ways to circumvent restrictions on such things as nitrous ammonia to manufacture ammunition. One group had even been able to distill nitrogen compounds from urine to make explosives.

On April Fools Day, (Sunday, the 1st) one group had managed to break into the UCLA restricted area and damage several key components of the "time machine". While the damage was quickly repaired, it created a critical shortage of back-up components. Labs in Seattle and Portland that made these parts were just now getting back in to production. Unfortunately, it would take at least six months to have replacement parts for back up. While all those that were involved were killed, it forced the Administration to change plans.

The date for beginning the mission was pushed forward to Thursday, April 19, the soonest date all could be made ready. By Tuesday, the 24th (Friday, in 1863), the travel phase would be completed. To make up for any lack of preparedness in equipment, all available ammunition, fuel stocks, etc. would be transported and reworked into usable replacements. Also, a total of 50 nuclear cruise missiles and bombs would be included, just in case. All personnel volunteering for the trip into time were carefully screened as well to insure the safety and integrity of the mission.

Emily List of NOW (National Organization of Women) was given responsibility in assisting Homeland Security Administration (HSA) Director, Les Lyberte, in the screening process. Donald Greens of the Environmental Protection Administration (EPA), Gerald (Geraldean) Corona of the Gay Rights Action League, and Black Jack Game Winner of (AIM) American Indian Movement were also on the panel. Barbara Boxer would take a temporary leave of absence as majority leader to help build the Legislative Branch in 1863. Steven Breyer and Ruth Vader Ginsburg would do the same for the Judiciary. Bill Clinton would help in the Executive Branch. Christine Todd Whitman would work with state government and be a Republican presence.

To assist in bringing the African Americans, or ex-slaves into full rights status, three key advocates would take center stage. Mary Berry would leave the Civil Rights Commission to lend her aid. Al Sharpton and Jesse Jackson also had volunteered for the mission. A significant contingency of Afro-American professionals would join them, among them several Moslem leaders.

In a fevered pitch not seen since World War II the nation, and world, made its final preparations for the mission. To even the most 'values neutral' philosopher or spiritual leader this had become a noble cause of moral righteousness. Only the fundamental Christian, ultra-conservative Jew, and a few other lunatic extremists were in opposition. The whole world held its breath as April 19th dawned. The first contingency was already in transport to Bonneville, four hours ahead of schedule.

Chapter 2

Tuesday, April 21, 1863 dawned like so many others before in Washington, D.C. An incomplete Capitol Dome rose above a Congress in almost constant friction with Lincoln's war policies. An old man, Chief Justice Roger Taney presided over a somewhat weak Supreme Court, pushed aside by a powerful Lincoln.

To the south, General Joseph Hooker was preparing for his first major campaign since taking command from Burnside only months before. His army, now before Fredricksburg, did not want a repeat of the mid December 1862 disaster that had cost Burnside his job. One part of his army, under General John Sedgwick would occupy Lee at Fredricksburg. The rest would swing west and flank Lee, or was the plan, and rout his army. All eyes would soon be on Chancellorsville, as its May 1st date with destiny drew nigh.

At 9:15 AM, the air over Washington was suddenly filled with mechanical chopping sounds. A startled population took to the streets. Some thought Lincoln, had some how, invented a secret weapon, others argued that Jefferson Davis had. Some likened it to the drums of perdition Napoleon had employed to unnerve his enemies in battle. Some wondered if the hosts of darkness had arisen from Hades now to flood the skies. But all perceived that something was stirring that would forever change the world as they knew it.

To those in the choppers, the sight of 1863 Washington was likened to a panoramic surreal movie. The sights and noises they had been accustomed to did not exist. Instead of freeways there were fields, roads, and farmhouses. Horses and carriages plighted brick, wood, and dirt roads where cars and buses should be. No skyscrapers, housing, or shopping complexes dotted the landscape. Some waved at those below as they flew towards a prearranged rendezvous point south of Annapolis. Others just stared in amazement.

A pre-constructed landing strip was being hastily set up off to the east. Already a significant force of Coalition troops were setting up base camp.

Others were soon to follow, with a key naval base at Hampton Roads as the anchor of the east coast command. Two other key bases would be set up, the one in San Francisco later that day and New Orleans would have to wait until April 23rd.

Lincoln immediately ordered three available regiments under General Winfield Scott to meet an unknown adversary in the Annapolis area. As they were en-route mysterious objects began to appear at multiple locations along the Eastern Seaboard and Gulf Coast. Multiple Confederate forts, port installations, and shore defenses were attacked. Scattered reports were already reaching both Lincoln and Davis by noon. Rumors of attacks on both North and South, of massacres, strange fire from the sky, of strange metal ships at sea, and "carriages" on land lent to mass confusion. It also led to some tragic mistakes.

In all wars there is the ever-present danger of attack from friendly fire. At Normandy in June, 1944, General Leslie McNair and 88 others died from a single bombing incident. Late that same year musician Glenn Miller, also, was lost due to another mishap. In the 1991 Gulf War in excess of one fourth of all US fatalities were the result of friendly fire.

An A-7 attack bomber buzzed Flag Officer David Farragut, on board the Hartford. His ship had survived the fires of forts' Jackson and St. Phillip south of New Orleans. Now, feeling that he was under attack, he did not flinch in the face of a daunting challenge. He ordered the Hartford, and as many other ships as possible, to open fire on the flying objects. The A-7, unsure of the situation and never in actual combat before returned fire. The Hartford was sunk. Ferragut was wounded, but survived. The same could not be said for 89 of his fellow crewmen. Another jet had set the Minnesota (battleship) afire, and she also sank with considerable loss of life. Nearly a dozen Union ships were sunk that afternoon.

To an already nervous nation, these errors constituted an act of war. Edwin Stanton scrambled to find units, much less any sort of weapons, to deal with this new threat. As the War Department scrambled under Stanton to fight, the State Department, under William Seward, sought to identify the enemy. Thinking Great Britain might have changed directions and suddenly gone to war, he sent a telegram to Canada in hopes of gleaning some information. He even wondered if all of Europe had joined France, already sponsoring a war in Mexico, and were now attacking America. But the weapons were beyond anything anyone had ever dreamed of, and that was the most troubling of all.

Meanwhile, at 1:30 PM Jefferson Davis sent a telegram to Lincoln requesting formal negotiations. He, also, had received mixed reports. Some said that the South was experiencing a massive attack by new and diabolical weapons the North had invented. Others reported attacks on both North and South by an unknown adversary. Davis wanted to know what he was up against, and act accordingly. He also asked for a truce.

From California, Joshua A. Norton, "Emperor of San Francisco", sent an urgent call to both men to "end the war before they brought an end to the earth". The "Copperhead" Peace Democrats feared that Lincoln had brought upon them all the evils the nation had most dreaded. As urgent pleas for help and requests for action poured in, Lincoln agreed to meet with Davis. He also asked for a fourteen-day truce so that the full nature of the situation could be evaluated. Lincoln left the time and location of their meeting open, but emphasized the urgency of speed. Both Kentuckians, while enemies, had every reason to believe they could trust each other to keep their word.

As Lincoln was sending his response to Davis, Scott arrived at "Base Camp Kilo", just south of Annapolis. Thankfully, Colonel Jamul Fresno of the 3rd Battalion, 2nd Brigade of the activated 4th Marines knew of some of these mishaps by the Coalition. As Scott's forces positioned themselves for an attack, Fresno came out to meet him under a white flag of truce. To Scott's surprise, he faced a fellow American.

Fresno's purpose was even more of a shock to an old general who probably felt he had heard everything. While time travel had been the thing of myth and muse, none believed it would ever happen. He expressed regret for Union casualties, but the ideas of collateral damage and friendly fire were not an unknown happening to an old general.

But, his request for a high ranking Coalition official to meet with Lincoln was another matter. Having a representative, even a high level one, meeting directly with Lincoln deeply concerned him. When two equals negotiate, they usually go through channels, embassies, secretaries, or other delegations. For a representative to negotiate directly with the "king" was either an entreaty for mercy or a demand to surrender.

Scott advised Fresno that Lincoln would be notified, but he could not assure what response Lincoln would give. Fresno presented Scott with modern communications equipment, and demonstrated its use to the Americans. Lincoln could relay his answer directly to the base. If possible, an answer was anticipated by midnight. Scott wired Lincoln immediately, and sent the equipment by carriage to Washington. Lincoln wasted no time in his answer. He would schedule a meeting. But as a sign of good faith he called for an immediate and total cease-fire. Scott conveyed Lincoln's response to Fresno.

A response from Davis caught Lincoln in an emergency cabinet meeting. He was leaving Richmond at 4:00 PM and with assured protection and escort by Lincoln's army could arrive in Washington late on the 22nd. Lincoln made the arrangements. As a sign of good faith Davis would be permitted a company of his own men as a guard. By now, both armies in Virginia knew the truce, but in some areas of Tennessee, Texas, and Mississippi, notice was slower in arriving.

For General Davis "Hawk" Taylor of the Coalition, the petition by Lincoln for a cease-fire met with open refusal. From Hampton Roads, now being established as a key installation, he ordered the roads north of Richmond to receive special attention. At 5:30 AM he launched an attack at Fredricksburg and succeeded in destroying much of Davis's escort. While Davis was uninjured, plans to proceed were now untenable.

From the other side of the Rappahannock, Hooker watched the attack. One day earlier and the pasting of the Confederates would have been met with shouts of celebration. The potential of the death of Davis would have elated the Union. But today, the world had been turned upside down. Hooker was fully aware of his president's purpose and he was not going to let Lincoln down. He ordered General John Sedgwick to cross the Rappahannock south of Fredricksburg to rescue a former foe. In what would have been treason only hours before, Union color bearers sported white and Confederate flags, as well as, their own stars and stripes.

Just southeast of Marye's Heights they met up with an embattled Jubal Early and the remnants of Davis's guard. The air assault ended for fear of firing on Union forces, bringing out thousands of thankful confederates. One Georgian scrambling to meet a Yankee exclaimed, "If y'all'd come yesterday, we'd been obliged to keels ya. But today, we's grateful beyond words. I's so glad we ain't keelt ya." Now, under joint North and South escort, Davis continued towards Washington.

Outside of General Taylor's command, the Coalition pretty well honored the cease-fire. While supreme operational command had yet to arrive, the various regional commanders welcomed the opportunity to consolidate their positions. But there was no respite in political pressure on Lincoln. When Lincoln had not responded to Fresno, or base commander General Eugene Newport by midnight, they initiated contact, pressuring Lincoln for a meeting.

Lincoln was able to stall for the moment. Due to a scheduling glitch, Barbara Boxer had not yet arrived at "Kilo" and would not until almost noon on Wednesday the 22nd. Edward Bates, Lincoln's Attorney General, was able to use as leverage the lack of a higher official to meet with Lincoln. While it would have been a feather in Fresno's cap to have already arranged Lincoln's cooperation, he was wise enough to accept the response.

But this did not stop efforts to meet with other governing authorities. At 8:00 AM, a chopper landed outside the Capitol Building. Before Union troops could be summoned to meet it, several soldiers dispersed to the Capitol and Supreme Court Buildings. Quickly seeking any leadership they could find they left communications equipment, and then departed as they had came. While this prompted Stanton to take immediate steps to improve security, little was available to fend off a helicopter incursion.

Boxer's arrival at Base Camp Kilo at 12:15 PM only intensified pressure on Lincoln. In his favor, the Governor of New York, Peace Democrat Horatio Seymour, pledged his support to Lincoln. So had the leading Peace Democrats (Copperheads) in Congress. The sudden "peace" with the Confederacy had shored up Lincoln's standing in every circle with the exception of the Abolitionists. But Frederick Douglass, a most eloquent Black leader recognized that Lincoln could only meet one adversary at a time and urged patience. Most of the Abolitionist community was willing to accept a temporary postponement to preserve Lincoln's leadership.

At 3:30 PM Lincoln, with the backing of his nation, agreed to meet with the Coalition leader at 10:00 PM. That evening Davis was due to arrive in Washington at around 6:00 PM, which would give him and Lincoln time for a private meeting first. Both resented the intrusion of this third party in the private affairs of the United States. Davis now even regretted his desire to have involved Europe in the war. This was a dispute between brothers, and as brothers they needed to settle their differences. And for now, the brothers would lay aside their dispute and negotiate, as one voice, with this Coalition intruder.

When Boxer arrived at the executive mansion (White House) she was not expecting Davis to be present. Davis represented the embodiment of bigotry and prejudice in her mind. With great difficulty she maintained a mind even open enough to allow his presence. But she made it clear that the narrow intolerance of his viewpoint was not something she, or anyone in the Coalition, could respect. For the present time, he wisely sat in silence.

Her position was clear. The world of the future had determined that the best way to solve its own problems, as well as correct past injustices, was to rewrite history. This point in time provided the best window of opportunity to do so. The first priority, of course, was to free the slaves, and then bring them to equality with the whites. Such rights must also apply for the Indians, Chinese, or any other racial or cultural group.

The Coalition was intent upon nation building, and 1863 America was the object of their initial agenda. Women must be elevated in their status, as even some in their time already were advocating. But, also, children must be protected from child labor, disease, ignorance, hunger, religious bigotry, and oppression. Social, legal, and moral oppression of those who seek alternative lifestyles must end. Workers, the environment, and all of society must be protected and the greedy must be more regulated.

Secretary of State Seward leaned over to Lincoln for a moment of silent discussion. Boxer interrupted them, reminding them that she had the floor and they were in a position to listen without disturbance. Secretary of the Interior Caleb Smith cut her off, "Who are you to march in here and dictate your demands like we are some defeated people? We will go to war before we kowtow to your decrees."

Seward spoke up in an attempt to maintain peace. "You have noticed, I am sure, that wherever our army goes, it acts as an emancipating crusade for those bound in slavery. Our institutions, however slow, labor as we speak to meet the wants of our people. Our ways may seem slow and primitive to you in a time yet to come, but they are our ways. We are a Christian nation and, as God is our leader, what is right will one day prevail. Now please be so disposed as to allow us to chart our destiny and pursue our own direction."

Boxer was justifiably incensed by this rebut of an unappreciative government. She, and those who took this crusade with her, knew of the gross failings and disgraceful, shameless injustices of America's past. They would prevail; human justice would be established, with liberty and humanities rights upheld. No assembly of old men with fossilized vision would stand in their way. But she would not act alone, Tom Daschle himself would make the call. She warned the Cabinet of the potential of 'dire consequences' for their foolishness and then departed.

Davis telegrammed Richmond. Boxer had been right on at least one count, this point in history was in the vortex of change. Even the Czar of Russia had freed the serfs from slavery in 1862. The social unrest of Europe, especially the revolutionary fervor of 1848 and following, showed that no people could forever be kept in subjection. Lincoln had already ordered the slaves of the Confederacy freed, Europe was enchanted by his vision and by all appearances, and the North would eventually win. Otherwise "modern" Americans would not be so openly antagonistic to it. In a move that could potentially cost Davis his position of leadership, he ordered the South to abolish slavery effective July 4, 1863. In exchange, Lincoln had agreed to abolish the restrictive tariffs against the South and to respect a degree of southern sovereignty.

Back in 2007, Daschle received Boxer's briefing. He was stunned by the degree of narrow-minded intransigence of those he intended to assist. If anything, though, this only exposed a greater need and call to purpose. Nation building, the rewriting of a flawed past must proceed. But now it must include a reeducation and social evolution of the North, as well as, the South. With a new and hostile landscape made up of a culturally primitive mindset, the mission would have to be revised.

At 10:30 AM on (Monday) April 23, Daschle held a joint Cabinet and Congressional meeting. With the adversarial status of the North several combat units that had been assigned to the South now were being shifted farther to the north. More fuel, spare parts, and supplies were ordered to be sent back in time. All available ammunition, even highly sophisticated antiaircraft and armor piercing missiles were included in the transport, to be cannibalized as necessary for producing bombs and bullets.

From the joint Cabinet-Congress leaders unprecedented steps were taken to insure the cultural success of the mission. Ten thousand of the best educators in America and Europe were now added to the mission. The Europeans voluntarily sent 850 and in the U.S. about 2200 volunteered. The "Joint Session" authorized Daschle to "draft" the necessary teachers to make up the difference. While time did not permit proper screening, the National Education Association recommended the 7000 "draftees". Paul Blake from UCLA was among those recommended. His exposure to, and repudiation of, creation dogma was one reason for his high consideration.

Another resolution of this joint session was a request of Daschle. Since his popularity remained high and no potential rival seemed reality he was in no danger of failure of his policies. All eyes looked to him as the clear choice of leader to assure success of an expanded policy. That Lincoln would have to be removed from power was a real possibility. If so, Daschle, as present leader would take the position of past leader as well.

The concept was very intriguing. To leave Feinstein as acting President in 2007 America was definitely a win-win proposition. If she succeeded, Daschle was a hero as a social pioneer with great vision. If she failed, he was still a winner for having given her the opportunity. And regardless of the speed of reform in 1863, he was a winner for his bold and courageous move. He agreed. Having no shortage of advisors and leaders from the whole spectrum of social and moral groups, from the ACLU to the ILO (International Labor Organization), his chances of success were overwhelming. This was humankinds' great opportunity, without the detractors of the narrow religious right, to prove its ability to save and redeem the human race.

For the time device engineers, the task had already been daunting. The damage from the April Fool's attack had placed strains on the system already. Several units were already down and being cannibalized for parts to keep the rest functioning. It would be at least April 25th before the whole assembly could be transported, and it could last until the 27th with the added surveillance and other electronic equipment. Daschle went through at 9:00 PM on the 25th. Scientists were warning of a complete system failure at any time, the last personnel passed through shortly before midnight. A short time later, while transporting critical electronics security equipment, it failed. The Coalition was on its own until at least late October. Daschle's last message was to Feinstein, "I shall return, victorious …".

Back in 1863, lines of hostility were hastily forming. By the morning of April 23rd, Coalition forces had "peaceably" established control over 40 bases across the United States. Most were in unpopulated areas. But New Orleans, New York City, Hampton Roads, and Pittsburgh were exceptions as bases extended into populated areas. At Hampton Roads, the Coalition presence was blocking in a significant Union fleet, while smaller forces were being held at bay in New York and New Orleans. Any miscalculation could lead to immediate hostilities, thus creating an air of great uneasiness.

Coalition forces were under orders to consolidate and provide security to bases, for now. While it was fascinating to watch the 19th Century lived out before them several things were troubling to those on the base. Seeing twelve to fourteen year old boys smoking and even drinking alcohol, or watching parents use belts and switches to punish their children aroused righteous indignation. Police arrested suspects without reading them their rights or following proper search and seizure rules of evidence. It was a rude, primitive, violent, and socially repressive time in history, desperately needing reform.

A strange, but undeniable bond was developing between former Civil War enemies. As they observed the mannerisms of the Coalition, they, too, were troubled by what they saw. Strange images, motion pictures as they saw them, depicted every manner of vile, immoral, and violent behavior coupled with language that even made sailors blush. The total disregard of patriarchal authority and lack of religious standards did not bode well either. The modernists lacked respect for culture and regard for righteousness. Even the Blacks of the South were filled will revulsion when they observed the Coalitionists' mannerisms. And fear of Coalition ambitions caused all Americans to view them with alarm and to view each other as comrades, out of necessity. Even the rash decisions by Jefferson Davis to seek reconciliation with the North and free the slaves were met with silence, an eerie silence from the South.

The Coalition, while confined to base, was anything but passive in its wait. US Geological Survey (USGS) maps of mineral deposits were being studied. Computer reconstruction showed locations of original oil, iron, copper, and other mineral deposits. At sea, naval contacts were made with other powers, most notably Britain and France. Communication equipment was disseminated, and requests made for contact with heads of state in the process. Feelers were also being sent, as best possible, to leaders in South America, Africa, and Asia.

Shortly before midnight, a small party of engineers and geologists from Base Camp Delta (San Francisco) left for a survey of the gold fields. Base Commander, Lieutenant General Paul Rupert had passed notice to Governor Leland Stanford of his intent. He also requested air reconnaissance from Bonneville Base Commander Verona Emory-Mills. She immediately dispatched air cover while Stanford offered a company of soldiers for protection. Rupert declined his offer, at which point Stanford warned him that their safety could not be guaranteed.

A little after noon on the 24th, the party of 18 scientists and 52 soldiers neared Oakland. Here they aroused the attention of a band of former residents of San Francisco. These "Sydney Ducks" (Australian prospectors), loan sharks, extortionists, pimps, and common criminals had been run out of town by the "Vigilance Committee". Now they survived, in part, by relieving passers by of their possessions.

Surprising the expeditionary party, they killed two soldiers and wounded seven others. Superior logistics and firepower led to the deaths of eleven and the capture of 23 other outlaws. Aircraft from Bonneville strafed the hills for hours as the party returned to base. But Coalition blood was shed and the truce was broken. By 6:00 PM, Washington time, attacks on American targets had resumed throughout the country. Although, far from an all out offensive, it threatened to isolate New England and close transport on the Ohio and Mississippi Rivers.

As details of the "provocation" became known, some in New England suddenly remembered the Pequot Indian War of 1637. The alleged killing of a white settler led to the burning of a Pequot village, and later nearly 700 others were burned alive in Connecticut. Throughout the rest of America other memories of wars against the Indians sparked by similar events began to trouble some consciences. Tecumseh's revenge, Sassacus, Massasiot, and others came to mind. If God were to bring remembrance of past deeds in this manner, Americans must somehow be accountable for how they had treated the Indians.

By early afternoon of the 24th attacks had again tapered off. From across the void of time Daschle had called for another cease-fire. He wanted to impress on Lincoln two things, first of all, that his forces were no match for the Coalition. But, he also wanted to convey the will of a civilized power to show restraint, even when they have totally superior capabilities. And realistically, Lincoln had no option but accept the status of a nation under reconstruction.

As soon as Daschle arrived, he requested an audience with Lincoln. Utilizing every tactical, diplomatic, and political skill in his arsenal, Lincoln was able to postpone the meeting until 9:00 AM, Monday, the 27th. While he struggled with the titanic issue of national defense, Lincoln called for a day of fasting and prayer on Sunday, April 26th. For Daschle and his military, it was 49 hours of preparation and planning. And this time, there were no off-base excursions, like the ill-fated one in California.

Monday morning saw a heavily escorted Daschle and Boxer in meetings with Lincoln, Davis, and their cabinets. As an equal to an equal, Lincoln was offered an executive leadership position in a nation building agenda that would not see defeat. A glorious future lay in store for America and the world. Lincoln could be a hero and a pioneer, or he could be the villain standing in the way of progress. Daschle gave him until noon, Wednesday, April 29th to get Congressional approval and come to terms. As Daschle was pressed for "terms" he responded, "For beginners, America will be freed from religious bias and become a truly free, secular, nation."

Maneuvering to a more secure location not far from Chancellorsville, a combined force under Lee and Hooker were also being readied for action. Since the South was expected to bear the brunt of renewed hostilities, Lincoln had asked General Pierce Beauregard to assume command in the East. In the West (Tennessee, Mississippi, etc.) General Henry Halleck was given by Lincoln, somewhat reluctantly, over-all command. In New England, he placed McClellan in charge, and in the Far West, Grant was given command, over the objections of Halleck. Lincoln feared that General George McClellan would fail in offensive efforts, but trusted his ability to posture for a good defensive struggle. Ulysses S. Grant was a good tactician, but he lacked an army of credible strength.

But Lincoln's greatest asset was the support of the people. On the morning of April 28th, the silence over Davis's peace and reconciliation was broken in the South. The Charleston Courier reflected what all had now come to believe, that the South would have lost the war even without the Coalitions interference. Slavery, as an institution, was doomed. Davis had done the only logical thing that could be done, however unpopular it might be, to preserve the rights, beliefs, and property of the South. While not surrendering on the issue of states rights, the need to unite as one against a greater threat was paramount.

Newspapers throughout the South pretty much mirrored the same sentiment, while in the North, the praise was for Lincoln. Horace Greeley, of the New York Tribune, saw Lincoln as a great leader who set personal pride and ambition aside for the nation. Rather than break the South, as history showed would happen, Lincoln sought a fair and just reconciliation. He went on to say that the people of the age to come (Coalition) had perspectives worth considering. He offered his paper and the services of the Associated Press as a springboard for dialogue on their ideas. But to attempt by force to impose their ideas would be an act of war. And in that, he threw full support behind Lincoln to uphold the cause of liberty.

In Richmond there was the memory of the April 2nd bread riots. The "Examiner" pointed to the still present lack of food and other necessities in the city. Only now, it was not the Yankees who were to blame, for they had lifted their blockades. If Richmond, and the rest of the South were to again be well fed, the new blockade by the armies of the future, must be ended. With Lincoln and Davis now united, this was hoped to soon become a reality.

The Macon (Georgia) Daily Telegraph quoted Governor Joseph Brown in his acceptance of the new reality, "While states rights must not be surrendered, a far greater threat to liberty now exists. We stand behind Davis in his decision to make peace with Lincoln to preserve our Godly heritage." At noon, April 29th, with a nation behind him, Lincoln refused Daschle's terms.

From their secured positions, the Coalition immediately sprang to the offensive. In New England, hastily prepared Union strong points were quickly bypassed and McClellan's strategy was undone. In September of 1939 Poland had quickly learned the fallacy of attempting to protect a number of critical positions with long defensive lines. It may have worked a generation earlier in 1914 against less mobile attackers, but not in a "fluid battlefield" of modern warfare. By Sunday, May 3rd, his beleaguered armies were confined to a few cities, most notably Boston, Providence, Springfield, and Albany. The Coalition had only to wait for the isolated units to fall into the basket like over-ripened plums from a tree.

In the Far West, Grant almost immediately gave up the concept of defending cities or strategic points. No effective combat force existed west of the Rockies, in most of the Great Plains, or in the Arizona Territory. A string of forts garrisoned by company sized (or at best, regiment sized) forces dotted much of the West. Grant chose hit and run tactics, and succeeded at one point in destroying five aircraft and several vehicles at Ft. Smith Arkansas. To help counter the infrared detectors in the Coalition's arsenal he made use of blankets, leaves, dirt, and other cover to avoid detection. His was the most successful campaign when adjusting for numbers.

In the "West", Holleck was captured in Tennessee on May 1st. The war effort focused on Vicksburg, Chattanooga, and Tallahassee. The Appalachians were soon to be the focal point of battle as many divisions, both Northern and Southern, were seeking cover in that region. To the north, from Iowa to Pennsylvania, little action had yet to occur.

Virginia and the Eastern Seaboard were aflame with conflict. Coalition helicopters and attack aircraft cut swaths through regimented formations. Armour and artillery units chopped up surviving companies and ground assaults flushed out dazed survivors. Quickly overwhelmed were Southern militias, seaboard forces, and Union troops in South Carolina. By May 4th Taylor's forces were poised to strike Beauregard in Virginia and Maryland.

In Washington, Sunday May 3rd saw Lincoln and Davis together in a special worship service. Abolitionist and minister Wendell Phillips, lawyer George Templeton Strong, and author Nathaniel Hawthorne were, also, present. There, both Lincoln and Davis committed their lives to God. They, also, pledged to die before surrendering their countries, or country, as Lincoln could again claim, to the Coalition. Lincoln recited those words written almost four score and seven years ago with a firm reliance on the protection of divine providence, "We mutually pledge to each other our lives, our fortunes, and our sacred honor." They vowed to each other and God, "death before dishonor".

As they met, Daschle met with his chief military and security leaders to bring a swift end to hostilities. A single blow, one overwhelming display of power and resolve was needed, before the Coalition would be forced to destroy the nation it came to save. It was 8:15 AM on August 6th, 1945 that the "Enola Gay" annihilated Hiroshima and Japan's hopes of averting surrender. One plane, one bomb, but history would never be the same. Reluctantly, Daschle consented to one nuclear detonation to end this war. At 5:00 AM, Monday, May 4th, Sharpsburg (Antietam) would be ground zero for a single nuclear blast. All tactical operations were suspended at 6:00 PM, Sunday.

Efforts to bring Lincoln into negotiations were proving fruitless for Daschle. Military operations were suspended. But a glitch in tactical maneuvers would prevent evacuation of all Coalition personnel from the target area. Another site offered better promise, Marye's Heights overlooking Fredricksburg, Virginia and the blast was postponed until 8:oo PM. The blast would illuminate Richmond, Washington, and the heart of Lincoln's resistance. It also cost America nearly 8,000 lives, half of them civilians.

Tuesday, May 5th, at 9:00 AM Lincoln and Davis rode in a carriage to a checkpoint north of Base Camp Kilo. There escorts were forced to disarm and they were then led to Daschle's headquarters. In the presence of Barbara

Boxer, Bill Clinton, and Les Lyberte, the two again met to discuss terms of an armistice. Daschle, again, made it clear the need for total compliance and cooperation to build a new America. Lincoln and Davis knew that victory was unobtainable. To accept the conditions of peace would mean the death of America and liberty, as they knew it. Lincoln looked at Davis and said, "Give me liberty or give me death". Both men pulled out concealed pistols and at a set moment shot each other through their hearts. As they died, so did any semblance of a future 2007 world as the Coalition knew it to be. Its future form was yet to be determined, but none of those currently in 1863 knew that yet.

Chapter 3

Press coverage of the deaths of Lincoln and Davis was nothing less than masterful. Dan Rather, Ted Turner, and others defused this potentially explosive news by covering it as a bizarre double murder. There had been an authority question raised concerning the new power structure of government under the Coalition. Not all details were known, motives could only be speculated, but there was undeniable proof that they had killed each other. How they were able to slip past security with their weapons, or why no intervention was made to halt the murders were discretely not mentioned.

Modern media had come to appreciate the value of ideology and were experts in its use. While news reporting makes objectivity its goal, this is not possible. Bias is what gives significance to news. When a dog bites a man, that isn't news, but when man bites dog, that is. Bias provides pertinence, empathy, and a sense of humanity. And bias shows our values and beliefs.

From this "story" as a springboard, the media saw as its duty to civilize a brutish people. Historic Americans were blinded by the greed of private ownership and misguided concepts of personal liberty. Much of their ignorance centered in their religious superstitions. They still believed that blowing someone's brains out to keep them from stealing was somehow different than to blow their brains out to steal. The success of the media in defusing this crisis would provide optimism for this broader mission. And it was successful. By May 7th, most Americans, while confused about the event, did not hold the Coalition directly responsible. It also planted a few seeds of distrust concerning the motives of Lincoln's peace efforts towards the South.

But this gave Daschle a window of opportunity to win over the American people. Coalition personnel began immediately to repair damaged transport systems to insure movement of goods and vital raw materials throughout the "Union" states. In the Confederacy and Border States hostilities continued to some degree, from both Northern and Southern forces. In April of 1863 the North had manned the largest army on earth and the South had the second largest. Over one half million troops were still in the field in un-liberated areas. But having either witnessed or hearing the story about the "Fire came down from Heaven" at Marye's Heights, most surrendered when confronted.

Their very presence hampered the Coalition and Daschle's opportunities in the South in yet another way. A number of leaders, especially in the South, had been prepared for a long, revolutionary style war. They did not readily want to surrender to anyone, and were ready to live indefinitely off the land. The cover of such a large army, even of dubious resolve, gave them that opportunity. It would be a long time before the Coalition could confirm the status of many such generals and leaders. And these leaders were also the ones who began questioning the events of the Lincoln-Davis murders.

By Friday, May 8th, Coalition people had taken occupancy of virtually every inhabited county or territory outside the South. In large cities, New York, Chicago, Boston, etc. they had set up zones of residency and bureaucratic offices. Medical centers were set up in New York City, Philadelphia, Washington D.C., and Baltimore. One of New York's specialties was to be its eye surgery clinic, run by Dr. Perry O'Brien.

O'Brien had been raised in an old Free Methodist Church and was well acquainted with the Fanny Crosby story. He also deeply resented having had religion forced down his throat as a child, and being forced to sing songs she had written. He had a special hatred for 'My Savior First of All' and 'Saved By Grace'. With her blindness how could she sing of seeing a Christ who never healed her of her blindness? He, himself, had suffered blindness in one eye because of an accident in infancy. In his early twenties a team of doctors from the optometry school he attended surgically restored his sight. Science and medicine had healed him where a distant, or non-existent God had failed. He offered now the same opportunity for Fannie.

She refused, responding that she was at peace with her physical blindness, it had opened the eyes of her soul and spirit. She was content to remain blind, and that the first thing she would see, "would be the blessed face of her Savior". But O'Brien was undaunted. If her religious blindness could be forced down his throat as a child, he could now force sight upon her. Surgery was performed on Saturday, May 9th. Anyone who would turn down a free opportunity to receive his or her sight needed to be locked up anyway.

On May 8th, another offer was made to several leading women of 1863. Emily List, Barbara Boxer, Susan Santag, and Connie Dumm (Planned

Parenthood Corporation) were able to bring a forum together. Over 100 feminist leaders were invited, and provided transport to this assembly, held at Seneca Falls, New York. Among those in attendance were Julia Howe (writer of the Battle Hymn of the Republic), Elizabeth Cady Stanton, Susan B. Anthony, and Harriett Beecher Stowe (author of Uncle Tom's Cabin). It was here in 1848 that Stanton and Lucretia Mott, at the first women's' rights convention, called for all the rights and privileges entitled them as citizens. And it was here, now, that the Coalition would work with them to secure those rights.

The immediate culture shock between sisterhoods was exposed over a request by Howe that the conference open with Scripture and prayer. Boxer and List finally relented to accept a moment of silence. With an eye toward unity the 1863 sisters reluctantly compromised. None could overcome their uneasiness over the unwillingness of the future sisters to commit their purposes to God or a higher good.

As the convention began with an opening address by List, their uneasiness yielded to open anxiety. History would show that when Wyoming became the first state to give women the right to vote in 1869, it was a moral uplift to the state. The women's vote was tied to a high moral code, closing saloons on Sunday, civilizing the state, and the West, and promoting decency. The concepts of free sex, abortion on demand, planned single motherhood, prostitution, and gay rights were not "their bag". The heart and soul of 1863 American feminism was not selfishness, but responsibility. By midmorning, all but five of the invitees had found ways to excuse themselves from the assembly.

Speaking for those who remained, Lucy Stone told Boxer that a united mission could not be established at this time. Too many differences separated the two camps. Women of the future did not share the same purpose as those of 1863.

To this, List replied, "And just what is your purpose? To allow your bodies to be the playground of domineering men? To be baby machines? To hold to the narrow moral confines of a God that either doesn't exist or cares nothing about your happiness? Trust me sister, one day you will grow up and find out that we are right."

Stone responded, "You may be". Then she and the remaining four others departed. They wanted rights, but they could not but feel disillusioned over their glimpse of the future.

Sunday, May 10th brought leaders of another minority group together. Mary Berry, Al Sharpton, and Jesse Jackson met in Philadelphia with leading Afro Americans of the current era. Frederick Douglass and Thadeus Stevens rose to the forefront of this delegation and were openly receptive to the Coalition leaders. Of the roughly four and one half million ex-slaves in America only a small percentage were in a position to function smoothly as freed citizens. Much needed to be done in education, housing, feeding, and finding employment, and the Coalition leaders were looked to with eager anticipation in helping those needs be met.

Stevens was very interested in the idea of reparations to the Blacks who had been slaves. He felt that their servitude should be repaid, even at the expense of confiscating the entire South from the Whites and giving it to the ex-slaves. Both he and Douglass were intrigued by the idea of organizing a Black Advancement League, like the NAACP. Stevens took particular interest in one of the earlier members of this League, George Washington Carver. The Coalition was able to furnish him with a couple of old books, including Linda O. McMurray's <u>George Washington Carver, Scientist and Symbol</u> and Holt's <u>George Washington Carver</u>. He held the books like a child would hold a precious gift, and immediately began to read them.

In another city, New York, four leading members of the modern mass media met with their 19th Century counterparts. Peter Jennings had joined the media team of Susan Sontag, Dan Rather, and Ted Turner. Horace Greeley was the leading spokesman for those of the earlier era who chose to attend. Any decisions would be sent out via the Associated Press to all others in the network.

Greeley had represented a wide spectrum of philosophies and beliefs. While "loyal" to Lincoln and committed to ending slavery, he also ran articles by women's groups, socialists, and even Karl Marx. He also had a tendency to "go with the flow", depending upon events or public sentiment. Caught between his convictions and politics, he opposed the Civil War after the Northern defeat at Bull Run, only to support it again later. The same vacillation had applied to ending slavery, policies toward England and France, and other policy issues. With this in mind, it was anticipated that Greeley would now see the light of day and throw his lot with the Coalition. If he made that step, others would follow.

Under Rather's eloquent leadership, the ideals and goals of the Coalition were laid out. The end of slavery was quickly celebrated for the success that it was. But this marked only the first step in building, "... one nation, indivisible, with liberty and justice for all". Social justice would extend to the emancipation of women and children, the establishment of equal treatment of all races, and the acceptance of diverse religious beliefs. Environmental, safety, and health care concerns would be addressed, as would criminal and civil law. By bringing these to reality in the future, Americans had built the richest, most advanced, and safest society in history.

When asked why the 21st Century saw the need to interfere in the process the media group had several points. Looking out a window, they could still see flocks of birds over the Bronx and the East River. By 1914, the newspaper leaders were told; the last passenger pigeon would die. The buffalo, whooping crane, even the bald eagle would come close to the same end, as would thousands of other species of plants and animals. The air and rivers would be poisoned, the climate warmed, and good land ruined. Countless lives would be crippled, destroyed, even ended because of social injustice. Now was the time to act, before it was too late.

Asked about the news media's role, the Coalition team struggled to avoid a mockery of those who should know better than ask this ignorant question. The whole purpose of a free press in a Democracy is to expose evil and advocate social change. The reporting of news is selective, and it needs to be. People need to know what is wrong with the system from a clearly defined perspective of right and wrong. In modern America, over 90 percent of the mass media elite and writers had a clear perspective of that society was supposed to be. News stories must be filtered to support these aims.

Again Theodore Tilton of the New York Independent addressed the issue of purpose. He argued that in a Constitutional Republic, it was the duty of the press as a sacred trust, to fairly and accurately report the news. The moral perspective must be based on our founding principles, and truth must prevail, regardless of any opinions.

He was cut off. In a Democracy, the will of the people, the moral direction of the nation, safety, and welfare, these are important above all else. The duty of the press is to promote these. If there are allies in government, they are protected and cultivated. It was no accident that over 90 percent of the media leadership voted consistently for the Democrats in modern America.

It was also no secret that these progressive visionaries were promoted by the media as well. The same media leaders that had so vocally demanded total disclosure of Nixon and Watergate ignored Koreagate under Carter. When special prosecutor Harvey Walsh, an avowed Democrat, "leaked" allegedly new information to the press four days before the election in 1992, it was to derail George Bush's presidential re-election bid. The press gave full coverage to this old news about the Iran Contra affair and Bill Clinton defeated Bush. While some might mistake this for bias it was nothing of the sort. Clinton was an ally to justice and social change Bush was not. The media was merely fulfilling its role.

Among those in the meeting was a Hungarian teenager who had been given special invitation and transport by the Coalition. Known for his future legacy, Joseph Pulitzer was recruited in anticipation of the benefit he could be in establishing a media base. His "yellow journalism" or sensationalism would one day propel both himself and the *New York World* to historical acclaim. But he also had built a reputation (according to yet to happen history) fighting political corruption as owner of the *St. Louis Post Dispatch*. His prompting led several others to question this Bill Clinton, even more so since he was in the Coalition mission as Secretary of State.

Again they were answered with a statement of purpose, expose evil, and advocate social change and justice. These take precedence over corruption or moral character. A good example was from 1932 when *New York Times* writer Walter Duranty won the Pulitzer Prize for his coverage of the Soviet Union. This prize, the result of an endowment by the Joseph Pulitzer now present, was for his bold and courageous reporting. It did not mention the Ukraine forced starvation of up to 7,000,000 people under Stalin because of their resistance to "Collectivism". Nor were any of Stalin's purges religious persecutions, violations of free speech or due process given attention. The greater good of social and international goodwill prevailed.

During the Clinton presidency this policy was refined to almost an art form. No major media source mentioned his record number of executive orders or proposed regulations. In the interest of fighting crime and tax evasion the "know your customer" policy was proposed. This would have required banks to note and report questionable transactions of cash, coin, or unusual requests. That this would have pried into the average family's financial activities was not important. The benefits to society outweighed the consequences. Another would also propose rules to bar religious bigotry in the workplace. Any expression of religion, Bibles, t-shirts, even humming a Christian tune would have been prohibited. Only leaks by a handful of independent sources prevented the implementing of these bold and beneficial policies.

Nor was such policy limited to political leaders. It also applied to social issues. The same press corps that showed mangled bodies in Afghanistan or Bosnia would not show, or even describe partial birth abortion. They labeled it too graphic, but once again, the social justice of abortion was more important than any concern for fetuses or full disclosure.

The editors and journalists of 1863 were aghast. Speaking for those present, Greeley acknowledged the media's proposals, and assured them that the various journalists would consider these in their dissemination of news. To this Peter Jennings replied, "This is not optional". To be part of the AP network, and ultimately maintain any control over local newspapers this policy was mandatory. The essential mission of supporting the Coalition must be satisfied. Each man present was asked to sign a contract of loyalty and support. On the pain of losing their positions, all refused.

Monday afternoon, the bandages were taken off Fanny Crosby's eyes. O'Brien tested her vision using video images of 21st Century America. Reluctant to receive her sight to begin with, she reacted in shock and anger at several of the images. Seeing two gays in carnal embrace she cried out, "I wanted to see Jesus, instead I am forced to see Sodom and Gomorrah." A few hours later as a nurse came in to check on her, she was humming "Amazing Grace." The nurse reacted in horror when she realized that Fanny had gouged her eyes out.

That same day saw a reconvening of the African-American Council in Philadelphia. Frederick Douglass was not receptive to any concept of reparations to the ex-slaves. He believed that by diligence, courage, and ingenuity his people would overcome racism and poverty to win acceptance in society. By doing so, they would win favor and respect without alienating the Whites.

Berry and Jackson reacted in disbelief. This was not how to address the needs of four plus million disenfranchised and unaccepted people. Racism was not limited to the South. When Lincoln had issued the Emancipation Proclamation, he weakened loyalties in Illinois and Indiana. Fear of cheap labor and an invasion by an inferior race long before (in 1851) had led to Indiana's outlawing all "Negroes" in the state. Ohio and Illinois also had "Black" laws to restrict the influx of freed slaves. Indeed much of the Midwest (heartland), Iowa, Ohio, and Michigan as well feared free black labor. On March 6, Detroit had been the scene of anti-Negro rioting. No, rights must be mandated and restitution made.

There was fear for another reason as well. It was no secret that 90 percent of the modern Black community voted Democratic, or why. Unlike the Republicans, they had seen the nation's responsibility to this oppressed minority, and this was reflected in a steady flow of financial and legal support. This base must not be compromised by the reactionary radicalism of Douglass. In the 20th and 21st Century, there was a small segment of Blacks who had sold out to the White culture, Clarence Thomas, Colon Powell, Sowell, or Keyes, to name a few, were a constant danger to genuine Afro-American equality and advancement. If this "Oreo mentality" (Black on the outside, white on the inside) could be rooted out now, much future grief would be eliminated.

Ignoring Douglass, attention was now centered on Thaddeus Stevens. With assistance, he had thoroughly aquatinted himself with all he had been given on George Washington Carver. Now, he raised the question of Carver's using the Bible as a science book in his discoveries. This source of embarrassment the forum leaders were able to work around, based on the prevailing intellectual ignorance of that day. Steven's had been touched by something else about Carver, his conviction that Carver would never allow anyone to force him to hate them. Stevens confessed his sin of hatred, and had come to accept the reality that two wrongs do not make a right. While bonds were made and ideals shared, the conference ended without success.

One success marked the day. By evening, Monday, May 11, all organized resistance had ceased east of the Appalachian Mountains. Attempting to lead his command through the mountains west of Lynchburg, George Pickett was forced to surrender with his 4,500 men. The end would have come sooner if not for rumors and false information. History has many tragic examples of lies, misinformation, and rumors and their consequences.

The Franco Prussian War of 1870-71 proved that false information and twisted truth can enflame nations. In this event Otto Von Bismarck acted deliberately to instigate war. Sometimes carelessness, ignorance or disregard for the values or beliefs of others was responsible. The Sepoy Rebellion in India in 1857 was case in point. Ordering Hindu and Mohammedan solders to bite open cartridges greased with pig and cow fat forced revolt. Little is held more dearly to a man or woman than their religious beliefs, as the Coalition was now only beginning to learn.

As Pickett surrendered, he made two pleas. As was now rumored by a number of generals of the American army, Lincoln and Davis had been executed by the Coalition. Pickett pleaded now for the lives of his officers, not to be executed as Lincoln and Davis were. Observing Coalition policies, he also asked that his men not be called upon to take an oath against their religious convictions. General Roosevelt Freeman on both counts reassured him, but suspicions remained.

The capture of Pickett brought the total capture from the Armies the Potomac, Virginia, and other seaboard forces to 113,000. A number of generals, Longstreet, Buell, John Gordon, Ambrose Hill, and John Hood were taken. Missing included Lee, Hooker, McClellan, Burnside, Jackson, and most other notables. Rumor had it many of these were incinerated at Marye's Hights, but no confirmation was available. Hundreds of thousands of soldiers were also missing. Many had deserted, others were dead, in time an accounting would be made.

By May 13, the Coalition had declared New England, the Atlantic Seaboard, most of the Midwest, and Great Lake areas as secured. A host of bureaucrats from EPA, OSHA, FDA, and the Department of Agriculture began to fan out in these areas. OSHA head Morris Safer and EPA Greens set up headquarters in Pittsburgh, Agriculture head Phil Dirte set up shop from Chicago. Others stayed in Washington or New York.

Overtures were being made to every social and political group in America from business leaders Isaac Singer to Charles Goodyear. The Astors, finance, or labor leader William Sylvis, authors, educators, railroad or relict organizations, all were sought for assistance. Even foreign notables such as Karl Marx, Herbert Spencer, Louis Pasteur were contacted. Most had adopted a wait-and-see attitude, although Marx expressed interest.

Several papers were now beginning to run articles sympathetic to the Coalition agenda. By Thursday, May 14, all major newspapers in the United States were on board. Susan Sontag was assigned to take over news dissemination in and around New York City. Ted Turner had general oversight of the Atlantic seaboard, and other cities and areas were assigned to other noteworthy leaders.

Ted Turner's vision was greater than media, however. He was a historian at least when it came to baseball. From sending a congratulatory not to Eddie Cutford of the Philadelphia Keystones (for his historical base stealing) to meeting with various owners he was working on the American pastime. His goal was to bridge a culture gap and establish goodwill and friendship, a critical mission to build bridges for 1863 American goodwill.

But because of his divided interests, he missed a detail that could have proven disastrous. The "Treasury Department," still under comptroller Hugh McCulloch, issued a report showing a drain of American gold and silver reserves to foreign powers, especially England. While the banking system was still afloat, major bank runs could capsize it. Efforts were being made to negotiate with London, and other foreign powers to avert crisis, but emergency policies were being contemplated.

An error was made by sending out this information through the AP "wire" service. Other Coalition media personnel were able to quickly pick-up on this and order the story purged from the news service records. But Turner was in Atlanta at that time recruiting potential athletes, and missed the release. The Richmond Enquirer was within an hour of publishing when Turner became aware of the leak. Moving immediately, he got the story removed from that paper and all others under his watch. If it had become public, it would have quickly spread nationwide, with disastrous results, especially in New York and New England.

As soldiers were being taken to internment centers; the Coalition was taking steps to insure their loyalty. Pickett had (as others also heard these rumors) heard of the compatibility profiling that was being done to these men. There were identified for informational purposes, each given a national identification number and a procedure called finger printing. They were required to swear allegiance to the government, or Coalition government. And some strange, what was called "psychological profiling" was done to determine their potential threat to society. Any criminal or unusual behavior or histories was documented.

Those who refused to comply were detained. This was not a new policy to America. Both the North and South had imprisoned those that they feared as political or military threats to their war efforts. Lincoln had drawn special notoriety in this regard. That he had suspended habeas corpus, the seizing and the holding without trial for any American deemed a threat to the Union, he circumvented the Constitution. He even used it against members of the press, governing officials, even members of Congress not being immune to its reach. At one point, at least, Lincoln had thought about detaining Chief Supreme Court Justice Roger Taney. Had the war continued the total number of detainees would well exceed 10,000.

While the Coalition was justified in holding its own detainees, the present keeping of almost 75,000 was cause for alarm. For everyone's benefit it was hoped that these men could be quickly returned to society. Postponing the surrender of remaining American forces was using up more Coalition fuel and equipment that had been planned. But the concern it was causing among the general population was just one more thing churning the pot of apprehension and distrust. To this problem the press was now devoting great efforts to ease public concern.

By Friday, May 15, the capabilities of the news media was already coming into question, however, diminishing its effectiveness. Part of this arose from the mass desertion by newspaper correspondents and writers. It was not that the Coalition had not made heroic efforts to overcome this.

In 1863, the newspaper publishing business was primitive by any modern standard. The rotary press invented in 1846 by Richard Hoe was slow and difficult to run. The continuous rolling process, where a roll of paper could be printed and cut from one large long sheet would not be invented until 1865. Modern computerized laser or video display techniques could not even be grasped by the 19th Century mind. Present technology only allowed for so much modern improvisation to begin with.

To overcome equipment and personnel obstacles, everyone who had any printing or publishing experience was called upon to help. Many of the reserve units were able to supply this need. Equipment, including copy machinery was brought in. Electric generators were set up to run printing and other necessary operations.

The loss of news gatherers and writers was not so easily overcome. While modern writers could produce a story that could appeal to a modern American, the 144-year culture gap provided an impediment to the 19th Century mind. Not only does a spoken language change over time, but also so does the word picture idiomatic point of reference. To say to an 1863 man "I made out with your wife" he would probably think of coming to an agreement or understanding. But to say "I knew your wife" would quite likely create an angry and jealous husband. To say "We are not rocket scientists" would leave them lost in space. Unavoidable impediment as it was, when the novelty wore off, papers sales declined.

No longer receiving news from familiar sources affected the populace in several ways. People had come to believe already that the Coalition was withholding information. Whenever folks believe that they are not being told the truth they tend to invent their own versions. Rumors ran rampant; news stories were twisted by a paranoid, sinisterish mindset. The ideas that Lincoln and Davis had been executed by the Coalition, that the Coalition wanted to destroy the Bible, that the Coalition hated families, etc... began to spread like prairie fire.

The loss of credibility created sympathy for media reporters and editors that no longer ran their papers. Their willingness to lose their positions rather than join a mentality they did not believe in elevated them to a position of respect. The weeks ahead would also see the advent and flourishing of a number of underground publications. It also created distrust abroad as other powers began to believe in the dishonesty of a government that pushed its agenda through the media.

May 15 also saw an increase in what was called secure zones. California and Texas were now pacified, but both governors Stanford of California, and Lubbock of Texas resigned. As Coalition department and agency heads continued to expand their activities into more of the nation, it was at the expense of American leadership.

Isaac Newton resigned his appointment as Secretary of Agriculture. Edward Bates, Attorney General and Montgomery Blair, Postmaster General had their resignations officially accepted. Salmon P. Chase was still Secretary of Treasury for now, but Lincoln's Executive Team was effectively gone. Efforts to "revive" Congress were equally fruitless. As Senators and Representatives were ordered back to Washington by the Daschle Administration, almost all declined. On pain of being expelled from Congress, all but a few refused to return. Among the very few who did was the core of peace at any price "Copperhead Democrats". Clement Vallandingham of Ohio suddenly found he was elevated to Speaker of the House over 16 other remaining representatives.

By day's end American elected or historically appointed government was limited to a dumfounded Supreme Court and Judicial branch, several governors, most mayors, and local officials. To the American people, the Coalition, and Daschle were seen more and more as an occupation government of a foreign power. That virtually all of the noble ideals of this government ran contrary to those of the people was beginning to create friction. Without collaboration in key positions from the Americans, the nation would soon have an underground economy, government, and social structure to go along with the press.

In New York, Susan Sontag had been performing heroically in her attempts to bridge this gap in the region's newspapers. The forever "peace monger" made every attempt to include feature articles promoting the values of 1863 America. The relatively low crime rate, respectful children, work ethic, and basic honesty were commendable, and praise worthy. Despite official advisories to the contrary, she included in the papers an acknowledgement of each key resignation, with a short biography and politically filtered explanation. All this was in an effort to win public trust.

But it was not enough. As she left her Tribune office that evening an older man met her. He pulled out a Colt pistol and shot her dead. As he did, another voice cried out, "She is dead, the Jezebel is dead."

Chapter 4

The death of Sontag hit Daschle especially hard. Her death was not in the battlefield; it was in a supposedly pacified big city. By all appearance it was not motivated by theft, no possessions were taken, her office was not entered. She was a friend. She also was oil in a hostile world filled with people who rubbed each other raw. And her death brought new security rules into government policy.

Plans for a registration of all firearms and national identification system went into an accelerated mode. As American troops were disarmed, they were requested to fulfill the identification procedures. That information now would be used to make a registry of all firearms owned by these men. All vendors of firearms or ammunition were to be licensed, and anyone purchasing these materials would be registered. A national ID number would be provided.

Any person receiving any form of government assistance would also be given an ID number, and required to furnish firearm information. All retained governmental employees, military forces, or those receiving government contract would also be included. Plans were in the works for a universal registration within a few weeks, using schools, bank accounts, places of employment, or property records.

The immediate need was to defuse a nervous population so winning the hearts and minds could come in a peaceful and prosperous environment. Daschle was mindful of history. A continued agitation, even by a tiny minority, was enough to disrupt even the best economic and political development plans. As the populace loses faith in the powers that be to restore order, little by little authority erodes and often is lost. This was especially dangerous to a power, like the Coalition, that advocated policies less that palatable to the common person. Time was essential to buy an opportunity to show the rightness of their cause.

No quarter could be given to any hostile force without unconditional surrender. A superior power, regardless of its advantage, still could be defeated. In 416 BC. Athens had money, a powerful army, much through superior alliances, naval superiority, a moral edge, and educated leaders. But in their quest to eliminate Sparta they committed many blunders, from attacking a neutral Melians, to squandering an army in Sicily. They were finally defeated, and only by the "mercy" of the Spartan alliance were not annihilated.

The American people were kind of like the Spartans. Armies, however hopelessly out matched still offered resistance from Kentucky to Louisiana. The longer it persisted the more international sympathy, and agitation would come into play, as France already was. Fuel, and to a lesser degree ammunition, was being depleted far more rapidly than anticipated.

Against this backdrop, friction was beginning to surface in the various Coalition agencies. No where was this more apparent than in west Pennsylvania. With drains on oil and demands for steel, OSHA and EPA were colliding with Homeland Security and official policy. Believing the war to be won, priority shifted to administrative and development in the minds of most policy makers. Like the old Chinese proverb, "A dog on a hunt ignores his fleas while a dog in a cage bites his", the hunt was over and the biting begun. Not even the death of Sontag, while it was mourned, brought back much concern for danger or alarm.

Monday, May 18th saw an official end to hostilities in the old South, at least on an organized military scale. Roscrans surrendered the remnants of his combined command at Bear Mountain, Kentucky. He had shown his staying power only five months earlier at Stones River when he had endured the loss of a third of his command. But his army's grit was no match for infrared scoping from helicopters beyond his range of fire. His only pleas were that his men not be forced to recant their faith in God or be executed like Lincoln and Davis. General Douglas Prescott from Memphis gave his assurances of fair and honorable treatment.

His 3,100 men brought the Coalition bag to 132,000 total prisoners. The balance of the American armies had disappeared. The best estimates place the death toll at 95,000, but history would later reduce this to 48,500. Against this the official Coalition losses were 267 dead and 139 still missing. A still illusive Grant had accounted for almost a quarter of the known dead. But with the surrender of Roscrans, his command nearly collapsed as well. He went into hiding and only a few die hard units remained in scattered settlements.

Daschle "celebrated" the news by calling a late afternoon cabinet and key leaders meeting. With the aggressive stage of military operations over, fuller attention could now focus on mopping up and sealing the borders. While cleared of organized resistance, many areas, especially in the South, Far West and Frontiers were infested with hostile stragglers. Along the Canadian border, a number of small adversarial groups were able to engage in hit and run raids. But while there was still danger, the process of saving America from itself should be accelerated.

Border sealing was quickly becoming essential for another reason. As the Coalition began to implement Daschle's new security and ID policies, one of the first steps was to put business leaders in the database. Richard J. Gatling, who less than five months earlier had offered his "Gatling Gun" to the world had left the country. So had Samuel Colt's interests, Oliver Winchester, and other key players in the arms industry. Nor was the desertion limited to the arms industry. Isaac Singer, sewing machine "tycoon", Cyrus McCormic, farm machinery, Gail Borden, processed foods, to name a few, had disappeared. So far, no noteworthy steel, oil, railroad, or banking mogul had fled, but it was only a matter of time. The Canadian border would receive special attention. Naval screening of the Atlantic shipping industries would also be stepped up.

Sealed borders also would isolate the vocal few who were pushing the limits of Coalition tolerance of freedom of expression on the 17th. Under the guise of religious services, a number of church leaders had openly criticized Coalition policies from their pulpits. Such political speech or the hate mongering of women's leaders, homosexuals, or atheists was illegal in 21st century America. Letters would be sent to the churches to inform them of their legal responsibility. But among the detainees in Coalition custody nearly 200 were considered civilian agitators. Another 3,000 had drawn special Coalition surveillance.

On May 19, William Lloyd Garrison joined the ranks of detainees. He had been advised by letter of the Coalition media standards that were adopted over the May 9-10 weekend. His paper, *"The Liberator"*, had been a bastian from Boston for the antislavery, or abolitionists. As one who also believed in women's rights, it was hoped that his paper could now advocate this moral good.

But Garrison chafed at the imposition of what he believed to be "the sin of Eve" or "Jezebel" morality on the nation. He refused. As the media authorities attempted to reason with him his response be came quite dogmatic. Having spent over three decades in bringing freedom to the slaves, he now employed his pen, and his paper, to oppose the evils of the Coalition. Peter Jennings tried to reason with him. His cause was morally bankrupt and soon to be on the fringe of society. But Garrison responded. "The success of moral principle has never depended on guns or popularity, but on devotion, justice, and resolve." Persisting in his stubbornness, his "devotion" now cost him his liberty.

Such surveillance, monitoring, and detaining of suspicious Americans was essential in preventing acts of aggression and sabotage. It also was creating a spirit of antagonism and distrust in the minds and hearts of the people. The arrest of Garrison was not received will by anyone, even the South, long seeing him as an agitator, was concerned by the reach of a Coalition that could arrest a high idealist pacifist.

On that same day official ground breaking took place at Franklin, Pennsylvania. The Coalition had in its possession USGS (US Geological Survey) maps of mineral deposits throughout America. Computer enhanced drawings also showed the probable locations of undeveloped cites as they would have appeared in 1863 for several regions, among them the oil deposits of the West Pennsylvania and its vicinity. With unanticipated demands on petroleum products, jet fuels, diesel, etc... Daschle was compelled to begin development and recovery two weeks early from his timetable. It also brought him full-blown controversy.

Rock oil, as petroleum was called, was brought to prominence in America when Edwin Drake drilled a well in 1859 at Titusvillie. By 1863, rock oil, at ten cents a barrel, had begun to replace whale oil. Wagons, river barges, and a growing network of railroads transported it to refineries out east. By 1862, US oilfield produced 128 million gallons of oil; exports to England alone were 500 thousand pound sterling.

Perry Noyah of the Environmental Coalition was concerned that accelerated oil development would crowd out the private prospectors. If this happened, and oil became short in supply, the whaling industry would increase its killing of whales. From his experience with Green Peace, he was fully aware that economic pressures were the enemy of the environment. Hugo Tree, formerly of the Sierra Club was concerned of damage to the oil field environment.

To this Greens of the EPA agreed. He had originally hoped for a postponement until at least July 1st for refinery construction to begin. This would provide time for the steel, and other industries to adapt at least somewhat more environmentally friendly alloys, procedures, and technology. Air samples form the area already showed alarming levels of pollution.

OSHA head Morris Safer was concerned with worker safety. While no official statistics were available; more Americans were dying in American farms, factories, and mines than on the battlefields. To accelerate oil and steel production would only make matters worse. Laws should be put in force, procedures modified, and safety equipment installed before any new construction should begin. Labor and women's groups objected to discrimination against minorities and women in any hiring plans. Department of Labor head Minnie M. Wage was concerned about wages paid the workers. Her concerns also were for work place justice and plant conditions. She also urged delay. With women's groups already concerned about policy, as other events of the day would show, these issues could not be ignored. Daschle agreed to an affirmative action effort to recruit women and minorities in oil and steel. But the timetable of contruction was nonnegotiable.

Property rights posed another problem. Many prospectors could not prove ownership of their land. Homestead rules could cover many, word of mouth contracts might cover others. But if the Coalition was to rapidly develop an oil field, it would have to some how settle accounts with all affected prospectors, legitimate or not. Time did not allow for a protracted investigation into bogus, or any claims. And land purchases must be done quickly.

Landowners were resistant to selling to the Coalition, at a fixed rate, while envisioning "good times a comin" in the oil business. From Titusville to Oil City only a score or so claimstakers sold out on first request. To confiscate the land could provoke open revolt among prospectors. It would also be bad publicity in a nation already unsettled by Coalition intrusion. To fork out the kind of cash most wanted for their land would threaten an already stressed financial system.

Daschle compromised with them instead. The Coalition would develop their fields at no cost to them to insure adequate supplies for refinery needs. The various prospectors would then be paid ten cents a barrel royalties on all oil taken. The land would remain theirs. By the 20th most had accepted the deal.

But no sooner had this agreement been reached then it resulted in even more controversy. The chief benefactors of this plan were white males, among them tycoons like John D. Rockefeller. Daschle had taken his first test on class fairness and flunked it miserably, in the minds of many. All he had done was to make the rich richer. This also would provide a continued friction for him and his policies.

On the 19th in an 8:00AM meeting, mission commander, General Reno Henderson, with HSA head Lyberte met with Daschle. The problem areas of resistance, rather than losing ground were if anything increasing in scope. In many areas, the populace was coming to the aid of the guerrilla movements. While generally confined to the South and frontier West, hot spots were beginning to redevelop in the heartland or Midwest. Ohio, Illinois, and Wisconsin had seen organized hostilities in isolated or wilderness areas.

A significant reason was 19th century sexual stereotypes When the men realized that many of the Coalition soliders were female, they were more unwilling to surrender. There seemed to be a macho problem of surrendering to a woman.

Such pettiness was not uncommon to the Civil War combattants. At Ft. Monroe (Hampton Roads), or South Carolina, and other naval incursions against the South, various commanders were reluctant to surrender to the wrong branch of Federal forces. During the civil war pride over not being defeated by the Federal Army (or vice versa) would force representatives of the other branch to receive a surrender.

The antagonism towards women had also been reflected in treatment of women taken as prisoners. Of the eighteen that were captured (at this point confirmed, others were still missing), ten had been molested by captors. While most occurred without knowledge of anyone but the attackers, two under the authority of Nathan Bedford Forrest were gang raped. Forrest, commander of General Braxton Bragg's cavalry, was unrepentant. "It is hoped that this will demonstrated to the Coalition that we Americans cannot cope with women combattants", he answered upon his surrender.

On April 12, 1864, Forrest would have used this same insanity to justify the massacre of 300 Blacks at Ft Pillow. But insane as it was, it represented the almost univeral ignorance of 1863 America. The danger of potentially unending hostilities, and the need to gradually prepare America for acceptance of reality were grave concerns. Some captured soldiers refused orders given by women, even at the risk of death. As a move to ease tensions, Daschle ordered women in combat or highly visible positions put in a less open view, for now. Those who dealt with the Americans were to act and dress in a lady-like fashion until the populace could be "incrementlly enlightened." Women in authority would remain in authority, but the appearance of male leadership, in dealing with the nation, was incouraged.

Reaction was immediate. Barbara Boxer was the first to confront Daschle, as initial shock was already turning into a firestorm of outrage. Women had not gone back 144 years in time, stand side by side with men, only to be reduced to a second class personhood. And she made her point quite effectively. The nation had once compromised in accepting the slaves as only 60 percent person. Islamic fundamentalists said women were only half a person, men being whole persons.

When Daschle argued that his intent was to protect women, while steadily upgrading their status, he cited Susan Sontag as an example. But Boxer, and the other Coalition women could not be won on this male biased logic. Susan was seen as a martyr to the cause, a cause for which they were willing to die for as well, equal rights. If Daschle did not move quickly to reverse the damage this policy was already causing, he would lose the 130,000 Coalition women. Daschle agreed to meet with a women's forum on Saturday, May 23$^{rd.}$

In the mean time, Daschle made several key immediate orders as a concession. While in some states, like New York, women already had the right to full property ownership, now, this was to be universal. The right of women to vote, at all levels, local, state, national, was also immidiately put into effect. Divorce laws would be liberalized, contraceptives disemminated, and abortion clinics opened. Boxer accepted this, as well as Daschle's commitment to affirmative action.

Breyer and Ginsburg met with Chief Justice Roger Taney on Friday, May 20th. They had been busily drafting an outline for a revised legal code for America. Advised by several advocacy leaders, they had conferred in great length with ACLU head Ann Junction. To free themselves of other legal responsibilities, they delegated authority to Elizabeth Patterson Roberta.

Considering the gross generalities and vagueness of American law in 1863 it did function with amazing effectiveness. Based upon English common law or more than a half millenium in making, it maintained social order, as much by tradition or custom as by written code. The primative

American system placed its foundation on the Bible, and laws were written to uphold the social fabric. While some evolution in the system had occurred, the Thomas Jefferson concept, "Government that governs best, governs the least," still held sway.

In the courts, a simple, common man could still carry his Bible into the proceedings, read from it, and say that an action or law wasn't right. Jury duty carried with it the charge, or responsibility, to overturn a law that was not believed right by the people. While rulings by precedent had their place, Andrew Jackson had argued, precedent used alone is a danger to the system. It would require total cooperation from Taney and the present court to bridge the 144 year gap of legal evolution.

Hopes were not high going into the meeting. This was the same Taney who had written the Dred Scott decision, which opened the door to slavery in the North in 1856. An old man, set in his beliefs that had been formed in a now dead past, he had shown rare life as of late, however. A paralell was made to Stephen Douglas. A foe of Lincoln and his policies, had spent his last year as an "ally", working dilligently to keep union and suppress the rebellion in 1860-1861. On his death on June 3, 1861, even Lincoln had mourned the loss. Now Taney had come to advocate the welfare of all Americans, Black and White. But he had yet to speak a kind word about Daschle and the Coalition.

As Ginsburg and Breyer met with Taney, they appealed to the ideal of welfare to all Americans. Presenting their case for social justice, Taney and his associate justices were concerned that no reference was made to God of the Bible. Ginsburg responded that even the ancient Greek thinker Protagoras in the 5th Century B.C. said, "Man was the measure of all things." Taney replied that he could not accept such a system. Being given little choice, he and all his fellow colleagues resigned.

This added to an increasing burden of government that was already leaching Coalition resources needed to meet other priorities. It was not that Daschle and his team had done nothing. On the 19th, he finally secured an interim counterpart president in the status of General Benjamin Butler. Offers had been made to Vice-President Hannibal Hamlin as early as May 6, but he refused, and resigned as Vice-President as well. Others who had presidential ambitions, according to the history books were also offered the position. "Pathfinder" John Fremont declined surprisingy, but did accept a military post. Another General, George McClellan was missing, but assumed in hiding in New England. All efforts to contact by radio, TV, or through friends were fruitless. Appleals to Thaddeus Stevens, past President James Buchanan, even Confederate States of America Vice-President Alexander Stephens failed.

Finally, in a chage of heart, John C. Fremont reconsidered and accepted the post. His reputation during the Civil War was known more for his policial than military exploits. In the fading summer sun of 1861, he became self appointed military dictator of Missouri. Devoutly antislavery, and antisuccessionalist, he almost succeeded in losing both Missouri and then Kentucky. Very possibly Confederate General Sidney Johnston, by his preemptively invading Kentucky ahead of Grant (under Fremont) saved both states for the Union. But, as a charismatic, and still somewhat popular figure, he would fill that position.

Samuel Barlow, a New York lawyer and a peace Democrat, agreed to switch parties and accept the Vice-Presidency. While his loyalty and integrity were questioned by many, especially Republican, his credentials were good. He was sworn in on the same day.

The cabinet, for now, posed a hopeless challenge. While Fremont was able to employ a few of his friends, not a few lesser European noblemen, Daschle refused to accept the appointments, officially, at least. Postmaster Montgomery Blair had agreed to stay on, and served as the only link to continuity that the executive branch could boast.

Congress was almost a deserted shambles. Not one Republican remained in either House or Senate. Only Copperheads, or Peace Democrats remained, six in the Senate and 17 in the House. Overatures to the CSA gleaned only one man willing to serve in the Senate, and five more in the House. The English Rump Parliament of 1648 under Oliver Cromwell was far more legitimate than that in Washington by June 1863 could ever hope to be.

For American military leadership two primary posts did need filling, the commanders of the Army and Navy. A standing army of 48,000 would remain. Some units, mostly ones in training or that had never seen battle would be retained. The rest would be made up of career, or the far west cavalry soldiers. For a brief time, Fremont was believed to take command. When he opted for Presidency, it left a vacuum of quality leadership. Of the captured generals and colonels only one, Benjamin Butler, had sworn loyalty to the new Democracy.

On Saturday, May 23 he agreed to take command of the American Army. As military governor of New Orleans (and formerly Baltimore) he had made few friends. The "Beast" as he was known, confiscated the possessions of those who refused to swear a loyalty of oath to the Union. He and his brother, had made considerable profit on the trade of contraband cotton while the city and area around chafed under his edicts. But he posessed the ability to recognize which side of his bread was buttered and who owned the butter supply. Now loyal to the Coalition, he commanded an army.

The size and shape of the navy had yet to be determined. The courteous, cultured Admiral Charles A. Davis, formerly head of the navigation department took the post. Sly, and somewhat ambitious, he also had been willing to accept Coalition authority. His age and lack of leadership were not an issue, loyalty was.

For those soldiers and sailors now being released back into society, each was given $50.00 in Union greenbacks. As an incentive to report any guns owned by themselves or family, Dashcle authourized payments of $20.00 more for each one decliared. The Coalition could ill afford upwards of a million trained and armed Americans out on the farm or in the factory. It was also hoped that this would encourage the now nearly 96,000 detainees to swear loyalty to the Coalition.

The resistance to Coaliton identification and registration policies were somewhat baffling to Daschle. In the late 20th and 21st Centuries, Americans willingly submitted to mandantory seatbelts, drug screening, airport and other security, video survellance, etc… Their 19th Century counterparts seemed to cherish their warped sense of liberty in ways beyond understanding. And they were not afraid to die for those beliefs, a reality most troubling to Daschle and the Coalition.

On that morning, Bill Clinton, Coalition Secretary of State, and a delegation of American and European embasaries headed for Europe. The first stop would be England for a meeting with "Lord Evergreen" Prime Minister Palmerston late that evening. The mission, to visit top powers in Europe and seek recognition and peace.

Peace was something Daschle could only wish for as he prepared for his afternoon forum with the women's groups advocates. Among those present Ann Junction of the ACLU, Connie Dumm, PPC, Emily S. List, NOW, Dept. of Education head Noralee L. Litterate, and Boxer. Others were allowed access, but all discussion was channeled throught these leaders. At the front of the room was a life-sized picture of Susan Sontag.

The meeting opened with frank discussion about the circumstances of 19th Century womanhood. With long hours of labor outside the home in poor working conditions without hope of advancements, life for women was difficult enough. Marriage was almost a life sentence. By 1870 Chicago would have one divorce to every 12 marriages, and many would argue that this was the highest in America. Women were forced to bear with drunkenness, infidelity, often abuse, and the financial mismanagement of their husbands. Labor saving devices were almost nonexistent. No access to birth control and poor wages kept them barefoot and pregnant. Lack of proper nutrition and healthcare offered an early grave, or at least chronic health problems. While this dismal picture was slightly exaggerated by the committee, what was most unsettling was the resistance by women to the freeedom now being offered.

Surprisingly enough, all assembled, while not everjoyed by Daschle's record, were encouraged by his orders on the 19th. More action was required to change altitudes and the social structure. Financial assisance, government purchasing and contracts, and emplyment opportunities must be given to women whenever possible. As for attire and profile, the sisterhood was reluctant to allow an archaic culture to dictate its scruples.

Pointing to the picture of Sontag, List praised her as a martyr for the cause of liberty. Womenhood would now "sounded forth the trumpet that shall never sound retreat." As she died for their freedom, they would allow noone to take it away. If the women of 1863 could not accept this freedom then they would just find themselves swept away by history. But their daughters would, and in this freedom they would prosper. The forum ended.

At 9:00 PM, Daschle received a briefing on food and other provision stocks in America. Of urgent concern, nearly 9,500,000 Americans faced food shortages within the next week. In the South, at least two-thirds or 3,000,000 of the ex-slaves were in danger. Mostly illiterate, several factors had left them destitute.

Economically, the South was in a virtual depression. "King cotton", as in the pre-war days this chief product was called, saw its flower fade even as war clouds gathered. The repeal of the English corn laws that kept out imported wheat had opened their markets to the midwest grain producers. King wheat had already begun to rival, and then eclipse king cotton, until by

1862 England (and Europe) imported 40,000,000 bushels of American wheat.

But the war sped cotton's decline as an export beyond anyone's expectations. The blockades of Southern ports at one point put as many as 400,000 English textile workers out of a job, and, to a lesser degree hurt France. But England quickly recovered by reliance on cotton grown in India and Egypt. Even by 1863 the fate of the South had irreversably been changed.

The banking and monetary plight of the south provided little hope for economic recovery. In addition to confederate currency each state had its own. Unlike the North where Bank Comptroller Hugh McCulloch had begun major reform, hundreds of private issue "shinplasters" were in circulation. Gold and silver were almost impossible to find. Inflation had taken the average family food bill from $1.50 a week to ten times that now. Banking and finance was virtually a joke.

Transportation posed another obstacle. Even before Coalition intervention, a bushel of corn that sold for $1.00 on the farm was going for $13.00 in Richmond. On April 2, 1863, the women of that city angrily responded by rioting. But two weeks of off and on attacks by the Coalition had disproportionately weakened an already troubled Southern transport system.

As early as May 15th, Dept of Labor head Minnie M. Wage had succeeded in implementing a ten cents per hour survival wage in the South. She also set a ten hour day limit even for farm labor. Wages were ordered paid in Federal greenbacks, gold, or silver, not Confederate or other monies. For the ex-slaves now employed on the plantations, this would have provided survival income for over 3,500,000 of the over 4,000,000 in the South.

But greedy Southern land owners retailiated by letting go nearly 2,000,000 of them from jobs, housing, and other provision. Using the excuses that they could not affort to pay that wage, or the lack of acceptable currency, they destroyed a beneficial program. They also condemned many acres of land to be taken over by weeds as crops would now not be planted or cultivated. When rich and greedy people can't have their way they take it out on the economy and the backs of the poor.

Another expample of selfish greed was largely responsible for the food shortages in the Northeast as well. Shortages of food stuffs was also aggrivated by shortages of coal and raw materials for manufacturing. New York City was potentially in the worst danger as shipments in and out were almost non-existant. Factories had less than a weeks worth of steel, coal, wood, or other stocks.

The infrastructure of railroads, canals, roads, and rivers was virtally undamaged, as Coalition forces had surgically struck at military targets. What was missing was the insturments of travel. Nearly three-fourths of the merchant fleet and barges were on their way, or already in foreign ports, mostly Canada and the Carribean ports. Rail traffic was down, as owners and investors, especially English feared sabotage or military actions. Many had been pulled into Canada, others sat in rail yards and depots. Even wagon travel was down. Owners complained about Coalition security checks, identification rules, new safety policies and controls on transport rates. The 19th Century America was not cooperative with a government truly interested in the benefit of all its citizens.

Daschle ordered a Sunday morning meeting, to be attended by his entire cabinet. A food and transport crisis affecting almost one-third of the population was priority. But so also was the continuing drain on governmental, and banking gold and silver reserves. And then again, there was the nagging problem of continuing armed resistance.

But one more problem was proving itself troubling to Daschle and his leadership. News of his women's policy had already made the news through the reporting of Rather, Turner, and company. Now Mary Berry and the Black (African-American) leadership demanded a meeting to discuss racial concerns. And a rumbling was also felt on every street corner in America, as the people, despite fear of detention, began to vocally assail these policies. Sunday, May 24 would be an important day.

Chapter 5

Nation building cannot be achieved without adequate military might. But it cannot be changed by that might alone. Every area of the economic, political, and social structure must also be addressed. To do otherwise is like leaving the roots of the weeds in a garden to return in the future. For those living in 1863 America, the economy needed reviving, food and essentials supplied, the money system secured, education and general welfare provided for, and national interests protected. To achieve these goals there were also logistical concerns, to provide adequate fuel, steel and oil needed fast track development.

Daschle's first action of the day was to address the growing food crisis. Food and raw material transportation was near a standstill. Fuel stocks had already been depleted at a much faster rate than Coalition plans had anticipated. The Coalition could provide transport for now to feed New York and New England. With effort, other essential shipments could also be made. Coal stocks could be diverted for industrial use for now, and rebuilt in the fall before cold weather heating demands set in. More on long term solutions would be addressed later in the day.

In the South the problem was not at present the availability of food, but distribution and affordability. The poor, especially the freed slaves, could not buy food. Daschle sought aid from the Afro-American leadership Counsel, headed by Mary Berry (of the 2007 Civil Rights Commission). The head of the Department of Labor Minnie M. Wage and Treasury head Cash also attended.

As the meeting began, Berry chided Daschle for his failure to more fully involve the counsel in his policy making. Daschle was including other groups (as women) to set policy, but only included the Counsel in implementing it. Racism was the reason for the mission to begin with, as Al Sharpton and Jesse Jackson weighed in.

For the Blacks of the South to be facing starvation proved Daschle's ignorance and insensitivity. Already thousands, mostly children, had died of hunger and disease. The toll would reach 500 a day by the end of the month.

The Coalition Blacks already had lost respect for Coalition leadership. Immediate action was vital.

To begin elevating the status of the ex-slaves, money must be put into their hands immediately. But the owners or ex-masters of the plantations should not be allowed to profit. To pay the ex-slaves to work the plantations would subsidize the very people responsible for the Civil War in the first place. In short order, these plantations needed to be nationalized, broken up, and distributed to the poor. But this would take months to fairly implement. In the mean time, let the owners suffer.

Coalition relief efforts would focus on providing a living income to the poor Blacks for now. Relief offices would be set up by Thursday throughout the South. Black households would be registered and daily payments of fifty cents per person begun. By Monday, June 8, the payments would be made weekly.

Many households were headed by women, and many men were poor money managers. To avoid gambling, drinking, or squandering of the money, payment would be made to the women. This also would aid the raising of the status of women. A number of Coalition construction projects were available to the men if they wanted money for themselves. Cash was commissioned with the task of making adequate money supplies available.

That construction was needed on the South's transportation system was above question. Even before the war, Southern rail lines were inferior in quality. In some cases the track gauge was not even uniform, the same trains would not fit on all the lines. Roads and bridges, even if not damaged by war, were inadequate. And all this was before the demands of modern transportation could be thrown in. The ex-slaves would be given priority status in hiring and promotions to all southern works projects.

To bring American commercial transport back, financial incentives were offered. Coalition Treasury Secretary, Preston "Prince" Cash, was forced to choke, as the monetary situation already was being strained, but necessity dictated policy. To bring tonnage back to American ports, owners would be given bounties of up to $5,000 per vessel. Owners of railroad rolling stock and wagons also were offered cash incentives. Mothballed "vessels", whaling ships, even military boats would be used, even if it was inefficiently, to get the nation moving again. And, as a last resort, Daschle issued a standing executive order to confiscate private shipping.

At 8:00 AM, Daschle and many other key members of the Administration broke to attend a universalistic worship service. A broad spectrum of religious beliefs was represented, Hindu, Moslem, Buddhist, Orthodox Jew, Wicca, and other New Age groups. All religions hold some truth, and since all rivers run to the same oceans, all were welcome. All that is, except for Christianity. The radical and exclusive Christian fundamentalist movement of the latter 20th and the 21st Centuries had alienated the open minds of the Coalition leadership.

Radical Christianity had driven Daschle to seek spiritual direction from an eastern spirit guide named Krishna Mahariji. In a personal meeting with Daschle he warned of the dangers posed by Christianity. The 1863 American, blinded by the narrow and intolerant teaching of the Bible, was poisoned to the truth. Jesus Christ was not the only way to God, as Christians claimed. For the Coalition to prosper the church must be discredited and the Bible disproved. Strangle it now in its cradle, or Christianity would prove his undoing.

Media leaders met with Daschle next. Americans had suddenly stopped buying newspapers; sales were off nation wide by almost half since May 10. At a time when it was vital to intensify the work of correcting Americans wrongful thinking, fewer of them were listening to the message.

A great 20th century visionary (Mao Tse Tung) had written, "To link oneself with the masses one must act in accordance with the needs and wishes of the masses." The Coalition would reach out to the masses on their level. But it would be unreasonable to expect media leaders to live on the streets with the common person. Therefore, a series of life story interviews would be conducted. These stories could then be regionally and culturally adapted to different parts of the country. A bond of understanding could be established, and the population would come to see the Coalition as people like them and learn to trust the media.

A series of these articles, used nation wide, would praise the acceptable values, beliefs, and accomplishments of the people. After a week or two, the media would then begin to subtly raise a few questions about the injustices, dangers, and wrongful values of the culture. At that point, selected individuals (or fabrications from the life stories) could be interviewed, and acceptable suggestions on how to amend these evils be advocated. This would disarm any claims that the Coalition was trying to impose its beliefs on the nation. Also, one more point, a systematic proof of evolution would be included, as well as discrediting of the Bible.

The price of newspapers would be set or reduced nationwide to a penny an issue. While inflation of the war years had dramatically raised the price of newsprint, an affordable paper was essential. The government would subsidize the newspapers to make up any excessive costs.

Also, Daschle explained to Rather, Turner, Jennings, and the others present the need for confidentiality of Coalition policy. On Friday the 22nd, an OSHA policy decision accidentally made it into print in the *Chicago Tribune* and a few other area papers. While all the goals were essential, and of exemplary nature, they could create a backlash. The American mindset was not on the wavelength of the modern mind. Safety chains, guards, barriers, goggles, all were foreign to the rugged individualism and belief in fate that Americans held. When enough stories and pictures of mangled bodies and grieving families could be run to shock the public out of its false concepts of liberty, then these rules would find acceptance. All present agreed to follow these policies.

Cash addressed the monetary problem with Daschle. In attendance were Esher Newbury and Ira Roth. Dr. Newbury was English, and had served as a banking and financial advisor to the Labor Party under Tony Blair, Prime Minister. As a "no-name" aide, she never the less had impeccable credentials as both an economic advisor and Socialist. She also gave credibility to the Coalition as an international effort. Roth was head of the Internal Revenue Service.

In an era of still circulating bank issued currency, "wild cat" and counterfeit money, bank booms and failures, order was needed. And Federal Bank Controller Hugh McCulloch, in his effort to help finance the war, had just began the long overdue process of reform. In 1863, 7,000 different currency notes, banks, business, or state and local governments were freely circulating. Estimates were that up to 6,000 bogus and counterfeit varieties of currencies also existed. Many of the nation's 1,600 or so banks saw their currency circulate nation wide. When banks failed, as frequency happened, their notes remained in the national money supply.

For the Mount Vernon Bank to have failed on Friday was really no big thing, under normal circumstances. But for the Coalition and its accelerated efforts to establish monetary stability, it was highly significant. This was especially true considering the growing nation wide run on the banks by account holders.

Working with McCulloch, Cash had continued to replace irregular notes with Federal Greenbacks. The process of assuming adequate bank reserves was in full swing. But the continuing demands, especially from Europe for gold and silver threatened the system. Not only did the American economy, but also such initiatives as the aid to the ex-slaves depended on a stable money system.

In the South, with Virginia as the only exception, the banks were allowed to function (or disfunction) on their own merits. The hyperinflation of Confederate Currency was doubling prices almost every six months. A barrel of flour that cost $5.00 in Philadelphia cost almost ten times as much in Richmond. The Coalition intervention had done little to improve the system. If anything, it hastened its decline, as Southern banks were forced to close or payoff demands in shinplaster (wild cat currency) or now worthless Confederate paper.

This did not evoke great sympathies in Washington. The South was to blame for all the ills of war, slavery, and poverty to begin with. Outside of the dire concern for the ex-slaves, the South could suffer. Also, over 80 percent of the nation's economic pie lie outside of the South. Little effort, outside of reparations and transportation improvement, would be directed there for now.

To preserve the northern banks, two immediate courses of action would be taken. One was diplomatic, with Bill Clinton in meetings even on that day in England to discuss European concerns. The other was to begin the immediate work of increasing mining of American gold and silver. Department of Interior head Landus D. Velepor would with USGS computer imaging, begin that process this week. More permanent proposals would be brought by week's end by Cash, Roth, and the rest of the team to provide long-term answers.

Late afternoon, meeting with Noralee L. Litterate of the Department of Education, Daschle brought up the immediate concern of worker training. The Coalition work in West Pennsylvania had already lain open the deplorable state of unskilled labor in America. Not only were workers having to be trained to run sophisticated (to them) equipment, many had to be taught algebra, geometry, and basic math, even how to read and write. In addition to a long-term educational agenda, worker skills training would be needed everywhere the Coalition hired workers.

Seven Score and Four

Litterate confessed that this was not a problem that her staff had been prepared to deal with. Credentials would have to be authorized and then given to upwards of thousands of unlicensed educators to train workers. Her teachers were primarily academic, and had been preparing an education curriculum, not a vocational one. The potential dangers and violations of Modern law and National Education Association Standards were legion.

Daschle gave her a free hand in education to take any and all necessary steps to begin training programs by June 15 at the latest and if possible the 8th. Procedural rules could be relaxed, and her staff would be exempted from any lawsuits for actions taken, for now, anyway. Daschle also authorized the necessary funding for book publishing, building procurement, or other necessary expenses.

In a final meeting Daschle met with his military and HSA Lyberte. A number of weapons, mostly small arms, had been captured. While in total little threat could be posed by the loss, one theft was troubling. At. Ft. Smith, Arkansas, the Coalition had set up and ammunition conversion center to disassemble antiaircraft and armor piercing missiles. On May 12 nearly a thousand of these portable missiles with launchers disappeared. Only two had been recovered yesterday, May 23 on a small boat on Lake Superior headed for Canada.

It was assumed that the technology to manufacture these weapons was beyond the grasp of anyone on earth. But there was no margin for error to allow England, Prussia, or France the opportunity to find out. While posing no match to Coalition weaponry, in the hands of guerrillas, they could cause substantial casualties and equipment loss. To prevent any possibility of counterfeiting these weapons, the borders must be sealed.

The next morning Monday, May 25 the first Coalition abortion clinic opened in America in Columbia, South Carolina. Whitney Gifford was the clinic director, and in the media zone administered by Marion Franklin. All services, abortion, contraceptives and health screening were free of charge, but no one came in that day. Franklin, despite his Moslem beliefs, saw the needed to promote its services and Coalition values. He launched a media campaign.

Franklin traced his ancestry back to a Moslem slave family that was almost wiped out in the 1860's. His grandfather, Dalton, was born in December 1863 near Durham North Carolina. He was raised by his mother, Henrietta, as his father, Stovall had died in April 1863 of pneumonia. An ambitious and resourceful man, Dalton virtually taught himself to read and write, and eventually became a schoolteacher. He died in 1934 while Marion was still in his infancy, but his determination had been the inspiration for Marion's own rise to fame.

Franklin was selected for the Coalition media team both for his efficient and effective media management skills and his impeccable liberal credentials. He was a moderate Moslem, one whose sect had severed all ties with fundamentalists. He had a profound sympathy for the poor, generally supported women's rights issues, and had rejected Moslem dogma against gays. "How could someone help what Allah caused him or her to be born with?" he would argue.

He and a significant number of the media corps also strongly disagreed with Daschle's agenda for media action. Seeing the media leadership as a club of old, conservative white men, he, and others believed that as a group they had lost vision. There was a terrible sense of urgency for action now. For the minorities and women, their pain was being ignored, and in the media decision, so was their counsel.

The abortion clinic gave him a cause to push, and he took full advantage of it. Within his area of oversight, most of Georgia, North Carolina, and South Carolina, he ordered feature stories covering the clinic and the plight of women. All other issues, including integration and education were put on a lesser priority now, abortion was the key issue in promoting rights, especially for women.

On May 14 when he initially took control of this area, many of the existing editors and writers had balked at his agenda. Ex-slaves who could neither read nor write replaced them in many cases. Coalition personnel were called upon to keep the papers running having to learn how to run a rotary presses not used since before their grandparents were born (except for Franklin).

Franklin was taken by surprise by the reaction of his new employees. At the Charleston *Mercury* one actually accosted him the next day, accusing him of hating his own people, of slaughtering the children as the Pharaoh of Egypt did. "If Pharaoh had his way the hero Moses would be dead in the river," the new editor said. The whole staff of ex-slaves joined in the chorus.

Franklin tried to reason with them using this same Moses to show his case. In "The Story" in the Koran, Moses was not understood, or accepted by his people when he was trying to liberate them. Now Franklin would have to establish a basis for trust.

"No my brother," he answered, "I am here to liberate you, as we all are." He knew the chains of bondage were not yet fully broken, and he hoped a vision of a better tomorrow would inspire an oppressed race to rise up and snap them. He spoke of a day when all children would live in peace and harmony, attend the same schools, have the same opportunities. All races would live and prosper in peace and equality, beginning with monetary reparations to the slaves. As Moses despoiled Egypt, now the enslaved peoples of the South would enjoy the wealth of the land. But they must also understand those tools of slavery, and how to stay free. Abortion was part of that freedom.

But for reasons unknown to the enlightened, modern mind, integration was no more popular in the minds of the ex-slaves than it was with the Whites. Even in 1896, when Plessy vs.. Ferguson legally allowed discrimination under the façade of "separate but equal"; there was no great outcry. The Blacks wanted the opportunity for advancement, acceptance in society, racial harmony, but not a loss of their own identity. Just as America saw ethnic German, Italian, Polish, Irish, Jewish, and other communities, many Blacks felt comfortable in their own. "Melting pot" would come, but not all at once, and not at a loss of identity or culture. Such change would come in time, but time was not something the Coalition had an abundance of. Franklin would not sit back and watch ignorance or prejudice from anyone keeps his ancestors down. His policies would continue.

The media bureau, or corps committee, also was not at ease with the policies of Franklin and other region overseers in the South. All districts except those in Virginia, Louisiana and Texas had taken a decidedly activist slant at odds with the corps leadership. But before the problem could be addressed, another media action caused even greater controversy.

Modern Americans cherish their freedom to read or view whatever they want to see without the interference of government censorship. When the Coalition arrived in 1863 America, thousands of movies, episodes of situational comedies, and other series came with them. Some were broadcast nationwide over the network system, others regionally, or even locally. While the chief audience was Coalition, all Americans were allowed to view from the TV rooms set up across America. Some even tried to use various programs to bridge gaps in several areas. "WKRP of Cincinnati" was played to a local audience, as was "Dallas" in Texas, "Matlock" in Atlanta or "The District" in Washington D.C.

On Tuesday, May 26, the entertainment group began a massive campaign to appeal to the 1863 Americans. The afternoon and evening airwaves were booked with back to back Harry Potter, James Bond, and "skin flicks" like "I Am Curious Yellow" and "Deep Throat." Americans were paid a quarter to come to the centers and watch. Nearly two million took the offer.

Viewing witches and wizards, spies and counter spies, heroes, villains, technological marvels both intrigued and angered. But the language, sexual situations, and challenge to the values of America created nothing but enemies. Mothers covered the eyes and ears of children as they attempted to rush out. Men's eyes locked on the images of sexual ecstasy on the screen, then most turned away in disgust. Unfortunately, the effort at cultural enlightenment was a failure, and only served to bring enemies together against the "wizardry" of the infidel Coalition.

Daschle moved immediately to defuse the situation before it could galvanize a whole nation against them. There was enough for the Coalition to change and reform without unnecessary antagonism. He ordered a public apology to go out both on the airwaves and in the newspapers. He made it clear that they were not there to mock or destroy the values of the nation, but to build a better society. No more graphic programming would go over the airwaves.

A potentially hostile people must be won over. Change would come, but it would take time, even if this was not something he had a wealth of. Just as the humanists had turned American beliefs in the 20th Century, it would come now. Control of the media, courts, and education system would already be in their hands, and in time their values would replace 1863 ignorance. Breyer, Rather, and Litterate would guarantee that. But for now, Dashcle ordered a limited censorship.

But in attempting to defer tension in one arena, he only created it in another. The ACLU led the way in criticizing Daschle's decision. Ann Junction contacted Judge Patterson-Roberta to file an injunction against the order. A number of other advocacy groups, including Gerald (Geraldean) Corona of the Gay Rights Action League was furious. One joked about Daschle taking off his mask to expose George Bush Jr. underneath. Others threatened civil disobedience if the censorship order remained.

In another policy, Daschle was finding opposition within his own ranks. His steel and oil program was becoming more critical by the day. Present fuel use projections showed that the Coalition would run out by August 28. Steel production was being accelerated to build a refinery, and this was one bright spot of cooperation with Americans in Daschle's agenda.

Meeting with the owners of the various steel companies he had struck a deal on rapid supply increases. Steel owners would keep ownership of their mills, but the Coalition would provide the technology and construction necessary to meet the demand. The new mills as well as the old, the Sligo works American, Birmingham, etc…would be upgraded. The mill owners would be paid a percentage based on total production, and when the Coalition management ended, would receive, at no expense, modern production capabilities.

Steel production was up over 50 percent from May 10 and climbing. A fully operational night shift would be in place by June 1, and present production would almost double again. Coalition generators and lighting systems were brought in, and prospective employees, many former slaves, were being interviewed and trained. As things now looked the refinery could be completed and begin production by August 4 and to full operations by the 15th. Any delays could be endangering to the Coalition.

That afternoon, June 26, Donald Greens (EPA) presented Daschle with air and water samples from areas around Pittsburgh. These samples had been taken over the prior 11 days showing pollution changes as production increased. Sulfur was up significantly. To a lesser degree nickel, fluoride, even titanium levels were up, as was silt from smoke. He also had data showing water and ground pollution in New York, Philadelphia and other cites from primitive America oil refining efforts. He and Hugo Tree of the environmental Coalition argued for an immediate cessation of American oil refining and increased steel production until environmental concerns could be met.

In the 20th and 21st Centuries, Daschle had complied an exemplary environmental record. In his Senate leadership he had even succeeded in hamstringing ex-president, or occupant of the White House George Bush JR's energy plan. He and his supporters kept Bush and the greedy oil companies from destroying the Alaska wildlife refuge. But now, the urgent must take priority over the necessary, the environment would have to wait. Oil was essential.

Dept. of Labor Wage then, with OSHA head Safer confronted Daschle with worker concerns. Safer reminded Daschle of the deplorable condition of job site safety in America. Like a growing tide of Coalition voices he also opposed Daschle's slow approach to making changes in America. The steel mills were a catastrophe waiting to happen, and should shut down immediately and be refurbished. The eight to ten week delay would have to be accepted.

Wage addressed the contemptible treatment of labor in American and worldwide. She reminded him of English Socialist Kier Hardie, who in 1866 at age 10 found out the heartlessness of business owners. He had arrived late a second time to his employment because he had been up all night caring for a dieing brother. He was fired and docked one weeks wage. Or so it would be if history failed to be rewritten.

But laborers were little better off then slaves, and maybe worse. A slave would have been beaten and sent to the fields. A fired worker often could not find employment anywhere. To improve worker's lots now would go a long way towards winning over the common person in America. A great leader (Mao Tse Tung) once said," Labor would provide an awesome force in making of history".

In 1914, the International Labor Organization almost prevented the guns of August and World War I. Only Germany wavered, as her labor was nationalistic, and allowed Kaiser Wilhelm II to mobilize and plunge Europe into war. In Russia, the Bolshevik Revolution and era of Communism rose from the working class. Only the religious bias of the American labor movement prevented a worldwide liberation. If Daschle would demand better treatment, shorter hours, higher wages for the oil and steelworkers, America would follow, and the masses would be his.

Again, to bring change would bring delay. And as Cash now would advise Daschle, could add millions in added costs at this time. Other social and economic needs were already on the list for financial support, education, safe food, the environment, etc... Again, this concern would have to wait.

From Europe there was good news. Bill Clinton, the master of charm and likeability had met with leaders in England and France, and was now on his way to Austria. He had been successful in establishing good will and in communicating the peaceful intent of the Coalition.

On the 23rd, he had met with "Lord Evergreen", Prime Minister Palmerston and select members of Parliament, including William Gladstone. Meeting Gladstone (a future Prime Minister), with his almost psychic personal appeal he had established basis for a friendship and common ground on many issues, including home rule for Ireland. On Sunday, he had a rare meeting with Queen Victoria herself.

Monday the 25th he had arrived in France to meet with Napoleon III. An opportunist and a populist leader, he had been quite successful in curbing opposition while making France prosper. Elected as President of France in 1848, by 1863 he was her unchallenged Emperor. Suspicious of the Coalition, he had dispatched nearly 20,000 additional French troops to Mexico to make Maximilian its emperor.

While in both France and England, Clinton had relayed the Coalition's desire to see an end to slavery worldwide. He sought a greater European political league, with England and France, and to a lesser degree Austria and chief powers. He also wanted the Coalition to have access to leaders in Europe, especially France and England. He had left several hundred radios and other communications units with these two for open contact with America. Microwave relay points were being set up across the Atlantic as he met with them.

And while he was in Paris, he made the acquaintance of a couple of French courtesans. This, surprisingly won him the acceptance of several ranking French figures, not out of respect, but in seeing him as a connesour of the finer things in life. It also brought a chiding from Daschle, as 19th Century Americans were not so receptive of such behavior. He reminded Clinton that there was no Janet Reno or Al Gore around to defend his zipper.

As Clinton prepared to leave Paris for Vienna on the 27th, one of his military guard also left something in Paris, a large brief case. Sergeant Henry Culpeper had left it, full of modern history books, in the possession of French Minister Henri Mercier. He had been temporary recall to Paris for French reassessment of American policy. Along with the history books, he also gave Mercier two very controversial right wing extremist books _How then shall we live?_ by Francis Schaeffer and _The Long War Against God_ by Henry Morris.

In the North Atlantic, the "Forrestall" battle group picked up on a radio communication between England and France late that evening. They were able to determine that something profound had been left in Paris, and that the French wanted the English to see. Washington was notified of a compromise of something, but no one knew what at the time.

That same evening other heads of state, Kaiser Wilhelm I of Prussia, Charles XV of Sweeden, and Tsar Alexander II held council with their own key national advisors. For Wilhelm, that included Bismarck, the Iron Chancellor. Larger powers felt offended in not having been on the Coalition diplomatic tour. All were concerned about this own security. Many would sent out feelers to others to form leagues of defense. At least one, Prussia, begin to consider war. Another, Russia was about to move to defend its eastern possessions, especially Alaska.

According to the history books, Russia was to sell Alaska to the United States in 1867 (for 7.2 million dollars). But the intrusion of the Coalition in history altered Russia's valuation of Alaska overnight it had gone from an untenable and empty possession to a potential frontier buffer zone between Russia and America. Now with Coalition foreign policy that seemed to ignore them, the Russian's became even more suspicious of Coalition motives. For Czar Alexander II of Russia, he had no choice but to take immediate steps to protect it. Nearly 40,000 soldiers would be sent east, to Alaska, Vladavostok, and eastern Siberia. In addition the Crimean Peninsula was reinforced, lest France and England again seek to fight over it.

For Prussia, plans were immediately in the works to seize the states of Holstein and Schliswig from Denmark. Again, according to history, Prussia would join with Austria in 1864 to take these states, but now that action would be solo. With Coalition overtures to Austria, France, and England, Wilhelm feared being hemmed in by hostile powers.

Gatling had set up residence in Berlin on May 23, having left America on May 6. He agreed to meet with other Prussian arms makers and now, on the 27th with Wilhelm. A deal was worked out for immediate production of his gun, with revisions based on captured Collation weapons as soon as possible. By June 15 Wilhelm would have enough to invade Denmark, and Gatling would begin shipments to American resistance fighters.

CHAPTER 6

On Thursday, May 28 Daschle ordered the dissenting media managers to bring their papers and other publications in line with approved media policy. Franklin responded with a powerful editorial on freedom. He started with a quote from a 20th Century revolutionary (Mao), "only when a man has killed his master,...master's wife....masters son, and...masters dog could be really be free." Not only the masters of slavery must be broken, but also its institutions, its traditions, and its economies. For all victims of slavery, the African race, or women, or those bound to religions bigotry, all chains must be broken. Reparations for past injustices must be made, and the rules of society rewritten.

Most of the Blacks in his area of oversight were illiterate, but many Whites were not. Those who did read it were outraged. Mobs of angry people began to take to the streets, and rioting broke out in Charleston, rural Walterboro, Hampton and Beaufort. But to the shock of the whites, a number of Blacks, ex-slaves came out to join them. They too were outraged by the attacks on their values.

To the Coalition, race or social stratum was not important at this point. Apache, Cobra, and other helicopter gunships were brought in, dropping tear gas and firing rubber bullets. The mobs were dispersed, but for the first time, Southern Blacks and Whites found themselves on the same side against a common enemy.

Under most circumstances, Franklin would have been relieved of his duties, or even arrested for inciting rebellion. But the Afro-American Leadership Council stood solidly behind him. Already upset with Daschle's insensitivity to racial and civil rights concerns, as well as a feeling of being slighted in policy, he was in no position to further anger them. He had Franklin verbally reprimanded.

On May 11, the Coalition had taken control of American arms and ammunition manufacturing. When workers had reported to work that day they were told not to return until May 25 and they were given roughly two weeks pay, or 25 dollars each. Returning on the 25th, they were again paid in advance and told not to return until the 28th, as the Coalition wasn't ready for them yet. Returning on the 28th, they found their factories had been turned into small fortresses, with guards and electronic security devices.

They also received an education in modern hiring and employment procedures. Employees lives had been to some degree investigated. Anyone who had a criminal, or questionable record was dismissed. Personality profiles were also conducted, those with potentially questionable or dangerous ones also were released. All workers under 18, or who could not show evidence of citizenship also were relieved of employment. Those who remained would be finger printed and given an ID number.

Realization of what was happening caused most of those remaining to quit as well. A reporter asked why they had a problem accepting a little security to prevent theft, robbery, or terrorism. The answer was a quote from Benjamin Franklin, "He who would trade a little liberty for a little security or safety will soon find that he has neither." But Coalition personnel knew that Americans had been trading liberty for security throughout the late 20th and the 21st century. And modern Americans were as free as they had ever been.

Alcohol Tobacco Firearms (A.T.F.) under Brandi Syntax was ahead of schedule in implementing national gun registration. On the 18th she had set up nationwide registration for anyone buying either weapons or ammunition. Purchasers were required under threat of perjury, to declare all their weapons and were given a national ID number as well. For failure to comply, nearly 2000 gun merchants nationwide were arrested, or under warrant to be arrested. Also, gun and ammunition sales had fallen to near zero. And in 60 locations at least, men were arrested for fraudulently buying for others, giving false statements, and being given multiple ID numbers.

With the decline in sales, and the present abundancy of war rifles, pistols, and munitions, demand for more was zero anyway. The arms factories were closed for now. In time, as Americans became accepting of security and registration, workers would be hired and factories reopened. By then, present stocks would be depleted or destroyed. But if most never reopened, it would only be for the best. Everyone knows that guns cause crime, the more guns loose in a nation the more robberies, murders, and violence they spawn. And right now, with an uneasy people, the proliferation of weapons in America was unsettling in itself.

Daschle again met with his monetary team. He had received a bit more bad news with the resignation Wednesday afternoon of Salmon P. Chase, Secretary of Treasury. David Wells, Commissioner of Internal Revenue resigned later that day. Hugh McCulloch, bank comptroller also agreed to step down, leaving the American assistance to the Coalition nonexistent. It also destroyed credibility of any partnership between the Coalition and banking or finance.

Chase had been a rival of Lincoln in 1860. A bit of or enigma, he never the less had remained loyal to Lincoln and to winning the war. A man of great vision and political savvy, he had overseen the development of the treasury from money keeping to the establishment of a national monetary policy. Under him, a national currency had come to replace gold and silver in the money supply. The circulation of bank and private notes was being restricted, a national income tax and modern internal revenue system began.

When Lincoln died, he was stunned. But while most of the cabinet resigned, he wisely decided to remain to see how the pieces of the puzzle fit together. Unfortunately, he had a bias for historic American values. And, with the ending of slavery and reunification of America found little other common ground with the Coalition. As the monetary procedures of the Coalition began to take form, he tried to modify them. But the Coalition knew best and Chase could not accept their policies and resigned.

Wells had successfully established a national income tax in August 1861, with a top rate of three percent at that time. Plans were already in the works to expand it to pay more of the war expenses of somewhat over $2,000,000.00 per day (by early 1863). In a day in which a nation had not yet come to grasp the concept at Gross Domestic Product (G.D.P.); he had began to tie tax revenues to the total economy. But he could not accept the idea of a comprehensive, or in his words "intrusive and anti-American" income tax system with rates up to 50 percent on the wealthy.

McCullock had brought a great deal of order out of the chaos in the American monetary system. With close ties to England, he had brought confidence as well to foreign investors, especially English bankers. His loss was a critical blow, and signaled weakness in Daschle's fiscal foundation. It would only fuel the drain of treasury gold and silver reserves.

One problem with money is that it likes stability. People who have money remove it from what they see as political, economic, or military threat. It happened in America with the Revolutionary War. With the French

Revolution of 1789, many aristocrats fled with their possessions, only fueling the ensuing Reign of Terror. Older Coalition personnel still remembered 1975 Vietnam TV images of terrified mobs in Da Nang and Saigon trading all their possessions for a few dollars. It was their Vice President Key who fled the country with tons of gold assets.

To prevent collapse of the America monetary system, and an already weak economy, immediate action was needed. One possibility would be to remove America from the gold standard. From an historical perspective, Franklin D. Roosevelt had done just that in 1933, helping end a similar crisis. That action had been part of a program that eventually brought economic recovery. While private ownership of gold was banned, foreign governments could still redeem dollars for gold. There was enough confidence in our policy that no great run occurred.

A Wall Street financier (from 2007) named Stewart Montgomery disagreed. Unlike 19th century conditions, in the 1930's several European nations had either directly or indirectly abandoned the gold standard. America had company, but in 1863 they would be going it alone. When Germany became a leader in abandoning it in the 1920's, they suffered incredible inflation. This devastated her economy as much as four years of war and the peace terms dictated by the allies.

A second proposal would limit the amount of gold or silver that anyone, except foreign merchants could remove from the country. The restrictions that McCullock had put in effect to promote greenbacks and discourage gold payouts would continue. Anyone requesting gold would be subject to monitoring, and no payouts of more than $20.00 in gold would be allowed. All bank accounts would be entered into a national data base, and this information could also be used in a tax structure as well.

Additional steps would be taken to secure the borders. People leaving the country could be searched. Once again, Lincoln had already set a precedent for such actions. By June 8 Coalition agents would be in position to enforce this at all known points of entry. Surveillance aircraft along the borders would be reinforced, despite a growing protest from Canada regarding border violations.

Yet one more proposal was made to address the pay out side of the gold rush equation. The composition of gold coins could be altered. A standard gold coin now contained 90 percent pure gold. Modern alloys could reduce this to 60 percent, and should be virtually undetectable. It would only apply to gold coins for American use only, not for foreign trade. A silver alloy could also be used, and cut from 90 percent to about 50 percent silver content. But the cost to benefit ratio would make this less appealing. A law could also be made to declare illegal the melting or material defacing of American coins. This also could discourage any chemist or assayer from "experimenting" on them.

The immediate application would be to restrict mintage of larger US gold coins, used for export abroad, but change the one dollar gold coin. All US gold transactions would be required to be done in one dollar coins. The new dollar gold coins would begin being minted by June 4 at Philadelphia and San Francisco. Branch mints in Charlotte, North Carolina, Dahlonega, Georgia, and New Orleans, Louisiana would be brought back on line as soon as possible. Steps to restrict inflation would also be taken.

Another step would be to increase the production of gold and silver bullion for coins. The problem lie in the sources of gold, most lay on Indian lands. The undiscovered Cripple Creek, Colorado deposits were borderline but Idaho (and Montana), South Dakota, Utah, and Arizona fields threatened Indian possessions. In all probability, California exploits could be sped up, but at a cost to the environment, which already was in trouble. Comstock in Nevada posed another option, but mostly for silver and not gold. Alaska, owned by Russia, was not at this time considered as a possible source.

The Black Hills of South Dakota offered an almost unlimited source of gold. Daschle immediately sent word to Black Jack Game Winner to ask AIM's assistance. If Black Hills gold was needed, he would need Indian (Sioux) cooperation. The only hope of winning their aid would be through the assistance of their descendants. For now, the Coalition was about to go into the mining business in California.

Steps had also been taken on a somewhat different front, but of assistance in monetary policy as well. The Coalition was rapidly gathering as much information as possible on 1863 Americans. The collection of bank records, interrogation of detainees, questionnaires given to national ID applicants were all a part. Lincoln's office had provided assistance in records that they had begun to keep. The Department of Agriculture in only one years existence under Newton, had already compiled significant data on croplands. Other agencies or private records showed production records, shipping invoices, or in counties, land ownership. The one exception here was homesteaders.

IRS leader Roth was ordered to draft an income tax program that would bring in at least 3.5 million dollars per day. To pay for a burgeoning Coalition shopping list, other taxes on commodities, imports, etc. would be reviewed and potentially increased. As had already been suggested, the income tax could go as high as 50 percent on the wealthy. The freedoms and social justice of liberty have a price, and America was about to learn this with their pocket books. If things went as planned, they would begin this learning process on June 29th, or at the latest, July 1.

Friday, May 29th, the abortion clinic in Columbia had its first customers, seven women, five of them Black, two White. Three of these women had been brought in from the Raleigh-Durham area of North Carolina, under Coalition protection. A number of silent protesters assembled, men and women, Black and White, all religions. Ignoring orders to disperse 17 ended up arrested.

In Washington, Daschle was becoming ever more concerned about the historical changes that were being made. To begin with Lincoln (and Davis) was not supposed to have died. The introduction of atomic weapons, at Fredericksburg 82 years before Hiroshima and 4,000 plus deaths, the ecological nightmare it caused raised alarm. Original plans had been for a second blast near Vicksburg, Mississippi. There was no contingency for the collapse of the Federal government, or growing unrest nationwide. The economic and financial crisis far outweighed all expectations.

Several important future leaders were unaccounted for. It was assumed that George Armstrong Custer, Jeb Stewart, Robert E. Lee, Stonewall Jackson, and Joseph Hooker (and others) were dead. Among the ranks of future presidents from the Ohio 23rd Regiment, two were missing, Rutherford B. Hayes and William McKinley. "Eyes of the Army," military intelligence officer, James A. Garfield also was missing and presumed dead. Business and industry leaders, and even the future inventor Thomas Edison, had fled the country.

One of those women from North Carolina was having deep second thoughts as she waited at the abortion clinic in Columbia. Her husband had died of pneumonia on April 14, leaving her with two young children. Being a slave, she trusted that Allah would protect her as she still had value to her master. But events after May 5 changed all that. She was officially emancipated on May 12. Now, facing hunger and the potential starvation of her other two children, she knew she had to be able to work. A pregnancy would interfere.

Seven Score and Four

As a Moslem she knew the "clot" inside her would not have a soul until she was four months along. But she had already come to love what was within her. The Coalition nurses and counselors all assured her everything would be ok, and then they sedated her as she struggled to make up her mind. But the hour drew late, and she could not decide. The child would have no future, only a tortured existence of disease and poverty a counselor assured her. She consented.

Late that evening, Franklin was given access to the clinic background data. Seeing Durham listed as home for one of the patients, his curiosity was aroused. Using his friendship with the regional medical overseer, he got access to her name. When he read Henrietta Franklin, his heart froze. She had just aborted his grandfather. Not knowing what else to do, he begged Allah for mercy, took out a captured Colt pistol put it in his mouth, and fired. His body was found the next morning.

Late that evening, Clinton returned from Europe. His final leg had taken him to Austria where he met with Francis Joseph the king. With his own knowledge of history, Clinton (and the Coalition) did not want to see the rise of a unified German state. On this point they were willing to change history, if not in keeping Germany out of Prussian dominance, then in not allowing unification at all.

He had assured both the French and Austrians that the Coalition would side with Austria against Prussia in control of Central Europe. Austria had found itself in a position of growing competition for influence and control of the Germanic states. Francis Joseph was not directly told, but was keen to interpret Coalition approval in his desires to rebuild the Holy Roman Empire under Austria protectorship. Once again, communication equipment was left purposely.

One failure of Clinton's trip to Europe was the response of the American diplomatic corps abroad. In nation after nation, the delegations had asked for amnesty. It was hoped that at least some of them, especially the three nations visited, could be persuaded to return to America. None of them did.

An old Roman historian (and many since him including Mayor William Tweed) once said, "to the victor goes the spoils." On Saturday, May 30 two important meetings showed the truth of this in two very different ways. The second one, Daschle had requested, the first was solicited by his army of interest groups.

At 8:00 A.M., a consortium of interest groups and Coalition department heads met with Daschle. Since there was no genuine legislative branch, Congress realistically did not exist, they felt justified in considering themselves a substitute. To maintain the spirit of democracy, Daschle agreed to hear their concerns.

The news media addressed the issue of confidentiality while they had only recently agreed with Daschle's proposals for gradual change and keeping a lid on policy decisions. But, Rather complained that too much access to governmental agencies was being denied to the media elite. Others also expressed concern that Coalition agenda might become tainted by the ignorance of the era. The 19th century mind was sedated by the opiate of moral absolutes. Much of the liberation of modern thought lie in the reality that there are no moral absolutes. Truth is what the ruling class determines it to be and that has no bearing on moral restrictions written in books by men long ago dead.

Asking for suggestions on how to avoid this pitfall brought an answer from the intellectual elite. The advancement of evolution must be a top priority in education. And the philosophy of existentialism (or as some ignorant minds claimed "religion of"), which teaches that truth is what we say or want it to be, should be taught in every college. The news media should step up its questioning of the claims or beliefs of Christianity as well. To fit right into the religious challenges of the time, it should focus on organized religion.

Women's groups were concerned about the speed of reform in society. They were aware of many of the legal changes that Breyer and Ginsburg were making in American law. But efforts to appeal with their message to American women were a dismal failure. They advocated media stories that promoted women as heroines and leaders. They wanted a more visible role in Coalition activities, and greater efforts at hiring of 19th century women in nation building projects. Daschle maneuvered for more time.

Gay rights groups complained that their agenda was being totally ignored. Corona protested that gay activists had been assaulted in Baltimore, Philadelphia, and New York City without anyone being arrested for these assaults. Corona appealed for a Gay Rights awareness rally within ten days in a major eastern city. List lent the sympathies of the women's movement to their cause, but Daschle again appealed for more time.

Hugo Tree, and Perry Noyah joined Greens in calling for immediate environmental safeguards. Their tour of the northeastern states had shocked them. Not only were the primitive oil refineries dumping huge amounts of sludge, tar, and other petroleum byproducts on land and rivers, but other pollution was appalling. New York City had seen the ravages of a fledgling iron working industry, the textile mills of New England had helped pollute many a river. The time to stop the war on the environment was now.

Daschle assured them that steps were in the works to protect the environment. But when pressed for details, he could not go beyond vague responses. There had not been time to take concrete steps yet. To the environmentalists, the response was inadequate. Greens was scheduled to travel to California to view what he expected to be substantial environmental damage there as well. He hoped for a moratorium on gold mining and other development until processes of extraction could be modernized. But he would need documentation.

Phil Durte (Dept. of Agriculture) had compiled a book of proposed agricultural regulations. Even by 1863, millions of acres of farmland had been depleted. Erosion and water pollution were already major problems. Crop production for 1863 would be cut, but it would not provide long term solutions. Again, homesteaders posed a problem of accountability.

From each agency or special interest group there was an agenda. The whole nation building program was supposed to be clear cut and decisive. But instead, a hundred different voices proposed a hundred different, and often contradictory courses of action. And if unity was lost, it would provide the 1863 enemies of freedom with a dangerous opportunity. At the very least it would extend the hostilities which was becoming a cause for concern in itself.

Over the last 11 days residual hostilities were actually increasing. There was a long history of wars that were expected to end in one swift, easy confrontation, but instead ended up quagmires. In 1914 all sides expected, and promised quick victories. But the guns of August reverberated for four years, three months and eight days, costing over 10,000,000 total lives. On July 21, 1861 civilians, ladies in fancy garb, even congressmen had traversed from Washington to Manassas to view a fancy fight. They anticipated a one day war at Bull Run. Instead they fled towards Washington as the Confederacy swept the day. One congressman was even captured. The war did not end that day, and if not for Coalition intervention would have lasted well into 1865. And who could forget Lyndon B. Johnson's 1964 Gulf of Tonkin resolution and a Viet Nam War that was only supposed to last a year or two. For some unknown reason, the images of that war era had begun coming back vividly to Daschle.

The meeting ended early that afternoon with only inconclusive results. Daschle agreed to take every proposal under consideration, but no action for now. Several grumbled about the loss of moral vision of their leader. Some would seek legal council to force action.

A short time later Daschle met with Game Winner. He had an extraordinary request, the potential opening up of the Black Hills for gold mining purposes. Daschle needed Game Winner's support, and was willing to offer several concessions in exchange, chief among them a repeal of the Homestead Act of 1862.

Under the Homestead Act, White (or American) settlers were allowed to claim up to 160 acres of wilderness (government land). It had already resulted in an increased torrent of settlers on Indian lands in the Great Plains, and showed no signs of abating. While it was a boon to settlement, it marked the death knell (along with barbed wire) of the old west.

Game Winner heard Daschle's request and then pressed him for evidence to support his claims of need for Indian gold. This caught Daschle off guard. He remembered back to the 1990's when then President Clinton attacked Afghanistan, the Sudan, and other targets. No one of importance ever questioned his rationale. That this same president put American peace keepers in more missions and causes than any other president had again went without questions. In fact, the mass media and other opinion makers rallied to his cause.

It was the radical right wing that warranted questions of motives or wisdom, when George Bush, Jr. (what some would call "president") got the nation into war with Iraq in 2003, his case for attack was never accepted as legitimate. When he ceased as occupant of the White House and the Daschle team took over, credibility once again should have been above question. Game Winner's challenge troubled him.

Putting feeling aside, Daschle presented, under strict confidentiality, the monetary challenges and possible sources for additional gold. He also reiterated the Coalition's commitment to rewrite history and save the Indian. He reminded Game Winner of the terrible atrocities that America, without intervention would inflict on his people. If a bargain could be reached with Red Cloud and the Sioux people, hundreds of thousands of Indians could be spared. And he would make concessions.

Daschle was more than willing to order an end to all homestead claims by July 1, 1863. Both he and Game Winner would like to see an immediate end, but fear of mass emigration to Canada or Mexico, the reaction of Europe, and a shock to the economy prevented that. Homesteading claims would continue until July 1. Daschle also offered cattle and other food needs, housing, and good jobs to any Indian interested. He also offered education and health care, and royalties on all gold recovered.

Game Winner accepted Daschel's offers and immediately contacted three capable Coalition Indians, two Sioux and one Crow, but fluent in Sioux. Carter Scenic Buffalo traced his ancestry back to Sitting Bull. Team spokesman was the other Sioux Ralph White Badger. Thomas Little Eagle was the Crow member. They would be transported by helicopter to a spot near Elm Springs on the Belle Fourche River. A large Sioux camp was there at this time, and it Red Cloud was not in that camp, the Sioux in it could lead them to him.

That evening, Daschle received an urgent phone call from William Tweed in New York City. On May 10 he had thrown his lot in with the Coalition, and when Governor Horatio Seymour resigned, he had volunteered his services. While many in the Coalition chafed at his historical record of graft and corruption, conventional wisdom said that imperfect government was better than no government. He had been admonished to desist from all corrupt practices and to behave as any honorable Democrat would. He agreed, and was appointed governor.

He had not been in a week until some of his alleged wrongful dealings from his time on the city Board of Supervisors, and later law office began to surface. Rumors of graft and corruption, "ownership" of elected officials and bribery topped the list. Most came from former and present business leaders from the city. On Tuesday, May 26 he had made public apology for past wrong doings and was granted clemency by the Coalition.

On the 27th Seymour called for Tweed's resignation, catching everyone by surprise that a Democrat would break loyalty and turn on one of their own. By Thursday the Astor's (businessmen and financiers), especially

William B., "The Landlord of New York," were calling for his removal. That evening a silent vigil of protesters assembled in the Upper West Side. New York police peaceably dispersed the crowd. Some fled to St. John's Chapel and refused all appeals to leave.

About 2:00 A.M. on Friday the 29th Coalition patience wore thin. Green Beret Colonel Nelson Lund, under command at N.Y.C. base commander Sidney (Sid) Dodson moved in. By 4:00 A.M. the church had been stormed with minor damage and the protest ended. Three protesters died and 74 others detained, including the Reverend Morgan Dix from the rectory next door. He had raised the issue of sanctuary and dared to protest the intrusion of the military into a house of prayer.

By early afternoon several thousand New Yorkers had assembled in the garment district to show religious solidarity. Men and women of all denominations and ethnic groups joined in the demonstration. Other groups began assembling to the south and east, and towards the old Tribune Building. By 5:00 P.M., estimates of a quarter million protesters had taken to the streets. To the Coalition garrison in the city visions of what the Draft Riots of July 12-16 would have looked like in an unaltered history of the era.

But there were critical differences, and but for the quick thinking of Dodson, would have taken over the whole city. This was not a draft riot fueled mostly by the poor and ethnic (Irish) immigrants against the Republicans (Lincoln) and the Blacks. Rather, it was a much deeper religious and political revolt against the Coalition and its standards. In the protest numbers were Black and White, rich and poor, Protestant and Catholic, all alarmed by perceived threats to their values and institutions.

Quickly bringing in nearly 60 helicopters and two brigades of soldiers, Dodson was able to cordon off the riotous area and avoid its spreading. But he also sought to remove the issues that spawned it to begin with. He publicly apologized for violating the sanctity of the St. Johns chapel and ordered the immediate release of those detained. He also issued, publicly, an order for William Tweed's arrest to face charges of corruption in New York City. Hearing the broadcast, either directly or by word of mouth, the crowds began to disperse. And Tweed, with his small personal guard vastly outnumbered by both Coalition and American opponents, sensing his own doom approaching, called Daschle.

Daschle, even in meetings, had been aware of ramblings from the city. But as the full weight of the clamor reached him, he ordered immediate reinforcements to the city and ordered a state of emergency. He had Tweed taken into protective custody in Washington DC and General Dodson brought in as well to explain his actions. Concerned about potential mismanagement, dereliction of duty in not quelling the disturbance before it started and a potential compromise of mission, Daschle relieved him of his duties. Colonel Nelson Lund was elevated to take his place.

But the whole issue of forgiveness disturbed Daschle. Back in modern history US Senator Trent Lott had fallen into disrepute over his racist insensitivity in praising retiring Senator Strom Thurmond. In 1948 the segregationalist Thurmond had run for President against Harry Truman. Lott made the remark that the nation would have been better off under Thurmond. No amount of apology could cover his sin of political incorrectness, and he lost leadership of the Senate over it. But he was a Republican and it was supposed to happen that way. Years earlier, Democrat Senator Robert Byrd had used the "n" (nigger) word applying it to all races. After an apology he was forgiven. Daschle could not understand why a contrite Tweed was not.

He could not linger long on the question, however, as trouble was now arising from another quarter. The mass media had made a report of the protest in New York in its 5:00 P.M. broadcast. Nowhere was it heard louder than in now deceased Franklin's area of oversight. The situation was already tense over the abortion clinic and moral challenges to the area.

About 7:00 P.M. groups began to assemble in the towns and cities of Charleston, Waterboro, Beaufort and Hampton of South Carolina. Initially, this was to be a show of religious solidarity with the New Yorkers. The two years of Civil War had seen a certain degree of mutual sympathies between the south and a poverty strickened city of immigrants up north. The same Irish immigrants lived in both north and south, the same Catholics, Protestants, ...and as events now stirred passions, "Americans" lived in both places.

Rioting is rioting, regardless of race, creed, color, or national origin. And mob mentality takes over. Granted, Christian or civilized people tend to be less brutal and destructive, but it was not to be tolerated. Daschle faced another emergency and ordered riot troops immediately dispatched to regain order. But as the evening progressed, not only did the intensity deepen, but so did the scope. The disturbance began to spill over in to Savannah, Georgia.

Daschle met in emergency session with his security and military advisors that night. Several facts were emerging. The rioting, and underlying discontent knew no regional, racial, or economic boundaries. The discontent was deep and spreading. And to regain authority, and initiative, a firm, even brutal hand would be needed.

CHAPTER 7

At a little after midnight, Sunday morning tear gas began to rain from the sky in special canisters on several locations in South Carolina and Georgia. In addition, ground units armed with both rubber bullets and live ammunition moved in. A steady discharge of flares lit up the area, providing adequate visibility.

By the time this action was launched, most of the rioting had died down. But those involved in the melee promptly declared the area free territory. Since Coalition forces placed most high ranking political celebrities under "protective custody" shortly after the demonstrations began, the leaders of the riots called upon George Trenholm to become their interim leader.

The Confederate Treasury Secretary had left his residence in Columbia two weeks before for Beaufort to escape Coalition detection. Caught by the demonstrators, he agreed to serve as governor-general and organize the scattered groups into one organized force. Pledging loyalty to America, he sidestepped any issue of Confederacy or Union. That could be dealt with later. For the moment, all that mattered was the preservation of their values and liberties from the "Heathens and Whoremongers" as they called the Coalition.

But before any genuine organization could be established, the Coalition returned. Ordering his "armies" to flee into the forests, fields, and swamps, he stalled for as much time as he could before finally surrendering at 6:30 A.M. On orders of Coalition commander General Cody Newcastle (from Jacksonville, Florida) he and the 17 captured with him were promptly hung. The rebellion was suppressed costing 87 rioters and civilians and thirteen Coalition lives (when their "copter" crashed near Jacksonboro).

Martial law was declared for the entire state of South Carolina and almost a third of Georgia. All assemblies were outlawed, including church services. Those who refused to honor the order were met with tear gas, water canons, rubber bullets, and riot dogs. The stubborn were arrested. An additional 46 deaths resulted from this crack down.

Daschle was saddened by the reports of the day, but all realized the necessity of the action. But 1863 America was not so understanding. By days end no elected governor or U.S. congressman was still in office. Only the appointed leaders remained.

At 11:00 A.M., Washington time, the USS Mount Whitney notified the Washington Command center of an intercept from London. The electronic surveillance ship was one of two primary information gatherers in European waters. The others was the Donahue. From a location near the Island of Borkum, just off the northwest corner of the Netherlands, she picked up communications to Denmark. Aging King Frederick VII was warned by England of Prussian intentions and of the legacy of a future history. European leaders were to have a heads of state meeting in Paris on June 3. The Donahue was off the coast of Cherbourg, France, and with aid of aircraft from the Aircraft Carrier Enterprise would gather information.

Out in (South) Dakota, Ralph White Badger, Carter Scenic Buffalo, and Thomas Little Eagle met with Red Cloud and his chiefs late that afternoon. The remainder of the evening was spent in conversation and supping around the campfire. Red Cloud expressed disappointment over the end of the Civil War. He had hoped that the war between the brothers would have wiped out white man and given the lands back to the Indian. He chided the "bird men", Coalition helicopters for having ended it.

Crazy Horse, a young warrior leader was quite outspoken. To him all white men were disgusting and loathsome, a pack of liars, thieves and murders. He minced no words in wishing all were dead. Others expressed anger over the continued encroachment of settlers on Indian lands, stealing the buffalo and taking their property. The three, White Badger and company, were told that (the Indian) Sioux would make no deals, nor even hear their requests, until they had a promise from the Great White Father (Daschle) to end the homesteaders, wagons, and soldiers from taking their lands. Red Cloud also wanted the Coalition to set up a peace council for him with the Utes, Crow, Cheyenne, and others to the west. White Badger agreed to attempt this as well.

Notifying Washington of their meetings, they proceeded by jeep transport the next morning into Wyoming and Colorado. On June 2 they were picked up on by Cheyennes near (what is present day) Cowdrey, Colorado. A hunting party met them, and finding out that they had been with the Sioux killed them. Their bodies were found the next day by Coalition searchers.

Sunday (May 31) afternoon Daschle met again with his finance team. With Black Hills gold still an unknown, the Coalition had assembled mining crews and computer projections to begin exploitation in California and Nevada. Maps of California lacked full detail that others had, but information was considered adequate. Silver supplies at Comstock alone were considered more than adequate.

This, however, sparked a serious debate. The United States was officially on the gold standard. Silver was accepted as part of this standard, with an ounce of gold being worth as much as roughly 16 ounces of silver. In this time of history, silver was actually worth more than the face value of many American coins, and often these were exported overseas and melted down. The Civil War, and its resultant inflation had also led to hoarding of silver (and gold).

As silver became abundant, according to the history books, by 1873 the U.S. official legal policy was to go to the gold standard alone. In 1878 Bland-Allison (legislation) modified this somewhat. But in spite of this and a populist demand for "free silver", or unlimited coinage of silver this policy pretty much remained. To put silver on the same standard would have been disastrous, as by the 1890's the silver in a dollar was only worth 70 cents due to America's massive supplies. In that same time, the world gold supplies could not keep up with demand, as the population of America and most of Europe effectively doubled.

Financier Montgomery was aware of this, and the problems that would happen if this area of history were unilaterally changed by America. He recommended not using silver as a gold substitute. But in politics, too often the immediate or urgent often takes presidence over the necessary, or essential. His position was sharply challenged.

Daschle needed no reminders that the very mission of the Coalition was at stake. For now, silver would be included as part of America's gold reserves, and would be paid out as such. The U.S.G.S. computer maps showed the almost exact location of the not yet discovered "mother lode" in Nevada. The exploitation of that area could very quickly put over 100 million dollars in silver, plus some gold into Coalition hands, and it was not on Indian lands.

Turning to the IRS, Roth was losing the confidence of the rest of the financial team. She was unimaginative, and not one who relished the opportunity to expand her authority or write her own legislation. She also was reluctant to force American businesses to comply with Coalition accounting procedures. All business customers who made purchases of over $20.00 at a time needed to be documented to help establish the national data base. By this time she still had not implemented this regulation.

Daschle decided to replace her. Treasury Secretary Cash recommended Morton Shelby. Shelby was an eight year department manager and had served on the Civil Rights advisory panel for federal employees. His field of expertise was gay rights, since he himself was. To promote him would not only put the IRS in capable hands, it would also send a message on tolerance. Civil rights were for all Americans and moral scruples had no place in government.

He immediately was commissioned to gather information needed to establish incomes, wealth, and accessibility of all Americans. He would recruit or appoint deputies in each community to document financial activities. Since much income, especially on the frontier, was in the form of goods or services, this would not be easy. The value of a chicken or pig paid to a doctor or preacher, the value of neighbors raising a barn or harvesting a crop, or even an apple to a teacher had cash value.

By July 1, the plan would begin collecting taxes at a half year prorated level. The demands of nation building were adding daily to the estimated costs. Revenues from all sources needed to be at least eight million dollars a day, three times what the country had been spending on the war. This would be twice what the North would have spent in 1865, when the American people thought they were about to be taxed to death.

Some solid basis of a Gross Domestic Product must be established as well. Additional welfare and nation building programs could be implemented if funding was available. America was about to go on the fast track of economic growth. And since the abundancy of wealth tends to mellow the soul, it should make governing a lot easier as well. But secrecy must be kept, at least until June 27. If America was experiencing wealth flight now, knowledge of a comprehensive tax system would turn it into a torrent.

Better border control would be needed. While Daschle said nothing to those present, this issue was causing him great consternations. The more effort that was put into it, the more pourous the borders seemed. And

Coalition flights over wilderness, especially Indian lands only agitated the natives. Solutions were needed, and speedily.

The food supply situation in American was becoming critical. Food and Drug F.D.A. head Newt Tricean reported that not only was flour in short supply out east because of transport breakdowns, the warehouses and train marshalling yards out in the grain belt were low as well. Faith in the markets was nonexistent. Millers had sharply cut back flour production. A barrel of flour that sold for $5.00 in Philadelphia on May 1 (or about 2.5 cents per pound) now was going for $15.00. But in Chicago on the Board of Trade, it was trading from mills in Minnesota at only $2.00 a barrel.

Shipments of wheat (and agricultural products) was also stagnant. To keep England, and to some extent Europe, neutral, they would have to keep them fed. Lincoln had learned that. When the dearth of cotton put their mill workers out of jobs it was King Wheat that deterred English alliance with the South. If Tom Bull (England) lost wheat as well, Europe could cast lots against the Coalition and greatly aggravate Coalition efforts.

Before any flour could be purchased and transported, however, it had to meet at least basic FDA standards. One problem was with the 1863 milling techniques. Stone ground flour, with present technology was not easily produced from higher nutritional hard wheat. Also, the flour had an intolerably high level of grit and stone. Back in 1863, flour (and bread) was rated, and priced on the amount of grit, mold, cockroaches, etc…it contained. The rich ate purer bread, the poor contended with more impurities.

Triseon was up to the task. His agency had already met with mill owners in Minneapolis to establish standards of purity. Grain with signs of mold was now discarded. Rodent control had been improved, but arsenic was banned for fear of potential human consumption. Step by step procedures of milling were implemented, and the milling equipment upgraded to cut stone and grit as well. Producers warned of price increases that would make bread unaffordable. Trisean responded, "No price is to high to guarantee our children have pure and wholesome bread."

And the standards that applied to flour purchased by the Coalition would apply to all flour produced. As the FDA and other agencies continued to involve themselves in the needs of the people, the flour would also be tracked throughout the distribution system. The customer no longer would have to settle for low quality bread.

On the Chicago Board of Trade, the next morning, the greedy, capitalistic spectators pushed delivered flour prices from 15 dollars to almost 30 dollars in the first hour of trade. On that day as well, June 1, the first Coalition flour shipment arrived in New York City. A one day supply, it was now valued at over 400,000 dollars. The cost of feeding 9,000,000 Americans could top 1,500,000 dollars per day just for flour. If the USDA was forced to buy for the whole nation, it would cost almost 5,000,000 dollars a day.

At 11:00 A.M. Daschle ordered suspension of flour trading on the Chicago Board of Trade. The USDA would deal directly with the mills, paying 11 dollars per barrel. It would be transported by sanitary carriers, either private or Coalition, and sold to the bakers and brewers for five dollars a barrel. Coalition subsidies would total about 1,000,000 dollars per day. This would continue until the mills could be upgraded to keep up with demand economically. Excess flour could be sold, or given to Canada or Mexico, as gratuitous foreign aid.

England would be promised at least 40,000,000 bushels of wheat, the same as in 1862, as would the rest of the world on 1862 levels. But no flour or other refined or processed wheat could be sold abroad until American needs could be guaranteed. All inferior grade flour would have to be disposed of (or used) by July 1 in America.

In another product safety issue, as well as supply, milk was addressed. In 1862 Massachusetts passed laws to prevent the adulteration of milk, and New York soon followed with similar rules. The dairies and milk producers had learned how to increase milk profits by adding water to it. The resultant "swill milk" not only was less nutritious than pure milk, it also was an incubator of disease. Even beyond the problems of drinking raw, or unpasteurized milk, the impure water caused thousands of cases of dysentery and other diseases, the main victims being children.

In Connecticut, Borden had developed a process to condense and purify milk. In France, Louis Pasteur was on the way to developing a process that would later bear his name, "pasteurization" to heat milk, wine, or other consumables to kill bacteria. Effective immediately Daschle outlawed swill milk. Within the month all milk would be pasteurized. New sanitary procedures were put into effect for dairy producers, and regulations that would force Borden, and other food processors, to make major changes in processing by October.

By weeks end, the Coalition, through the USDA, would be regulating the entire food industry. It would be subsidizing milk, butter, cheese, bread, rice, beef, pork, lamb, sugar, and vegetables, at a cost of over 2,500,000 dollars per day. To implement and enforce these new procedures, and prevent fraud and corruption, would require at least 20,000 bureaucrats. For now, Coalition personnel would do the job.

A little after noon on June 1, Daschle met with Noralee L. Litterate of Education. She now had 10,000 teachers and 15,000 aides feverishly preparing for the education of 10,000,000 children and adults. In some states, especially northern ones in rural areas, school was held from spring to fall, over the summer. In Minnesota, for example, several schools already had Coalition observers who would take a more active role by June 15.

Already existing, mostly church based programs to educate the exslaves in the south would be taken over by her educators. At least a significant number of colleges and schools of higher education would hold special session beginning the middle of June. The immediate need was to provide a technologically literate core of workers who could keep modernized factories running. The rebuilding of America did not allow time for the Faraday's, Edison's, Einstein's, or Gate's to make their discoveries. America was on the fast track to her destiny.

There was also the opportunity to rewrite history for real. One embarrassment to many a modern scientist or educator was the reliance on religion in America's dark past. Many, for example, cringed at the knowledge that the "father of synthetics" George Washington Carver, used a Bible as his text book for scientific discovery. This part of history was now to be rewritten, officially.

Special efforts were also made to reach out to minorities. In 1863 the nation and the world belonged to the white male. Women would be recruited for educational advancement, as would the black. Any modern thinking American would be recruited for assistance. One name highly mentioned was evolutionist educator Asa Gray. The perverting influence of Christianity would be substantially eliminated.

Late that evening, Surgeon General Sam Unella met with Daschle. An unknown strain of the small pox virus had surfaced in the New Orleans area. On Friday, two Coalition relief workers at Paulina had come down with a skin rash, fever, and other symptoms of the disease. They were hospitalized.

By Sunday, nearly 50 total personnel were ill, and by Monday evening, the numbers had risen to 100.

A brief report of other disease exposure and infestation was given. In the Four Corners area of the Painted Desert, five cases of Bubonic Plague among the native Indians had been documented. Cholera, typhoid fever, diphtheria, and pertussis (whooping cough) were making their presence felt, even affecting some Coalition personnel. But the main concern was small pox.

Prior to their time travel, every Coalition participant was immunized against every known communicable disease possible. This genetic maveric strain of small pox defied prevention efforts, and could impede the Coalition's objectives in the area. The Louisiana Parishes, or counties of Lafourche, St. Charles, Terrebonne, Orleans, and Jefferson were known to be affected. This included the city of New Orleans.

To quarantine the whole region would place the whole city, its shipping and transportation facilities, naval base, almost completed air base, the mint, industries, and people outside Coalition jurisdiction. It would weaken Coalition presence in a strategically vital area. It also would foster civil unrest and sedition at the very time it was already becoming a national concern.

At a time of heightening concern about pourous borders, New Orleans was a critical base. Nothing else like it was available in the Gulf of Mexico. Another base existed at Tampa Bay, but that base was almost 900 miles from Brownsville and the Mexican border. New Orleans was 500 miles away, and its port facilities were also superior. A base was under construction at Houston; the Buffalo Bayou was not now adequate, and would take time to be improved. A base at Corpus Christi was for now a pipe dream. With a French army already in Mexico, and bafflingly pourous borders, the base could not be abandoned.

To the people of New Orleans, disease was not new. During this era up to one in ten of its residents died in any given year, a great number by disease. If a base was to be maintained, it would have to be separated from a seemingly unconcerned people. The whole region would have to be quarantined, and only accessible to Coalition personnel with a special access. A zone around the base would have to be evacuated and its residents relocated. The neighborhoods of Algiers, Behrman, Holy Cross, and Desire would be vacated, and if necessary, at least partially leveled. The mint would be closed, local industry lost for now (and the tax revenues), and checkpoints set up.

The next morning, June 2, Daschle received word of the deaths of his AIM Team in Colorado. Contacting Game Winner, he sought assistance in assembling another team to continue the mission. Game Winner could furnish only three remaining members of his entourage who could speak fluent Sioux (Marco-Siocian). One was an Osage, Florence Blue Bell, and would be chief spokesperson. A Shushoni, Henry Swan Lake, and a lone Sioux, Irene Rosebud agreed to go. They would depart on June 5 (Friday) for South Dakota.

Lyberte (Homeland Security) reported the capture of two armor piercing missiles near Memphis, Tennessee. They were from the shipment stolen at Ft. Smith. Also sporadic radio broadcasts were being picked up in the west (far west) and south. The users showed surprising sophistication, the broadcasts usually were less than ten symbols in length making tracking the point of origin extremely difficult. Also, one radio near Washington was giving frequent broadcasts.

The remainder of the Coalition anti-aircraft and anti-armor missiles were being transferred to safer locations out east for now, Hampton Roads and Jonesville in Virginia, and Wilmington, Maryland. The workers needed to convert them to other ammunition were presently tied up in other needs. Ft. Smith was still in a hot zone, and a capture of more could prove quite damaging to military operations.

In the south, the financial assistance program for the ex-slaves began. It had almost been sidetracked at the last minute due to Coalition infighting. The question was over money, as 50 cents per person, per day was not deemed adequate payment. Based on present prices, "the Herald" (New York newspaper) had estimated that the average family of six needed a minimum of 16 dollars weekly to afford necessities. In 1863 that was food, clothing and shelter.

At 50 cents a day this gave the poor black family of six only 21 dollars a week. With bread costs already threatening to rise, this was barely adequate, especially to people who even now were on the verge of starvation and many without shelter. Poor sanitation practices had already led to several outbreaks of cholera and typhoid fever. The Civil Rights Commission was most vocal in objections, but in the end they finally relented to allow payments to begin. With a black death toll approaching 20,000, Daschle also requested all available medical aid brought in.

In Selma, Alabama, the hastily established relief office began to hand out cash allotments at 9:30 A.M., from the city hall. Men were either turned away or informed of work details paying 10 cents per hour. Some argued that their wives or mothers were dead or whereabouts unknown. They were instructed to find a woman next of kin to receive payments for their families. In addition, each woman was required to register each member of the family by name and (approximate) birth date. A nine digit identification number was furnished for each, and other pertinent information was gathered including a list of any or all firearms. This in itself created several heated debates, as slaves in general owned no weapons, and the few who had succeeded in getting them wanted to keep that secret.

By 2:00 A.M., an angry group of men had collected just across the street, upset by what they viewed as humiliation. Most 1863 Americans, despite their race or religion or economic status viewed the man as provider and head of the home. Regardless of who spent the money, and in general women spent more than men, at least token acknowledgement of man's authority was a given. He was viewed as being responsible for the economic destiny of the family. In Selma it was no different, and males of both black and white races were offended, and tempers were beginning to rise.

The processing and providing of allotments was not proceeding as fast as the administration had hoped. News had spread rapidly throughout Dallas County about the money grants. A long line of women ran out from City Hall into the streets. Adding to the frustration, all white women were also being turned away. But this created another bit of deceptive ingenuity, as many a white woman smeared herself with coal tar or other dyes and reentered the line.

Not to be outdone by the fraudulent deception of the Southern Belles, one of the black recipients decided to go for a second allotment. Identified only as Ellisa, she took her place at the end of the line as she left the City Hall, federal greenbacks in hand. At about that time, the relief workers began a second line to try to speed up the handout process. When they did, Ellisa saw her opportunity to go almost to the front of it. When she did, several of the other women who had seen her come out money in hand began to jeer her.

The men across the street joined in the shouting, and another woman, Thelma, feeling a little bit courageous by their shouts got out of her line and cut in front of Ellisa. Almost immediately Ellisa began to shove her out, and several others joined in. All order was lost as both lines broke down into a pushing and shouting melee. The men quickly joined in and rocks began to fly. Within minutes the mobs anger shifted from Ellisa and Thelma to the Coalition Office.

Alarmed by the disturbance, two marine guards quickly stepped out, weapons in hand to restore order. But before either could ready their M-16's to fire they were overwhelmed, beaten to a pulp, and stripped of weapons and ammunition. As screaming rioters attempted to break in, the other soldiers responded with tear gas and a volley of fire over their heads. The mob stopped, and the two marines, one dead, were pulled back inside the building.

At that point order might have been restored. But two women who only an hour earlier had received their money came up. They complained that the grocer was only giving them half credit for their money, or 50 cents on the dollar for their purchases. Over night, prices had doubled in the south.

Inflation was not new to people either of the north of the south. Some estimated that the consumer price index had virtually doubled in the north from 1861 to 1863. The average price of beef had gone from nine to 16 cents, mutton seven to 14, sugar seven to 15, rice five to 11. In the south the rate was over twice that, or 10 percent per month.

Complaining loudly about the worthless paper they had been given, they again incited the mob. As the two neared City Hall, they were ordered to disperse. Ignoring the order they complained loudly to the soldier guards at the building doorway. A mass of humanity joined them. The soldiers inside fired their remaining tear gas, in vain at the mob chanting from the streets.

About a half hour later the mob began to disperse as cooler heads prevailed. As they did, "chopper" reinforcements began to arrive. Tear gas and rubber bullets filled the air. One child, hit by a rubber bullet in the head died. But the mob was finally dispersed and the Coalition retook control of the town.

About an hour later, Military Psychologist, Colonel Chelsea Mendon was visiting with one old black man helping to clean up debris. She tried to reason with him about what the Coalition was trying to do. She also was at a loss as to why the very people who were benefiting from the help were so angry with their benefactors.

The old man Rufus replied "Ya can't puts a man on his feet by keeping him on his back." The pushing of men out of what was seen as important did nothing to raise their self respect or esteem in the eyes of their families. And handouts don't meet the need of a person to value himself (or herself) and feeling a sense of purpose. Unfortunately, Rufus had the misconception that the three things his people needed most was God, family, and a work ethic, and no amount of reason could dissuade him. Hopefully the rest of the people were more open minded to reality and less steeped in religious bigotry.

A number of other southern communities had also experienced civil unrest, although Selma was the worst. In some communities, Birmingham, Shreveport, Chattanooga, and a number of smaller towns sporadic rioting lasted well into the night. Some local officials made claims of avenging the deaths of Davis and Trenholm and the sanctity of the church. A few, surprisingly enough even included Lincoln and northerners in their sympathies.

As Daschle met with advisors, the term "infatada" came to mind. The Palestinians, by strikes, violence, and suicide attacks on Israel had succeeded in wearing down a whole nation. While they were in session, the second marine from Selma died in surgery. A.C.L.U. head Junction was present at the meeting, as was Daschle's economic team.

It was of no benefit to the Coalition that the observable agricultural business of the south had realistically collapsed. The plantation owners were now required to pay for any labor in planting and harvesting. They could not grow crops, and several fields already planted were being taken by weeds. The southern banking system in reality was non-existent. No money was available for loans. For those who had cotton or other crops, transportation was in short supply. Even if bank capital, or financing could be made available, no one wanted to benefit the plantation owners. Any plan to nationalize, or break up the plantations depended upon a fair and equitable distribution plan. That, in turn, was contingent on information gathered from the needy ex-slaves, and they weren't cooperating.

The financial relief riots defied reason. Most people valued their pocketbooks, or full stomach highly enough that they would willingly sacrifice a few scruples. The great moral melting pot (or melt down) of modern America had succeeded because of something called instant gratification. Any hunger, or desire for pleasure or comfort could be very quickly met. Cold religious values, moral scruples, social values, all lost their relevance. And this was how the Coalition needed to win over America. Irrationally, though initial efforts had met with failure.

As Junction and Coalition ethicists saw it, much of the problem lay in the inferior state of the 19th century mind. The necessary cultural standards for personhood had not been met. The distinguished author and ethicist Ashley Montagu had said that a human being did not become a person until they were molded by cultural influences. The 19th century Americans had not yet been properly molded, therefore they were sub-human, like unborn fetuses. If stern measures were needed, then there was no need to worry about civil rights. Those who are less than a person do not have any.

In addition, modern Americans frown on civil disobedience in general. Some still remembered the Civil Rights Movement, antiwar, women's and gay rights protests and marches. But society had changed, truth and justice had prevailed, and the need for protest no longer existed. The extremists of the right, like Operation Rescue, or the Christian demonstrations of the 21st century were dangerous and a threat to society.

There is or was no room in a tolerant American for fundamentalist radicalism. That both Operation Rescue and the Christians were broken with massive fines, long jail terms, even torture and occasional deaths at the hands of police was justifiable. Those Christians, as more tolerant Americans compared to the Taliban or al Qaeda, had tried to poison American culture with their bigotry. As for rights, those protesters who had cried about a violation of their rights were the very reason anti-hate laws, to protect gays and abortionists were passed to begin with. And because of their protest, laws against terrorism also were passed putting thousands in jail for trying to impose their views on the nation.

One lesson learned in dealing with them was that the sooner a firm response was made, the quicker the protests crumbled. A second was that it didn't matter how nonviolent the protesters, as both Operation Rescue or the Christians were. Any protest posed a threat to government policy. America, as a democracy, was above all else a nation of laws. The state, not church, was the most important power in the land. And obedience to conscience must be subservant to government and its beliefs about what is right and wrong.

An example of modern social control was needed, and Selma would be used as that demonstration. On June 3, the Coalition would covertly hold a "prayer meeting" for Christians of all denominations and races. A few Coalition personnel would mingle in the crowd and become instigators. When anything resembling a riot broke out, troops would put it down forcibly. There would be fatalities, and a strong message sent to the nation.

CHAPTER 8

By Wednesday, June 3, the Coalition was ready to get into the mining business. USGS maps showed locations of proven gold mining cites and projected 1863 fields. California, with its gold was the primary objective, and Nevada with its silver the secondary one.

The Coalition was operating at a disadvantage. The scientific party that had been ambushed on April 24 was ordered back to San Francisco and remained there. When hostilities seemed ended, the USGS had hoped to resume ground exploration of California, as well as begin aerial photography. But the continued hostilities and increased demands for border surveillance prevented this as well.

Now as the U.S.G.S. crews fanned out along the foothills of the Sierra Nevadas, a deep anguish sat in. From these hills and trailing for a long distance down towards San Francisco were the scars of mining abuse. In some fields, miners had diverted river water to literally wash away whole hillsides in their quest for riches. In other places creeks and forests were in death convulsions from mercury poisoning. Since mercury bonds with gold, miners would use it to extract the gold from ore. Then they would boil the mercury away to distill the gold. In the process, they left horrible scars of mercury poisoning behind as well.

Most of the easy gold had long since been recovered. Placer, or gold deposits that had washed away from the original ores had been depleted. The remaining miners, mostly in the form of businesses and corporations had gone to more sophisticated quartz mining. But even these were primitive by modern standards and contributing to the ongoing pollution of the region. Traveling with the group Greens (EPA) was appalled by what he saw and urgently pressed the administration to halt all California mining operations.

The needs of the hour took priority over any other concern. Instead of halting operations, Daschle ordered the confiscation of all mining operations. Because of the gross contempt shown for the environment, the companies "North Star", "Empire", and others were given nothing for their businesses. And to offer as much environmental care as possible, as well as speed the process, new methods were to be used, as the more modern zinc-cyanide extraction process.

The Nevada mines, suddenly elevated in importance, would be the next target. Cherry Creek, Colorado would soon see USGS teams. The "undiscovered" Cripple Creek deposits were on disputed Indian land, and for now were off limits, without their permission. But the California disappointment and the deepening banking situation was pushing Daschle ever closer to dependence on Black Hills gold.

Out east the banking situation continued to deteriorate. Two more northern banks were forced to close due to bank run insolvency. And even the Durham Merchants Loan and Trust of Chicago was facing difficulties. Agricultural clients were demanding immediate payment, in gold if possible. The suspension of wheat and flour trading on the Board of Trade had sent panic through the investment and farming sectors. Efforts aimed at averting crisis seemed to only fuel it instead.

In Richmond, Virginia, one businessman took a bag full of greenbacks to a federally run bank. Being informed of the $20.00 gold redemption limit, he read the "promise" on the bills out loud to the teller. Printed on the bills it read that they were redeemable in legal tender" on demand. The teller reminded him that even under Lincoln or Davis the banks were not freely giving out gold or silver. His response stirred the memories of stories the older generation had heard from their parents. "If they aren't redeemable for gold then they aren't worth a Continental (Revolutionary war currency) damn", he shouted. Then security escorted him out.

In the street outside the bank he began to offer passers by 20 dollars in paper shinplasters for 10 in gold (or silver). He got no takers. Even two who came out of the bank with their gold were not willing to trade at a "profit." His comparison to the virtually worthless Continental (American Revolution) currency had made an indelible impression. Nor was it limited to Richmond. Americans throughout the nation were increasingly making the same connection.

Out of urgency Daschle was able to schedule the AIM team's departure for the next day, Thursday the 4th instead of the 5th. Their meeting with Red Cloud was taking on new concern. But the concessions Daschle had to offer were beginning to shrink. Not only could the Cherry Creek mines not be abandoned, but "King Oil" was now making demands that would soon threaten other disputed lands.

The Pittsburgh steel mills were now operating ahead of schedule. In Alabama, Birmingham and other steel producing centers were also adding to the volume. The scheduled data for the Coalition refinery had now been pushed up to August 1 or at the latest the 5th. This was good news, as present fuel reserves would run out by August 24, at present rates of usage. But this increased demands for iron ore.

In America, two areas contained vast iron ore deposits. In northern Michigan, the Marquette and Menominee ranges contain large deposits. In Minnesota lie the Mesabi, Vermilion, and Cuyuna ranges. The Menominee Indians had already been promised some of the Michigan lands, and the other areas increasingly were at risk from guerilla bands with captured weapons. The Mesabi also proved more easily exploitable. The Coalition could no longer offer northern Minnesota back to the Sioux.

In Selma, Wednesday June 3, a crowd began to assemble on Coalition approval at 9:00 A.M. Three ministers, two white and one black were in the town square to offer prayers and words of strength. They had been advertised as traveling evangelists from Georgia who had come over in solidarity with the Christians at Selma. In reality, they were Coalition agents.

As the crowd assembled, which ultimately would number 20,000, the ministers and area choirs led in singing a number of hymns. Among them were several by Fanny Crosby, who was experiencing nation wide sympathies. By 1:00 most of Dallas County (and Selma) were present, as well as surrounding areas. The assembly was totally peaceful. One of the ministers got up to speak.

As he did, the instigators, strategically placed, raised questions about the identity of the speakers, claiming that they were Coalition personnel deceiving the crowd. After a few minutes, the speaker himself fueled the crowd, praising the Coalition moral standards, welfare policy, and separation of church and state. The crowd began to murmur, but remained peaceful. Feeling deceived some began to depart.

Fearing that opportunity was slipping out of their hands, the agitators took a more direct route. Loudly heckling the speaker, they began to pick up stones and throw them at the platform and City Hall. Some youths began to join, and a few other hotheads chimed in as well. As most of the crowd watched in confusion, one of the agitators hit one of the Coalition guards with a board. The scene deteriorated as people began to run every which way in massed confusion while a small number began a full-fledged riot.

On a preset signal, the agents sought cover while over a thousand well-armed Coalition soldiers surrounded the scene. The soldiers began to saturate now panicked and screaming people with water cannon tear gas, and rubber bullets. Then someone opened up on the soldiers on one side of the square with a captured M-16. Six were hit, two fatally. The soldiers immediately responded with live ammunition. After about 20 minutes of slaughter it was over, 17 Coalition and over 1,100 terrorists lay dead.

Sometimes change (in how one people views another, or philosophy or beliefs) takes centuries, and sometimes it happens as a result of a single set of circumstances. As this miserable and wounded mass of humanity left Selma, it could be felt. A young black, just recently freed from slavery stopped to pick up two little white girls, crying over their dead parents. Then there was the white merchant who had loaded his most valued wares on a wagon and began to head out of town. Coming upon an old worn out black woman hobbling with her wounded husband he made room for them, at the expense of some of his goods. As he went along more good were jettisoned and his wagon eventually held over 20 refugees, mostly black.

Those who have been in the military can relate to foxhole bonding. In Vietnam, all became brothers, regardless of race or social standing. So also in the Gulf Wars, or the 9-11 terrorist attack, whenever a group is threatened with death from another quarter bonding happens. So also in Selma. As this weary mass of humanity began to leave it also pulled together. All were American, almost all claimed to be Christian, and all were human beings. Even the most orthodox racist could not look at the fear turning to heroism and not see a man with a soul, regardless of race or national origin.

Facing a common enemy, the Coalition, they all agreed to go west, to a land of homesteads and make a new beginning. The joining of Selma was in only one corner of America, but as news of what happened there got out it began as well to galvanize a nation. No longer were there black and white, Irish "spudheads" or Anglo-Saxon "wasps", they were American, north, south, rich or poor, they were becoming one.

And to some the issue went beyond that. Especially in the Selma area, many remembered the "Trail of Tears". Under Andrew Jackson (and others) thousands of Creek, Cherokee and other Indians were forced to leave their possessions and relocate in Oklahoma. Thousands had died along the way. Indians had souls too, and maybe this was God's way of showing America that they, too had a place and belonged. The Selma survivors vowed that if they made it to Indian territory, they had an atoning to do with the Indians.

As for the Coalition, order had been restored. An example had been made for the south and for the nation as well. It was very troubling, though, the willingness that 19th century Americans would give up their lives for their beliefs. It was very troubling indeed.

All intelligence eyes were on Europe that day. A multinational summit was under way in Paris. Napoleon III of France, and Lord Palmerston (Evergreen) of England had called it after they and several others had read some "history". Heads or representatives of more than a dozen powers were present.

But significant changes in the flow of history had occurred in the few days since Clinton had visited. A few have already been noted. But of great significance was the change in the hearts of several leaders. Both Palmerston and Napoleon III had given their commitment to "live for the God of the Bible and His son Jesus." Several ranking people in both countries made the same pledge. Frederick VII of Denmark committed his throne, and nation, to the providence of God. Ranking men in Russia, Germany, and Austria were becoming Christians, and their rulers were looking favorably upon it.

Also technology was already taking a giant leap. With many American business leaders, including Richard Gatling, Oliver Winchester, and Colt's heirs in Europe, American know how met European. Several captured Coalition weapons and other equipment were already in the first stages of duplication. And technology leaks were feeding a frenzy of very infant "technological industries."

Daschle feared for a united and potentially hostile Europe. While Coalition might could blast much of Europe back into the dark ages (as 49 nuclear devices on key cities), it would destroy any hope of mission success. The Coalition needed the European empires as vehicles for changing the world.

A modern debate among the educational elite was over the values of all cultures in the world in the 21st century. It was agreed that no culture was any better than any other, with the exception of religious fundamentalist ones. These alone were inferior and needed to be redeemed by western humanism. But it was also realized that some cultures offered better opportunity to advance humankind than others. This was how the Coalition viewed Europe in 1863, as an opportunity to reach the world. More about this will be mentioned later.

In New York City on June 3, a second Family Planning and Abortion Clinic was opened in America. The location, like the one in Columbia, South Carolina was no accident. Family planning advocate Margaret Sanger had envisioned such services to the poor and non-white races as a means of enabling women to be emancipated from unwanted child bearing. While some had erroneously branded her as a racist and pugonesist (trying to build a superior race) they were wrong. She was a heroine to the helpless. And modern America proved that. The abortion rate of blacks far exceeded that of the general public. So it was not surprising that abortion should first be made available to them, and the poor immigrants of 1863.

By late afternoon, Coalition personnel were accompanying a USGS crew at the outskirts of Virginia City, Nevada. Up to this point, the miners and settlers had only seen a few aircraft and heard rumors about those "Coalitioners from perdition." And that suited them just fine. They were a group long known for a free spirit, rowdiness, and frontier roughness. They were also known for their frontier justice, a "shoot first, ask questions later" legal system. Mining communities were not for the frail or "civilized" none of them had ever heard of a "nation of laws", much less accept the notion.

USGS and administrative bureaucrats entered town at 5:30 P.M. (Nevada Time) and immediately requested records of all mining claims. Other Coalition personnel did the same in every other community in the Nevada City mining district, Carson City, and Mormon Station (Genoa). When told by various town officials that the desired information could be obtained the next day, the USGS and bureaucrats ordered it given then. Under fear of arrest, the various town officials had no choice but to comply.

At 6:30 A.M. the next morning, Coalition people fanned out into the mining regions. By 7:00 Captain Sharon Quincy and seven support troops arrived at a dry gulch near Gold Hill. Near the top of the hill were three miners, an Irish immigrant named O'Mallery, an Australian, or Sydney Duck named Barney, and a veteran named Farley. A short distance off was a burley Texan with two colts and named Rusty. O'Mallery asked Quincy what her business was on their land.

Quincy said that she was there to take possession of their improperly made mining claim. As O'Mallery frowned she added that even though their claim was not documented, the Coalition would pay them for it. O'Mallery responded, "Ain't sellin, and get off our land". Quincy said that they (the Coalition) were the law now and unless they wanted trouble they would pack up and leave.

Rusty had come over to join his friends. He knew he was next, and felt it better to stand together than stand alone. Quincy informed him of the same demand. An older man, he had been in Texas back on October 2, 1835 and remembered a similar demand by the Mexicans for a cannon at Gonzales, Texas. When the force of 100 or so Mexicans uttered their orders the Texans replied, "If you want it, come and get it." They never made it. Now Rusty uttered those same words.

As the Coalition guard went for their weapons, the four cut loose with their weapons. Only Quincy survived unhurt, and was captured by the four. Later that day Barney decided he needed a woman with a little spunk. With the others to officiate and witness a literal "shotgun" wedding was held.

A Coalition attempt at negotiation with the miners ended in failure throughout the area. The military was to have taken a back seat in the operation. Those soldiers involved were reservists, mostly support and administrative. And the Coalition paid the price in two ways. They did not make any friends in Nevada. The reservists also paid heavily in blood, 322 died or were captured against around 120 miner and other deaths. Valuable weapons and equipment were lost as well.

Coalition forces retreated back to Virginia City and waited for reinforcements. As helicopters began to fly in, the miners wisely headed for the hills, or mountains along the border with California. In the process, they destroyed everything they left behind, caving in productive mines and camoflaging their fields. The next morning a first class military took possession of a desolated land without opposition. But then again so did Napoleon in Moscow (Russia) in the summer of 1812. No one wanted to make the comparison.

Thursday, June 4, Noralee L. Litterate again met with Daschle. Teacher standards were discussed. In 1863, virtually anyone who could read and write could find employment in teaching. In many places, and especially on the frontiers, a high school diploma was not needed. A sixth grade education was all that many had. In modern America, a janitor in a school required more education than that.

The curriculum for American schools was a hodge-podge of unstructured mythology. There was no national standardization, and few states had made any efforts to set even minimum standards or goals. The Bible was even used as a textbook. How America was able to make the advancements it did with the education system it had was truly beyond belief.

She had been able to arrange for publishers to print enough of her text books and curriculum for the June 15 deadline. Darwin's <u>Origin of the Species</u> had only appeared in America about three years ago, and now every student in America would have one. Most books would be modern, however, as the McGuffy reader (and others of the era) contained altogether too much religion. And 19th century Americans needed to develop sensitivity to women's and gay's issues, the environment, and new age values. They had a lot to learn about rights and true freedom. And to her, this had to be top priority.

Her key staff had spent much of the past two weeks in Massachusetts. As the first state in American to require primary education for all its children, Litterate was greatly interested in the workings. Also, several of the book printers she had contracted were in that state, Boston being the hub of activities.

As they spoke, a tempest was brewing, and Boston was its hub as well. In 1863 Massachusetts was proud of her Christian (Calvinistic) heritage. In many ways, she was the moral beacon for the nation. Now resigned Senator Sumner, most vocal abolitionist and civil rights advocate was from that state. So also was William Lloyd Garrison, the steady, militant moral giant, author of "The Liberator". In 1850 Worchester hosted the National Women's Rights Convention. Harvard was known as a center of higher Christian thought, and of organized religion. Now, in 1863, a great spectrum of Christian theology and philosophy had assembled to debate a Christian response to the Coalition system.

In 1863 the primary religious debate was between the doctrinal, intellectual, or formalists and the transcendentalists. Both believed they were the form and substance of Christianity. Harvard was still on the side of those who put their faith in knowledge, evidences, or doctrine. The transcendentalists, like Ralph W. Emerson were more existential, their faith in feeling, experience, or intuition. The north, and east tended to be empirical, or form centered, the frontiers and south more transcendental.

Both arguments now seemed overshadowed by a challenge to the very survival of Christianity. Again thoughts turned to that old Chinese proverb "A dog in the cage bites his fleas, a dog on the hunt ignores his". As various concepts were brought to the table of religious thought, Harvard again would play the leading role.

By late morning, a consortium of representatives of Christendom began to arrive in the city. Every significant denomination and sect had been invited. Even the Mormons were offered opportunity. Brigham Young had expressed interest, but on the precondition of Christianity accepting polygamy and of Joseph Smith as a high and inspired prophet of God. The requests were denied and he refused to attend. The conference was scheduled to begin late on Saturday, June 6, but Coalition security was already on alert.

Also in Boston, a few pages of one of those modern history books were captured by agents. What astounded Lyborte, and also Boston base commander General Austin Lane was the speed of them arriving in America from Europe. But speculation quickly shifted to a second set of books, "circulating" in America. Security agents were immediately assigned to track them down, if they existed.

Boston was also known for its whaling industry. In 1846 the American whaling fleet had numbered 700 ships. Over the years foreign competition and depletion of several species had taken a toll. During the war Confederate marauders had not been kind, either. But the rise of "rock oil" or petroleum had dealt the industry a serious blow. Whalers from along the New England coast suffered, but Boston more than any others. And with the war accelerating the trend, the whole shipping industry itself was suffering, with foreign competition quick to fill in the difference.

To compound this, Springfield and much of the rest of the state was feeling the shock waves of a cotton shortage. The rise of wool had helped to ease the loss of cotton. And contraband trade between North and South, even at high levels in both administrations had helped as well. But the price was dear, helping to fuel inflation in every product that used cotton, from newsprint to a new shirt.

Nor was the damage limited to Massachusetts (although that state was especially affected). In New York City, for instance, a seamstress who was paid 17.5 cents per shirt in 1861 would now receive only about a dime (if the war had continued, only eight cents by 1864). Add to this the return of soldiers and sailors looking for work, the decline of the arms industries, like Oliver Ames and Sons shovels, and the state was falling into depression. Memories of the 1857 panic paled in comparison. The manufacture of Coalition textbooks was a boom to the area. But that was not without troubles, already two workers were being prosecuted for sabotage.

This economic crisis was compounded by the efforts of the FDA to improve the food quality. When the first flour shipments arrived in Boston on June 2, the result was higher bread prices the next day. With so many unemployed, and the highest prices ever, the city of Boston was becoming increasingly restive. Though most of this economic turbulence had happened before May 5 (or April 24) the Coalition, already seen as an adversary, took the blame.

To this add the rumor mill. On that morning rumors of the Selma massacre hit town before the Coalition morning news. As Dan Rather provided the nation with an official toll of 1,143 dead and up to 4,000 injured, scuttlebutt put the toll at 10,000. The very image of such uncivilized barbarism shocked even a war numbed people. Rather was perceived as a liar, and the Coalition like Attila the Hun and his "Golden Horde." But the rumor mill did not stop here.

As with any government or political system known to man, no matter how tight the security, there are policy leaks. On Monday, IRS bureaucrat and Army Reservist, Captain Hope Bristol angrily reacted to her bosses removal. As she complained to a reservist friend she let it slip that, "Shelby is like an opportunist vampire … and would be eager to bleed Americans dry with taxes." It was also overheard by residents in Fall River, Massachusetts. This time the story tellers had it right, an "income tax" would take up to half of people's incomes.

For those of modern vintage, Massachusetts had well earned the nickname "Taxachusetts". But the state also had a long history of resentment to exorbitant taxation as well. In 1772 the Boston Committee of Correspondence was formed in response to English taxation policy. The Boston cry "No taxation without representation" became a motto of the Revolutionary War.

A little over a decade later, Massachusetts passed another oppressive assessment to pay off the state war debt. In response to Governor James Bowden and the General Court's actions in 1786, Captain Daniel Shay led a populist rebellion. Only the Confederation of States (early US government) army restored order. But probably the original 10 Amendments (Bill of Rights) owe the existence to Shay's sympathizers (and North Carolina's great refusal). It was hard to believe that states rights started in the north.

The compound anger of economics, inhumanity, and taxes had even the most refined Bostonians in a stir. The city was a powder key waiting for a spark. The religious leaders hoped to bring a sense of responsible resolve with a statement of purpose. The social and moral issues that all Americans cherished were threatened. The 19th century concept of liberty, however misguided, was under fire. In a state and city where in 1770 the first blood in the War of Independence was shed, it was even more poignant. It was also symbolic that in that Boston Massacre", both black and white blood was shed.

It was more than a coincidence again, many felt, that of all the units of American soldiers left intact was the Massachusetts 54th. An all black (except for officers) regiment, it was commanded by Colonel Robert Gould Shaw. In a public relations move, it was brought to Boston to help maintain order.

In Washington, the Civil Rights Commission demanded a meeting with Daschle. Outraged over events in Selma, they demanded the court martial of everyone involved. Daschle responded that he as well was appalled by the violence, but tried to be philosophical. The growing threat of civil disobedience was either going to be ended, or it could end them. By a display of force, the hopes were, the nation would take note and settle down.

Mary Berry protested that Daschle had no understanding of the needs or feelings of Afro-Americans. Of course they would be somewhat combative, after centuries of abuse by White Supremacists. An abused animal needs time to warm up to a benefactor, so also a person. When Daschle tried to reason, philosophically, that 19th century man had not yet evolved socially to personhood all three cut him short. "That might be true of your white male Neanderthals, but the Afro-Americans were, and better be treated as humans." Daschle agreed to order an investigation into the Birmingham fiasco.

In New Orleans there was also a significant outcry. To the Coalition occupation personnel, the French Quarter had become quite popular, especially the social houses. But five of the smallpox cases had come from there (as well as a few cases of communicable social diseases). The six weeks Unella was asking for time to develop a vaccine seemed like an eternity.

In Pittsburgh, another crisis was brewing. The situation was not as physically volatile, but it posed a critical danger of another sort. William Sylvis of the National Organization of Unions had come to town. His goal was to organize labor in the steel mills. He had been listening to Rather, Turner and Jennings each night as they gave the news and commentary, and was moved by what he saw as a dedication to the rights of all, including labor. His appreciation for Daschle's commitment to social justice was turning into admiration and support. He also saw in it an opportunity for action, and intended to test that in Pittsburgh, and then Franklin, for the few oil workers hired there.

Even Karl Marx was now showing some enthusiasm in what he saw as the Coalition Revolution. At this same time the eyes of Europe's leaders were opening. Already the English hierarchy was becoming more sympathetic to labor's concerns. Now Marx was upping the ante, as he spoke favorably of a society founded on and for the benefit of the oppressed. With his own contempt of Christianity (some even argue that he had sold his soul to the devil), he rejoiced in the Coalition's contempt of it as well. While he was becoming anti-Semitic (Jew) and anti-black, he was beginning to view these as points for negotiation with Daschle. For now, his workers paradise seemed to be coming close to reality. He urged Europe's labor to rise up and cast open the continent of Europe for its advent.

But for now, Daschle's focus was on Sylvis. Labor was in its infancy and sorely needed Coalition approval. According to "Fincher's Trade Review" there were fewer than 80 total labor unions in all of America. If steel was unionized, it would launch a tidal wave of labor organization, and fast track Coalition aims as well.

On Tuesday and Wednesday, he had been able to meet with a few key sympathetic employees from every mill in Pittsburgh. He was able to recruit agents who immediately began soliciting others. Promising better wages and working conditions they found immediate success. They also found some unwanted notoriety.

Thursday, June 4, as they reported to work (on their various shifts) they were called into the offices of those mills. They were informed that their services were no longer needed. By mutual consent, the mill owners had also had a meeting, late Wednesday afternoon, and agreed to fire the organizers. As they left, they went to Sylvis. He ordered an immediate wild cat strike, and had those who were fired positioned outside the mills as the second shift came into work. Nearly a third of the shift joined the organizers in the strike. When they did, the owners ordered them fired as well.

The union organizer remained undaunted, and as third shift began to arrive a large mass of strikers were there to welcome them. Over 90 percent refused to cross the picket line, black or white. But this time the workers were confronted by police and the owners ordered the organizers arrested.

This left the mills woefully short of workers, especially skilled, experienced ones. This also meant that steel, which took precedence over even gold or silver, was also threatened. Already, Coalition procurements had cut inventories of steel, and threatened to crowd out other demands. With the increased demands for fuel, a delay in the refinery, now scheduled for August 1-5 was unacceptable. To crowd out other uses would further weaken the already fragile economy. John Deere and James Oliver needed it for thousands of plows and planters, Cyrus McCormick for reapers. And there were thrashers. Steel was essential for railroads, cables, ships, etc… Steel was the skeleton and oil the life blood of America.

Daschle sought compromise. Even though no union officially existed, and the organizers had broken the law, he ordered provisions of Taft-Hartley put into effect. The fired workers were ordered reinstated, for now, and the strike was halted. While a strong base for a union had been established, Sylvis was halted for two months at least in bettering the lot of the workers. In addition, the organizers were marked men.

A few days later, mill owners offered the workers a five cent an hour raise, and efforts to improve safety and working conditions. In exchange the workers were asked not to unionize. They agreed. A defeated and dejected Sylvis left for Philadelphia. His vision of organized steel was destroyed. And so was his vision of Daschle and the Coalition. Across the Atlantic, Karl Marx and European socialists felt defeat as well.

As darkness graced the evening sky in Washington, Florence Blue Bell, Henry Swan Lake, and Irene Rosebud departed for Aberdeen. At dawn they would meet an Indian escort. That escort would hopefully take them to Red Cloud. All eyes of Washington watched, and waited in hope as well.

CHAPTER 9

On Friday, June 5 a steady stream of religious delegates was arriving for the interfaith council at Harvard. While the Coalition publicly affirmed a hands off policy, Daschle, and Lyberte knew that they could ill afford to not be involved. Daschle remembered the words of Krishna Mahariji and the dangers posed by the scourge of Christianity.

Daschle was already working with Emily S. List of N.O.W. She was compiling a record of present (1863) and past clergy abuse of parishioners, especially sexual. In the process she also documented thousands of under age marriages, girls as young as 12 or 14 that the church had performed or sanctioned. While the volume of actual sexual abuse among the clergy was very low (just like it was in 20th and 21st century America), she found several hundred cases of documentable or alleged misconduct. Some cases of abuse were up to a half century old, but some were ongoing as she investigated.

In that morning's news broadcast the story was aired, and a few of the clergy were mentioned by name. That evening, or late afternoon, it was aired again, with a few more names. Then the issue was raised as to why the various denominations were tolerating such abuse from the church leaders. The next mornings broadcast included as well the troubling problems of church sanctioned child marriages and marriages contracted by parents or others. And Saturday evening, the report was on child and wife abuse, and the church stand on divorce that locked victims into these situations. This was in addition to more allegations on clergy sexual misconduct. The story was ended with mention of the meeting in Boston, and a question as to whether the participants cared enough about broken lives to address the issue.

Daschle had also requested that key members of the Coalition religious community also be allowed to attend as delegates. Four he had in mind were a Moslem, a Buddhist, a Wiccan, and his friend Mahariji. He also, under pressure from Gerald (Geraldean) Corona submitted his (her) name to represent the alternative lifestyle believers. They would also need to be afforded the opportunity to worship as they saw fit in any community services.

The response Daschle received angered him, and exposed the Christians for the narrow, self righteous fanatics they were. The five could come, but only those who believed in Jesus as the Christ could be delegates. As for worship, it would have to be God and Christ centered. Armed now with proof that the Christians were not willing to comply with the religious freedom standards of the tolerant Coalition, he now had cause to interfere as he saw fit.

Daschle imposed a curfew on Boston to begin at 8:00 P.M. that evening. By that time the Massachusetts 54th would be in position to guard the south and west approaches to the city. Four Coalition warships would blockade the harbor (with help of a few motor boats). The company of Coalition soldiers in the city could be in place to block the north entrances. No minister would be allowed to pass without first signing a loyalty oath.

Four men in a carriage neared West Roxbury from Dedham at 8:30 that evening. Three of them had an early morning discussion engagement at the Old North Church before heading to Harvard for the council. The fourth was an author, but curiosity brought him along to Boston.

The first man was a spunky young traveling evangelist named Dwight Moody. He already was immersed into his calling, even at the beginning of his ride. A second man, Alexander Campbell, was a man near the end of his. After 50 years of leadership in the Church of Christ Disciples of Christ "Restoration Movement", he was warmed by the growing tide of Christian unity. A third was a Roman Catholic, and the first black American to rise to priesthood. His name was Augustine Healy. He was returning to Boston after a brief visit to Albany, New York.

The three preachers were sporting in a friendly way as fellow soldiers headed for battle. Campbell, who in debate had once called the Catholic Church the Beast in Revelation 17, had struck up a conversation with Healy. As they conversed Melville, a somewhat Puritan Calvinist engaged them with a challenge." If God has predestined all things, what accountability does He have for the evils of hate, war, famine, and the Coalition barbarians?" All eyes turned to Campbell.

Campbell responded to Herman Melville that God has total foreknowledge, but does not predestine our actions. We choose good or evil, just as Adam and Eve did, and bring its consequences on ourselves. Citing an example in Melville's *Moby Dick*, "Just as Captain Ahab had a choice, but he was driven by his own emotions and stubborn heart. And his consequences came at the hands of the great whale he so fervently pursued."

So also with the Coalition, as Campbell reasoned. The age of great expectations had dawned. America, and much of the world looked with glowing spirits towards a gilded future. With the rise of humanism and evolution, the social moores of society were being altered. The future is the result of the paths of history. Maybe this is God's way of bringing our consequences back on us, like a great and dreadful whale.

At that moment the carriage was halted. A young sergeant named Brooklyn Stratford ordered the four out and told them that Boston was off limits to religious extremism. To enforce her authority was a unit of the Massachusetts 54th under Sergeant William Carney. She offered the men an opportunity to take a loyalty oath. "Christ or Caesar?" Moody replied.

Stratford had a deep contempt for Moody for poisoning her great grandmother's mind at one of his crusades. Her hatred for Campbell was even greater. He started the church much of her family had attended. When she chose an abortion and live in boyfriend the church could not accept her lifestyle. Healy she knew very little about, but Melville was one of her favorite authors in her early life. She gave him permission to pass.

Melville locked arms with two of them and proceeded. Campbell followed up the rear. Stratford ordered Carney to have them stopped. According to history, Carney had gotten his stripes early. But as revised history would have it on May 8 Col. Shaw had been given a copy of "Glory", the story of the 54th. After viewing it himself he showed it to his regiment. It changed their character and led to early promotions. Unfortunately, it did not bring any sympathy for the Coalition cause. And also, due to bureaucratic foul ups, no loyalty oath was requested of the 54th or any of the American holdovers in the northeast, army or navy. In fact in reality, of the 42,000 men of the American military only 6,500, mostly in the south, took the oath.

Now confronted with an order that ran against his beliefs Carney refused to obey. He had never killed a man of God and wasn't about to start now. She (Stratford) then ordered the guard to open fire one of them, Wendell, said he "ain't never shot a nigger priest either" Stratford corrected him and said "Afro-American." He responded again "I's a free Christian

American nigger and I's a gonna stay that way. And I'sa be proud if I'a stand with them (ministers)".

Without support, but unwilling to be defeated Stratford pulled out her weapon. Campbell saw it and for an old man jumped quickly between her and the other three. Before she could get off another round, a cloud of bullets from the platoon cut her to pieces, almost literally. As Campbell lay dying Melville again began to ask why God would ordain evil if He wasn't to be held responsible for this deed. Only this time Healy and Moody responded that God had allowed them to see the result of their own evil devices. Campbell smiled as he died.

A few moments later Col. Shaw arrived to investigate. His men said that they would take the firing squad, if he ordered, but they could not kill the preachers. Remembering his own past at Antietam, he had vowed never to shrink again in the face of danger. He ordered his men to go retrieve the carriage for Campbell's body and to escort the others to Boston.

In Europe, the meeting of the European powers had concluded the first and most critical series of discussions. Each nation had come together out of self interests except France, and to a lesser degree England. As an invited guest, Pope Pius IX also attended. Despite intense Coalition eavesdropping (almost the entire arsenal of surveillance equipment was employed) little information leaked out. To all heads of state or representatives who as of yet did not have the modern history books, copies were made available.

France, with English agreement, opened with a bombshell. With borders that allowed autonomy for Poland and other ethnic groups, Prussia was to be granted rule over a unified Germany. As Napoleon III had read about the rise of Prussian-Germany, he was incensed. But seeing life and history unfold ahead, he saw opportunity to benefit his people and all Europe. If history had continued unaltered, Prussia would defeat France and topple him in 1870. With Gatling in Berlin now, if anything, German nationalism would be accelerated. For Europe to preempt a strike at Prussia would only serve to benefit the Coalition. It would occupy Europe at a time when concern for the Americas was crucial. And it could provide political and other leverage for Daschle in Europe.

About that time Napoleon III also began to think more of the future of France and Europe than his own prestige. Committing his life to God, he set a course for peace, justice, and good will. Bismarch of Prussia was so stunned that he was momentarily undone, leaving the room to regain composure, and change history.

Sending a dispatch (encrypted) to Kaiser Wilhelm, he give him good news, but also a personal retreat. From that day forward his first loyalty must be to God. To do less would cover history in blood. Having been informed of the great 20th century wars, even he did not want any responsibility in the deaths of at least 40,000,000 Europeans. Wilhelm had no choice but to concur.

Austria was shocked by Napoleon's offer. But their delegation, also with encrypted communication, found an unexpectedly open Francis Joseph. He, too, had done some reading, and was quick to see half a glass as far better than an empty one. But it wasn't all loss for Emperor Joseph. As soon as word came of his acceptance, most of Europe dropped all tariffs or restrictions on trade to Austria, most notably Russia, Turkey, Italy, and "Germany". England also vowed technological advancements, as already much Coalition technology had been compromised at the Canadian border. Turkey and Russia, more out of concern for each others armies, and the common fear of the Coalition, also extended commonwealth concessions. The states of Romania and Bulgaria now were in Austria's sphere of influence. Being promised territorial integrity by all three powers, the two accepted.

Italy and Russia saw new markets and opportunities open up from Turkey to Canada as all Europe was caught up in a spirit of cooperation. This also benefited England. With the volatile economic situation in America, English investors were looking for alternatives. The populations of central and southern Europe, oil of the Middle East, Black Earth of Russia, all offered opportunities. Russia needed railroads just as America did, and southern Europe needed employment.

For the lesser powers, Belgium, Netherlands, Denmark, Norway etc…the promise was for security. Denmark ceded Schleswig and Holstein to Germany. The Kaiser gave Denmark partnership in what was a now European sanctioned involvement into Namibia. The rules of colonization were different, however, from past European policy.

All nations involved, including Turkey, immediately abolished slavery. For Russia, the Czar had only the year before freed the surfs, but the end of slavery, world wide, was irreversibly set. For the lands now colonies of Europe, there was also an agreement to raise the status of the colonial peoples. Some were even given the right to vote for the leaders of European powers. Property ownership laws were also strengthened for the "natives."

Spain and Portugal made little tangible gains in either national or territorial development. But they now had access to English and French markets and technology. The isolation of the peninsula also ended, and the establishing of cordial relations throughout Europe was a great boost to both nations. And their colonial empires, as they still existed, now had the sanction of all Europe against any possible Coalition tampering or invasion.

On paper, the Ottoman Empire (Turkey) appeared to be the biggest losers. She had lost virtually all her European possessions. In addition, she opened to English French, and other European "protectorship" of much of modern Iraq, Kuwait, Saudi Arabia, and Arab Emirates. Her empire also opened to religious freedom, and the Christian Armenians were elevated in status. In Palestine, Jews and Christians were exempted from Moslem rules and law.

Turkey had lost much of her empire already, however. Halted in several attempts to invade central Europe, by Poles, Austrians, Russians, and Italians, since 1783 she had been driven out of most of Europe. Dubbed "the sick man of Europe," and with an eye on the future, she was grateful for what she retained, Tunisia, Cyprus, and much of the Middle East. She also gained access to a developing European economic union and a respected status in the European community.

Finally, Czar Alexander II of Russia saw his star rising. He had conceded, along with Germany and Austria for the formation of an independent Polish nation. He also restored some autonomy to Latvia, Lithuania, Estonia, and the Finns. He also opened Alaska and Russia's Far East possessions to British military and economic presence. He gained English and French economic assistance, a host of foreign investors, markets, and technology. He also gained a room full of friends. Past offenses, even the joint French, English and Turkish war against him over Crimea less than a decade before were forgotten.

Everyone came away winners. Palmerston, despite concessions to the continent (the rest of Europe) held support of every political spectrum from Labor to Tory. Granting a degree of autonomy to Ireland also brought her on board. Europe had come to look with great respect on England, and France. A growing partnership with France was underlined by a mutual opening of each others ports to economic, and military vessels. A similar friendship was possible with Russia, an old enemy as well. And a joint European voice now stood in the path of potential Coalition imperialism.

France was also a major winner. Her prestige established as well, she had a solid ally now in England. All Europe looked with favor on her tampering in Mexico, as a counter weight to the Coalition. But she was obliged to push Maximilian into some humanitarian and democratic overtures to Juárez' camp.

All Europe powers came away feeling stronger. Personnel issues and ambitions had been put aside. Good will was established. With growing concern for the masses, and, Daschle's ill fated venture with American labor, the radical socialists lost much of their "radical" as well. All Europeans sensed a growing camaraderie against a powerful and unknown potential adversary.

Old animosities with the 1863 Americans also vanished. Many in Europe had family and friends living in America. There was also a sense, among most Europeans, that they had more in common with those upstart Yankees than with their Coalition over lords. And such things develop strange alliances. A few older Coalitioners remembered at least reading about Winston Churchill. A devout anti-Communist, he made no effort to cover his dislike of Stalin and the U.S.S.R. But when Hitler's Germany invaded them, his tone immediately changed. When asked why he quipped "If Hitler invaded Hell, I would at least make a favorable reference to the Devil..." The uncouth Americans would receive any assistance Europe could give against the barbaric Coalition.

The moral and social impact on Europe was also profound. At the meeting, several delegates made commitments to Christianity. Pope Pious IX was openly vocal in assailing the tenets of evolution and humanism. The various delegates and heads of state agreed.

In a move that smacked of censorship, several burned copies of Herbert Spencer's *First Principles*, Darwin's *Origin of the Species*, Marx's writings, and others. A public book burning "of Marx's" Communist Manifesto" was held in his home town of Chemetz (Germany). Also from Germany the "KKK" (for women), church, children, and kitchen was becoming vogue in even cities like Paris, France. The liberating drift of secular humanistic intellectualism suddenly reversed back into the archaic, narrow minded religious straight jacket. But oddly enough, Europe's under currents of racism and anti-Semitism also had fallen into disrepute. For 1863 Europe had seen the future and were terrified by what they saw. To them, technology without moral absolutes was like throwing a lit firecracker into a gun powder room.

As this stage of meetings ended, Palmerston returned to England, allowing the rest of his delegation to carry on talks. With the consensus reached in Europe, he sent a set of proposals to Daschle. Of first importance was the continuation of food and oil shipments to England and Europe. Uncertain about the new political order in America, or the continued availability of American products he offered to buy a two-year supply of grain. Any available cotton, oil, or other goods would also be taken if terms were acceptable.

Palmerston also was concerned about English investments in America, especially in banking and transportation, He reminded Daschle of a prior source of friction from two decades before. In 1839, English citizens held about 200,000 dollars in American securities. Within two years 60 percent were at risk. England had asked the U.S. government to assure them, and were refused. It led to foreign refusal to loan money to the U.S. the next year.

Now the potential English and European loss was in the hundreds of millions in all their investments and trade agreements. Palmerston asked that all foreign assets be secured by the Coalition government, and any property "insured" in gold for their April 24 value. Already England faced substantial threat from the stock market collapse triggered by financial tremors. Money had already been lost on the Chicago Board of Trade as well, and in the banking concerns, especially in New York. He offered to keep railroad rolling stock in America, or push for its return as a carrot. If no guarantees were made, he would have to move unilaterally to protect them.

To guarantee the territorial integrity of the rest of the world, he also asked for a covenant of sovereignty. All lands outside of present American possessions would be respected and not invaded or violated in any way. Only the elected government of the United States would be permitted to enforce any of its policies, like the Monroe Doctrine. And there would be no border incursions.

As he had this proposal presented to Coalition ambassador Erwin Newbern, he received word or a collision of the coast of Plymouth. In a bizarre set of circumstances, Coalition intelligence had reported that the H.M.S." Trent" was carrying a number of 1863 diplomats and aides that had refused to return to American as ordered. The USS. Bainbridge, on assignment in the area, sought to intercept. As the Bainbridge neared the Trent, she was able to run into an early morning fog bank. Neither ship was aware of the closeness of the USS Mount Whitney. The Trent saw the ship and veered, just clipping the Mount Whitney's stern. But the Bainbridge was unable to turn in time, tearing a mortal gash in the Mount Whitney's side. As the Trent limped to shore the Mount Whitney, with all its spy gear sank. Nearly 90 of her crew had perished as well. Palmerston dispatched an immediate formal protest. He also sent word (incripted) to his agents in Canada to get as close to the border as possible.

Saturday morning, June 6 the underground newspaper Liberty II (named after John Hancock's Liberty of the 1770's) ran two front page stories. One reported on the Coalition execution of Lincoln and Davis on May 5. Right beside it was an article with in depth detail on the coming income tax program. The inner pages dealt with issues such as the attempts to halt the ministerial council, and the murder of Campbell.

Daschle felt the uncomfortable position of response. To deny all would be impossible. When the tax system did go into effect it would destroy any credibility on the other denials. To acknowledge a coming change in the tax structure would only accelerate the flight of gold and silver from America and intensify the banking crisis. Daschle decided to ignore the "Liberty II" issues for now, and intensify the efforts to shut down all unauthorized press publications.

This made the media corps uncomfortable. While they did not like the underground publications, they were uncomfortable with a governmental power having such authority, even if it was Daschle. Asking for a meeting with Daschle, they reminded him of what could or would have happened if Nixon had held such power in 1973. He may well have become dictator.

Daschle reminded them of Clinton's control in the 1990's as President, of news stories that involved government actions. He was able to even use the covers of something being classified, or of national security to defy congressional subpoenas. No one could rightly compare Clinton to Nixon. Clinton made up rules as he went along, but he did so to do what was necessary for the good of the country. Nixon was clearly a crook and was evil.

In their hearts Rather, Jennings, and Turner agreed with Daschle. But the fear of a future "Richard Nixon" troubled their minds. Not able to come to agreement with Daschle, they consulted with Ann Junction (ACLU). On her advice, they took the issue to Judge Elizabeth Patterson-Roberta.

Out west, on the Rapid Creek, near a future Caputa, South Dakota, Florence Blue Bell and entourage joined with Red Cloud. When asked about the first delegation, Blue Bell responded that they had died well, attempting to make peace among the Indians. Crazy Horse expressed contempt that supermen from a flying bird could die at the hands of the Cheyennes. Camping there for the night, the council would move west the next morning into the sacred mountains, near modern Bear Butte. They would be witness of all the Indians said, and covenanted to.

In Boston, the ministers began their church council at Harvard. Outside, surrounding the delegates, was the Massachusetts 54th. The loyalty and intent of the regiment was not known by General Lane. Because of the weakness of Coalition presence he recommended an immediate reinforcement force sent in.

Daschle wanted to use his channels through Fremont first. If the 54th was to respond positively, it would do so through the orders of Benjamin Butler. If it didn't it would be accountable to the Fremont administration, and they would suffer for treason under his rules. And if this was not enough to bring them into line, Coalition reinforcements could be brought in early Sunday morning.

That evening, in New Orleans 473 men (and 78 women) were arrested in a sting operation. Partying in the French Quarter against orders, they openly defied rules that they felt deprived them of their rights. One sergeant, now fearing for his military career echoed the sentiments of all, "What I do with my zipper is a private matter, just as it is for our leaders." And even as he spoke, Clinton himself was being escorted out of that same New Orleans district.

But it was different. He had an official pass and was on Coalition business. In his Secretary of State role, he was on a mission to establish good will. Those caught in the sting were guilty of breaking the law. He as leader had special consideration, just as when he was President. When he lied to a grant jury over his alleged relationship with Monica Lewinsky he was justified. It was a private issue. So now his visit to New Orleans was for official business. There was no wrongdoing on his part.

As for the revelers and their excuses, they would be charged with disobeying a direct order and for now put in detention. "Free people don't break the rules, they keep them for the benefit of all," they were told. But unfortunately, they appealed their arrest and sought a higher legal authority, Judge Patterson-Roberta.

In New York City, two noteworthy feminists were arrested. They, Reverend Morgan Dix, and about 200 other non-violent protesters were taken into custody outside the abortion clinic in Lower East Manhattan. One was Harriet Beecher Stowe, and the other was Susan B. Anthony. These two had been present for the May 8 Women's Forum at Seneca Falls.

Harriet Beecher Stowe had written *Uncle Tom's Cabin* which had done much to enflame America against slavery. She also advocated women's rights and the uplifting that it could bring to society. Susan B. Anthony was a known pioneer in the women's movement. Her bravery and relentless quest led her to be honored in the 1970's with a portrait on the Susan B. Anthony dollar. Their involvement in opposition to such a key women's rights issue defied rationalization.

Only a week before, Republican Christine Todd Whitman had met with Anthony. The women had discussed implementing women's suffrage, or right to vote on a national scale. Anthony also was offered a prominent position in the rebuilding of the American government. Whitman also made an offer to Stowe for a position as well. Strangely, both had refused. What was even more bizarre was the lack of enthusiasm Anthony seemed to show on the suffrage issue. Then, strangely enough, both Anthony and Stowe went into a recluse status, as had so many other key women's advocates.

When the second abortion clinic opened in America on June 3, few in New York fully understood what was happening. By the 5th, however, Mayor George Opdyke made a personal request of now General Nelson Lund, district commander over New York. His petition to close the clinic was denied. Showing backbone (for almost the first time in his political life), he called for a city wide day of fasting and prayer for Saturday, June 6.

His proclamation brought an immediate admonition from Lund, warning him of potentially dire consequences for his impudence. He responded by stressing that he and his fellow Americans were not children but responsible adults. While those who saw them in retrospect could easily see their failures, blunders, and imperfections, his people were content to make history their own way. If modernists didn't like what they saw, they could correct their own age, but leave the past alone. Let it be lived and written as it was intended to be, not as future generations might want it to be. "And who knows", he added "you might find that we were right after all."

Lund called him a stubborn, ignorant fool, and told him to clean out his office. Conferring with Lyberte, both began to seek a more open minded and tolerant replacement. Unfortunately, the whole city Board of Supervisors resigned in protest as well. It would take time to sort the situation out and find replacements.

But the city responded to Opdyke's appeal. Saturday dawned to a city of closed shops and businesses. From thousands of windows 1863 American flags were displayed, as well as the first appearing of flags of white sporting a large, scarlet cross in the upper corner. A group began to assemble at the abortion clinic, and Coalition troops dispersed them. At 3:00 P.M., a persistent group assembled, and while peaceful and orderly, they still posed an unacceptable challenge to the Coalition. The Reverend Dix led them in prayer while all assembled were on their knees.

At 5:00 P.M., riot equipped military police moved in and arrested the lot, and took them to the Coalition detention center near Central Park. A larger barracks was under construction in the park itself to house up to 30,000, but it would not be ready until the 15th. Crowded in to the incomplete detention center, they continued their prayer vigil. No family members were allowed to visit.

The presence of Stowe and Anthony posed a major embarrassment for the Coalition, and anything that might lead to their release was encouraged. Elizabeth Cady Stanton was allowed to visit the ladies, and Connie Dumm, Planned Parenthood leader was also present. Stanton was another highly respected women's advocate. Her, probably more than anyone else, was instrumental in finally getting women the right to vote in 1920 (even though she died in 1902). A short time later the two were joined by Emily S. List of N.O.W.

When asked how these two got involved in the abortion clinic protest they answered that they had helped to organize it. A stunned List asked why. Stowe spoke first. She had always stood on the side of defending the rights of the oppressed. She could not stand by while poor and helpless unborn babies were consigned to perish in an even greater injustice. Anthony agreed. Abortion was a reprehensible evil that would not only destroy the unborn, but ultimately, the very foundations of society itself. It was not a woman's issue, but a man's feeble excuse, allowing them to escape responsibility for their lust. It was men who wanted to cover their indiscretions at the destruction of their children. It was of no benefit to women, but only gave them grief. "Sweet...has been the joy to me to help bring a better state of things for mothers in general...so their unborn ones could not be willed away from them."

Dumm cut them off, asking if they had ever seen one of these unborn lumps of tissue. Before they could answer she added that this "product of conception" was not a baby and no one knew for sure when it became one. To protect viable poor mothers must take priority over something that might one day be human.

"Might be human?" Stowe asked. You mean like the black man that is six tenths of a white man? or a woman who is considered even less in some states? Humanness is not yours or mine to grant as we wish, but it is the gift of God."

Dumm and List tried to reason with such religious ignorance. Abortion was an essential pillar in the temple of women's liberation. It allowed them full equality with men. And turning to Stanton, they praised her for a relentless campaign to win women the right to vote, paving the way for all sisterhood.

Stanton then reached to embrace Anthony and Stowe through the bars. As List and Dumm continued, they pleaded for unity on this issue. To free womanhood from the shackles of men's expectations and childs demands women needed freedom from the marital chains and oppression of motherhood. But Stanton had seen enough. Over the last month and a half, she had observed the lifestyle and attitudes of Coalition women. Their lack of morality, respect, or lady like culture distressed her. The frequent use of the "f___" word, and appeals for abortion made her ballistic. "If the fulfillment of my mission is this vile evil, I recant. I no longer want the right to vote," she cried.

Refusing to sign any loyalty agreement, Anthony and Stowe would not be released. But even worse, now Stanton had chosen to join them to the total repudiation of their ideal of women's equality, and a rejection of the light of liberty the Coalition offered, the three joined in prayer. A dejected List and Dumm walked out as the words "Our fathers chained in prison dark, were still in heart and conscience free" rang in their ears.

CHAPTER 10

Sunday, June 7 saw a nation in prayer. Nearly 28,000,000 Americans, or 90 percent of the population attended worship services. Even in the Jewish community, synagogue numbers rivaled anything seen in a millennium. In many places, no church building existed. A barn, city hall, even saloon suddenly became a house of worship. Mary a newly converted itinerant preacher gave whatever message they felt laid on their heart. In a show of unity, many preachers were called upon to preach in churches outside of their denomination. Even Catholic churches open to Lutherans and vice versa. Old animosities were put aside.

Hospitality was practiced as almost never before. In the heartland and far west local folk were confronted with over 800,000 migrants. Headed to the wilderness were almost three quarters of a million homesteaders. Many were ex-soldiers seeking anonymity and a new life. To the Coalition they were still unknown, and wanted to stay that way. Some were ex-slaves, recently freed and mostly illiterate. An increasing exodus of skilled workers, professionals, and civic leaders were among them. And from Selma and vicinity there was a mass of about 18,000, holding together as best they could out of fear and mutual support. Besides the "homesteaders" there was another group, upwards of 50,000 mostly black southerners headed north.

Indiana was typical of a revolutionized national perspective. In 1851 the state had outlawed Negritude. With great southern sympathies from Indianapolis south, the state wavered in 1861 on whether to remain loyal. It was also a perpetual hot bed for the "Copperhead" Peace Democrats. But now, as 30,000 plus southerners headed north from Kentucky and Tennessee, hearts and doors opened to them. On their way north to Chicago, Detroit, and Canada, many were held up with special offerings and prayer in the churches of Indiana. In western Pennsylvania thousands more flocked to the steel (and oil) centers seeking employment, mostly from Virginia and the Carolinas.

But the Selma "Trail of Tears" seemed to touch lives most deeply. As they trudged west, now mostly along the border with Mississippi they were provided food, clothing, and even wagons and horses (or mules). While 350 of the injured had died, donated medical care had saved many others. When asked about destination, they replied "freedom", either Indian territory (Oklahoma) or Kansas.

Jews as well as Christians, mindful of their own history of oppression, opened their hands and homes in kindness. Without distinction for race or nationality, or religion, they too sought to ease the myriads of hurts that encompassed them. And like the Gentile Christian, they also looked to God for guidance and direction. Increasingly another question began to be asked. If God hated slavery, and if it was the reason for the Civil War, as many now were concluding, what evil had brought upon them the Coalition invasion?

In New York City Irish immigrants worshipped side by side with English Wasps (White Anglo-Saxon Protestant). Catholic and Protestant joined hands in common worship. Even the estates of William and John Jacob Astor (now residing in Montreal) were opened to help their fellow Americans. A rent holiday was declared in the city as well, that Sunday morning.

Coalition intelligence had hinted at a possible record church attendance and felt serious attention was needed. In over 10,000 meeting places someone from the Coalition was present to observe. What added to concerns was the presence of 90,000 or one of six Coalitioners also present in church, to worship. Even in South Carolina, where the Coalition was attempting to discourage worship, many of their own attended, totally voiding the effort.

At St. Johns Contius in Chicago, in another display of ecumenicism, Ira Norris was invited to speak. He was a Methodist minister and a newspaperman. He was also a Copperhead, having incurred the wrath of the Lincoln Administration. Since May 10, he also was incurring the wrath of the Coalition, as he denounced their policies as well. From the pulpit he directed a challenge to the Coalition to renounce godless immoralities and oppression of the American people.

Coalition agents had no choice but to arrest him. As he was "escorted" from the sanctuary, he called upon the people hold firm in resisting the evil that flowed from the new Babylon (Washington). Such sedition arrests were not new to America. John Adams, the nations second president was responsible for the Sedition Act of 1798 that led to the arrest of many journalists and others. When General Fremont took control of Missouri for the Union in 1861, he made no apologies in making similar arrests. While his dictational policies alienated thousands, and almost lost Missouri and Kentucky for the Union, it ultimately succeeded in its goal of supporting the Union.

Abraham Lincoln also was responsible for thousands of arrests. He suspended habeas corpus, holding many indefinitely without legal evidence. In the Baltimore riots (April 1861) Lincoln was not afraid to order the detention of a mayor and 31 legislators and keep them in prison for two months. In Kentucky, after the state rallied for the Union, he arrested former governor Charles Morehead and Louisville Courtier editor Reuben Durrett. They too suffered indefinite internment.

But Americans have never taken kindly to violations of their basic rights. Adam's Sedition Act cost him the White House in 1800. Lincoln's actions fueled opposition, and gave ammunition to the Knights of the Golden Circle (Peace Democrats). Even members of his own party condemned his actions. Now, for the Coalition to arrest a minister in the pulpit for preaching his conscience violated the decency of even the most callously un-churched. And Norris was not the only minister arrested. Nearly 700 others also were taken for preaching hate doctrines and denouncing the police action in Selma.

In Boston, there were no morning arrests. After a standing room only service at the Boston Music Hall, and another at the Old North Church, delegates assembled at Harvard. The 54th provided protection as the 11:00 A.M. session began, picking up where they had left off the evening before. They had previously agreed that unity would be based only on the Bible, not human councils or other writings. Now they sought to establish a statement of belief. From the Coalition's perspective, this was the worst thing that could happen, a potentially united Christian voice.

Even without unity there was much to fear from religious activism. The 19th century church was a nursery of social change. Abolition, women's justice, child labor laws, the rise of hospitals, youth programs, all found roots in the church. When Frenchman Alexis Tocqueville had visited America in the early 1830's he was deeply impressed by two things. The first, the power to own and develop private property by the masses was essential to the nation's health. But even more, the strength of the church in holding the social and moral fabric of American together was critical.

Even a divided church on social issues still welded a profound power in holding the nation together on moral principles. America in the 18th and 19th

century was anything but a nation of laws, civilized by any modernist standard. Observing the shortcomings of the humanist French Revolution of 1789, even Deist, Thomas Jefferson had been blinded by its deceit. He saw critical the role of religion in the establishment and security of America. When he saw the results of French seizure of church possessions he wrote of the need for a wall of separation between church and state. Unfortunately, he intended it to keep the state out of the church. It took the enlightened wisdom of a much later Supreme Court to interpret it the other way around.

But he was not alone in his misconception. All Americans had followed the irrational logic, among them James Iredell an original justice of the Supreme Court. He claimed that "the people wanted no Anglican (Church of England) establishment, but neither did they want to see the United States as less than an openly Christian nation. "And to 1863 America, the intent was still to allow Christian ideals to rule the land.

To fast track nation building in America, this would have to change. Our greatest advancements as a nation could not happen until the country was freed from Christian fundamentalism to face a brave new world. And who knows better what standards we should live by, an ignorant carpenter from 2,000 years ago, or intelligent, educated people living in the real world?

By 2:30 P.M. two battalions of Coalition military had arrived in Boston from New York City. As mediators, Al Sharpton, Democrat, and Thaddeus Stevens, the black Republican statesman were brought in. Amnesty would be given to any black soldier or minister who broke ranks with their white deceivers. Of the 106 delegates inside, only three were non-white (two were black and one was an Indian).

At 5:00 the already tired Coalition troops were in positions around the city. Two companies under Colonel Elmira Locke were deployed at Harvard. Stevens appealed for the 54th to stand down and allow the Coalition time to improve things. Hatred and violence were not the answer, but alluding to George Washington Carver, he appealed to the Christian standard of turning the other cheek.

Carney answered, We can do that sir, but what about the preacher men inside?" Sharpton told him that the Coalition would deal with them in a fair way, but he need not worry about defending white men's beliefs. Carney protested, they were not defending white men's beliefs, but were defending their own. With patience already thin, Locke ordered her force to move in. Delay would only risk spreading of the insurrection into the city at large.

The 54th would not retreat, shots were fired at them, and they responded. By 5:30 it was over, 416 lay dead, including Colonel Shaw. The Coalition had lost 53. But caught in the crossfire, both Stevens and Sharpton were also dead. A copter borne "swat" team swarmed the meeting hall, blind folded and handcuffed the ministers and removed them.

For the ministers, however, their work was done. Alexander Campbell had been a nemesis to many of those inside in his life, his beliefs often publicly vilified. But in death he had become a martyr, and those very ideas now were almost entirely incorporated as the statement of belief. But their first test now awaited them, they could only be released when they recanted their narrow minded belief in Jesus and made a loyalty oath to the Coalition. All refused.

At the infirmary now detention hall, a lone black man approached the guard. Minister Charles Bennet Ray asked for the release of the delegates. Unfortunately, Coalition lawyer, Murray Irvington was present. Reviewing the charges, he had all released on a lack of evidence. By 8:30, when an official statement of Coalition policy for church leaders arrived, most were already on their way out of Boston, via the underground railway. Only fingerprints remained in Coalition hands. But the mission was clear, the church would have to be broken.

Out west in Dakota territory, Florence Blue Bell met with Red Cloud. He chided her and the Great White Father for sending squaws to do a chiefs work. Others, especially the outspoken Crazy Horse expressed outward contempt for the mockery of the Sioux. Henry Swan Lake would take her place, even though he was not as fluent as Blue Bell, nor an experienced negotiator.

Blue Bell understood, but was grieved that such sexual bigotry was practiced by such a noble people. She was allowed to accompany Swan Lake as an advisor, for now. Washington was made aware of the turn of events, and Red Cloud's misgivings.

Sitting Bull was given opportunity to speak. He made it clear that the Sioux were a proud and independent people. They were free and were one with nature, having no need for white man's houses, cattle, farms, clothes, or slavery to firewater, stolen land and killed buffalo. Let white man give the land back, rifles, and twirly birds (helicopters) to protect it, from Lake Superior to the (Rocky) mountains. Then there would be a treaty.

Red Cloud was more conciliatory, but warned that an agreement would be hard. The Black Hills were sacred to the Sioux, and the very thought of white man desecrating it was abhorrent. All white man's promises had been empty, just as they had emptied the wigwams where Sioux widows lament.

Swan Lake vowed by those hills themselves that Coalition white men would not set foot on them. Only people with Indian blood would do any mining. Daschle, the great chief would protect the Indian, and his people would preserve the land. It was not his wish to mine at all, but he was in danger of running out of gold and silver. If this happened, enemies at the Indian would throw him out of power and replace him. With war and treachery they would wipe out the Sioux.

Red Cloud promised an answer in seven days. Swan Lake knew time was short. By July 1, if not sooner, refined gold needed to be flowing to the treasury. But he (and Blue Bell) had no choice but to wait. The Coalitioners were returned to the Rapid River, but this time with Sioux escort.

As circumstances would have it, a half breed named "Lucky" Luke was in that camp at the time, overhearing the whole conversation. Not fully trusted by either white or red man, he proved invaluable to both. To the white man he provided information on Indian movements. His warnings to Minnesota settlers had saved hundreds in the 1862 attacks by Little Crow. To Red Cloud and the Indians he provided guns and ammunition. He also left camp that night, by horseback to Ft. Garry (Winnipeg, Canada).

With the Coalition restrictions on weapons purchases, he was headed across the border. He had hoped to arrive by Saturday, June 13 to barter Indian gems and gold for guns. Now he intended to sell information instead. Unknown to him, Coalition intelligence had picked him up as he left the camp. Not knowing his business, though, they would offer no hindrance, so as not to anger the Sioux.

Early Monday morning (June 8), the night shift had just gotten under way at the Sligo Works in Pittsburgh. The previous Saturday afternoon, day shift workers had noticed that a furnace was not properly heating. A note was left for workers to check on it first thing Sunday night (10:00 P.M.), but it was lost. Now, at 12:30 A.M., the furnace exploded, setting off a chain reaction of fire and more explosions. The fire quickly spread into a nearby neighborhood, made up of ex-slaves and poor whites. By 7:00 A.M. the fires were mostly out, but 300 workers and about 900 other residents were dead.

At 9:30 A.M., Daschle faced another "explosion" from his labor and environmental team. Greens of EPA, Wage of Labor, and Safer of OSHA were of the belief that their concerns had been short changed by the Coalition agenda. Over Daschle's better judgment, they also were able to maneuver Dirte of Agriculture into the meeting. All openly condemned Daschle's negligence of people issues. To maintain leadership, Daschle was forced to give broad authority to implement a comprehensive safety and environmental program. In exchange, they would not publicly attack policy.

For Daschle the issue now was damage control. The 24 hour a day six day a week production schedule was succeeding. In addition, steel was soon to start flowing again from Alabama factories. A small surplus was on hand, and the oil refinery was now doable by August 1. The drilling for oil had, despite efforts at sabotage, also exceeded expectations. As inefficient as they were, American refineries could also be tooled, in time, to process crude oil, maybe by October.

As for safety, it could not be ignored. In modern America, it was not until the 1970's when OSHA came into existence and began to flex its muscles that worker safety became a major concern. It was an embarrassment that even during the first seven months of declared war, US worker deaths exceeded military deaths in World War II. But the progressive forces of OSHA (and tort lawsuits) had by 2007 made worker safety a model to most of the world.

For Daschle, however, there was also a public relations issue with 1863 Americans. Labor was only too often viewed as mere capital, like a cam in a machine. It worked until it broke or wore out, and then was replaced. And in the case of Pittsburgh, the nation blamed the Coalition as well.

To this Lyberte of Homeland Security gave Daschle an out. Even before any investigation was begun, he raised the specter of sabotage. Daschle reported this as a definite possibility in the evening news broadcast. Unfortunately, it did not play well with his safety environmental team. This would haunt him later.

Daschle sent proposal back to England as well that morning. Temporarily he ignored the issue of borders or sovereignty, but responded to Palmerston's protest. He made it clear that American diplomats were no longer authorized to represent the nation and were illegally overseas. Any aiding or abetting of this illegal action only strained relations. But he did offer to buy all English transport and manufacturing assets at 150 percent of value in green backs.

The gold situation was not good, as reserves began to reach dangerous levels. But from Philadelphia, the first 60 percent alloy dollars hit the banks that morning. In California, the first Coalition gold was being extracted as Daschle had his 9:30 A.M. meeting. In a gesture to shore up his environmental record, this was only a temporary operation. Attention focused on Comstock.

The damage the miners had done there was substantial, but USGS workers were closing in on the mother lode. A small city of nearly 11,000 Coalition personnel were setting up complete refining operations. The existence of pockets of disgruntled miners, drifters, scamps, ruffians, and city slickers was not unknown. But the Coalition lacked the available chopper presence in the west to monitor the region. This allowed unrestricted movement for the small numbers who lived there. Among them were the beginnings of a substantial force still under the command of General Grant. They were seeking supplies and horses to aid their movement from a miner camp at Walker Lake, Nevada. They met there with mining engineer (and future governor in 1867) Henry Blesdel.

Prodded by the violence in civilized Boston, Daschle also met with Brandi Syntax of A.T.F. and Les Lyberte of Homeland Security. The registration of firearms was not meeting expectations. Black market weapons, some becoming quite sophisticated, were pouring in from Canada and Mexico. Many were repeaters of the Winchester and Colt design. But two Gatling type guns had been intercepted just west of Detroit, and counterfeit M-16 rifles were recovered near Buffalo, New York.

Lyberte was suspecting a mole in the government who was leaking border patrol schedules to smugglers. He wanted to discharge all his 1863 staff and go it alone on Coalition personnel, but the 558,000 of them were getting stretched thin. He suggested a raid on Toronto, Montreal, and other Canadian cities where weapons might be getting manufactured. Daschle resisted that request for now.

Syntax reported on a growing fraud in implementing the national identification policy. Even with the threat of huge fines and imprisonment, people were not using their given numbers legally. Some were transferring their numbers to others. Some had been issued as many as 20 or more from different agencies or offices. Some were using primitive, but sophisticated counterfeit numbers. The requirement of numbers being issued still was not being implemented in much of the nation.

These numbers were not only essential to gun control, they were critical to almost every modern program. Any comprehensive tax policy required personal level monitoring. The tracking of potential trouble makers, discovery of missing persons, enforcement of environmental, safety, and other laws rested on identification. Even small problems, like school truancy, were more easily solved.

The proper credentialing of professionals also rested heavily on this system. Unfortunately, America's founding fathers had a fear of licenses and certificates. They saw danger in their usefulness as a tool of government control. They wrongly believed that the soul of the nation was unbridled liberty, and once forsaken or lost to government, would never return. How little did they understand true liberty as 21st century people did. That liberty was preserved by the very security and monitoring of an interactive government through licenses, certificates, and identification policies. They also better society.

Some modern right wing extremists argued that those were too restrictive. They had claimed that creativity and advancement in education, science, or business was stifled. Such fools forgot that the unrestricted idiocy of Benjamin Franklin, flying a kite in a thunderstorm, could have cost us his life. Only a properly trained and credentialed person should be allowed to do anything. The concerns of the environment, economy, civil rights, all proved the need for tight control. And this did not even include safety or security. Free wheeling people are a danger, not a blessing to society.

Licenses also provide a means of changing behavior and social concerns. In modern America, for example, the driver's license had been used in this way. Most states used it as a tool to force young people to stay in school or get good grades, avoid alcohol and tobacco, obey curfews, or even use birth control. It was also used to enforce payment of certain taxes (along with vehicle registration), child support, and prevent criminal activities, as well. And license plates were equipped with a tracking device so its whereabouts could be monitored.

Syntax pointed as well to the growing exodus of professionals from the cities as those policies were being implemented. Many had submitted to fingerprinting literally at gun point. Many others just disappeared. In 1863 birth records were incomplete or even non-existent. She appealed for a temporary moratorium on this and loyalty oaths until stability could be maintained in the cities. Daschle, facing tax and security issues, was forced to deny her request.

In the south, the welfare offices again opened that morning. Military security was tight, and in all places scores of white woman were turned away. The claims worker numbers had been greatly increased, but still the offices were overwhelmed by "new" claims. By days end nearly 11,000,000 new numbers had been issued for payments, in addition to the 3,000,000 in the prior week. Something was clearly amiss and the offices were ordered closed until further notice.

Tuesday morning, as the lines again began forming, Coalition guards with bull horns ordered them to disperse. With little fanfare they complied. No one wanted another Selma. But it was here that a significant discovery was made.

Following the black women as they left the welfare centers, agents found them congregating to meeting places with men of both races. They had been giving the men the money, and they in turn were using much of it to buy contraband weapons and military supplies. While the greenbacks were highly discounted for inflation, it was obvious that the arms business was all too healthy. And in exchange for the money, whites with any resources at all were opening their homes and property to support these women and their families. Even the "closed" plantations served as living quarters for many ex-slaves and poor whites.

A barter system was developing. As many of the men, both black and white were becoming armed they needed training. Old Confederate and sometimes Union officers volunteered their services. Many whites were already experienced military men, and they performed agricultural and maintenance work while the others trained. Plantation owners, gladdened by protection and at least some crop planting were only too willing to provide food and shelter. Outside of the initial mass immigration, most of the remaining southerners chose to stay, and build an underground society.

Migration was accelerating in the north and midwest (Heartland). Pittsburgh was being inundated, Buffalo and Detroit had seen some increase. New York, Baltimore, and Philadelphia had experienced a net loss. Other cities were suffering major decline, some like Chicago drastically. Throughout most of American history, the flow had been to the cities. In modern America, it was to the suburbs and gated communities. But this migration contradicted all conventional wisdom as mostly skilled or professionals were leaving to live on relatives' farms.

Since those leaving were skilled, added pressure was put on Coalition personnel to run railroads or factories, waterworks, and stores. Often vehicle and aircraft mechanics were called in to fill the void, either reducing their availability, or threatening the safety of operators.

In New Orleans, the first sting defendants were up on charges. This was the first significant court case involving Coalition personnel. As a local case, though, it drew national significance, and an opinion by Ginsburg and Breyer. Coalition Judge Elizabeth Patterson-Roberta was brought in to rule on the issue.

As a member of the 9th Circuit Court of Appeals in modern America she had gained respect for her reputation as a defender of judicial activism. It had helped earn her the premier legal office in the Coalition, second only to the Supreme Court. And she was not afraid to use that office to insure that proper rulings were made and procedures followed.

Arguing the administration's case was Attorney General, Ida B. Derapp. ACLU head Ann Junction had volunteered her services to represent the defendants in a class action defense. She questioned not the violation of a law, but the constitutional legality of it.

Three arguments were offered. The first regarded what Junction began to label as Daschle's "imperial presidency". In the absence of Congress and a duly elected legislative branch none of his executive orders or policy making rules were subject to review or challenge. At the very least, the court should review all his policies before they became "law", and he should be forced to consult with the various interest groups in making rules.

Secondly, as defined by modern court rulings, sexual intercourse is a constitutionally guaranteed right. People may be warned about the dangers of sex, but could not be kept from it. The AIDS epidemic of modern times was a good example. All diseases can kill, but AIDS threatened a lifestyle, especially the gay community. The 1863 standards of morality were not constitutional to either modern or historical Americans. Warning of consequences was all Daschle could do.

And one more point. The people in question were off duty. Only security or religious bigotry rules could be enforced. They were free to access the nation, have sex with anyone 16 or older, or use any language, they saw fit. They could dispense pornography if they so desired, or hold gay worship services. Liberty, as the Coalition was granting America, cannot be promoted by denying the basic rights of those establishing it. A ruling was expected that week.

By Wednesday, June 10, the USGS had opened the mother lode in Comstock for exploitation. On that day Ulysses S. Grant arrived in Genoa with a small group of his troops. Traveling nearly 50 miles a day, he had planned to set up base in the Sierra Nevadas. Having been in California a decade before he had observed many places to hide an army. Arriving in Genoa, he was immediately approached by civil authority and mining engineer Henry Blasdel. Under his auspices was an assembly of irregulars scattered in camps around Lake Tahoe, and some of Grant's men.

Grant agreed to take command. His small escort had a few captured grenades, rifles and a dozen surface to air missiles. In the days ahead more would arrive in small groups as his army followed him. On that afternoon he began organizing the 850 irregulars with the 200 of his own men present. But as soon as the news of his arrival got out, he was inundated by hundreds more. Among them, an ex-confederate named Samuel Clemens, better known as Mark Twain.

Grant was always a man who was more concerned with how he would hurt his enemy than what his enemy could do to him. He immediately began studying the town of Virginia City and its base, and planning an attack. Samuel Clemens immediately was employed to keep chronicles for the general.

In Mexico, Maximilian captured Mexico City from Juárez. This had come early by the history books largely because French forces in the country now numbered 50,000 (instead of 30,000). He was now in pursuit of Beuito Juárez, the "elected" president, as he retreated to the northwest. In the northern part of the country, a mass of soldiers and refugees loyal to Juárez was fleeing towards El Paso, Texas. They also were under pursuit.

Further south, a number of European powers were making power moves on other Central and South American nations. England had opened her Caribbean ports to French and other European battle and transport vessels. An English frigate had docked at the new (1860) Russian city of

Vladivostok, enroute to Alaska or Victoria. The need to pry England from Europe and into the Coalition sphere was becoming vital.

As Daschle prepared a strategy, Judge Patterson-Roberta issued him a verdict in the New Orleans sting. She had every reason to believe destiny had chosen her for this role. Back in the late 1970's as she was about to enter puberty she had an experience while playing with a Ouija Board. Over the next few years of contact with the occult she learned that she was a reincarnation of Joan of Arc. Her mission begun in the 15th century was someday to be made complete in an altering of time. The climactic visions came at the time of the Planetary Alignment and dawning of The New Age Movement in the 1980's.

She then began to look for her reincarnated Charles the VII. She saw in America that the forces of peace and true justice were gradually winning out over Christian injustice. By 2005 she was coming to believe that her visions were a hoax, until the events of January 20. Then she was asked to be Superior Judge in the Coalition effort. She now had her mission, and in Daschle her Charles VI. She would not be burned at the stake this time, her authority would uphold her mission.

Her verdict was the first step in guiding her Charles. She struck down his quarantine of the French Quarter. Raising the question of Daschle's unrestricted use of executive authority, more rulings were promised as well. Without a Congress, Daschle could not make law and impose regulations.

She also stated that he could not abridge the authority of Federal agencies to fulfill their duties. The EEOC (Equal Employment Opportunity Commission) and Civil Rights Commission were free to set their own standards. So were OSHA, FDA, and all other agencies. All American laws restricting civil rights, including birth control, modesty, abortion, divorce, pornography, and gay rights were null and void. The Dept. of Education was to proceed with standards reflecting 21st century values. Any Bibles, school prayers or Christian propaganda were prohibited. This included gay intolerance or creationism.

Just as this order was presented to Daschle, he was in the process of issuing another order to discourage the population exodus. He intended to return the migrants to their point of origin. But no sooner had he issued it than she struck it down as well. Daschle was in a collision course with the Judiciary.

CHAPTER 11

An early morning meeting on Thursday, June 11 with Litterate showed a program ready to begin, at least in part. Instructors and curriculum were in place and ready to take over the unorganized private programs to educate the ex-slaves. This would begin in Tennessee on Friday. By the 15th, a number of colleges and universities would reopen, most for an unprecedented summer term.

Already acting on Judge Patterson-Roberta's ruling, she said that the children's education agenda would have to be postponed. Not enough of certain Coalition texts, as <u>Jennifer Has Two Moms</u> were available. To make matters worse, a worker in a factory had read a copy of that book, returned to the publisher with a gun and killed two Coalition advisors. He also damaged the line causing a seven hour delay before being shot.

There would also be a problem with adequate teaching staff. When Massachusetts became the first state having compulsory primary education, class size was 50 students per teacher. But the 19th century mindset relied on child brutality to keep order. Since no civilized society could sanction child violence or abuse, the fear of beatings and spankings was gone. But in unlocking the creativity and self esteem of these children, more personnel would be needed to keep order. A September target date was to be set.

Even while the Civil War was being waged, a number of individuals and religious groups had taken a faith based initiative to educate the ex-slaves. With the end of hostilities, this accelerated. Henry Turner of the Israel Bethel Church arrived in Little Rock on May 18. He was offered the opportunity to continue using Coalition literature. To this he refused, adding "Our Constitution was made only for a religious people, and is wholly inadequate for the governing of any other." Being chided for his narrow, biased, and unconstitutional viewpoint he was asked the source of his foolish opinion. He responded "John Adams."

In Nashville, Tennessee, J.C. McGee of the Western Freedmen's Aid Commission arrived at George Peabody College for a day of instruction. As he carried his McGuffy Reader into his class area, and his waiting students, he was stopped. He was given alternate books and told he now would use better materials that the Coalition was furnishing. Due to his love for his students and his work he took the texts.

As he began to thumb through the text of a reading book he was handed he was aghast. Jennifer had two moms because they were homosexuals. The Coalition literature was teaching tolerance and acceptance for a lifestyle his narrow mind could not accept. He ordered his class to return their copies to the front of the room, and he attempted to hand his back to Coalition educator Maurice Covington.

Covington tried to reason with McGee. The books he wanted, the McGuffy Reader or Blueback Speller violated their constitutional rights. They contained too much religion and were intolerant to the rights of others. If religion were allowed, this would not comply with the First Amendment "separation clause". McGee said that he had never seen those words and wanted Covington to show them to him. Covington responded that "you just have to believe it was what the words are intended to mean."

McGee argued that he could not use such repugnant material. Covington told him it was essential to use values neutral literature, and that McGee had no right to judge or dictate his religious bias. Sexual expression was a fundamental right, and he had no right to deny them liberty. Anyway, if he really was a Christian and believed God loved everyone than he should, too.

And just one more point. In 20th and 21st century America experts, who knew more than either of them, wrote textbooks. These experts had extensively researched education, and had come up with the best methods and materials to teach with. It was their superior system that had made modern Americans the brightest and best educated people on earth and in history. That was why the Coalition was superior and successful.

McGee could not argue with what he had never seen or experienced. But his belief system would not allow him to accept what he was being told. Covington gave him an ultimatum. He could either teach the Coalition way or be removed. McGee asked how the government had abandoned its duty to defend his beliefs, and now instead define them away and punish them. He began to address his class leaving Covington no choice but to have him arrested.

Covington tried to explain to the class that McGee was no longer willing to teach them. He refused to use the best text books available because he wanted to keep them inferior. The 800 students, about two thirds men and the rest women and children began to murmur in disbelief. Covington promised them that he would give them the best education possible, if they would give him the opportunity. The books were returned to the students.

As McGee was being taken out he heard two Coalition soldiers discussing the stupidity of a shopkeeper. The one complained that he had purchased a 37 cent item with a silver dollar. The shopkeeper had only given him 63 cents back, not the 73 that he should have. McGee marveled in disbelief.

Back in class, the question was raised as to how Jennifer could have two mothers. Covington eloquently explained that not everyone could be happy in a conventional marriage. Some people, due to feelings that they are born with and cannot help, can only be happy with some one of their own sex. As the group began to murmur he stressed that such choices were normal, morally acceptable, and constitutionally practiced.

An old ex-slave known as Uriah ran into the room shouting "Theys arrested McGee and I thinks theysa gonna keel em." One of the students began to argue about what he had just heard Covington say. Uriah answered "Ya all know McGee loves Jesus. He only wants to learn us to read and he ain't tellen no lies to nobody." And as he looked around he said "Wes gots to save him now!"

As a number of men got up to run out, soldiers took defensive positions to cut them off. Panic set in. The students began to fear that they would be slaughtered like in Selma, and began to stampede through the guard. In self defense the soldiers began to fire on the crowd. In a matter of minutes 14 soldiers and 58 students were dead. By days end order in Nashville was restored, but at a cost of 11 more soldiers and 51 more citizens. Another 200 citizens were arrested, some indefinitely.

At Comstock, Grant deployed his forces, now numbering 1,500 into three groups. One was to hit the mine, a second, the vehicle storage area, and a third, the barracks. Security was lax, all but 300 of the 11,000 Coalition personnel were now demobilized from combat support to city building. Downgraded intelligence failed to pick up any signs of a problem. At 12:15 P.M., Friday morning (Comstock time), the attack began. Caught flat footed, Virginia City was overwhelmed. All mining and processing equipment was destroyed or severely damaged. Over 350 vehicles were destroyed, vast stocks of weapons and equipment was captured. Worst of all, over 2,000 Coalition personnel were dead and 6,000 others captured.

As helicopter gunships arrived at 5:00 A.M., three were shot down. But order was quickly restored, and 31 terrorists were captured as they retreated. Some Coalition captives were released as they fled in haste with other booty.

Unfortunately, in war their are atrocities. In this case the righteous indignation led to the terrorists being tied to a wall, doused with diesel fuel and set on fire. Their screams were heard by Grant's retreating men. In vicious revenge Grant ordered half the remaining Coalition prisoners, of 3,100 total, shot. The rest were released. Against the 3,000 plus Coalition dead the insurgents had lost only 114. Among them, though, was Grant's records keeper, Samuel Clemens.

The media report on Comstock was almost as stunning to Daschle as the event itself. He was blamed for failure to properly defend against an attack that permanently crippled Comstock operations. Probing questions were raised for his "George Bush Jr." like blunders, both at Comstock and in his executive policies.

He should have seen it coming. As his policies began to compromise, even temporarily, commitment to civil rights the environment and social engineering, the media began to question him. Rather had stood loyally by Clinton in his darkest hours as President because of his unwavering support for these ideals. And the media elite invested itself heavily in the Democratic party. Over 90 percent voted Democrat or leftist in every election. They systematically slanted their reporting to influence public perceptions, Bush bashing and Clinton or Daschle coddling. Daschle would have to recommit to moral purity to win them back.

To add to Daschle's problems was the action of Grant after the raid. He had observed Coalition tactics and was a quick learner. He knew he was expected to retreat towards Taho in the west. Instead, he retreated into the desert to the south and east. Blasdel took the 150 or so injured with him towards Taho, leaving an obvious trail. Coalition forces followed, killing or capturing all by noon, but Grant and over 1,200 others escaped.

News media response portrayed Daschle as a man distracted by his political blunders and failing to discharge his rightful charge as leader. The intent was to prod Daschle to comply with Patterson-Roberta's orders.

Instead, it only entrenched him in what he saw as a constitutional confrontation over authority. For the first time in his executive role he was deeply concerned about the Founding Father's intent.

The media response also had a second and unexpected effect. By this time in Coalition occupation nearly two of three Americans were at least somewhat knowledgeable of what was broadcast each day. Hearing of the embarrassing setback at Comstock gave new spirit to the general population.

In any contest of wills the psychological edge is just as important as any other factor. The old saying "It doesn't matter the size of the dog in the fight, but the size of the fight in the dog", has been borne out many a time. On May 5, most Americans were convinced that the Coalition was invincible. Now that mystique was shattered. And Americans, north and south alike cheered a man famous for his victory at Shiloh 14 months before, Ulysses S. Grant.

The defeat of Comstock had yet one more repercussion. It only accelerated the migration of critical American know how from the cities and weakened the work ethic and loyalty of those who remained. To keep the nation running more and more aircraft were grounded, warships docked and ground forces cannibalized to fill in the cracks. Remaining units began to feel stretched, gaps created, this at a time of increasing demands to pacify a people. As in Boston, Butler's army was of questionable worth.

As the Coalition took over education of the freed slaves that Friday, Comstock cast its long shadow over the south. In community after community class ended abruptly in a walk out, shouting match, or open revolt. In all 67 communities saw violence, 130 Coalition and 1,100 student deaths (almost all black) resulted. In several communities the violent reactions spread into the general population. Six armories were breached and weapons stolen before order could be restored. But in 177 towns and plantations, for the moment, the rebellion had taken control.

And Comstock had not just inspired Americans. Like the 1775 Lexington Commons shot heard around the world, it gave the Europeans renewed spirit as well. More testing of Coalition resolve, meddling, even potential for brinkmanship was inevitable. It was essential for Daschle to regain the initiative. As Lenin once said, "To make an omelet you have to break some eggs." Daschle began to coordinate a military response.

Meanwhile the EPA and USDA wasted no time in discharging their agency responsibilities. In over 1,000 farming communities throughout the heartland, agents checked out farms and procedures. Of special concern was the late plantings as returning soldiers and the ex-city dwellers struggled to get a crop in.

Corsica, Ohio was no different than any other village or town. For the last couple of weeks farmers and field workers had been pushing to get a crop in. At 7:00 A.M. Warren DeWitt, USDA supervisor arrived with 11 assistants in the village. An armored personnel carrier with four soldiers had brought them in. To the vexation of the farmers, they invited themselves to fields and pastures, taking notes and samples of plants and dirt. At 3:00 P.M. they gave a list of 46 farms to the local authorities where all or part of the land could not be planted. Crops already growing would have to be plowed under and replaced with pasture or trees. Also, an extensive list of regulations were to be given to every land owner.

At 5:00 P.M. they were ready to leave town for near by Marion. An angry mob approached. Fully aware of events at Comstock, DeWitt was not taking any chances. He ordered the soldiers to fire warning shots over the heads of the mob as his crew scrambled into the A.P.C. (armored carrier). As they did, one of the mob believed they were about to be killed and shot back. His bullet killed DeWitt almost immediately. The APC turned its guns on the mob, killing nine and wounding 17.

In the crowd was a young man named George Harding. He had always wanted to be a doctor, and as the wounded fell he immediately began to render aid. As he did he was struck down and killed. Had he lived, his first son would have been born two years later. His name was to have been Warren, and he would have become President in 1921.

When military control was established the next day, the Coalition became aware of his death. But since Warren would have been a corrupt Republican, damage was minimal. In this case the rewriting of history was a definite improvement.

As for the village of Corsica (or Blooming Grove), an example would have to be made. The population was rounded up, women and small children were taken to boarding houses in Columbus. All the men and elder boys were put in trucks to be transported by rail to North Platte, Nebraska. At that point they would be coded into the Coalition data base as native Americans and sent to mines of Deadwood by early July. But before the deportation, everyone was stripped of every possession but the clothes on their backs and the town with surrounding farms was torched.

That Saturday morning, June 13, Patterson-Roberta added to her decisions from earlier in the week. She went all the way back to the 1803 Mabury vs. Madison decision that "established" the court's authority to confirm the Constitution. The courts had legal stewardship of the government, and everything done by the government was subject to its oversight. The executive branch lacked authority to act alone.

She ordered a stay on all Daschle's orders until they could be fully reviewed. With that said, she gave official approval to his military, monetary, and identification policies. She chided him for not taking a stronger stand on religious bigotry and social issues, with guidelines to follow. Any refusal to accept her authority would be viewed as contempt of court. And even appeals of her rulings would have to go through her for approval.

She did order Daschle to take immediate steps to crack down on religious extremism. The narrow minded intolerance of the church was a breeding ground for sedition, terrorism, and hate crimes. All churches must be registered with Coalition approved bylaws. All preachers would be required to make a loyalty oath and be licensed. Only when freed from the dungeon of religious slavery could America find the glorious liberties, truth, and justice of her modern era.

The blame of Comstock was settling on General Verona Emery-Mills of the Bonneville, Utah base. Her choppers were supposed to run reconnaissance for the territory from California to Missouri, and Canada to central Texas. She protested that the reduction in her aircraft for service elsewhere had hampered her mission. But on Saturday she also provided evidence that an air strike near Durango, Colorado had destroyed virtually all the captured antitank and antiaircraft missiles stolen from Ft. Smith. What she, or no one else knew was that they had rather destroyed a large stockpile of fire works. But at least for the moment her position was more secure and the Coalition more at ease.

The actions of another general, although unknown at the time, proved very troubling. As midnight passed, Lieutenant General Roy Scofield, commander over the nuclear arsenal ordered its transfer. From bases in now Anapolis, Bonneville Flats and San Francisco he ordered them transferred to the Forty Mile Wash at Yucca Mountain, Nevada. One cruise missile was brought to his base at Clarksburg (West), Virginia. He also had the detonation code for that missile programmed for his activation only. The other 48 remained under Daschle's control.

While he did not want to face charges for high treason, he feared even more that the arsenal might fall into the wrong hands. With the showdown between Daschle and Patterson-Roberta threatening leadership stability, he was taking no chances. If chaos or a coup were to happen, he would launch his one missile, aim it at Yucca Mountain, and detonate the whole arsenal. He, if he survived, and any of his command would evacuate to New Orleans, Hampton (Roads) or San Francisco. There they would wait on the reopening of the time channel in October or early November.

Sunday, June 14, saw America in church. Along with now nearly 30,000,000 Americans, nearly 150,000 Coalitioners were inside as well, to pray. A joint worship service was again held in Washington. Again Krishna Mahariji gave Daschle counsel. Reminding him of the words of Lincoln himself he said "A house divided against itself cannot stand." He urged Daschle to make honorable peace with Patterson-Roberta as soon as possible.

The forces of darkness were indeed growing stronger, all agreed, and must become the focus of everyone's energies. As a wise visionary (Modern China) once said "It is expedient to strangle the baby while it is still in the cradle." And Daschle was not about to be caught flat footed. The arrests on June 7 proved that.

This Sunday, New England was the central focus of Coalition observation. With armed escorts, agents attended every major worship center from Maine to Connecticut. While the Coalition presence was intended to establish good will, they were viewed as enemies. With a deep and uneasy calm, both sides pondered just how far the other would go to honor their convictions.

This question was answered in Boston. At the Baptist Tremont Temple, the Coalition had brought in a guest speaker in the interest of a tolerant spirit of religious harmony. With so many ministers in hiding or detention from the Harvard revolt, most pulpits were empty anyway. The "Great Agnostic", Robert Ingersoll, famous for his eloquent criticism (denial) of Christianity was that speaker.

Before the service began, a Coalition spokesperson informed the congregation of new, and hastily implemented rules. Here, and throughout New England the church learned that each minister would have to be licensed by the government. The churches would be registered and required to draft compassionate and cooperative bylaws that had respect for everyone's rights. Women would be recruited for leadership, gays accepted, and other religions welcomed. To refuse to comply would result in arrest and state seizure of church property. The June 7, Harvard Covenant was publicity condemned.

All Coalition eyes were on Ingersoll. With great dismay they had watched as each group they had hoped to rally to their cause had become adversaries. Blacks, women, labor,...But Intersoll and those of his belief system, John Fiske, Asa Gray and others, were warming to the Coalition's overtures. As a lawyer he also showed political leadership potential as well as being a rationalistic visionary.

Political leadership was something Daschle sorely needed. Not only was a functioning congress desperately needed, Fremont was not proving to be a quality leader either. He was seldom cooperative and seemed more concerned in exercising his own authority than in setting to any workable policy. Rather than winning support from underlings, he was only interested in lording authority. He was also under suspicion for security leaks. To relieve him of his office would only further alienate Europe. But if someone like Ingersoll could defeat him in a special election, that would boost the Coalition both at home and abroad.

As Ingersoll rose to speak he was ready to answer those who were claiming that the Coalition was sent by God as a punishment and warning for national sin. To them the unholy greed and rejection of Christian principles that seemed to be breeding in 1863 America (and Europe) were made manifest in the Coalition evil. He believed that the future offered much good, and if Coalition avarice, immorality, arrogance, and perversion could be held in check then there was no cause to fear. Men did not need a god (God) to save him, he only had to listen to the inner voice of goodness and reason. Deep down he believed the heart of the Coalition had to be in the right place. After all, man was basically good.

But as he began to speak, the church was entered by Geraldean (Gerald) Corona and 28 other gay and lesbian worshippers. Asking for the opportunity to give the congregation a special worship testimony, Ingersoll stepped back from the pulpit. On a preset signal, they came up to the altar and began to act out their own version of the "love feast." The homophobic congregation could not accept this liberating and constitutionally sanctioned worship. As a fracas broke out, the two squads of soldiers attempted to restore order. They were forced to evacuate taking the surviving 21 gay activists with them.

Attempting to take Ingersoll, he refused. Totally undone by what he had just seen he fell to his knees and wept. Now he turned to a God he had long ago rejected and begged for forgiveness. As he did, the church mob embraced him as a brother. For the Coalition, there was yet one more tragic loss to the shackles of outdated morality.

The Coalition effort to stifle the Harvard Covenant was also a failure. When the preachers had left town on June 7 they were preceded by ham radios and telegraphs. While Patterson-Roberta had not helped by striking down Daschle's travel restrictions, no one could have foreseen the zeal of the general public in the cause.

As a result, Americans were finding that they could stand united as one throughout the land. This would also provide them with a greater bond of brotherhood and courage. Sharing common religious beliefs, as minds were quickly converting, the Bible, family, liberty, and morality joined all Americans together. If they still doubted, news of the Baptist Tremont Temple riot dispelled any contrary opinions. The once gaping differences between north and south, rich and poor, black and white now had all but vanished.

For church leaders, the Harvard Covenant also provided security and continuity. If they were arrested, someone else from any church could step in to fill the gap. And they saw that as a reality. The Coalition seemed to them as a modern Caesar demanding them to renounce their faith. Now there was no shortage of leadership. And since many "new leaders" had homes large enough to accommodate several families, if church property were lost, the church could still meet.

Over Patterson-Roberta's injunctions Daschle sent a fresh reply to England. Having received nothing but assurances of English considerations, he now raised the possibility of a future Anglo-American partnership. If England would pull the Coalitions direction, all the benefits of modern technology would be theirs. The resulting prosperity would make English merchants the masters of Europe. He also agreed to meet the English requests of June 5, except for accidental violations of borders, but on condition. As a measure of good faith England would have to close her ports to the French military and join America in upholding the Monroe Doctrine. Specifically, pressure must be applied to drive France out of Mexico.

Daschle was beginning to feel internal pressure to take action on Mexico. Hispanics comprised the largest minority group, 18 percent of the Coalition force. The vast majority of these were from Mexico. Maximilian was leaving a tidal wave of death and chaos in his wake, even with French pressure to respect human rights. Hispanics sympathized for their ancestors, and, in altered history began to wonder if their own existence might be jeopardized.

If England agreed to this offer, Daschle could establish a blockade to keep supplies and reinforcements out. He also sent Coalition agents into Mexico to offer logistical and tactical assistance to Juárez. Sanctuary was offered in the United States for refugees. Camps were to be set up in Texas, New Mexico, and California.

As Daschle's most recent proposal winged its way across the air waves to London, Lucky Lucas arrived at Ft. Gregg (Winnipeg). He was the immediate center of attention as bushrangers, or frontiersmen pressured him for news from America. His newfound friends escorted him through town, provided him lodging, and began filling him with Canadian brew. His tongue began to loosen. As circumstances would have it, English agent Lord Robert .... Salisbury was present, and he was all ears.

As a Conservative Party member in Parliament, Lord Salisbury was on good working terms with "Lord Evergreen" Palmerston. With the Coalition challenge, "Evergreen" tapped him, as well as others, for their assistance. And, after reading the history books, his perspectives also began to change. Once an opponent to total democratic rule, now he saw the need to win all segments of English society. He also had a religious conversion. Giving over half his possessions to the lower classes, he advocated governmental purchases of half the land holdings of the English lords, to be given to the peasants. He also wanted greater freedom for Ireland.

Due to this and his keenness of foreign policy, a reformed Lord Evergreen asked him to "keep an eye on those Yanks." He still held to the need for a representative republic, and was himself curious to observe the end result of unbridled democracy. Such emphasis was placed on this mission that Palmerston furnished him a set of radio equipment with a special code.

To Canada Lord Salisbury gave a sense of security. By his presence, he showed English resolve to defend her. To the Canadians, there had always been questions about American intentions. In both the War of Independence and of 1812 America had invaded. In 1846, the American slogan "54-40 or fight" potentially could have resulted in war over British Columbia. While Polk was otherwise distracted with Mexico, a treaty setting the 49th parallel was negotiated. A decade later, America and Canada inked a 10 year trade agreement. But western Canada was open and vulnerable, and American treatment of the Indians lent reason to question her intents. Now with a new and potentially aggressive overlord, the situation was even more volatile.

When Lucky staggered out of bed the next morning he found a wagon filled with the finest new Winchesters and ammunition, courtesy of England. Lord Salisbury had already informed London of America's monetary crisis. England had power to either prop up or force the collapse of the economy. To pull the plug could risk war. England needed to find a weak link in the Coalition armor before she took that chance.

Red Cloud met again with Henry Swan Lake, in the Badlands and without Florence Blue Bell present. As Red Cloud and his chiefs negotiated, they could sense weakness in Swan Lake. Lacking in diplomacy skills and the full language of the Sioux he began to crumble. Red Cloud, taking advantage of the situation, said that the Sioux had grave misgivings and would not give an answer for another seven days. Again, Daschle was notified.

As this and other events crossed his desk that evening, he could see a plan in the process of unraveling. Everyone seemed more intent on persuing individual agendas than Coalition goals. And in the meantime, objectives were not being met. The power struggle between him and Patterson-Roberta had opened this Pandora's Box of woes. He requested a meeting with her at her earliest convenience.

Late that evening, as Christine Todd-Whitman was walking in Philadelphia she paused at a shop that drew her attention. On one side of the window was a picture of Tom Daschle facing towards the middle. It was slightly, elevated. On the other side a picture of Elizabeth Patterson-Roberta, also elevated and facing down towards the middle. In the middle was a copy of Les Miserables by Victor Hugo, still in French. Sticking up from the book were two miniature flags, one an 1863 American and the other a Christian one like those from New York. The American spirit, like Jean Valjean, was a hunted fugitive, but it was still very much alive.

As midnight approached, Daschle received two memos. The first was via radio communication from the USS Enterprise off the French coast. The Coalition's only "Orion" EC-3 surveillance aircraft had suffered engine failure and had crash landed near Bordeaux, France. The fate of the crew was unknown, and Napoleon III could not be reached.

The Donahue was still on duty, but another intelligence hole was opened. In addition, the USS Coral Sea in the Pacific was suffering malfunctions in reconnaissance equipment. Several American based units would have to be redeployed to keep an eye on Europe and the Pacific. And that was at a time when Coalition surveillance was increasingly being challenged by American know how. Rebel units used thermal blankets to frustrate infrared imaging, or tinfoil to blind electronic scanners.

The other memo was from Patterson-Roberta. She would meet with Daschle, but on a precondition. If Daschle would acknowledge her rightful authority, including the right to intercede in his military and foreign policy actions, they would talk. She made specific reference to the 1973 War Powers Act. Otherwise there would be no meeting and she would file charges of contempt against him if he stepped out of line.

As he pondered his next step with Patterson-Roberta, he went over last minute details on action in the south. At 37 points terrorist guerillas and rebels still held power. Nine would be attacked at dawn and other 28 located in east Kentucky, Tennessee, and north Alabama would be surrounded and isolated, for now.

From San Francisco came yet one more challenge, this one from the self proclaimed Emperor of San Francisco, North America (and Protecter of Mexico), Joshua A. Norton. As a friendly and beloved eccentric, he had a mission of daily inspecting the city for safety, cleanliness, and proper behavior. His bizarre behavior had not been limited to San Francisco, however. When the Civil War began he had sent orders to both Lincoln and Davis to come to San Francisco for mediation. Both respectfully refused, but his efforts brought respect and notoriety to the city. When the Coalition arrived, he urged calm. And when General Paul Rupert arrived in town he had offered protection by the police and twice activated vigilante committee that in the prior decade had brought most of the city from lawlessness to respectability. Now, he was circulating an invitation to a peace assembly, at 11:00 A.M., June 16, 1863. The military base was placed on alert by Rupert.

CHAPTER 12

Monday, June 15 brought Coalition education to the colleges and universities. Many, especially in the south, had been closed during the war. Now they were the focus of a Coalition effort to quickly train those who already had a basic education. Speed was becoming increasingly critical to fill the gaps between 1863 society and 2007 industry. For the qualified, education would be free.

Unfortunately, white males would be the primary recipients. While some girls and coeducational facilities existed, the ratio of those showing interest was about seven to one. Even worse, less than one percent of all enrollees were nonwhite. Daschle had personally met with Barbara Boxer, Mary Berry, and Christine Todd Whitman, but for present, no viable solution could be found. Several rights groups activists were led to believe Daschle was not doing enough, but Patterson-Roberta remained silent on the issue, for now.

At 8:00 A.M., Eastern Time the first students had assembled for their first classes in schools east of the Mississippi. All assembled were given opportunity to hear Don Rather's morning news broadcast. The feature story was on the reestablishment of order in nine lawless cities in the south. Though fighting continued in four, the report stated that these communities had all been pacified. No mention was made of casualties, probably because the loss of a Coalition transport off Mobile, Alabama with sophisticated electronic gear and 500 lives. By days end over 850 rebels and 594 Coalition fighters were dead, all objectives reached, but that count was kept confidential.

The news had a sobering affect on the students. All went to respective classes without incident. One such college was the Furman Academy (and Theological Institute) in Greenville, South Carolina. Reopening on its own on June 8, a total of 473 young men and 99 ladies had enrolled. Many, in light of the ethical earthquake that had hit the nation with the Coalition's advent, had come to study religion. Only a minority were there to attend the law and medicine schools which had opened two years before.

The college itself was the dream of a Revolutionary War era man named Richard Furman. He had been inspired by the English General Lord Cornwallis, who "Feared more the prayers of Godly young men than the armies of (Americans) Sumter and Marion." Finally begun about a generation before the Civil War, it then in the 1850's merged with a state university. When forced in 1862 to suspend normal operations, Professor P.C. Edwards had continued with a small school for boys on campus. Two others, Charles Furman and Charles Judson were able to keep a small female school open as well. Now, five Coalition educators with military support were in charge.

As students assembled and roll was taken, each was given an ID number. Also, both men and women would attend class together. The students were told that the national crisis would require help from both men and women. While some murmurs were heard, restraint was the rule. As for the ID number, the instructors did not know their students and this would help guarantee fairness and good record keeping. Again, despite rumors of ID horror stories, the students kept their peace.

They were challenged by a fearful vision, one of a nation beset with famine and pestilence, impoverished by ignorance and war. They, if fervent in their studies, could in three months learn of modern marvels that would lift America from this calamity. They were assured that they would not be forced to renounce their beliefs in God or the Bible. They would need to have an open mind to accept truth, wherever it can be found, and also respect the constitutional rights and beliefs of others. To please God and help His children, they would need to devote full time to this study, only one hour a week, on Sundays, for personal or collective worship.

One of the professors was Paul Blake, the UCLA scientist. He was to hold the first class of the day, and all 572 students attended. To attempt to hold everyone, the school chapel was used, and speakers were set up outside for those who could not fit inside. The students were given two books, one a modern physics text and the other, Darwin's *The Origin of the Species*. During a short break some of the students read excerpts from Darwin's book.

Returning to class, Blake was asked how a Christian could reconcile the Bible and creation with evolution. Blake reassured them of his faith as a Southern Baptist, as also was Bill Clinton and many other Coalition members. Science had proven beyond a doubt that the world was over four billion years old. God had used trial and error, just like any intelligent scientist, and man was a product of this process. He then showed them pictures of an embryonic fish, frog, mouse, monkey, and man. The similarities only proved evolution. Each animal recapitulates, or reverts back to the one cell stage, and each basic stage of evolution as it grows.

One young man then asked how a wise, loving, all powerful and all knowing God could be so cruel. To use life and death struggles for billions of years to experiment made God heartless and distant. Blake answered back "How could your vision of a loving God allow war, famine, and calamity?" The student argued back that Adam and Eve's sin, not God, were responsible, as well as everyone else's sins.

As he was about to answer, an old memory suddenly flashed in his mind. He remembered a lecture that he had once heard, by an archaic creationist, Dr. Thomas Sharp in the late 1990's. While at the time he dismissed it as pseudoscience, unfortunately the creation "virus" had been implanted in his brain. But now, as he debated with these scientific "Neanderthals" the incubated disease of Sharp's words emerged. All the arguments for a young earth, impossibility of life existing by chance, of organs evolving, now flooded into his mind. Now, in a critical hour, he began to waver. In a rejection of science and truth he crumbled. "Yes, you are right" he said. "And I am just an old man who has lost his way" leaving the chapel, he walked out into the nearby woods. It would not be until after noon that Professor Dorothy Pomona would step in.

Taking a no nonsense approach, she resolved to settle this evolution versus creation nonsense. She began by explaining the ethics and religion had their place in society. Back in the pleistocene, or 100,000 B.C. as she explained, humankind needed a code of values to hold a social unity, and an explanation of the purpose of life and of a hereafter. Now, it was a cultural fossil, hold over from past eons and no longer pertinent or of value to America and needed to fade.

Then she took on another form of vestigal bigotry, that of sex discrimination. Even the female members of the class were showing unease, or hang ups with her authority. With thick skinned dignity, she proved the development of men from a single cell in the primoral sea. Showing pictures of primitive man, she returned to religion, and God's role. She argued that God was just a concept these stupid primitives came up with to explain disappointment, death, and the unknown. But we were as much god as God existed, our life force combined with matter and somehow continues after our deaths. And it may be that this life force lives over and over again in one life form after another.

At this moment a former rebel soldier known as "Jake" stood up and cried out "For to me to live is Christ and to die is gain." As all eyes fixed on him he added "Lets take back our college and our nation." But no match for Coalition steel, they were driven into the woods. Five had been killed and nine injured. But the rest, and another 400 residents at Greenville headed towards King's mountain. But Furman was only one of an almost total educational failure, and yet another nail in the coffin of winning the hearts and minds of the people.

By days end Daschle was now planning a massive offensive, mostly in the south, against at least 177 towns, cities, and plantations now in revolt. Almost every available helicopter and most other air units would be needed. Other Coalition posts and missions would be drawn down, some to a point of being dangerously understaffed. It would also seriously deplete fuel reserves. Daschle's HSA chief, Les Lyberte also urged the use of one higher yield nuclear device. Detonated at Crossroads, Mississippi, near Corinth, it would paralyze resistance for 100 miles. Daschle reluctantly agreed. Fortunately for Scofield, not all of Bonneville's bombs had been moved to Yucca Mountain. His secret was still safe.

Daschle was also preparing for another offensive, as Patterson-Roberta issued more rulings. Challenging his legal authority to use Taft-Hartley to gloss over unsafe steel mills, prevent union organization, or extort a wage increase for the workers. She also assailed him for failure to provide any cash payments for the Pittsburgh victims.

Using his own version of history, he determined to challenge her assault on his Commander in Chief powers, especially military and foreign policy. Using the Prize cases, just ruled upon by the Taney Supreme Court in March 1863 he began a case for executive authority. The court had recognized Lincoln's authority to blockade the south (economic as well as military) and defend the nation without congressional approval. Even without future, or post 1863 rulings, that should be enough. But they were included since modern warfare had shown that social, economic, and homeland security were often as important as actual combat. Broad authority was essential to the successful completion of the Coalition mission.

Tuesday (June 16) morning Joshua Norton with his beloved dog Lazarus was among the first to arrive at Mission Delores for the Peace Rally. By

11:00 A.M. over a third of the 100,000 residents had assembled thousands carried modern American and white flags. After prayers, the group began a march to the Hall of Justice. At that point they were four miles form the Coalition Naval Air Station at Hunter's Point. For over an hour they sang hymns and gave speeches. They appealed for all sides to peaceably work together and show restraint.

But General Rupert was not in a position to show patience. The Comstock attack and southern revolts left little margin for any organized demonstrations. Soldiers took strategic positions around the group. As Norton rose to speak the order was given to disperse at once. Norton objected, claiming they had come in peace and good will. An attorney who was present, William T. Shaw attempted to give a soldier an American flag. He was shoved back into the crowd.. Norton, fearful for his city, in his eccentric way pulled out his famous sword, and immediately was shot dead.

Seeing their beloved leader fall, the crowd lost composure. Order and restraint died with Norton and a wild stampede began. The Coalition opened fire with machine guns, grenade launchers and tank shells. By 3:30 order was restored. Against no Coalition deaths over 800 protesters had perished and 1,200 more were arrested. San Francisco grieved, but for many tears of sorrow began to turn to cries for vengeance. Bill Clinton and Barbara Boxer, on Daschle's request immediately arrived to try to console a city.

That evening on the news, Patterson-Roberta was given a live interview. She expressed her deep sympathies for the people of San Francisco, and demanded an official investigation of the Coalition action. Chiding Daschle for failure to properly deal with the nation's problems, she promised a more compassionate plan forthcoming. And for the victims of the Pittsburgh disaster, she ordered an immediate fifteen hundred dollar payment to each of 8,600 survivors. She suggested it be paid in gold, as a symbol of the value of their lives.

Wednesday morning (June 17), Coalition headquarters in Philadelphia sent a call for police or military back up. The entire police force resigned following the Tuesday release of a suspected rapist. He was arrested on the 13th when two men heard a woman's screams and caught him in the act. After ruffing him up a bit they turned him over to the police. A search of his home uncovered Coalition pornography. But Coalition judge Christiana Walker ordered him released. He had not been read his Miranda Rights, and the search of his home was without a warrant.

Colonel Roxana Yorklyln ordered martial law as the police commissioner resigned. Already angry over a crime wave that had begun shortly after the Coalition invasion, he and the police chafed at her rebuke of official policy. And not just policy was assailed, she had begun to void many of the city's laws especially Blue laws and those governing moral behavior. Unfortunately the 1863 mindset could not grasp the need for reform, and a large city was now without protection.

To respond, Daschle asked Fremont to use a regiment of federal troops. In classic style he agreed, but at a price. His military command would increase to 60,000, and they would be getting a stock of old M-1 rifles. While primitive by modern standards, in less than two months the U.S. Army had taken an 80 year leap. Unfortunately, over the next few days a number of other cities would also see their police forces resign. By weeks end Butler's (Fremont's) garrisons were maintaining order in 18 other cities.

As Christine Todd Whitman walked the streets of Philadelphia again that night, she paused at the shop she had noticed Sunday evening. In the back, visible from the doorway was a caricature of 1789 Paris. A "nobleman" in a carriage was throwing a gold coin to a ragged woman whose son had just been run over. A woman in the carriage was throwing two more. Her face was that of Patterson-Roberta, and the nobleman of Daschle. A book was held in the poor woman's hand. It was a copy of Charles Dicken's *A Tale of Two Cities*. Again the message was chilling.

At 10:00 P.M. Daschle had made final plans for a Thursday morning assault in the south. Task force commander, Major General "Dusty" Valdez San-Juan and Washington DC base commander four star General Craig Walden attended. A nuclear device detonated at 6:00 A.M. at high altitude (30,000 feet) would open the offensive.

While they met, Daschle's office was informed that Judge Patterson-Roberta, with a breach of security, had become fully aware of the operation. She ordered an immediate stay, subject to a legal review of his domestic riot control scheme. This was to avoid any reckless threat to lives of both Coalition and American. And in a public statement, heard throughout America, she called on the south to end its rebellion to avoid dire military consequences.

While the military was bound to obey any legal order given by the Commander in Chief, all felt obliged to await further orders. However, at Bonneville, General Emery-Mills ordered a total halt, and refused to obey any orders without Patterson-Roberta's assent. Daschle was forced to delay for at least one day and deal with both a judge and a general.

At about that time Red Cloud and his chiefs were again meeting with Swan Lake. This time, Florence Blue Bell, while not able to address the chiefs directly, was his advisor. Irene Rosebud was also with them, in camp at a place near Cherry Creek on the Cheyenne River. All groups of the "Seven" Nations of the Sioux were included, and it seemed as if the whole mass of them was assembling with their leaders.

Crazy Horse and a number of braves were still off on a raid against new homesteaders in southern North Dakota. Red Cloud was barely restrained in his words. There was much cause for anger. While the number was not known at that moment, almost 180,000 land claims had been made since April 24. An area of 45,000 square miles, more than the whole state of Pennsylvania had been occupied. He not only rejected any thought of Black Hills mining, he demanded a token of peace and good will. Tepee Rock (Chimney Rock, Nebraska) must be returned, and all new settlers must leave at once. They gave until June 20, Saturday for an answer or there would be war.

Around midnight, two men emerged from hiding in Virginia to make a preemptive strike. One was Jeb Stewart, a Confederate Calvary commander under Lee who had been forced to join with union Captain George Armstrong Custer. Freak circumstances in north Virginia weeks before found both under attack by helicopter gunships. In a daring move, they joined commands to save their men. Traveling west to the Allegheny Mountains of western Virginia, nearly 700 of their men followed.

In a food raid on a small depot at Big Stone Gap they acquired a few weapons, some communications equipment, and six prisoners. Now, about seven miles from their camp, the Coalition maintained a support base at Jonesville. The prisoners were able to provide their captors a great deal of valuable information. To the now lightly garrisoned vehicle maintenance base at Jonesville, this would prove lethal.

The 900 mostly support and repair personnel there had labored non-stop since Monday to ready a logistical transport group. Most had not slept in over 60 hours, but their unit was readied and left for Mt. Alry, North Carolina at 9:30 P.M. Coalition intelligence had not picked up the rebel force, and in spite of the Big Stone Gap raid two weeks earlier, considered the area safe. Only two Coalition men were used to guard the base as the others slept. From a visual surveillance center, they watched as cameras and sensor devices scanned the perimeters. Sgt. Kelsy and Private Marion had not slept in well over 48 hours.

At 1:00 A.M. Marion tapped Kelsy on the shoulder and asked him if he saw movement on the southwest monitor. Both men, now on the borders of mental endurance focused full attention on that set of monitors. After a few minutes they were trying to decide if they were observing deer or small horses. Suddenly five men burst into the room and overwhelmed them. While the two were looking west, attackers had snuck in from the east.

In just over an hour it was over. The base was totally neutralized, 513 Coalition personnel were dead, 186 captured and the rest scattered into the night. Enough small and medium weapons were captured to arm a thousand men. Custer and Stewart had lost seven, 200 locals volunteered to take their places. Among the booty were over 500 armor piercing missiles.

On Thursday morning (June 18) Daschle got Blue Bell's message from Red Cloud. Lyberte advised him that two things might bring the Sioux around. One would be the immediate termination of the western movement of settlers. This would be difficult, and would require pulling border patrol units for the task. The other thing was a massive incendiary display above their encampment. One B-2 Bomber could do the trick. The only need was to keep the Sioux in that camp until Saturday. Swan Lake would inform the Sioux that at 6:30 A.M., Washington time, they would get a sign from heaven.

Urgency of mission was now coming from another quarter as well. The raiding party of Crazy Horse had brought a flux of refugees to Ft. Berthold (North Dakota). Among them were survivors of the Gros Ventres, Rees, and Mandans. These tribes, once masters of the Sioux, and generally friendly to the white man had been devastated by a small pox epidemic in 1837. Now they sought white man's protection.

Offensive action was to commence in the south on Saturday, with another B-2 dropping a high level nuclear device, also 6:30 A.M. Washington time. In the meantime, Daschle took all steps possible to isolate Patterson-Roberta. Her access codes were changed, communication lines curtailed, and escort guard reduced. All commanders were told to ignore her interference. For the moment Breyer and Ginsburg remained out of the feud, but Patterson-Roberta was using their office to maintain contact with a new friend.

General Emery-Mills, verbally reprimanded for Comstock, had now come to question Daschle's strategy and legal theory. She was willing to cooperate when Patterson-Roberta requested the nuclear armed B-2 placed under the judges jurisdiction. She did proceed with the order to arm the second B-2 with its less than lethal cargo.

Friday brought the Coalition one of its few successes in the field of education, at the University of Michigan in Ann Arbor. The education of 123 male and 27 female students could be attributed to a cooperative Asa Gray. Once a professor there, he now returned from Harvard after the June 7 skirmish and a resulting administration return to religious fundamentalism. He feared that his scientifically progressive views no longer had a place there. On June 15 he took over as dean in Michigan, as that school's administration resigned in protest of Coalition policies. To open for class he had brought in several like minded men.

Othniel Marsh, a devout evolutionist had recently returned from Europe (by plane) as they, especially Germany, now headed into an intellectual dark ages. He would head the paleontology department. Social Darwinist William Sumner left Göttingen to join him. A Harvard class of '63 graduate John Fiske also accompanied Gray. These men would head the ethics and history departments. Gray would use his own *Manual of Botany* as a textbook. Classes were held without incident except for the debate between a Social Darwinist and Marxist Darwinist perspective.

The same debate now raged, interestingly enough, in the Coalition camp. Social Darwinists, those who believe in the survival of the fittest, like Treasury Secretary Cash, saw a national sorting out process as healthy. He was not concerned with present American hostility. In time, a superior mentality would arise and the nation would praise the Coalition. Inferior businesses and processes would die out, and be replaced by a superior people.

The Marxist Darwinists, like OSHA head Safer, felt that the only way to succeed was through the system. By standardized education, safety, health, and environmental policies, a new mindset would be created. The weak would be transformed, under social protection by the state into a strong new world. The only reason the Communists did not succeed was that they had stifled personal rewards for their labors. A little personal gain and society could be mentally regimented, the People's Republic of China proved that.

But for now, Daschle was trying to remain above the debate. He had other things to worry about.

Late that afternoon, Daschle ordered Emery-Mills relieved of her command. Brigadier General Cody Worland took her place. He immediately ordered the B-2 for Mississippi, readied for its mission. But the power struggle with Patterson-Roberta continued throughout the evening, creating confusion and a mix up. The B-2 loaded with incendiaries was given a target in Mississippi and the one with the nuclear device, South Dakota.

In San Francisco, in an effort to comfort a city, a funeral service was held for Joshua Norton and 800 unfortunate victims. Over 50,000 people crowded in and around the St. Francis of Assissi Church in San Francisco. An uneasiness could be felt as the service concluded and Lazarus was given to Attorney William Shaw. Outside, a "Cemetery of Innocents" was set up with 813 little white crosses with one in the middle, for Norton and the others for victims. By the next morning General Rupert had removed them. They were "too graphic" as a reminder of an action the government felt was justified.

At 6:30 A.M. Washington time, Saturday, June 20, dawn came with unnatural flame. Mississippi and the surrounding parts saw a fireworks display that alerted all of a coming invasion. In South Dakota, everything within two and a half miles of Cherry Creek was incinerated. Among the dead, Red Cloud, Sitting Bull, Swan Lake, and any hope of reconciliation with any of the plains Indians. Also mortally wounded was any hope of cooperation from a stunned world.

In the south, the unorganized, but determined resistance was ready for an assault. Under loose leadership of men like General Benjamin Prentiss, an escaped Bedford Forrest, and Pierre Beauregard cooperation was universal. Since Monday, eight armories had been raided (outside of Stewart's group). Captured Coalition personnel provided much valuable information. Numerous security and monitoring equipment cites were destroyed and some captured weapons, including the missiles captured from Ft. Smith were shared between the many groups. And thanks to Patterson-Roberta, Rather and company, many of the targets were already known.

As the sky filled with the sight and sound of aircraft, defenders at over 40 locations were ready. With veteran nerve, learned at places like Shiloh, Vicksburg, Fredericksburg, and a hundred other battles they waited. When the helicopters were most vulnerable, as they began to unload, the veterans opened up with rocket launcher and rifle, machine gun and mortars. The choppers become the epicenter of a tremor of fire, the focus of a ground turkey shoot. At one landing cite near Milledgeville, Georgia alone, six choppers went up in flames in two minutes. Surviving units pulled up to higher elevations and attack jets, many armed with napalm, saturated surrounding areas. Even some of these were hit by the incredibly sophisticated ground fire.

By 10:30 most of the fighting had ended. At 3:00 P.M. all initial objectives had been met. Nearly 5,000 Americans were dead, many were women and children. Of the combatant dead, nearly a quarter were black. The actual white rebel body count was about 1,500. Against this, Coalition losses were 79 helicopters and nine other aircraft. Nearly 1,600 were dead or missing, and in some locations units were still perusing rebel units.

Not knowing how to report casualties, all American losses were listed as hostile. 4,893 confirmed dead and over 4,000 others suspected as dead. A total of 161 locations were listed as secured. The guerrillas were reported to have been virtually annihilated. But to the loosely organized freedom fighters, this was a great victory. Americans were finding a resolve, and a growing order in their struggle to reclaim their nation.

The press release from South Dakota was anything but kind, however. As a stunned Washington heard the news of the day, Cherry Creek brought nothing but finger pointing and recriminations. While the pyrrhic victory in the south deeply bruised the psyche of the military, Cherry Creek splintered any sense of a unified mission. Cries for Daschle's resignation, from Patterson-Roberta and throughout the civil rights groups made national news. And so did Daschle's and the military's blame of Patterson-Roberta.

Krishna Mahoriji asked for a meeting with Daschle. He assured the great leader that all was not lost. For the Sioux, their souls would find another channel to be reborn. They would be enlightened and would forgive. But Daschle would have to take control from Patterson-Roberta or all could be lost.

The defeat in the south was due to bad karma. Too many on the Coalition were joining with the American people in a retreat to religious intolerance. They were giving power to their spirit force and that was working against the Coalition. It was time to close ranks and outlaw their beliefs. Then their would be an early dawning for the New Age, and Daschle could ride in its light to glory. If not, the future would be condemned by history.

On a side note, Minnie M. Wage, Dept. of Labor met with Daschle. She pointed to statistics that showed a wage price strangulation of the nation during this era. Without intervention, prices would more than double during the Civil War era, while wages would increase by less than 50 percent. She proposed setting a base national wage for both agricultural and manufacturing labor. It would help win support of the working class. It would also put more money in the consumer's hands at a time when the economy was languishing. Since the Coalition had already put one in effect for the ex-slaves in the south, it would only take a few added steps to make it nationally universal. Daschle agreed.

Late that afternoon, Lyberte gave Daschle the full insight on Europe's history leak. Sergeant Henry Culpeper, one of Clinton's entourage had been responsible for leaving a set of nearly a dozen books in Paris. These subversive books portrayed history from the 1800's though early 21st century from a radical right wing viewpoint. They lay the blame of world war, Communism, moral decadence, and genocide at the feet of the evolutionist, humanist, and atheist. Now Europe was being swept by censorship and religious extremism.

An example would be made of Culpeper. He would be publicly stripped of rank, and dishonorably discharged. All his books that he still possessed would be bundled up with him and parachuted to a spot near Wall, South Dakota. The surviving Sioux should take care of him.

As evening came, a crisis was brewing in Baltimore. Thursday morning one of Butler's federal troops had made an arrest. Coalition business consultant Archie Horton was arrested as he left the Peale Museum. On his possession were several artifacts. A legal search of his Charles Street off base apartment turned up many more. Taken into Coalition custody from the Federals he was given a Friday hearing, before Judge Walker in Philadelphia.

He at first denied everything, but in light of the evidence quickly changed his strategy. He placed full blame on a wide open and security ignorant America. He was enticed and entrapped by the undue temptation it offered. Also, 19th century laws were too vague concerning theft and should be struck down anyway. As far as prison, 19th century prisons were cruel and unusual punishment, and unfit for incarceration. And it was the

Coalition's fault, not his, for not taking proper action in preventing his weaknesses from controlling him in such an environment. After confiscating all the relics, Walker had no other option but to drop charges and let him go.

Baltimore was known for its willingness to display civil disobedience. In April of 1861 it was the scene of riots against Union troops' presence in the town and the state. On April 19, a mob opened fire on troops headed for Washington resulting in 13 deaths in an ensuing battle. Now, on June 13, 1863 a group of nearly 400 vigilantes headed by merchant John Hopkins patrolled the city. Two found Horton as he left the historical Edgar Allen Poe house. A single bullet left him dead.

Butler's troops quickly arrived in the form of the Maryland second regiment. But seeing virtually every civil leader on the side of vigilantes, they refused to take action. By nights end, a company of Coalition troops with Christine Todd Whitman spokesperson appealed for the guilty to be surrendered. Instead gunfire broke out. Baltimore was in a state of revolt, and the Coalition force retreated to their base near Ft. Mc Henry.

CHAPTER 13

Sunday, June 21 was the longest day of the year, and for Daschle, one of the longest of his life. At 2:00 A.M. he was awakened to be told that insurgents had overrun two bases in the south, one at Lynchburg, Virginia and the other at Birmingham, Alabama. The southern steel centers were in jeopardy. An uneasy peace prevailed in Baltimore, without Coalition control of the city. Fighting continued at several other locations in the south.

Calling an immediate meeting including economic and environmental advisors, the value of the Appalachian and deep south regions were considered. If the military was unable to restore order by noon, Monday, a large section of the south would be isolated. All railroad and road lines would be severed and bridges destroyed. A Sherman style scorch the earth approach would destroy any recognizable industry or manufacturing centers. Food stocks and animal herds would be ravaged.

Insurgency would have to be broken and to do that the rebellious spirit of the people would have to be crushed. Food, medical care, and education had failed to win them over. To do without anything might bring them to a little more appreciation for the Coalition's generosity. And when they came to realize that no God could save them, they might open up to the compassionate ways of the Coalition.

Throughout America everyone who could attend church did so. In a zone from New York to Illinois churches were advised of the new rules going into effect on the 28th. Worshippers were given leaflets warning them of the danger of attending churches that failed to meet government approval. Although the agents were backed up by armed soldiers, most of the leaflets were rejected. When Coalitioners rose to give warnings in some of the churches, parishioners would turn their backs in contempt.

In the Black Hills, the Coalition wasted no time in setting up a mining camp. Using modern computer imaging, they had identified two key veins by nightfall. Back in Comstock, production was again at 50 percent of pre-raid levels. In Colorado, both Cherry Creek and Cripple Creek were seeing

USGS action. Within a week enough gold should be flowing to end the monetary crisis.

Bill Clinton and Barbara Boxer were pushing a diplomatic offensive in California. Speaking to whoever would listen they hit San Francisco, Los Angeles and a number of other cities. Before they would leave the state they would also worship in the first Buddhist Temple in America, in an outreach to the Chinese.

Meanwhile, Ulysses S. Grant decided against returning to California and went south towards Goldfield. Using thermal cover by day and moving by night they had evaded Coalition eyes. They had not escaped notice of prospectors, settlers, and adventure seekers. Along with more units of his army moving west, the added numbers brought his command to almost 2,000 by days end. Among the new recruits was Orion Clemens, Secretary of the Nevada Territory, and brother of Samuel Clemens who had died at Comstock.

The surviving 43 Coalition captives were very helpful in training Grant's men. They also directed a party to a stash at Spring Mountain (near present day Las Vegas). Grant spent long hours studying Coalition maps of the western territories, planning his next actions.

Late that morning in Washington, Daschle received the 30 year old Spencer Compton Clavendish, English consulate. As First Lord of the Admiralty, he was personally entrusted by Palmerston. Both had seen the role Clavendish was to play in history, and felt a sense of destiny in his commission. He was a persuasive speaker with the ability to weigh all sides of an issue before committing to a position. He was also loyal to the Crown, and now to God as well.

Studying the modern history books, he was intrigued by Adolph Hitler and the Nazis. Given the historical cultural and religious roots of Germany, it deeply troubled him that a man and system so devoid of both could hold such power. From his perspective he had come to view the Coalition in the same light.

Hitler had played on Germany's animosities over the outcome of World War I, anti-semitism, and a sense of destiny. Jews and other subhuman groups (including the Church) were blamed for impeding the fulfillment of German destiny. Hitler also appealed to Europe's desires for peace and prosperity. After he struck without warning to retake the Saar (Rhineland) in

1936 he appealed for peace. Later he did the same after Austria and the Sudetenland were taken. Appealing to the west's fear of communism as well as peace, he seduced English Prime Minister Neville Chamberlain at Munich. And later, after the war began, he attempted to drive a wedge between France and England, while he demonstrated on Poland how brutal his war could be.

Clavendish viewed Daschle in the same light. Seeing abortion and hearing about Montagu's philosophy on what defines a human being smacked of historical parallel. And the Coalition policies towards the church reminded him of the Nazi treatment of Diedrich Bonhoffer and the German Christians. Like so many of America, he was seeing a divine warning. They could not understand the vast philosophical differences between the Nazis, or Stalinists, and the Coalition. And as he saw Daschle seeming to drive a wedge between France and the rest of Europe from England, his beliefs gained credibility. After his meeting he retired to accommodations wired with all modern convenience. As he viewed a T.V., he saw a replay of the hideous blast at Cherry Creek. His fears seemed to be confirmed.

He also observed footage of the downing of two choppers near Birmingham. The vulnerability of those metal monsters while loading and unloading did not escape his notice. It had not escaped Daschle's either, as his generals plotted strategy. Nor had Emery-Mills claim of having destroyed most of the deadly missiles. The possibility of a primitive manufacturing cite would have to be investigated. Meanwhile, chopper units elsewhere were drawn down. The Navy would have to open a base in Seattle, against a policy of not developing the area. Border patrol would rely now on fixed wing aircraft and ground units.

In Atlanta and 17 other safe communities, baseball was the entertainment of the afternoon, as 34 of the now 42 teams met to play. In one short month Ted Turner had made a dream into reality, as the National Association of Baseball Players was transformed. Begun in the 1850's, it had reached a level of 25 teams, mostly of amateur quality. During the war the league survived, but like all civilian activities had faced war's challenges.

Turner had convinced Daschle of the value of building up the sports past time program as a means of entertainment and goodwill. He had been given a green light, literally, with government green backs. Keeping most of the present owners in the fold, cash incentives lured new ones, and money also built teams of more quality players. A schedule had been worked out for each team to play three games a week through October 10 and playoffs to follow.

To no one's (Coalition, anyway) surprise, he had taken personal responsibility for the Atlanta Braves. He also would have the honor of throwing out the first ball. Admission was free to Atlanta's debut with the Philadelphia Keystones as it was for all games that day. But attendance was low, only 2,258 were in the stands and 1,646 of them were Coalition. Games out west were slightly better attended, but most Americans still legalistically honored the Sabbath.

As Turner threw out the first ball of the first game of the first season of his new league a shot rang out. A lone assassin had his in a shed near the makeshift playing field. The beloved philanthropist, social giant, and pioneer for freedom fell dead. Though the dastardly coward was immediately killed, the damage could not be undone.

In Detroit, border guards nabbed a group of 26 attempting to cross over to Windsor, Canada. Among them was the author Walt Whitman. Apprehending him caught the attention of two disabled veterans. One of them, Cyrus, had lost a leg at Antietam. While he was in the infirmary, Whitman had come to visit him and read Scriptures to him. He was most encouraged by the words "A friend loveth at all times and a brother is born for adversity." Now it as his turn to be a friend.

Hobbling up to the two guards, he pleaded for Whitman's release. He and the other veteran even offered their medals of honor and other citations in exchange for his release. Hearing the exchange, a group of about 30, mostly veterans, gathered to press the cause. Among them was a young Wisconsin named Arthur MacArthur, who had also made plans to leave the country. In a flash of courage, he offered himself in exchange for Whitman.

More security troops arrived, and ordered the mob to disperse. Instead, MacArthur began to sing the Battle Hymn of the Republic and the others joined in. The demands of the gathering crowd also were escalating, now they wanted all detainees released. Among them was Thomas Buchner. On March 6 he had brawled to keep blacks out of Detroit, but June 8 he was arrested for attempting to smuggle them in.

Troops begun to arrest the veterans, causing Cyrus to cry out, "Give me liberty or give me death." But base commander, Colonel Lilly Penbrook was determined that no one would be a martyr. Cyrus did not get his wish.

Instead he, MacArthur, and 50 some others were arrested. Penbrook then implemented a novel plan. She had them, Buckner, and ten other detainees fed a meal. In the process, unknown to them, they each swallowed a tracking device in the form of a vitamin pill. They were released but every move and conversation was monitored.

As evening descended, Judge Patterson-Roberta ordered Daschle arrested, and brought to her for legal action. The charges were incompetence, dereliction of duty, and failure to uphold the Constitution and oath of office. She had legal president as no Commander in Chief was above the law. Andrew Jackson had been the subject of Congressional censure, Richard Nixon forced to resign due to Congressional probing. Two presidents had been subject to impeachment proceedings, Andrew Johnson and Bill Clinton. In Clinton's case, the courts were also involved, as he was called to testify before a Grand Jury. Since there was no functioning Congress now to take action, she took action herself, as a voice of reality in an unraveling mandate. She notified Bill Clinton, still in California, of her action, as he would take over leadership from Daschle. But his loyalty was to Daschle, and he immediately notified him of her actions.

With her entire force of five federal marshalls and 18 deputies at her immediate disposal she made her move. Daschle had been alerted, however, and met them with over 70 military guards. Out numbered three to one the marshalls surrendered. Patterson-Roberta was now ordered arrested for high treason. Despite strong words from both Ginsburg and Breyer, she was placed under house arrest.

Events of the day prevented Daschle from sleep that night. The compound failures and disasters of the day distressed enough. The confrontation with the Judiciary vexed him. He no longer felt that he was the democratic head of a nation, but somewhere over the line as a dictator. His worries were as much for himself as for the fate of the nation. And he wondered how history would remember him for his actions.

Monday morning, June 22 Crazy Horse joined his war party with a band of Sioux survivors near Eagle Butte, South Dakota. Many of these stragglers suffered blindness and serious burns. They were about seven miles from ground zero. They spoke of how the white chief had made the sun touch the earth, and mother earth had groaned and shook in agony. They had managed to put almost a dozen miles between themselves and the cursed ring of death. Others had not been so lucky.

Crazy Horse was now chief over a people few and trembling. His hatred of white man was well known. He had just completed a successful raid on homesteaders along the Heart and Cannonball Rivers in North Dakota.

The few squaws and children that he took captive all had the same story. They had come to Indian lands to escape the same white chief that had just destroyed over half his people. For all the evils of the settlers they were less a danger than the white chief. An old sage once said that "The enemy of my enemy is my new friend." Crazy Horse began to think the unthinkable, a deal with the homesteaders, the Pawnee, the Mandan, against the new invaders.

Later that day, ex-sergeant Henry Culpeper was dropped off a chopper near another surviving Sioux camp in the Badlands. Still in handcuffs, he and his gear were soon discovered by the Indians. It was assumed that the Sioux would end his life. But they were curious of one who had become an enemy of the Coalition. An English speaking tribe member interrogated him. Accepting him as trustworthy, they broke off his cuffs and shared their provisions, and named him "Bird Man." In exchange, he treated their sick, taught them new ways of doing things, and about the God of the Bible.

With insurrection spreading in the South, Daschle approved of Lyberte's plan to cordon off the areas of greatest resistance. The Mississippi and all coastal areas remained in Coalition hands. The massive invasion of Saturday now was a search and destroy mission. Livestock and food stockpiles were destroyed, over 300 towns and cities were burned, bridges blown up, and the earth scorched. Atlanta was the largest city destroyed. The death of Ted Turner and discovery of six different weapons caches were avenged.

Losses had been heavy. In three days nearly 12,000 terrorists and their supporters had died. But Coalition dead numbered almost 2,800. Worse yet was the erosion of discipline. Nearly 1,800 Coalition fighters (and support troops) faced court martial for failure to obey orders. Another 1,900 were missing, most having deserted over to the rebels. Much of the south resembled descriptions of historical lore on Sherman's march to the sea. Nearly three and a half million people, almost half of them black, faced famine and disease. But critical times called for extreme measures. Daschle had no way of knowing at that moment, but to a slew of American generals and commanders in hiding, this was their wake up call as well to extreme measures.

Tuesday brought Clinton and Boxer back from California. With the realistic failure of the education effort, Daschle had asked her to take a direct role. A minimum of 700,000 trained Americans would be needed by October 1 to have any hope of keeping nation building hopes alive.

Noralee L. Litterate was immediately concerned about the direction education would take. Her program had lost Daschle's support, but she had not lost her supporters. Together they drafted a list of concerns and proposals to keep the spirit of modern America alive. Of major concern was the poor results in bringing women and minorities to a more prominent role in 1863 America. But in lieu of Sunday's judicial "decapitation" no one felt comfortable pushing the issue too hard. She did take her recommendations to Boxer, however, and found her openly receptive, especially on gay rights concerns.

The next day Clinton was able to meet with Clavendish. With Daschle's growing concern for domestic concerns, he turned even more heavily to his old friend. He hoped Clinton's charm and almost psychic appeal could win over Clavendish and a significant foothold among the English ruling class.

Unfortunately, English hierarchy was in the vortex of great change. Gone was the "agnostic by 20 atheist by 40" mentality among the English elite. They believed they were seeing the hand of God and were returning to the outgrown obsolete scruples and narrow religious confines of their past. The Coalition still hoped for a more open minded class, and intended to appeal to the yearnings of its heart and soul. The Coalition was more than willing to share its technology and knowledge to bring liberty, life, and pursuit of fulfillment. All could be theirs if they would join hands and help build a brave new world.

Clavendish may have been a "youth" at 30, but he had an ability beyond his years to play the game. He nodded attentively with Clinton's enticements and played to his charm. As Clinton offered the bait, Clavendish acknowledged the need of modern health care, nutrition, and living conditions. But he did not take the bait, he viewed it as concealing a deadly hook of perversion.

Clinton was not aware of the depth of change since May 23 in the ruling class of Europe, and England in particular. More and more they viewed wealth and power not as a privilege, but as a commission, or responsibility. The whole social order seemed to be turning upside down, as each one seemed intent on outdoing the next in benefiting the less fortunate. Personal comfort was no longer a priority. He also was well aware that England now knew of the monetary difficulties, oil demands, and insights in Coalition schisms.

The Coalition crisis of confidence and growing disillusionment within gave Clavendish an edge on Clinton. Something was going terribly wrong, and the Coalition needed England far more than England needed what the Coalition had to offer. He responded to the request to close English ports to France and to joint partnership by asking for a token of American goodwill. Clinton provided him with a dozen modern computers. They would meet again after Clavendish consulted with Palmerston.

Late that evening, Wednesday, June 24, a cluster of Mexican refugees were making a crossing just south of Del Rio, Texas. They were met by about 350 Texans, dressed as Indians under the command of General John Pemberton. The refugees were turned back. No one in Texas wanted the problems of Mexico to spill over into their state. Many remembered the War for Independence in 1835 and 1836, and Santa Anna's invasion again in 1846 after the state joined the United States. They had enough memories of invasion from the south and, with their own problems with the Coalition, were short on sympathy.

Daschle immediately called for an air strike against the offending Texans. Jets and high level bombers were called in from Ft. Smith, San Diego, and New Orleans. By the time they arrived, Pemberton's men had faded into the hills and the bombs fell on empty lands. Ground troops could not be spared.

On Thursday morning, June 25, Colonel Penbrook's tracking devices paid dividends. In Detroit, it led to the apprehension of 113 plotting terrorists, snipers, and sappers. Arthur MacArthur was killed in the process. Had he lived, he would have been the grandfather of World War II and Korean General Douglas MacArthur.

As Daschle received news of events in Detroit, he received news of the death of another family in Elizabethville, Pennsylvania. The family of Jacob F. and Rebecca Eisenhower (Eisenhouer) perished when they were caught in the crossfire of an ambush. Had she lived, she would have given birth on September 23 to a son David, who would have been the father of Dwight D. Eisenhower. This led Lyberte to respond "so many Republicans, so little time." But Daschle was not amused, too much was changing, too quickly.

Dave Spiering

In Detroit, the "sting" yielded even more results. In Ann Arbor, Walt Whitman had opportunity to meet with Asa Gray. Both men had come to seriously question their agnosticism. Gray confided that he had come to believe in the Devil, and the Coalition, with perverted culture and ethics had to be his offspring. Whitman agreed, and would dedicate his pen to destroying the invaders. Gray had taken up the study of Creationism. Both vowed to see the Coalition fall, and to let America fulfill its destiny. The poison of American blindness had destroyed a virtual last hope for enlightenment.

That day, the leading columns of wagons and carriages from the Selma Trail of Tears had arrived in Indian territory (Oklahoma). They were camped on the Canadian River (near Calvin). There, former adversaries, the Cherokee under Chief John Ross met them with food and provisions. Offering them a place of refuge, they humbly accepted.

Three races, three cultures, three peoples joined in a time of confession of sin and repentance, of forgiveness, of tears. All were guilty of something against each other. The Indian White hostilities were confessed and released. Some of the Indians had been guilty of slavery towards the blacks. This also was forgiven. What emerged was one people committed to Christianity, and the building of a truly free and united nation. From the Coalitions perspective it was tragic that these people could believe unity could be achieved from anything but a humanist foundation.

Farther to the west, troubles were brewing between the Indians and other white homesteaders. Since Daschle's order to end the Homestead Act effective July 1, nearly 400,000 land claims had been made by June 26. Almost 100,000 square miles, or an area roughly the size of Colorado was claimed. Most of these claims were west of the Mississippi, and New Mexico territory was not immune. The Indian was forced to take action, for self preservation if for no other reason.

One man had stepped forward to take charge, Cochise, the chief of the Chiricahua Apache. His hatred of white man and his military prowess were well known. Two years earlier he and some companions were captured by the Army and charged with kidnapping. While some of his companions were hanged, he escaped. Since then he had carried out a hit and run war of revenge. The "war between brothers" (Civil War) had provided him many opportunities.

Now among the Indian old enemies had become allies. Out of a fear and need for common defense, a massive confederation was emerging. Even the peace loving Hopi had joined the Apache, Comanche, Navaho, and a host of others.

Sensing an Indian war in the making, homesteaders were anxious for peaceful resolution. As the Indians had made raids, the settlers practiced restraint. Texas ex-governor Francis Lubbock had been elevated as leader of a large block now in the southwest. For attitudes among these new homesteaders had changed as well. The Coalition occupation had made once enemies to become now friends and allies. Having had a taste of their own medicine, being driven from land and possession had forced them to think. Now they could sympathize with the Indian and offered flocks and herds, corn and wine in exchange for peace. Realizing war to be unwinnable against so mighty a host, both sides came to an uneasy peace.

Throughout America it was becoming increasingly unsafe for Coalition people. They were the object of verbal abuse and scorn, many were pelted with rotten vegetables, rocks, even human feces. Those who dared travel alone were at risk of being accosted, beaten senseless, or even killed. Arrests could not stem the violence, and Americans in detention topped 180,000 by day's end. The nation was running out of prison space.

Lyberte gave Daschle data projecting at least 40,000 church arrests that Sunday. The churches had failed to take the Coalition policy seriously. Even the most progressive, or open minded of them were refusing to comply with licensing requirements. And ministers already in detention were refusing offers of freedom for their cooperation. Incredibly, they advocated resistance from their jail cells.

At 8:00 A.M., Saturday, June 27, Daschle made a stunning policy shift in an open meeting with the advocacy groups. The June 28 deadline for church and minister registration would be indefinitely postponed. Voluntary compliance was a dead hope. All attention for now must be focused on ending the growing revolt, but he did hold out the possibility of a church tax at a later date.

Coalition reaction was swift and deep. Ann Junction of the ACLU was philosophical but deeply troubled. To allow an unconstitutional establishment of religion would only continue to undermine freedom and poison minds. Freedom can only exist where Christian beliefs are kept from interfering with personal lives and government policy.

Perry Noyah and Hugo Tree of the Environmental Coalition were livid. Touring just the farm belt of the heartland with Phil Durte of Agriculture and Donald Greens of EPA they were appalled at the blatant disregard for the environment. While most 1863 Americans had become far more environmentally conscious, they were resistant to governmental controls. Their religious scruples made them far more concerned about spiritual and moral values than in protecting a fragile five billion year old planet.

Emily List of NOW was outraged. NOW (National Organization for Women) with help from Planned Parenthood Corp. and others had researched 1863 abuse of women. In just a short time, and with limited reporting they had documented over 200,000 abuse situations. Most were ongoing conditions of discrimination in employment or property rights. Some were church sanctioned rape, where marriages had been performed on underage girls. A few cases involved spouse beating. No open access to birth control or abortion were allowed. And the women hating church was at the root of the problem.

The rights of children were trampled upon by a hateful and narrow religion. Child abuse, in the form of spanking had damaged the psyche of almost every young person. All were forced to undergo religious brainwashing by parents, teachers, and peers. For a compassionate and open Coalition, which had outlawed such injuries, to even consider allowing them to continue, was criminal.

A strong church posed a peril to issues of moral and social justice as well. Gerald (Geraldean) Corona protested the poisoning of minds against gays and lesbians. Black Jack Game Winner of the American Indian Movement joined in on rights issues, as did all others. Abortion, gambling, divorce and cohabitation, all were constitutional rights threatened by the church. Alternative religions, wicca, Satanism, spiritism all were persecuted by it. John Adams was wrong. Our system was made not for a religious people, but can only function best when religion is muzzled.

Daschle's retreat on this fundamental issue alienated most of the Coalition interest groups. The timing could not be worse. July 4, the day that Americans celebrate as a day of liberty from tyranny was just one week away. While no one spoke openly, a conspiracy was in full swing. All agreed that Daschle must go.

To American church goers, however, this was a great victory and cause for celebration. That evening church bells rang throughout the nation. And most also saw it as only the beginning of a long battle to take back their nation.

In a less controversial move, he also postponed for one month the new income tax. In the south, it was un-collectable at that time anyway. In the north, a shortage of treasury agents impeded any hope of enforcing it at that time. Americans had quickly learned how to cook their business books. While the economy itself was in depression a black market flourished. The scope of the underground economy could only be speculated on by the Coalition. As of that time, enough gold and silver were flowing to the mints to avoid a monetary crisis. Even the Pittsburgh survivors had been paid off, in silver. By August 1 the nation would be ready.

In a surprise move, Alfred Wallace showed up on American soil. From Canada, he had arrived in Buffalo that morning. A devout evolutionist and spiritualist, he finally converted to Coalition orthodoxy. His belief in a great spirit influence on the dealings of man fit with many in the Coalition. They, like him, were open to this cosmic force, or intelligence, and had rejected the confines of a Christian God. His coming brought hope that there might yet be some way of winning over world wide supporters.

Such hope was in short supply. While internal strains threatened to tear the Coalition apart, external adversaries threatened defeat. Each defeat, or less than successful military campaign only fueled public unrest. All the groups who Daschle had courted, and counted on to sympathize with the Coalition were instead adversaries. Women, labor, the poor, and most distressing the ex-slaves fueled the ever growing inferno of unrest. While some tolerated Coalition presence, virtually no one welcomed it. Hopes of winning the hearts and minds of the people, were indeed, in short supply. Alfred Wallace was paraded around like a superstar celebrity.

At 11:30 P.M., two ships passing in the night met in a fatal attraction. The nuclear cruiser Bainbridge had been on patrol in the Grand Banks area off Newfoundland. Although she had been reactivated from retirement for her Coalition mission, she still was more than a match for any 19th century vessel.

That evening at about 10:30 a large vessel was observed sailing in a somewhat erratic manor. The Bainbridge was on assignment to intercept any vessel that threatened unauthorized intrusion into American territorial waters. This large vessel, the 700 foot iron sided "Great Eastern" aroused suspicion. That she was headed for Halifax, Nova Scotia was not known at that time.

The Bainbridge used a bull horn to order her to stop for boarding and inspection. The "Great Eastern", with protection of the international law of the sea proceeded on. The Bainbridge then used flares and finally a warning shot fired across the Great Eastern's bow. Fearing that she was under attack, she raced for a fog bank. The Bainbridge followed, firing two more warning shots.

One shot hit close enough to damage her stern and upper deck. Three men on board were injured. Now in the fog bank she came to a complete stop. The Bainbridge was not able to stop in time and broadsided her. Rescue efforts began at once, but 93 lives, all English, were lost. Ship logs showed no weapons, ammunition, or fugitives were on board.

Also, just before midnight, a mass of nearly 15,000 Mexicans fleeing Maximilian began to enter modern day Arizona. Journeying west from El Paso they followed the Butterfield Trail in the state. An alarmed Cochise began to assemble every Indian who could carry a gun as he prepared for one massive strike.

CHAPTER 14

Sunday, June 28, the church bells pealed with an ardor not seen for years. The nation seemed to be on a path of rebirth and renewal. The victory of their religious standards was celebrated. But it was, in their minds, just a beginning. Words turned increasingly of the next step, the next battle, the next triumph.

For the Coalition, the mood was somber. The cause of truth, liberty, and justice had suffered a great defeat. Their leader had caved into the pressures of a corrupt and evil "empire." He had violated the very rule of law they sought to ordain. The hopes of a democratic nation of laws was in detention, Patterson-Roberta. The Supreme Court justices, Breyer and Ginsberg were unable, or unwilling to correct the crisis. Any hope of victory lay in their hands, but how or what to do would require great skill and wisdom. If nothing else, the military was solidly on the side of Daschle, and the policy maker's pens were no match for the Army's swords.

A host of logistical problems also would face any new leadership. The monetary and fiscal (tax and spend) problems were only under a temporary solution. There were still fuel and spare parts shortages looming, economic dislocation, transport strains, and the flight of skilled labor. The south (and increasingly the rest of America) was in rebellion, hunger, pestilence, and crime were rampant. The pinions of 1863 government had all but disintegrated. The world was increasingly distant and hostile. A steep bigotry of a reactionary and intolerant people undid any progress made by the Coalition.

Combat and other deaths were increasing by leaps and bounds. In the last six days nearly 2,200 Coalition personnel had died in establishing and containing the zone in the south. From the Piedmont of the Atlantic seaboard to roughly the Tennessee River, and southern Kentucky to (about) Montgomery, Alabama was in the zone of rebellion. In the rest of the nation nearly 1,000 more had died in abductions, assassinations, and ambushes. Total Coalition dead now exceeded 9,500. The American death toll now exceeded 150,000, of which almost a third were black. The deaths resulting from disease and malnutrition now exceeded 5,000 a day, mostly black.

A vocal challenge was now coming from the Black Relief Union headed by Mary Berry and Jesse Jackson. They were mortified by Daschle's apparent indifference to the looming demise of half of America's black population. They demanded an immediate end to the siege. They did not believe that the rebellious conditions of the region warranted such dire measures. Nor did it matter that whites were dying with them. The rebellion would have to be broken another way, or risk loss of Afro-Americans.

Daschle appealed to the need of survival itself. In life and death struggles, all targets become legitimate. That had always been accepted policy. During the Cold War, the doctrine of MAD or mutually assured destruction, deliberately targeted civilians. It, more than anything else probably prevented the Cold War from becoming a hot war. For many, this was a phony question. Communism was never the real enemy and the imperialistic war mongering of the nation was barbarically insane.

For Daschle to argue mission survival was a cop out for a failed war of aggression. Oil stocks were not being depleted by southern aggression, but by a failure to win a people. The real enemies were the church, capitalism, white supremacy, and male chauvinism, not two million starving blacks.

At a little after noon, Clinton met again with Clavendish. Clinton had been briefed about the Great Eastern. England had failed to mention it, so it was assumed that the collision was not yet known. This would give Clinton opportunity to mention it first, and put a positive spin on it. He did not know that he was disarmed before the meeting began.

Back in 1961, when Clinton was a teenager, President John Kennedy met with Nikita Khrushchev. For those who remembered as well, a U-2 spy plane was shot down over the Soviet Union, and pilot Gary Powers was captured. Khrushchev used it as a club on Kennedy and the United States, giving him tremendous leverage, and prestige in negotiations.

Clinton now hoped to pressure Clavendish and England for concrete action, to prove their good faith in negotiating a pact. The trap was set. The English also now knew history, and at 6:00 P.M. Clavendish had been contacted by Lord Evergreen on how to play it.

For the English the Great Eastern was a provocation for greater than the Trent affair. When Lincoln's Captain Charles Wilkes of the San Jacinto boarded the Trent to seize Southern Embasaries it brought the two nations to the brink of war. It was only a slight exaggeration that 999 of every 1,000 Englishmen were eager to defend their national honor. If radio and TV had been in use in 1861 there probably would have been war. But in time calmer heads prevailed and the crisis ended. Lincoln wisely let the diplomats go free. This time, an unarmed merchant man was fired upon and sunk with considerable loss of life.

While England, and Lord Evergreen knew she could not hope for an easy time of it in war, she could not let this pass. And neither could the rest of Europe as they lined up "to a man" as they learned of it, behind the English. The Prime Minister began to talk with parliament about the nature of any ultimation or action. He also had told Clavendish that his meeting with Clinton would determine English response.

As Clinton talked to Clavendish about an English step in "good faith" Clavendish responded by asking what "good faith" entailed. "Did that mean the deliberate sinking of a merchant ship in international waters?" he queried. Clinton, caught by surprise assured Clavendish that it was an accident. The two ships were on a collision course and the Bainbridge had fired warning shots to get the Great Eastern to turn. Clavendish told Clinton that England was at the brink of war. At a minimum, all international transport was off limits to Coalition intimidation, all ports closed and territorial waters closed to Coalition ships. And no Coalition aircraft or persons would be allowed over any foreign territory without permission. Also, England would now demand full payment, in gold, for all English assets. Clinton could only nod in acceptance.

In New York City, Alfred Wallace was on tour. The English naturalist had a joint share in Darwin's work in proving evolution. While in the area he stopped at the D. Appleton and Company publishers. Publishing works by great men like Darwin, Herbert Spencer, Thomas Huxley and other modern free thinkers, they also now did much Coalition work. Since earlier that month when Boston saw violence and the book factory bombing, almost all printing was now done there, on a round the clock seven day a week schedule.

When William H. Appleton began publishing such works, one extremist clergyman wrote him. "Divine wrath would be visited upon him in this world and through all eternity" he was warned. Like most rational thinkers he dismissed the admonition. But this day an Irish employee of unknown status had planted a bomb in the publishing house. Yelling "remember Saint Patrick and Tim O'Laggerty" he set it off. He did not escape the blast and fire, nor did Wallace or Appleton. Wallace's spirit guides could not save them. Beset with a misguided and unconstitutional concept of liberty and rights, an ignorant populace preferred darkness to light.

Good news came from Pennsylvania. While the southern rebellion was draining oil, the refinery was ahead of schedule. Oil stocks would last until about August 4, but by July 27 it would be on line and fully producing. A second one could then be begun using the same equipment, to fuel all the economic and technological programs.

The border patrol situation was continuing to be a failing effort. Even with state of the art technology and experienced Coalition border guards, weapons and other contraband continued to flood in. As of yet no proof of collusion between smugglers and the Fremont government was found, but suspicions were high. The timing of the various crossings could not be coincidence. Only when patrol units were off schedule were they able to catch smugglers.

Among the weapons now pouring into America were several new Canadian manufactured counterfeits. A few of Prussian and English versions also had made their way across the Atlantic. Along with Colt, Winchester, and Gatling were modified M-16s, land mines, grenades (of modern, not 1863 versions), and antitank weapons. Of dubious quality, but alarming never the less were primitive hand held, heat seeking surface to air missiles. While unequal to Coalition originals, they posed a menacing array of firepower.

How these weapons were being smuggled into such areas as the isolated south also defied conventional explanation. Southern smugglers did their part. The "railroad" of contraband trade that had flourished so well in providing the north with cotton and the south with finished goods during the war was alive and well. James A. Garfield, who had helped organize his "Eyes of the Army" lent his tactics and men. Even Coalition deserters assisted the operations.

The Coalition was not totally unsuccessful in arms interceptions, though. Two occurred that evening, one at Sault St. Marie, and the other near Lake Champlain. Both bore English involvement. To Lyberte this justified the sinking of the Great Eastern. He contacted fleet commander Jordon Conrad, and ordered any command by Daschle modified. It a vessel was reasonably suspect of carrying weapons to America, it would be halted.

Late that evening two youths, one 13 and other 15 were captured by Coalition forces at Reading, Ohio. They had been involved in a fire fight with Coalition soldiers who had stumbled upon their camp near the town. With old flint locks they had managed to hold out for a half hour before running out of ammunition and being forced to surrender. Coalition agents interrogated them to find out how they had obtained weapons and ammunition. The guns were their fathers. But for ammunition they had scraped lead off the back of a mirror. To make gunpowder they had distilled urine. It was a common practice to many in the south even before Coalition involvement. Now it had nationwide appeal.

On Monday, June 29, Jeb Stewart and George Custer joined up with an already growing army under Robert E. Lee near Chambersburg, Pennsylvania. That the two, with a growing force of now nearly 2,300 moved over 300 miles in 10 days was a marvel of military achievement. It also showed how two egos had come to work together as a team, and come to regard each other almost as brothers.

It also owed to a growing breakdown in Coalition reconnaissance. Part of this was due to a lack of air and ground units available to keep track of such movements. It also owed to the pulling of monitoring equipment to Europe, the Pacific, and the border regions. But to a growing degree, it reflected the growing rifts within the Coalition. More and more monitoring equipment was tied up in keeping track of Coalition personnel. Several interest groups were ignoring rules on communications and travel. Unauthorized frequencies were employed and private activities strained security. This allowed a number of rebel movements to occur without detection.

For Lee, his command now numbered in excess of 9,600 in that area. Volunteers were pouring in almost constantly. A few hours later, he made contact with another force under Joseph Hooker's command from West Pennsylvania. From camps centered in Clarion County, he now had about 6,800 including 106 Coalition deserters under his command. By days end, Hooker, having learned from his Coalition deserters about how history would have been, placed his forces under Lee's authority. When he did, 1,100 others in Ft. Littleton also joined Lee. Other smaller groups were joining hourly.

Farther south, another general was picking up support as he traveled. Clarksburg (West) Virginia, in addition to being base for General Scofield had yet one other claim to notoriety. In 1824 it was the birthplace of Thomas

J. Jackson. Despite being orphaned at an early age, he was a man of deep Christian conviction and strong drive. In 1842 he was accepted into the United States Military Academy. Seeing service in the Mexican American War, by 1861 he had become a Confederate leader. At the Bull Run (Manassas) he picked up the nickname "Stonewall" for his men's stand, and by 1863 was Lee's "Right Arm."

But on May 11 he had walled himself up in Charlottesville with about 200 stalwarts. With a touch of hypochondria, he spent most of his time recuperating from a slew of imagined maladies. But he also visited the Monticello, where Thomas Jefferson had lived, during his stay.

On June 24, he came out of seclusion and began to head east. As he did, he picked up a number of veterans and also blacks, now eager for the chance to confirm their own freedom. On this day he was joined by Jubal Early and 600 men under his command. With now around 2,200 men, he headed towards Mechanicsville. Nearly 40 Coalition deserters also had joined him.

On Monday, June 29, the 15,000 Juárez refugees made camp at Paradise, Arizona. Cochise had assembled his Indians to the west and north, and at dusk, he attacked. It was a very unorthodox attack, Indians did not like to fight at night, but it caught the Mexicans totally off guard. Within hours over 3,000 were dead and the rest scattered in the desert and retreating back into Mexico. A Coalition surveillance plane picked up the slaughter.

It was immediately assumed that those responsible for the massacre were either Pemberton's men or others dressed up as Indians. High level bombers and attack jets were again called in. Cochise had gathered his braves together to the northwest of Rodeo, New Mexico, in plain view. The high level bombers carpet bombed the assembly, and were followed by low level napalm. It was then that one of the pilots realized that a tragic mistake had been made. The targets were not whites dressed as Indians, they were actual Indians. Fewer than 500 of the many thousands in the camp were still alive. Among them were a number of women and children who also had perished.

Black Jack Game Winner, already embittered by the "nuking" of the Sioux and tolerance of the homesteaders, now went ballistic. He demanded the impeachment and execution of Daschle quite vocally. He called for an immediate release of Patterson-Roberta from her house arrest, and every general involved in this massacre arrested. He was given a live interview with the mass media.

In unrestrained criticism of Daschle, he called upon all with Indian blood to openly revolt. He also appealed for those of any race who loved justice to join in on this rebellion. The media made no attempt at censorship or offer of defense for the administration. Daschle had few allies left.

Instead, Jennings and Rather raised the moral bar even higher. They spoke of a lost crusade. "How could something so right, so noble, so just and true go to terribly wrong?" they asked. The slaughter of the Indians was one of the very things they had come to prevent. Now no leader in American history had destroyed as many Indians, not Grant, Jackson, or Theodore Roosevelt. And the record against blacks was not much better. The death toll of other Americans now exceeded 170,000, of which one third were black. But Rather and Jennings stopped short of demanding Daschle's ouster. They were beginning to sense a real danger, and did not want to lose his leadership.

Black Jack Game Winner, however acted out his words. On the guise of claiming that he wanted to go to Arizona to investigate, her secured a C-130 transport and went to San Francisco. Using his security clearance he accessed arms storage and had it loaded with weapons and ammunition. Having it then flown to a remote location in southern Oregon, he had it crash landed. With a limited fluency of Nez Percé and other Penution languages, he joined the Indians and began to unite them in one force against all white man.

In Germany (Prussia) on June 30, Tuesday, an amazing discovery was made. German physicist Hermann von Helmholtz was demonstrating an acoustic, or sound travel experiment to some colleagues. In the process, he accidentally spilled some cold hydrochloric acid on a new US gold dollar that he had received as a gift. As he, and they, observed an unexpected reaction by the coin, they determined to know its composition. By 10:00 A.M., Washington time, the knowledge of American "gold" only being two thirds gold was known to every major financial institution in Europe.

In 1863, many still remembered Templeton Reid and Gainesville Georgia in 1830. He was a private citizen, and also owner of a private mint. Unfortunately, the gold coins he made were slightly low in their gold content. He was assailed by the press, the public lost confidence in his money and he was forced out of business. His coins ended up as nothing but an historical relic.

Now in Europe panic set in. Confronted with the potential loss of billions in liquid assets and business, fear quickly turned to rage. Many saw this deception itself as an act of war. To all it was a wake up call. English businesses, many still hoping to weather the storm of political uncertainty, now scrambled to protect their assets. Railroads refused American money, a move quickly followed by all foreign businesses. Foreign banks suddenly pulled assets, now losing value by the minute. Loans were called or sold to anyone willing to take a chance on speculation. US money was converted to commodities, precious gems, gold and silver bullion, or land.

By days end, an ounce of gold dust, officially valued at $20.67 in 1837 dollars, and $42.10 in greenbacks as late as June 29, now brought almost $200.00. Even pre-Coalition US coins were severely discounted. They now were worth only about 60 percent of their day before value. No one could be sure that if gold content was bogus, the date on a coin could be also. In addition, all American assets abroad were frozen, and many foreign nations experienced bank runs.

While the days ahead would bring some stability, and even restore some value as calmer heads prevailed, the damage was done. Confidence had been lost. In America, no amount of gold or silver could prevent the banking collapse. A parallel could be made to post World War I Germany, with inflation, banking and monetary distrust, and economic ruin. But only to a point, as in America, the collapse of an entire nation's economy happened in a single day. Wealth was evaporating and values melting like snow in July. Businesses either closed or went to a barter system. Manufacturing was in chaos. Anyone old enough to remember the Great Depression of the 1930's was even appalled at what they saw.

Daschle tried to calm the nation, to reassure the world that the nation was financially sound. After all, all money only has value because people believe in the value of gold, silver or paper to buy what they want. He used the term "fiat", or value by decree or acceptance to explain his position. The only difference between gold, silver, paper, or gold alloy was in people's heads. American money, regardless of composition was worth what it was promised to be worth and worthy of good faith.

This drew a response from Benjamin Disraeli, who since May 29 was Palmerston's (Lord Evergreen) Minister of Commerce. A member of parliament he had served as Chancellor of the Treasury in the 1850's under Prime Minister Lord Derby. Now he challenged Daschle's logic. England was a nation of merchants and shopkeepers. Merchants deal in gold and silver, and not bogus money. It would be preposterous for them to put faith in a government of bankrupt faith, values, and gold. No, the Coalition can keep their money of faith" which is as counterfeit as their whole system of counterfeit truth. And they can keep that, too.

Baltimore entered its tenth day of uneasy truce. Two regiments of American troops, under General William Vandever held the city. The Coalition force under Colonel Sherman Gilmer and Christine Todd-Whitman confined itself to base. Todd Whitman functioned as liaison between the two commanders, and gave semblance to claims that the Coalition still controlled the city.

That afternoon Coalition intelligence captured two militia insurgents near Hagerstown, Maryland. They confirmed evidence of a substantial guerrilla force in the area. They had been "recruited" from Baltimore on June 25 by General Phillip Sheridan along with nearly 3,500 others. Orders were issued immediately to reinforce the garrison at Baltimore to retake the city on July 1 or 2.

General Sheridan, or "Little Phil", of Irish ancestry, was raised in Somerset, Ohio. As a Union General, he had distinguished himself in the Tennessee theatre during the war. Evading Coalition apprehension after May 5, he had hid in Red Lion, Pennsylvania. While getting word to his family of his safety, he also accumulated a few die hard followers.

When Baltimore went into revolt, federal commander Vandever contacted his old ally. Traveling to Baltimore, he picked up more recruits. By the 24th, he arrived with 1,100 of his own men. Helping Vandever organize a city militia as well as bolster his existing two regiments, he left town on the 26th with a total of almost 5,000. By the 28th, as he headed west, he heard of other armies organizing in south Pennsylvania, and determined to link up with them. Now, with a force of almost 7,500, he was on course to link up with Lee. Along with 70 Coalition deserters, he was headed for a rendezvous at a town called Gettysburg.

Late that evening, an army patrol just east of Danville, Virginia confronted about 30 refugees fleeing the cordoned zone to the west. While they were not the first, they were caught. Staff Sergeant Morris Boswell had no choice but to order these emaciated black tobacco laborers and families to turn back. They begged to be allowed to cross over. There was no food in Danville. Finally Boswell ordered warning shots to be fired. Of his squad, five were black, three hispanic, and three white.

The five blacks refused the order. One was a descendent of tobacco farmers and feared that one of his ancestors might be in the group. The hispanics also wavered, leaving only Boswell and three others to fire. Fearing for his ancestors, the one black began to fire in Boswell's direction. A melee ensued when the smoke cleared only Boswell and one other, a hispanic, survived to return to base, just west of South Boston.

Hearing of the confrontation, Jesse Jackson used the privilege of his office to secure transport to South Boston. He arrived by 11:00 P.M., and using executive authority, was present for the interrogation. What he heard convinced him that the war in the south was turning into black genocide. Taking a helicopter back to Washington, he would have a live interview on the morning news before meeting with Mary Berry.

Decrying the failed policies of Daschle and Lyberte, Jackson demanded an immediate end to the hostilities in the south. An immediate pouring of food and medical supplies, for humanitarian purposes, was essential to prevent genocide. If Daschle would not act on his own, conscience demanded that all soldiers, especially black, disobey orders. But while he addressed the racist hate policy of discrimination and genocide, he could not but feel uneasy. The ex-slaves were making their alliance with their ex-masters, not the Coalition. Not even Al Sharpton could convince them to leave their misguided beliefs for the open and compassionate ones of the Coalition.

Black reparations must be enacted now. In his meeting with Berry this issue took front burner. While the economy was already in shambles, now would be the time to confiscate all the plantations of the south and distribute the land. They also reached out to the Coalition hispanics. Both were victims of a "white cultural patriarchy", run by the values of mostly dead white men. Both were entitled to their own land, own culture, religion, value system, their own space.

Blacks would be recruited from the south with the promise of land. If Daschle was not willing to act now, then the Black Relief Union would act alone. When warned of being charged with sedition and rebellion, Berry accused the administration of "Hitler like" racial genocide. They began to contact black commanders to act against their Coalition orders.

The message got out to the Coalition's 62,000 blacks. Over half of them were in military operations, mostly in the south. By noon, July 1, many were resisting orders, even at gun point. That Dan Rather announced a probable cholera out break in Tennessee and Alabama only added fuel. A mass mutiny was eminent.

Daschle requested an immediate meeting with Jackson. He hoped for a workable solution to save the blacks without losing the south. But Jackson was unwilling to meet with Daschle. Sensing victory for his cause, he set several preconditions, including a power sharing arrangement, in exchange for cooperation. The escourt was insistent, however, which led Jackson to remark about "White Facist Storm Troopers". One of his two personal aides picked up a pistol to defend him. In a tragic shoot out, Jackson was mortally wounded.

Seeking to avert a melt down in the Coalition military, several commanders took action of their own. Among them was General Scofield. Unable to reach Daschle, as Lyberte was for now holding all calls, they ordered all available cargo space made ready for humanitarian assistance. Mass rebellion was halted, but Daschle's strategy was in shambles.

At about that same time, late morning on Wednesday, July 1, Coalition forces discovered evidence of Hooker's forces in Western Pennsylvania. General Roosevelt Freeman was now in Pittsburgh, and was assessing the situation for possible needs. Meanwhile, General "Dusty" Valdez San-Juan and his forces were to be withdrawn from the Carolina seaboard and brought to a base at Wilmington, Delaware. From there he could restore order in Baltimore.

Of top priority now, for Daschle, was damage control, and holding his grip on power. The action of the military, and General Scofield in specific, had opened the floodgates of policy alterations and breakdowns. Daschle ordered all military operations unless otherwise noted to be ended at once. Border patrol, base security, the area from Washington to Pennsylvania, and mining operations would continue. In Seattle, a base the Coalition never wanted to open, facilities were about to be expanded. At 4:00 P.M., an emergency meeting would be held with all agencies and interest groups to assess and redirect.

One thing was certain, Scofield would be replaced. He was given until noon on July 2 to transfer his command. Fearful of the nuclear arsenal falling into the wrong hands, he proceeded with plans to destroy it. Fully aware of his decision, his subordinates obeyed his orders, even in the face of high treason.

But as preparations were being made, Scofield discovered Ulysses S. Grant and now nearly 3,500 men just southeast of the arsenal. A nuclear detonation at Yucca Mountain threatened their existence as well as residents of Goldfield and the surrounding territory. Knowing history, Scofield was not willing to annihilate a future president. With the political fabric of 1863 America in shambles, he also had no faith in Butler or Fremont in restoring it. He postponed the nuclear eradication until Grant could be saved.

Under a flag of truce, one lone helicopter landed in Grant's territory at 4:00 P.M., Washington time. Grant was told that he, his army, all weapons, and any surrounding people were offered safe transport. Scofield also had Grant told that he was destined to be president in 1868. Though rumors, he had already heard that. He was also aware of the power of nuclear weapons, having both heard accounts of Fredericksburg survivors, and observed T.V. footage.

It was also common knowledge that things were not going well for the Coalition. He was in possession of more than one radio, and his men would collect at news time to hear the reports. For Scofield to have made such an offer was either gross treachery or his army was about to crumble. Trusting his instincts, he agreed. But he also sent a special message to Generals William Anderson and Sterling Price, in joint command, at Hutchinson, Kansas. Anderson was the union commander who would have burned out a large stretch of southwest Missouri, had the war continued. Price was an ex-governor of Missouri, and Confederate leader. They were informed of Grant's offer and looked forward to joining him against the Coalition.

Grant and his men were transported to Ft. Robinson, Nebraska. The rest of the evacuees were transported to Ft. Hayes, Kansas. True to his word, Scofield had transported weapons and all. By 7:00 A.M., July 2, the final group of Indians left the Yucca Mountain area, bound for Ft. Hayes.

In Mexico, Maximilian was making news of his own. Under pressure from France, he sent a messenger to Juárez with an offer for power sharing and soon to be announced elections. Juárez, after the Paradise massacre had come to doubt Coalition promises. He too, was ready for peace. Maximilian in return received a promise from France and other European powers for the financial rebuilding and modernization of Mexico. On that day, all parties came together, by radio, and agreed to truce. Daschle and the Coalition were now more alone and isolated than ever.

At 4:00 P.M., a grand assembly began in an unfinished capitol building in Washington. All agencies and special interest groups were present to establish a leadership consensus. Even Judge Patterson-Roberta was released from custody and allowed to attend. Barbara Boxer and Bill Clinton would jointly chair the session, Daschle took a back seat role. Daschle was fully aware this might be his last convocation as Commander in Chief. With the best interest of the mission, and nation at heart, he would step down if necessary.

CHAPTER 15

As of noon, Tuesday, July 1, the siege of the south was over. The Coalition kept bases at Houston, New Orleans, Tampa Bay, Miami, Charleston and Hampton Roads. On the Mississippi, Memphis was still in Coalition hands, as were a few other bases, Nashville, Jackson, Monroe, and further west Ft. Smith, and bases in Texas. Otherwise, the 11 states of the confederacy, and most of Kentucky and Missouri were free of Coalition presence. By 6:00 P.M. most other bases or towns were ordered evacuated.

Civil authority was beginning to reemerge. From John Milton of Florida to H.R. Gamble of Missouri, governors were again reemerging and establishing political leadership. The actions of these leaders showed the profound depth of change in a national perspective. Having seen the future, they now resolved to change the present.

Governor John Letcher of Virginia was a prime example. As he came out of retirement and headed towards Richmond he made several proclamations. Until a state legislature could act, he ordered several environmental and health reforms. He initiated food and product purity rules. But what drew the most attention was his extending the right to vote in Virginia to everyone 18 years old or older.

What was also of interest was the reaction. By evening a number of leading Virginia women spoke concerning the right to vote led by Sally Tompkins, of the Richmond relief service, a nurse who cared for the wounded. They had seen how future women acted and wanted no part of their "un-seemingly" behavior. If obtaining the right to vote was the cause of such vulgar behavior, then it was a luxury they could do without. The issue of women's vote was put on hold for the time being.

In Richmond, Thomas "Stonewall" Jackson was not willing to wait for the Coalition to officially evacuate the city. With a force of now nearly 3,800 men in and around Mechanicsville he struck at 3:30 P.M. as the evacuation was in full swing. For the defenders, no air cover was available, and they themselves were support units, not actual combat units.

In the city was a large depot filled with provisions, weapons, and vehicles. The 1,500 Coalition soldiers were loading up as fast as they could for a convoy exit at 5:30 P.M. As Jackson led his force into the city, any resistance quickly crumbled. In just over an hour 254 Coalition personnel died and 731 others were captured. Jackson had lost 79. Jackson was able to capture almost intact, weaponry to arm nearly 5,000 men. His prisoners eagerly helped train his men on weapons and equipment. An additional 1,800 Virginians also joined his ranks.

In Oklahoma, or Indian Territory, the Selma survivors had journeyed south to the junction of Muddy Boggy Creek and the Red River (Gay, Oklahoma). A few Cherokee accompanied them. Early in the day they received the first of three visitors, a Colonel Arthur P. Bagby and 44 of his Texas cavalrymen.

Col. Bagby, born in Clairborne, Alabama, had attended West Point to be an Army officer. But in 1855 he returned to Alabama, passed the bar, and practiced law until returning to Texas in 1858. He there distinguished himself with his "Horse Marines" of the 7th Regiment of Texas Mounted Volunteers. Surrendering his command on May 8, he intended to take up Texas law. But with the new Coalition legal theory, he traveled north to Paris, Texas instead. There he became a homesteader. With his Alabama roots, his sympathies ran deep for the Selma survivors. Hearing of their arrival only about 20 miles to the north, he traveled there to meet them. With him went the remnant of his command, along for the ride.

Several hours later, about 2:00 P.M. Texas time, Cheyenne chief Black Kettle and several braves arrived on the west bank of Muddy Boggy Creek. He led a confederation of plains Indians to the Selmanites land. Already inundated by homesteaders, he hoped to keep peace, and keep them off their land. He sent scouts to arrange meeting the camp leaders.

Col. Bagby offered his services and crossed the creek to meet Black Kettle. Black Kettle had heard of his reputation and held him up in honor. He invited Black Kettle and the almost 400 with him to come to the camp for a covenant meal. There they assured Black Kettle that they would remain where they were. They did not intend to steal land from anyone.

As Black Kettle and his men offered tokens of a treaty, he and Col. Bagby became blood brothers. But the people of Selma had nothing worthy to offer as a token of friendship. One brought out a new Bible. Bagby took his own sword and one of his men had brought their regimental banner. He offered these as tokens.

In the late afternoon sun, as all parties were ready to disperse, a small convoy of vehicles approached from the west. In them was a clan of 52 white supremacists. They also were Coalition personnel who had slipped through the security screening.

No security device or system invented by man is foolproof. Using lies and deceit, they had been cleared for the Coalition mission. Now their intent was to recruit disgruntled whites and establish a separatist white nation. They knew enough about American history to know the depths of racial prejudice throughout America. Being stationed together at Wichita Falls, Texas, their strategy was to hang loose until the Coalition mission ended in October or November to return to their time. Then they would desert and emerge to build their own world.

Before they could complete their plans, Daschle issued orders to close their base. They were ordered to report to Ft. Smith Arkansas. They happened upon this settlement just as the assembly was breaking up. Leaving their vehicles, they approached Bagby and his men. Recognizing him, they urged him to join them and offered him military leadership. They would help him to rebuild a new nation, one without the inferior races. Bagby responded that the rebuilding of the nation had already begun. And that nation, America, was one people, not black, white, or Indian, but American.

Not taking "no" for an answer, several pulled out weapons and began to shoot at the Indians. But before a slaughter could begin, Bagby's horse marines and the Selma refugees with weapons returned fire. Since most of the supremacists were taken by complete surprise, they were quickly defeated. Leaving 28 of their comrades behind, the rest fled. A total of 13 Indians, nine Selma refugees and one of Bagby's men had died. Most of the vehicles, loaded with food and supplies were captured, and their contents distributed.

At 4:00 P.M. in Washington D.C. security was tight. It was so tight that only with great difficulty one of Lyberte's aids was able to enter to provide some critical information. Coalition Air Force General Anthony Goodland, in command of the border patrols was the source of a security leak scandal. He had been selling flight and cruise ship schedules to General Benjamin Butler. "Pathfinder" John C. Fremont was not involved in any way.

Goodland was captured but Butler escaped to Canada before he could be caught.

As the meeting commenced, the first item of business was a challenge over chair leadership. Patterson-Roberta, with a sizeable sympathy support, asserted that there should be someone representing the judiciary on the chairmanship board. Supreme Court Justices Breyer and Ginsberg were in agreement. The preservation of Constitutional law and authority were paramount. All three were nominated for the post, but Patterson-Roberta received more votes than either of the others and was now a joint chair.

The next chair leadership challenge was over Bill Clinton's position. He was immensely popular to everyone in the room and was viewed as a likely successor to Daschle. Although no one said it out loud, it was virtually assured that Daschle would be replaced. With the potential of Clinton becoming chief executive, it would be awkward for him to serve as chairperson at a meeting that could put him in that position. He was removed and replaced with Mary Francis Berry of the Civil Rights Commission. She also would fairly represent minority rights at a time when Sharpton and Jackson were both dead. She was approved overwhelmingly.

A third challenge then erupted. Both Patterson-Roberta and Berry were Washington insiders, as was Barbara Boxer. In the interest of balance, someone was needed to better represent the special interest groups, business, and other private concerns. Emily S. List of NOW was nominated to replace Boxer. She also was approved.

In everyone's mind was the issue of mission. Many now questioned the practicality of continuing the nation building effort. Krishna Mahariji now saw the effort as a lost cause. The American people were blinded to reality by their religious darkness. Reciting Satanist Anton LaVey "the world was kept ignorant by its religious (Christian) orders." It was not until the Age of Aquarius in 1967 that these chains were broken. And even with that, LaVey's prediction that by 2000 Christianity would be a well known folk myth was not fulfilled. Christianity proved to be a virulent disease with deep roots and a relentless hold. To try to win now, in 1863 against it would be hopeless. The Coalition should retreat to their bases and wait until the time gap opened again and they could return to 2007.

Connie Dumm of Planned Parenthood disagreed. She argued that the nation's turn to enlightened reality had to start somewhere. The nation was confused. In some ways they accepted their humanity, they questioned God, they wanted a better way. The Coalition had failed in explaining its mission to the people. Once people saw how much better accepting their humanity and rationalism would make things, they would change. Sigmund Freud was able, at a later date to prove that their instincts were "in themselves are neither good or evil." The Coalition's mission was to prove this to humanity a couple of generations sooner. They would have to "suck it up" and act. The eyes of humanity, past, present, and future, were on them.

Noralee L. Litterate of Dept. of Education warned of nationwide and worldwide reactionary pressures. Clinging to a misconception of alleged divine intervention and judgment, faith in God was now stronger than ever. In Europe and most of the world, the growth of Christianity was explosive and panademic. It there was any truth at all to this Judeo-Christian God myth, God was winning. To pull out now and return to 2007 would be a death sentence for the ideas of Freud, Darwin, Nietzsche, and John Dewey. Not only would 19th century humankind continue in blindness, that blindness would extinguish the light of the future. Just before 8:00 P.M., an overwhelming majority voted to reaffirm the mission.

Before the assembly could continue, they were given another intelligence report. The rebel forces in West Pennsylvania were estimated to number 6,000 (actual total closer to 10,000). Also, another force (Lee's main body) was in south central Pennsylvania, with status unknown. But the reality of such strong enemy forces so close to the vital west Pennsylvania region was unsettling.

Pittsburgh was now garrisoned by 6,000 military personnel. The grouping of the rebels pointed to a probable attack on the city. In Wilmington, Delaware, a force of 40,000 capable, but exhausted troops under General "Dusty" San-Juan from the south was available. They were needed in Baltimore to restore Coalition authority. In places like Harrisburg, Reading, and Philadelphia, others were following the lead at Baltimore in rebellion as well.

But a show of force is a show of force. If they were to travel cross country from Wilmington to Pittsburgh, the same affect would be achieved. In the process, Pittsburgh would be saved as well. San Juan was ordered to ready his force and move west.

Ann Junction of the ACLU raised the issue of civil rights and the rules of warfare. Again she argued, as she did with Daschle, that 1863 Americans were not culturally developed enough as of yet to be full fledged humans.

Especially with their attachment to primitive values, their personhood was not established. And, just like a fetus, their survival should depend upon their potential usefulness to society. Many agreed. Personhood was not a right but a rite. Passage was achieved by meeting acceptable criterion of humanhood, and that was an acquired characteristic of evolution.

But Minnie M. Wage rose in disagreement. While abortion rights were not to be challenged she did argue for the value of Americans as they were. Social engineering was needed. But in any given organism one part must provide a service for the sustenance and development of another. If one part is injured, like a broken leg, the rest must nurture it back to health, not cut it off. Americans were like this broken leg, they had to be set right and healed into the body."

By a narrow vote, human status was enacted for the 1863 Americans and world population. However, actual combatants might be incorrigible and field commanders would be at liberty to judge their "rite" to human treatment. The same rules applied to the political detainees.

Then, taking up the leadership question, Daschle was officially impeached and removed as Coalition head. While Clinton was the favorite for the post, Lyberte had gathered enough support to block, at least for now, Clinton's election to the post. The filibuster he led lasted into the next morning.

The economic collapse at the nation proved to be the volatile fuel of rebellion. The swelling ranks of unemployed and despoiled men from Maryland, New Jersey and east Pennsylvania fueled local militias. Lee's force by 6:00 A.M. on July 2 had swelled to over 15,000 men in the Waynesboro area. Over the next few hours several other groups under generals like John Fulton Reynolds, John Gibbon, and Daniel Sickles joined him. By the time Phil Sheridan met him in late afternoon (with now nearly 9,300), he had just under 22,000 already in his camps. A "prison break" of detainees from Wilkes-Barre was headed his way with 6,500 men, including over 300 Coalition defectors.

Lee's western arm under Hooker now numbered about 9,700. The deserters had furnished a wealth of information including several override systems. Hooker had enough modern weapons to properly arm almost half his men. Smuggled Colts, Winchesters and others were available for most of the rest. With Lee's confirmation, he would feign an attack on Pittsburgh while his main army would be north. The Coalition center at Butler would be disabled, but the real target was the refinery at Franklin and the oil wells to the north and east.

Lee's plan was to "make noise" in the Harrisburg area, and lead the Coalition to believe his main targets were to the east. His main force would head west to link up with Hooker north of Pittsburgh. He also had substantial modern armament, enough for almost 6,500 of his men. He also knew that he was no match for the Coalition in the open terrain. He would train and prepare at Gettysburg until after Sunday, July 5.

But Coalition actions forced Lee to reconsider. Late that evening a Coalition defector picked up on a large Coalition troop movement from Wilmington headed Lee's direction. They probably would be in the Gettysburg area sometime on Friday, enroute to west Pennsylvania. He could not escape ahead of this force, and he could ill afford a reinforcement of the Coalition in Hooker's theatre. He had no choice but to dig in and fight.

At 10:00 A.M. a lone cruise missile launched from Clarksburg hit its target in the Nevada desert. The arsenal at Yucca Mountain ceased to exist. Called from the capitol meeting, Lyberte was briefed on Scofield's high treason, and immediately ordered the three B-2 bombers in Bonneville loaded and dispatched to Clarksburg. Briefing those inside the Capitol Building all agreed. Scofield had already made contingency plans. Base personnel were given the option of going with him to join Grant, or flee to the Coalition base in Washington. All but 13 of the 3,604 personnel were committed to Scofield. One of the 13 was communications specialist, Felicity Shreve. Devoutly loyal, she relayed Scofield's scheme to Washington.

Bonneville General Verona Emery Mills had the complete confidence of Patterson-Roberta. All charges and investigations against her were dropped. In her renewed role, she ordered two squadrons of fighters to intercept Scofield's transports at the Mississippi, while the bombers would neutralize his base. But in a chess-like countermove, an alerted Scofield ordered a change in flight plans. He ordered his troops to airdrop over Bonneauville, Pennsylvania. The transports then would be put on autopilot and sent west, empty and crewless. His 23 helicopters, loaded with weapons and equipment followed them to a "landing zone" just to the west of Bonneauville. Just before midnight on July 2, he met up with Lee and offered his command against his former compatriots.

A short time later his transports were intercepted near Peoria, Illinois. Refusing to respond to orders to surrender, they were blown out of the sky, spewing flaming wreckage along the Mississippi. The attack on Clarksburg lit the sky and sent a message to what was becoming a torrent of Coalition turncoats.

In Washington, the Capitol Assembly was still deadlocked. News was bad. To plan a counterattack, Berry, Patterson-Roberta, and List were excused and Lyberte temporarily took charge. They ordered General San-Juan to proceed with his full 40,000 troops from Wilmington by noon on July 2. It would proceed through Gettysburg enroute for Pittsburgh.

The operation, Keystone Crossing, was beset with impediments from its onset. San-Juan was reluctant to act without the order of Daschle. Patterson-Roberta was incensed, and wanted him replaced on the spot. The rest of the leadership committee were more understanding of his reluctance and were able to reason with him.

After establishing authorization, the leadership committee needed to set direction for the mission. To avoid fuel depletion, most heavy vehicles, all but a very few tanks, and armored vehicles would be left behind. The route would be clearly marked and a high visibility would be kept. Civilians along the path would be warned to avoid casualties. Other agencies had other requests, seat belts would be used at all times. Weapons would not be loaded until the convoy was fired upon. Environmental laws must be honored. The multiple regulations frustrated and confused the force. They also led to a mission threatening disaster.

Bureaucrats were convinced that the Columbia Bridge at Wrightsville was capable of supporting trucks. They also discounted reports of heavy rains at Harrisburg and resultant flooding. The historical weather records gave no such account, but some allowance for climate change was needed. The steel production increases at Pittsburgh and Coalition fuel hydrocarbons were blamed for any climate changes. To expedite transport the bridge was ruled as safe, and pontoon bridges were also laid to the south of it.

Initial units had no difficulty in crossing. But when the ammunition trucks and sophisticated electronic systems were strewn on the bridges trouble struck. The main bridge crumbled, and in its wake all the pontoon bridges were broken as well sending every truck on them to the bottom. Over 100 lives were lost as well. While most of the material was sealed in water tight containers, it would be days before they could be salvaged.

The pontoons were quickly repaired, and the rest of the force and most trucks crossed the Susquehanna. Over 4,500 personnel would remain behind to salvage. The rest were ordered to move on. For San-Juan, already frustrated and hampered by agency interference, this order could not be safely obeyed. He was relieved on the spot and replaced by, now promoted, General Roxana Yorklyn. She was brought in due to her successful handling of affairs in Philadelphia after the June 17 police resignation crisis. Now, the eyes of the Coalition were upon her to crush the rebel force assembling near Gettysburg, save Pittsburgh, and restore morale and momentum.

Generals San-Juan and Scofield were not the only casualties of the day. The news of Daschle's impeachment had angered and alienated many loyal to him. One group of soldiers under Annapolis commander, Gen. Eugene Newport attempted to rescue him. His plot almost succeeded, but in failing cost over 1,000 lives and several critically needed combat jets. Nationwide, 26,000 Coalition personnel were now in detention, and 23,000 had in all probability, defected, a loss of almost 10 percent of all their numbers.

In Washington, the issue of leadership was becoming even more critical. One thing was certain, whoever took leadership would have to take a firm hand on two fronts, military and religious. As they met, and as armies braced for battle, reports came in that across the nation, millions were making this a day of prayer and fasting. Even military units with tear gas were not able to dissuade these fanatics.

Hugo Tree of the environmental Coalition was especially outspoken. He upbraided these ignorant Neanderthals and their babbling ignorance with talk about God. If their God was real why did he allow the catastrophic pollution of Love Canal, or Three Mile Island, or Exxon Valdez? What God would allow war or starvation, or forcing poor women into marital or child bearing slavery? Why are children born into disease and poverty? Why would God condemn someone to Hell for a sexual preference they were born with? Or two young people on a date for doing what comes naturally? And how could a loving God sanction such hate mongering by these bigots who oppose any effort to end such misery? No real God could allow the defeat of a compassionate Coalition intent on bringing love, peace, healing, and enlightenment. All this proved that the God of the Christian did not exist. Man (or woman) was his own god, and truth and destiny is in man's hands.

Perry Noyah, also an environmentalist agreed. The hate crimes against witches and Satanists was also cited. A good example, he argued, could be seen in the Californian's persecution of the Chinese Buddhists. In the name of peace and harmony with nature and the spirit forces, Christianity must be crushed. To this the educators and others joined in agreement. As Bill Clinton was now gaining in support, he agreed to abide by a policy to squelch any form of Christian fundamentalism.

Another major military confrontation was brewing as they spoke. Stonewall Jackson had left Richmond for the large Coalition base at Hampton (Roads). He had learned in Richmond that by historical accounts, he was supposed to have died on May 10 after Chancellorsville. Believing that God had given him borrowed time for a purpose, he planned to do as much damage to the enemy as possible.

His ranks had now swelled to about 7,300 by the 2nd. They saw their purpose not in prosperity, comfort, or a long life, but instead, in fulfilling a purpose. Life was not an end to them, but an end to a means. This was their testing grounds, or field of service to prepare them for eternity. God was not glorified in their pleasures, but their purpose, a view shared by a nation they were ready to die for. By days end, Jackson had established positions along the Pamonkey from White House to the east.

Without consulting Fremont, the Coalition committee acted to replace Benjamin Butler as American (Federal) military leader. The former Confederate Secretary of War James A. Seddon was selected. He had shown a cooperative "bipartianship" in relations with both north and south during the war. He had maintained business contacts on both sides, helping keep the north in cotton and the southern army fed and equipped. But as a condition, he only agreed to use his army in a nonpartisan way to maintain order, not defend Coalition bases. Reluctantly, the Coalition accepted. This limited support reinforcements in the east to troops in Washington, Hampton, and Philadelphia. And for now, there they would remain.

At 2:00 A.M., Lee received one more major player in his main body. General William T. Sherman and 3,700 others joined camp. He had achieved notoriety in Tennessee and Mississippi during the war. But he was best known in history for what now would never happen, his 1864 devastating march through Georgia.

When the Coalition invaded, he evaded capture and, with 450 die hands, made his way to just outside Harrisburg, Pennsylvania. On June 29 he had infiltrated Harrisburg and plotted a Baltimore style revolt. Instead, as events unfolded, he picked up an army and learned of others in the area. Now he would cover Lee's left flank on the west of Cemetary Ridge. Scofield would cover his right. Lee's force now numbered about 39,200 against almost 36,000 headed against him.

At this point Lee divided his command. He ordered Stewart and Custer, who every day functioned better as a team to head west. Somewhere in the Chambersburg area they would link up with forces headed from Wilkes-Barre. If the Coalition force either bypassed Lee, or annihilated him, they would wait in ambush. About 3,800 were under their command.

The group from Wilkes-Barre was a queer assembly of its own. Gen. Dodson, who was relieved of his Coalition command in New York had become greatly disillusioned with policy. While committed to the mission, he was intrigued by American rejection. From what he had read in modern school history textbooks, he expected their beliefs to closer mirror modern Americans. It troubled him that the 1863 Americans were regarded as second class persons. He had difficulty with the belief that "to make an omelet one has to break some eggs."

After the nuking of the Sioux and invasion of the south, his loyalty was lost. Seeking out any leadership among the American people he found General Dix. As the Coalition plan began to unravel the two hit on a plan to rescue detainees at Wilkes-Barre. With a handful of trusted experts, they were able to plan the break on June 28, just before midnight. With stunning success, they were able to release the prisoners and escape to the west and south of Plymouth. Now they were in the Blain-Waterloo area, and it was here that Coalition intelligence began to track them.

Coalition reconnaissance picked up Custer-Stewart and force headed west as well. Plans were changed. A show of force would still be made in Gettysburg on this historic date. But Lee's main force appeared to be making a run for west Pennsylvania, and would be caught out in the open. Victory should be quick, low cost, and decisive. Spirits soared in Washington.

Lee, with Scofield's advisement, determined to make his main stand at Gettysburg, where the ground favored the defense. Holding positions south of town. Sherman was to cover Cemetary Hill, and Sheridan was now positioned on Culp's Hill and along Rock Creek towards Hanover Road and Benner's Hill. Scofield's troops paralleled the Baltimore turnpike on the west bank of Rock Creek. His helicopters were now hidden about half way between Fairfield and Gettysburg. Lees main body was along Cemetary Ridge and the Taneytown Road. With weapons from Clarksburg, now half his force there had reasonably modern weaponry, and 23 serviceable helocopters. Best estimates showed the Coalition's arrival from Hanover via the Hanover Road at sometime around noon, July 3, 1863.

In the early morning hours, Washington discussed battle strategy. No air support was available. The Bonneville craft either were in the process of refueling and rearming, or were on assignment. Border patrol had been stepped up dramatically. Other units were involved in redeployment-evacuation campaigns in New England, Texas, and Florida. Remaining available units were on security alert to cover key installations along the Washington and Hampton areas of command.

List was concerned about casualties. Before any show of force an offer to surrender must be given. Lyberte, now included in the chairperson planning session advised that without armor and major firepower it would be difficult to show much force anyway. The loss of ammunition and equipment compounded the problem. List was forced to agree.

Berry was concerned about minority advancement, especially for Afro-Americans. She did not want a white man's (persons) war. With events in the south she believed a rise in black heroes and leaders could woo back the ex-slaves. She abhorred the possibility of another Colin Powell, who had done just that in the 1991 first Gulf War, and then betray his people. His radical right wing extremism had led to his rejection for consideration in the Coalition mission. But the Afro-Americans needed a hero. A promising young Colonel Perry K. (Pickett) Thomas would be promoted. He would command the hastily organized second combat group in the "Keystone Crossing" expeditionary column.

Patterson-Roberta was concerned about environmental and legal issues. The salvage operation on the Susquehanna also underlined the need for safety. The evacuation of civilians would be continued. Travel routes would be clearly marked, and the easiest, most direct routes used. Vehicles must be properly spaced, seat belts and safety devices used at all times, environmental equipment in proper use. Some had argued that safety rules were an impediment in battle, but this mission would prove their worth. Vehicles would run with lights on and even back up beepers must be properly functioning.

Yorklyn was given a daunting task. Her force must reach Pittsburgh by midnight July 4-5. In 70 hours she would have to take her force over 240 miles. Patton, of the U.S. 3rd Army had impressed the world with his ability to bring his forces against the Germans in the Battle of the Bulge. She was going to go over four times as far in less than three days. Truly, the best man for this job was a woman, and she was that woman.

In Washington, the losses of the last two days were tallied. The nuclear arsenal, one fourth of the heavy air cargo fleet, well over 40,000 personnel headed the list. But Keystone Crossing was about to restore momentum. General Verona Emery-Mills had destroyed Scofield's force but his helicopters were not accounted for. It was only assumed that they were destroyed at Clarksburg. But her air force was about to destroy Ulysses S. Grant's force as it was believed to be, in Ft. Hayes, Kansas.

For the committee in the capitol, a decision on leadership was now imminent, and none too soon. The political gridlock could not be kept secret. The very fact of it betrayed a crisis and undermined morale. At 8:00 A.M., Friday, July 5, "Pathfinder" John C. Fremont came to the capitol to take his official role as leader. Promising a middle course that would restore the republic while avoiding a blood bath against the Coalition, he began to issue orders. Finding no one responding, he paraded into the Capitol Building where he was halted by an unyielding security guard.

CHAPTER 16

In the early morning hours the last available fighter and bomber units took off from Bonneville Flats in Utah. At 9:30 A.M., Washington time on Friday, July 3, 1863, Ft. Hays, Kansas felt death rain down from the skies. After a half hour, virtually nothing remained but flames and craters. A few choppers from Ft. Smith flew in assault troops. But before they landed the town and surroundings were raked with machine gunfire, with a deliberate and deadly efficiency. The same treatment was given to an encampment on the Smoky Hill River.

When the assault troops landed, they found fewer than 500 survivors in the town and camp. Nearly 3,800 residents of the town and camp were dead. Camp survivors were prospectors, merchants, refugees, and a few Indians. Grant and his men were nowhere to be found.

As Coalition soldiers reported their findings, a surveillance plane picked up evidence of another camp near Ft. Robinson, Nebraska. With its proximity to the Black Hills, concerns were raised of a possible hostile force. But with the dismal record of killing Indians and civilians, Lieutenant General Craig Walden in Washington ordered it investigated before any attack would be mounted.

Last minute rebel groups streamed into Gettysburg ahead of Yorklyn, making up for over half the men he had sent west with Stewart and Custer. Now, with 37,500 some men he prepared, and waited. At 11:00 A.M., advance units of Keystone Crossing came up the Hanover Road towards Gettysburg. Anticipating little resistance, loudspeakers echoed orders to surrender. All prisoners, including Coalition deserters, would receive humane treatment. As they entered Gettysburg proper, the main body followed closely behind, vehicles in neat rows.

In Washington, an important announcement was made. The symbolism of Fremont's assertion was not lost on those inside. The challenge of Lyberte was disintegrating. Bill Clinton was approved as Coalition president in place of Tom Daschle. He had pulled the nation together before, and America had prospered. Under his leadership freedom had grown, the environment had been cleaned up and America was made safer. But for all the good he had done, he had no legacy. He now had the opportunity to build one, as the most important leader America had ever had. And for all the ominous events of the times, he knew that he would have to build it quickly.

At 11:15 A.M., the announcement of Clinton's election hit the airwaves just as Yorklyn's first columns neared Benner's Hill on the Hanover Road. As they did "Little Phil" Sheridan and Scofield set off fireworks of their own. The vehicles neatly lined up were slaughtered like ducks in a row. The Coalition returned fire, primarily against Culp's Hill. There a regiment of about 600 under Maine Colonel Joshua Chamberlain was deluged with hot steel. But the regiment held. Sheridan sent in reinforcements.

As Yorklyn brought more forces up the road, she ordered them to leave the road. Scofield's choppers began to attack. Several were downed or disabled by ground fire, but not before inflicting substantial loss on the Coalition column. In a break with safety and environmental rules the second battle group under "Picket" Thomas took matters into his own hands. He swung his second battle group off the road and south to Two Taverns. Flanking Scofield from the south, he crossed Rock Creek south of Little's Run and raced southwest. Crossing Taney Town Road one company continued to push, now with heavy resistance, against Scofield's chopper base. Those on the ground were destroyed. By 1:30 P.M. he had swung with most of his command around Big Round Top and behind Seminary Ridge, along Willoughby's Run. He took position along the ridge and pushed towards the Peach Orchard. Disregarding environmental concerns and potential loss of vehicles he faced Cemetary Ridge. He had no artillery support or heavy weapons.

At 2:00 P.M. he ordered his 13,000 weary men, many now low on ammunition, to attack Cemetery Ridge. Yorklyn was about to order him to hold his position instead, but the situation along Hanover Road was deteriorating. She approved his attack. "Picket" Thomas' men faced murderous fire from a panoply of weapons, M-60 machine guns and M-16 rifles to flint locks and muskets. As they neared Emmitsburg Road, rebel artillery blew holes in the lines, but ranks were quickly closed. Vehicles were tossed like toys by explosions. Then Sherman's forces attacked Thomas' left flank from Cemetary Hill, often in hand to hand combat. But the Coalition lines held and surged ahead. With murderous fire on both sides, "Picket" Thomas fought to the crest of Cemetary Ridge, and plowed into Lee's defenders and raced towards Culp's Hill. Sherman was cut off, and Sheridan forced to retreat. Scofield covered Lee's retreat and extracted as much of Sherman's force as he could. With 11 surviving helicopters, now low on fuel they retreated, cutting "Picket" Thomas' thin line to the south.

A defensive line was formed south of Plum Run to cover their retreat. As night fell, Lee made camp. In breaching Thomas' line a large quantity of medical supplies were captured. They were immediately put to use. He still had nearly 19,400 who could be used in another fight, and he regrouped his command around them.

The battle had cost him 2,800 dead and 6,300 wounded, with 4,700 others scattered. He had lost 4,300 captured, including Sherman and Reynolds. For them, the Coalition had two very reasonable requests, identify the Coalition traitors among them and sign a loyalty oath. Following Sherman's instructions, all refused, to a man. They were all in mass tried for treason, and, including wounded, ordered executed. Sherman protested this inhumane order, to which Yorklyn responded "You know what they say Sherman, war is Hell." Reynolds was able to escape with about 500 men, but the rest were executed before they too could do so. Victory was complete.

But Yorklyn had paid a high price for victory. Half of "Picket" Thomas' 13,000 main assault force was dead or wounded. Lee, by capturing most of their medical equipment sentenced many of the wounded to painful death. Air resupply came too late. Of her 6,000 deaths, two thirds could have been saved. Of her 24,000 uninjured survivors, half were left to care for wounded and finish off Lee. She began to race towards Pittsburgh.

In Washington, Dan Rather reported a major victory, as, Coalition courage had rewritten history, and succeeded where no one of this (1863) age could." But in reality, the cost of victory provided no comfort. And the actions taken in violation of safety, environmental, and military codes of conduct fueled dissent within the Coalition. Patterson-Roberta wanted the court martial of Yorklyn and Thomas. Several civil rights groups and the environmentalists joined in. Safer of OSHA and Greens of EPA were troubled. Berry and List were sickened but they had come to realize their survival depended on success. The ACLU was supportive, necessity dictated the action. Clinton, although abhorred himself, met with Patterson-Roberta and the environmentalists and won their acceptance.

In Oregon, AIM leader Black Jack Game Winner was holding council with a number of Indian leaders. Most of the tribes of the Penutian group were present. Several of the Aztec-Tanoan, and the California Pomo also sent leaders. The Bannock and Shoshone, friends of the white man were in attendance. By far the most influential delegations were the Modoc and Nez Percé. Old Chief Joseph became a chief spokesman across tribal and group lines. Old animosities between rivals faded.

Game Winner grimaced at the thought of a Christianized leader as head of an Indian council. He accepted it, though, knowing that Joseph held the trust of all present. If unity was to come, he was the key. What bothered him, though, was the presence of two white men. One was a trapper, the other sported Confederate officer's garb. Both were unarmed.

Old Chief Joseph rose to speak of a troubled history. The white man had once been a visitor, now he owned the land. His encroachment had been relentless. He spoke of the Walla Walla Valley Treaty of June 11, 1855. But white man was never satisfied, before the "ink was dry" the treaty was void. His appetite yearned for the valleys and mountains still possessed by the Indian. The last few weeks had brought a flood of new ones who consumed the land like ravenous wolves. He did not legally know what homesteader meant but he knew what it meant to his people, and to all the tribes present, death and destruction.

One by one, tribal leaders and representatives rose in agreement. Even the Shoshone, long a friend of white man, joined the union of spirits. Game Winner, struggling to conceal his elation, fixed his stare on the two white visitors. All the others soon joined him. At that point he asked "What about these?" Chief Joseph again spoke, saying that they should be heard before any action was taken against them.

At that point, the Confederate officer, using the trapper as an interpreter, rose to speak. His name was Earl Van Dorn, an ex-Confederate general. He had served on the western (Mississippi) front during the war. He was utterly humiliated at Corinth and was relieved of his command and reassigned to the cavalry. He had drifted into moral dissipation, wine, women, and song. But the Coalition intervention forced him to change his life, and ultimately save it. He found out in early June that history had given him an appointment of death on May 7 in Spring Hill, Tennessee at the hands of a jealous husband, Dr. George Ritters. Instead he fled to Arkansas to escape the Coalition, and with 39 of his cavalry men came west. He also brought enough gold and silver to purchase weapons for at least 300 more. Now, as head of a delegation of 160 homesteaders and their families, he had come to make peace with the Indian.

They blamed the Coalition for their plight. All would still be out east had the Coalition not driven them from their livelihood. This Coalition was also the enemy of the Indian. He had heard about Cherry Creek and Paradise, and Game Winner was forced to agree. In his possession he also had several mementos from his days of leadership over Cherokee and other Indians. He offered their services in any action against the Coalition. Game Winner rose to assert that this was an Indian matter and it did not concern Van Dorn or the white intruders. Game Winner and Van Dorn were excused from the meeting while the others discussed in private.

By late afternoon, July 3 Old Joseph was endorsed as leader. Two commanders under him were Keintepoos, or Captain Jack of the Modoc and young "Chief" Joseph. Young Joseph had considerable knowledge of white man's ways. Game Winner would be chief advisor. Calling Van Dorn back in they asked him if the Indians would be allowed on homesteader lands. He responded that they would be welcomed to hunt, to attend schools and churches, and to learn their ways. They made peace.

As Game Winner waited, he listened to the daily news broadcast on his radio. It was almost 4:00 P.M. (7:00 Washington time). What he heard was a live address by now Coalition President Bill Clinton. A true friend to Game Winner's cause, he had been given opportunity to meet twice with him. Suddenly, with Clinton as leader, Game Winner's loyalties shifted. He knew with Clinton at the helm, everything would be all right.

Being called back to the council, he said that he had been given a revelation from the box that talked. The enemy was not the Coalition but the Oregon intruders and homesteaders. If the Indians would wage war on them, the Coalition would help them get their land back. Van Dorn and his settlers should go to Seattle and settle there, if they wanted peace, if not, death.

This took Young Joseph completely by surprise. With his own native beliefs and training in Christianity, he was a man with deep moral conviction. After extending the hand of peace to Van Dorn, it would be treachery to kill him. "The Father of all spirits", he argued, had given many laws. One should never be the first to break a bargain. It is a disgrace to tell a lie." It was also wrong to trick, or steal from another. His people had made a treaty, and must honor them if they wanted the giver of these laws to prosper their ways.

Game Winner argued that these men already had, that they were deceiving the Indians. They were worthy of the death of the treacherous. But Chief Joseph cut him off. To make peace and then kill is the greatest of treacheries. Captain Jack added that if anyone was treacherous and worthy of sentence it was Game Winner. His loyalty to the Coalition after calling for death was of deceit, as his sudden call for the death of Van Dorn. Game Winner began to plead his case for his shift. Captain Jack replied "You talk too much. You cover one lie in many words of another. Your words form circles like a rope to snare the simple minded." As Game Winner began again to explain his cause Captain Jack struck him dead. The council consented to his death, and accepted Van Dorn as military advisor.

Two reconnaissance craft were sent over Ft. Robinson. The presence of Grant was not proven, but ground to air missiles downed one of the aircraft. The other plane then spotted what looked like Indian dwellings near by. An attack was ruled out, for now. Grant had deceived the Coalition into thinking there were Indians present.

Out in the east Atlantic, the USS Donahue was experiencing navigational and tracking system failures. She was the newest ship in the Navy, equipped with state of the art spy capabilities. At 1:30 A.M. (8:30 P.M. Washington time) she was off the southern coast of England near South Hampton. The electrical systems began to malfunction as well shutting down almost all lighting. A low, rolling fog had hidden the ship from view.

A short time later, the English "Scotia" with 850 aboard cut into the same fog bank. The Donahue became aware of the Scotia's presence and sent up flares in warning. The Scotia, feeling that she was under attack sped up, right into the side of the Donahue. The superior engineering of the Donahue minimized damage, but the Scotia was not so fortunate, she sank in a matter of minutes.

Fearful of a gross intelligence compromise the Donahue hesitated in rescue efforts. But Washington was immediately notified. When the order came from Washington to do so, only 91 survivors were rescued. Other English vessels in the area began to arrive about 5:00 A.M. (London time) and the survivors were transferred.

Efforts to contact England, either by radio dispatch with London, or direct embassy contact in America only met with silence. But radio chatter throughout Europe was lively. At 4:00 A.M., Washington time, on Saturday,

July 4, the English delegation began closing their embassy. France, Russia, and most other European powers followed suit. American embassies throughout Europe were ordered vacated as well, to Coalition personnel. American personnel could stay, but midnight was set as a deadline for Coalitioners to be removed. Only the Swedish embassy remained open in America, and vice versa.

One other event of significance on the evening of July 3 was the presence of jubilant crowds in cities now free of Coalition occupation. Even in cities still occupied crowds would begin to form, only to be dispersed. But a spirit of reckoning and expectation could be felt. Coalition forces felt more alone and alienated than ever. In Baltimore, a steady stream of fire was being traded by the city militia and the Coalition units around Ft. McHenry. And yet the modern American flag still flew. Francis Scott Key would be proud.

At 12:15 A.M., July 4, Yorklyn's column had made excellent time as avante-garde units were already in Chambersburg, now the home of a melancholic James Buchanan. Born a few miles away at Stoney Batter, he rose to become America's 15th president. Now he spent days in solitude, grieved over a nation, once torn by war, now torn by two worlds so far apart. As Coalition columns pushed through town he had risen to go out and watch.

Moments later he heard explosions as two trucks just outside the west edge of town burst into flame. The column lurched to a halt and troops poured out of vehicles into the streets. As shots were fired outside of town, Coalition personnel began to return it from the city. Buchanan tried to get back to a safer place, but not in time. His death came five years early.

Outside town Stewart and Custer had sprung an ambush. The force from Wilkes-Barre had been unable to link up. The few helicopters in Pittsburgh, Buffalo, and New York City had launched an attack against them. Acting alone, though as a team the two had become almost brothers. The cavalier Custer who was head strong and consumed with his own greatness, and a Stewart with the common sense of a Black Labrador who tended to wander off now fit like hand in glove. Together they surpassed what both could do separately.

As the Coalition force at Chambersburg battled an ambush, Custer and Stewart had set their main body to the east of town. There they struck the now vulnerable middle, left lightly guarded as troops poured to the north and west of town. With modern hand grenades, far superior to their 1863 union counterparts, they set over half the fuel trucks on fire. Quick reaction routed the cavalry, and with heavy losses. Over 400 cavalrymen died in the attack, including a mortally wounded Stewart. As Stewart transferred his command to Custer, the gallant ego broke down and wept. But he regained composure and led over 3,000 men to safety at Ft. Littleton.

Yorklyn tallied her losses. She had 374 dead, and over half her fuel was lost. Loading 10,500 into as few vehicles as possible, she pressed on towards Pittsburgh. The other 13,000 were left to deal with rebel stragglers and wait on more fuel from those still in Gettysburg. She proceeded now unimpeded, Lee's last ditch stand had been brushed off.

As the Keystone Crossing column picked up steam. Lee did have one more card to play. Scofield still had 11 choppers. Dividing them into two groups, he sent five to strike the Coalition nerve center at Butler. The other six would attack the refinery complex at Franklin. At Altoona, the six headed for the refinery were intercepted and shot down. But the five headed for Butler made their target and, at 5:00 A.M., devastated it. Running out of fuel, they were ditched near Grove City. As a result of the raid, all transport between Pittsburgh and Franklin was indefinitely suspended.

Yorklyn had read the historical accounts of the Battle of Gettysburg and knew that rain would come that day and frustrate Lee. Her force in the area would be able to annihilate him in the rain. But for some unknown reason the rains did not come. Lee's army was able to make a complete escape as Scofield's force covered his retreat.

Saturday, July 4 dawned in Washington with Bill Clinton in conference. With the attrition of Keystone Crossing, concerns were raised over its capability to defend Pittsburgh, if indeed it even got there. Lyberte offered a contingency plan that involved borrowing up to 10,000 soldiers from Hampton to offset Yorklyn's losses until her fall force could arrive.

Another issue was one of leadership and of ethnic and social advancement. While women and blacks were being advanced, gays, and alternate religious views were not. While Buddhists, Hindus and Wiccans (witches and wizards) did not have anyone of a noteworthy military record, the gay community did. Gerald (Geraldeen) Corona had been an army major under Clinton, and achieved colonel status under Bush until sexual orientation led to discharge.

To head this operation, Corona was selected. A veteran of the 1991 Gulf War, air transport was Corona's area of expertise. Speed, precision, and coordination were critical elements, and Corona was up to the task. While eight senior officers at Hampton were passed over for Corona's appointment. Clinton believed the mission was in good hands.

Code named "Zodiac", 9,600 ground troops would be pulled from Hampton (Roads). Equipped with the most advanced of the weapons and gear there, they would be transported by air to Pittsburgh. To do this, virtually every transport and helicopter craft on the east coast would be used. When Yorklyn arrived with sufficient force to protect the area, they would return to Hampton. To avoid hot spots in south Pennsylvania and Baltimore, an Atlantic route would be taken, up the Delaware Bay and to Reading and then west.

Included in Zodiac would be a civilian force of about 300. It would include 85 gays, 16 Wiccans, and several Buddhists, Hindus, and Moslems. Corona paralleled this command to Alexander the Great and his bisexual army that conquered the world. The very idea of returning to 2007 and reading his (her) name in the history books exhilarated and inspired him.

One other debate of the morning centered on the treatment of prisoners of war. Mao Tse Tung once said "our policy towards prisoners captured…is to set them all free, except for those who have incurred the bitter hatred of the masses and most receive capital punishment…" The ethical and legal question of prisoner treatment had pitted Patterson-Roberta against Junction, Lyberte, and Coalition ethicists. It was agreed that any rebel who favored the beliefs of those who had abducted and murdered some 328 (or more) Coalition civilians shared in their crime. As such, they had incurred the hatred of the masses and deserved death.

Clinton continued to make efforts to contact England. He also called Paris in hopes of staving off the ominous rumblings now coming from Europe. He hoped to build on the friendship he had made with Napoleon III of France in his May 1863 visit to avert war.

He and Napoleon III had shared much in common. Both were left of center political leaders who trusted human instincts more than religious creed. And both enjoyed the things human instincts and cravings had to offer. Both were willing to restrict a few political excesses of their opponents to secure their power base. And both had ruled over prospering economies. And they had established a "chemistry" with each other, similar to what Clinton had built with English Lord William Gladstone.

Now, however, it would take more than chemistry, or even "alchemy" to turn dross to gold. And from Europe's perspective, the Coalition covered America like dross. Two hours later, Lord Lyons, English consulate, handed a letter to one of Clinton's deputies as he was leaving Washington. Clinton's appeal for a last minute meeting with Clavendish was rejected. As the letter was handed to the Coalition Lyon's added that this was a formal statement by the English. But it had the assent of every power of Europe, at least in spirit. Even the Irish Sinn Fein saw the Coalition as an enemy. They promised a truce in their war for self rule until the Coalition was dealt with. But in the interest of neutrality Sweden, Switzerland and the Netherlands withheld official statements.

The radio chatter of the previous hours was European response to perceived Coalition aggression. Many details get lost in history. That the sinking of the U.S. Battleship "Maine" in Havana in 1898 had absolutely no Spanish involvement, was of no consequence in the Spanish-American War. Now, the reality that the Scotia had run into the Donahue was a non issue, European sovereignty was. All Europe agreed strong action was needed.

And all looked to England for leadership. She was now viewed as first among equals. Even Wilhelm of Prussia (Germany), after reading the history books left in Europe feared his own nation's ascendancy. France, so frequently a rival of the English now feared a future without them. While each gave advice and personal concerns, Europe lined up behind England and her actions towards the Coalition.

War sentiment was high. Lord Salisbury quipped about the Trent affair and how 999 of every 1,000 Englishmen had wanted war. Now 999 of every 1,000 Europeans wanted war. Their honor and sovereignty was at stake. And so were the moorings of a Christian civilization against what they saw as the perverted science of the Coalition. All except Sweden, Switzerland and the Netherlands were willing to back up any war with the Coalition by England. Even Turkey pledged 150,000 men, provided transport could be made available.

While Europe talked the talk, walking the walk was a little more difficult. While Europe could mobilize millions, there would be an obstacle in arming and training them against a futuristic enemy. While strides were being made to modernize, they still would realistically be no match for

Coalition capabilities. Then there was the problem of trans-Atlantic passage. If the March 1862 battle between the Monitor and Merrimac at Hampton Roads had made English warships obsolete, how much more aircraft carriers and guided missile frigates.

While any effort to invade American would be defeated, all Europe would be open to attack. While several of them were now making counterfeit rifles, machine guns and rocket launchers, aircraft and armor were years from development. With naval and air force mastery, the Coalition could sit back and pick targets at will. Canada would be lost, as would all European interests in the Americas. From their ships, Coalition admirals could pick and choose which city or factory in Europe to obliterate.

A formal declaration of war was reluctantly ruled out. Instead several other steps were taken. First of all, Sweden closed its embassy in Washington and the Vatican embassy would remain open in its place. Any mediation would have to be made through those very religious channels the Coalition loathed. Pope Pius IX hated rationalison, evolution, communism, moral decadence, and all other manifestations of humanism. But he also hated war.

The Coalition was not the legitimate government of America and would not be recognized as such. Until lawful and honest elections could be held, the Fremont administration was regarded as the government. All foreign holdings of American property would be given to the forces of opposition to the Coalition in America.

All the nations of Europe (including Sweden, Switzerland, and the Netherlands) jointly purchased Alaska from Russia. It was now presented as a gift to American homesteaders, rebel armies, and the Fremont government. As peace keepers, a small force of English, Canadian and Russian military would occupy it. Any effort by the Coalition to invade would be met with fighting.

Payment had not yet been made on European investments and property in America. Now much of it was at risk with hostilities. The loss of such assets would be written off on the condition that the blockade of American borders to refugees and trade be lifted. If not, the destruction of European property was viewed as a grave provocation.

Palmerston's government also demanded a 200 mile nautical zone around Europe and all European possessions. Any Coalition vessels or forces within that limit would be viewed as hostile and dealt with accordingly. All Europe stood together as one, and an attack on one was seen as an attack on all. The Coalition had until noon Sunday, July 5, to reply.

The demands of Europe were viewed by the Coalition leadership as a provocation of war. For Clinton, however, circumstances did not leave much promise of successfully fighting another war. The nuclear arsenal was gone. Ground forces were already overcommitted, air power had suffered serious loss. The refinery was not yet complete and it would be at least a year before any real supply of ammunition and some weapons could be manufactured. The earliest reinforcements could arrive via the time channel was October.

To meet Europe's demands would be surrender. Lyberte advised Clinton to ride it out and let Europe make the first move. But Coalition vessels would stay out of the English Channel and at least 30 miles from land. The only exception would be at the straight of Gibraltar. As for Alaska, the carrier groups Midway and Coral Sea would blockade Alaska and protect the west coast of America. The base at Seattle would take on even more importance. Coalition hopes to end settlement there had met with failure. All that could be done was warn the nation of future consequences of living there.

Most of Alaska was uncharted wilderness. It was believed that the Gulf of Alaska, Beaufort, and Bearing Seas could be easily patrolled. To the west the ocean was almost more a barrier than blessing, and Europe lacked power to bring any force to bear. The 600,000 square miles was not hard to patrol. But the hastily built or expanded settlements at Victoria and Vancouver and between would have to be isolated. Prince Rupert was only 25 miles from the Alaska border and was rapidly being built into a naval base. If England really wanted to go to war, she would have to make the first move in running the blockade.

As for the rest of Europe's demands, they would be ignored. The actions of Fremont had shaken any Coalition confidence in his ability to govern. A replacement was being sought while the Coalition tolerated his presence.

The evacuations in New England were proceeding on schedule. These had not been according to any official order or policy, but had been done out of necessity. New England was becoming increasingly hostile, and the forces were needed at critical points elsewhere. The bases that remained were strengthened, as were Buffalo, New York and Detroit, Michigan. A base in the Duluth area of Minnesota was greatly expanded to protect the new iron mines.

Coalition trucks and other craft now no longer would supply flour or other goods to the cities of New England. To the contrary, they now would impede transport. When hunger began to set in, the refined New Englanders might be a little more willing to accept Coalition generosity. And no one would complain about a few starving whites. The closing of the last businesses and impoverishment to a people would also hit the pocketbook. And New Englanders have always been concerned about their pocketbooks.

In the process, the Coalition took great care to take the nearly 6,600 detainees with them as they left. These were union officers, defiant soldiers, political and church leaders and other dissidents. They were taken to the New York detention center, already crowded with a capacity 30,000 others. But shallow graves marked the final resting place of almost 300 Coalition turncoats. It was only a miracle, at least for now, that all the others hadn't joined them. There were still some in Washington who felt that they might yet be rehabilitated. But things were changing with a fury in the Coalition ranks. Soon, all things would be negotiable.

CHAPTER 17

While the Coalition was contracting in New England, the rebel influence was expanding. And so were their armies. Ambrose Burnside, once the Commander of the Army of the Potomac, now headed 17,000 men. After his humiliating defeat at Fredericksburg in December of 1862, he was replaced by Hooker. He craved the opportunity to redeem himself and his reputation as a general. Now in upstate New York his chance was near.

In Massachusetts, Winfield Scott Hancock had assembled another 14,000 men. A native of Pennsylvania, he had headed for Canada after the Coalition takeover. He came to realize that his purpose was to fight to restore his nation so he returned to America and began to organize a force in Massachusetts. Courageous to a fault in battle, his reputation quickly amassed him an army. He now moved towards Boston, one of the few cities a Coalition force still remained in.

John Sedgewick was in Maine. He lost his command when Coalition firepower cut his VI Corps to pieces east of Chancelorsville. Now he had collected about 10,800 men. He wanted one more crack at the Coalition, as did his men. He was about to move on Portland Maine, another remaining Coalition base. Other Coalition bases at Burlington, Vermont and Bridgeport, Connecticut would face harassment by small groups under local leaders.

A few units of federal troops under the command of military commander James Seddon were left behind. Among them was Col. George LaFayette Beal of the 10th Maine Regiment. Learning of the presence of Burnside southeast of Albany he joined him the morning of July 4. Despite Burnside's defeat in December, he was an able commander. Very soon he would be leading all the armies of New England. But at this moment he was headed south for New York City.

In the south, food shortages were again critical. Scofield's food shipments had ceased, as had all others, with his defection. Where food was available, salt was scarce, making storage and transport difficult. But the reemerging governmental powers were rising up to meet the crisis. A well organized militia was being assembled to build and repair roads, bridges, railroad tracks and telegraph lines. With available resources scarce, corderoy, or timber highways were quite common, but progress was being made.

In the rebuilding effort, the ex-slave community was critical. Nearly half of all the militia east of the Mississippi were black. This was true of those in combat roles as well as reconstruction. And many were earning and being promoted to positions of rank. Among them was William Carney.

In Boston, he had been a sergeant with the Massachusetts 54th. Although he had been wounded, he had survived the June 7 battle and had been moved south with the aid of many both black and white. Now in Murfreesboro, Tennessee he was colonel over a mixed regiment.

The rebel forces massing around Coalition bases at Memphis and Nashville were well over half black. Other combatants from Louisiana to the Carolinas were almost half black. In some cases not only were ex-slaves with ex-masters in the same unit, but in at least three companies, the ex-slaves were in command.

The value of the contribution made by a people only so recently freed was beyond measure. Their participation in the southern insurrection was essential to its success. Inspired by the stand of the church leaders in Boston and elsewhere, they found a purpose in standing for their religious values. They found that the brotherhood of God was stronger than the barriers of race or position. So also did their white neighbors, who had lost much of their wealth in a war among brothers. In May, their values became threatened by a new enemy, one that challenged the very pinions of their society. They too, had found brotherhood with their former slaves in defending values of mutual concern. Their bond was now being ratified in the blood of both races.

Without the black participation, the rebellion would have been crushed. The losses of two years of war had already reduced the white manpower pool. Their numbers filled the gaps and provided needed strength. And the zeal of the newly freed slaves pumped up morale in a region worn by conflict.

The southern revolt itself was vital to the success of the uprising in the rest of the nation. Southern foment was responsible for the drawing down of Coalition forces elsewhere. If Comstock had not been depleted to garrison the south, Grant would have been thwarted, and either killed or captured. Any hope of success anywhere in America depended upon actions in the south. This was one more reason for Coalition vexation over the wrongful loyalty of the ex-slaves to their ex-masters. And it underscored the sinister hold that religion had, and its dangerous potential to destroy the truth.

The sacrifice of these ex-slaves was also not ignored by southern whites. On June 26, famous black abolitionist Frederick Douglass was in Columbia, South Carolina, urging an end to the cordoning off of much of the south. He also touched on the issue of providing land for the ex-slaves, as had been mentioned during his council with Berry, Sharpton and Jackson. But in his remarks, he angered Coalition base commander Wayne Romney, who attempted to squelch the challenges by his fellow Afro-American. To the contrary, Douglass became even more vocal, and a mass demonstration was beginning. Romney had three soldiers nab Douglass and transport him to a cite unknown, where he would be permanently silenced.

Learning of this plot, a group of vigilantes, 26 ex-soldiers and slave owners intercepted the assassination party in transit. At a cost of four of their own lives, they abducted Douglass. Expecting to be lynched, he instead found himself transported, under their guard, to a safe location near Rock Hill. A mixed militia force took over from there to transport him to west Tennessee. As he was being transferred two of the ex-masters asked him for a detailed plan to get land into the hands of "his people" and see what would happen from there. By July 4 brotherhood had replaced racism in almost all of Dixie.

This provoked Mary Francis Berry to complain. She was dumfounded that her people were dying by the thousands to defend the outmoded scruples of old dead white men. It was painfully obvious to her that the fate of the Coalition hung in the balance, and that the Afro-Americans could tip the scales. Neither her nor anyone else could understand this perverted bond of religious blindness and "symbiosis" with their ex-abusers.

Meeting late that morning, Independence Day, with Clinton, she appealed for one last chance to personally plead for their alliance. He consented, making a transport available to take her to Nashville. But in the back of both of their minds was a nagging, and growing question. Was the past really worth saving?

Berry and Clinton were not the only ones asking that question. Feminists watched in consternation as they saw the 19th century suffrage and rights movements headed in reverse. In areas evacuated by the Coalition it was women who were objecting to their right to vote. Many 19th century women's leaders were in prison and detention. And the others were in a prison of Neolithic moral codes and social values. Their minds seemed unable to grasp the concepts of liberation and justice that their modern sisters offered. Darwin was right, we are the products of evolution, the 19th century mind hadn't fully developed yet as their 21st century counterparts had.

Labor, environmental, and civil rights groups were coming to the same conclusion. Something was wrong, inherently wrong with the 19th century mind. They could not break out of the fog of their outdated values. The Coalition had brought light to this darkened age. But the brighter the Coalition light shone the more it had exposed the hypocrisies, and ignorance of the age, the more they loved and clung to the darkness. One of the beliefs of the new age was that all cultures were equal. But that can only be true if the people in it have evolved to a higher mindset. The 1863 American, and European, had not gotten there yet.

This past America was also more united now than ever. Not only were the races in collusion together in the south, the whole nation had found purpose in opposing the truth. If it weren't so tragic it would be comical. In April 1863, and before Rebels killed Unioners as a service to God, and Unioners killed Rebels in the same way. No one stopped to ask this so called God what He wanted or why He took pleasure in everyone killing everyone.

Some misguided historians claim that they were seeking God's will. It was alleged that one day Abraham Lincoln was asked if God was on the Rebel side or the Union. He supposedly answered that, "The question isn't what side God is on, we should rather ask if we are on His side." But any real modern historian relegates this story to the myth heap of history.

There was still one hope. But this would require revisiting issues of humanity and civil rights. The Coalition would have to break the American spirit. Only when the old was crumbled to ash could a new one rise in its place. Kindness had not worked. Instead it had been interpreted as a sign of weakness.

Berry would be given an opportunity to win over the ex-slaves. In the meantime, a decisive victory was essential to dampen the fanaticism of the host of hostile armies forming throughout America. Lyberte with eyes on

Pittsburgh, began to draw up a plan to do just that. Baltimore rose to the top of the list. But he did not inform Clinton of his intentions.

As Operation Zodiac departed Hampton (Roads), a frightful discovery was made at White House (New Kent), Virginia at about 9:00 A.M. Stonewall Jackson and a sizeable force (nearly 8,000) had been identified. He was headed towards Hampton. A diversion or delay action would be employed against him to lure him into a trap from which he would not escape.

American know how had created a generation of modern weaponry that was marvelously sophisticated. But much of it, especially hand held killing machines, were made easy to operate. Jackson's forces were quickly trained in how to use them. He also learned, through his Coalition deserters of the defenses set up at Hampton.

What he soon learned was the Coalition plan to take him out. At a little afternoon a battalion of soldiers had departed from Hampton to meet him. Commanded by Col. Shirley Anderson, its mission was to lure Jackson to the east, towards Mathews. The Battleship (reactivated) Missouri was steaming back from the mid Atlantic. By evening it would be in range to blast Jackson into the next world with her 16 inch guns.

Jackson, the great tactician that he was, brought his left flank under Jubal Early down the York River driving a wedge in Anderson's force. The battalion fell apart and Jackson cut it to pieces. As 400 plus stragglers retreated towards Hampton, base commander "Hawk" Taylor pulled together his remaining forces for another fight. With a fully armored force, 9,000 strong, supported by 14 attack helicopters, he sent his entire combat capability northwest.

Jackson shifted most of his army to the west of Barnhamsville. A small, highly visible force of 500 was arrayed on the Pamonkey River to draw attention. Another 360 armed with surface to air and surface to surface missiles were camouflaged to the east and north of West Point. Early dug in along the York River.

At 4:30 P.M. the Coalition force under General Chelsea Livonia-Baldwin, after a massive barrage pushed towards New Kent. At 4:45 Jackson struck with about 5,000 men on Livonia-Baldwin's lightly guarded left flank, ravaging resupply and support units. Barnhamsville was quickly encircled and captured, netting over 800 prisoners (most now defectors).

As this was taking place, the attack helicopters came in from the north east, in an attempt to surprise the defenders from the rear. As they neared West Point, in a low attack formation, a barrage of surface to air missiles devastated the command. All but three were hit, and seven were hit fatally.

Fearing a trap Livonia-Baldwin pulled her main force against Barnhamsville. Jackson was forced to withdraw to the northeast and, while cutting completely through the Coalition brigade, link up with Early. Early, with about 2,000 men, covered Jackson's crossing of the Pamonkey to regroup. Total losses to Jackson were 344 dead, and 286 captured or missing. Coalition losses were 11 choppers, 635 dead and 917 captured. Under changing policy, all white prisoners were shot. Blacks were given the opportunity to swear allegiance to the Coalition. All but one refused, and were shot.

Lyberte, with Clinton's support, determined to make a full end of Jackson and his army. By late evening the Missouri was in position to cover. With other events of the day, all favored a complete elimination of him and his army. An assault was scheduled for 11:40 P.M.

By 9:30 A.M. July 4, the first elements of Zodiac arrived in Pittsburgh. By noon, the whole force had arrived. By 3:00 P.M., making incredible time, advance units of Keystone Crossing also arrived in the city, traveling at over 10 miles an hour through hostile territory.

With their arrival, Bill Clinton gave a live broadcast to the nation. He spoke of the decisive and historic victories over Lee, Stewart, and a short time later, Jackson. He made a (premature) announcement of Grant's demise in the west. But his greatest praise was reserved for the relief force in Pittsburgh. He magnified the victory for gays, women, and blacks in making it happen. This Independence Day had truly seen the liberation of all Americans and everyone should join in the celebration of freedom.

All at once the spirits of the Coalition were revived. A grand celebration was hastily planned in Pittsburgh, and a number of Coalition leaders would attend. Each of them had played their part in achieving this day, Barbara Boxer, Christine Todd-Whitman, Ruth Vader-Ginsburg, Peter Jennings, and Stephen Breyer. At 10:00 P.M. they were scheduled to land for an 11:00 P.M. honor ceremony and celebration.

The announcement of Grant's demise came from a report sent by Emery-Mills from Bonneville. At 4:00 P.M. Washington time, her attack aircraft bombarded Independence, Kansas. It was assumed that the estimated force of about 450 whites were meeting with General Watie and his force of about 300 Cherokee. Unknown to the Coalition, the whites were under the command of William Clarke Quantrill.

On May 13, Quantrill and his followers went into hiding with General Sterling Price and about 2,500 of his men. North of Joplin, Missouri, they were fed and supplied by sympathetic locals. Price was a hero in the Mexican-American War, and a former governor of Missouri. He was also a Confederate, and his Civil War prowess included his victory at Wilson's Creek in Missouri. On May 22, he set out for Mexico with all but Quantrill's band. Unfortunately, he was confronted by a Coalition force on the 25th and forced to surrender. He later escaped, virtually alone.

But for Quantrill, the Devil on Horseback, opportunity knocked and he answered. Price had promoted him to Colonel before he left, and an army soon began to collect. Unlike most Americans, he still openly supported slavery and opposed black-white brotherhood. By July 2 nearly 4,000 proslavery southerners and northerners had joined him. He became the self proclaimed governor over almost half of Kansas, a fourth of Missouri, and several counties in Arkansas.

General Stand Watie also had ambitions and opportunity. As commander of Cherokee and other Indian forces at Pea Ridge, Arkansas he had incurred both a reputation and experience. His Indians had been accused by many, as recorded by George Templeton Strong, of indiscriminately scalping northerner and southerner alike. But he was an able commander.

The Coalition had provided opportunity for both men as well. Even at the zenith of Coalition involvement, its involvement in the region was almost entirely limited to Jefferson City and Kansas City, Missouri, and Ft. Smith Arkansas. This allowed Chief John Ross of the Cherokee and civilized nations to repair his own bridges. During the Civil War, Chief John Ross had been coerced by circumstance to cast his lots with the south. Some of his own people had owned slaves.

But his sympathies were with the north. In addition, he abhorred slavery. He remembered that he and his own people had once lived in the Appalachian Piedmont before the "Trail of Tears" took them here. He had made it his goal to educate and civilize his people. This created some friction with his own, and provided Stand Watie the opportunity to take advantage of the discord.

Leading 300 of his ex-soldiers to Independence, he met with Quantrill ot cut a deal. In exchange for pledging loyalty to him, Stand Watie sought to use Quantrill's army. The Devil on Horseback would join with Watie and approximately 2,000 others loyal to him. Together, they would oust John Ross and drive out the Selma survivors. Their plan was to set out after dark on July 4 for Cherokee territory. But at 4:00 P.M., Emery-Mills surprised them with her air force. In less than 15 minutes of carpet bombing they killed Quantrill, Watie, and almost 2,000 others. The rest were scattered. Among the survivors were two brothers, Frank and Jesse James.

Back in West Pennsylvania, General Joseph Hooker and his now 10,600 men were ready to act. The last few days had been spent carefully deploying his forces without disclosing either the size of his army or its objectives. He took a page out of history in plotting this deception. Back in 1781 then General George Washington had convinced British General Clinton that his army was in New York while it headed south. Washington had kept a small force behind to build huts, bread ovens, and fortifications. By building false camps, Hooker had convinced the Coalition that his main target was Pittsburgh, with a potential secondary one at Butler. Then he moved his main force north.

By the evening of July 4, 8,300 of his army was at Franklin, where the oil refinery was now due on line by July 24. There, sprawled out on both sides of French Creek and the west side of the Allegheny was a mini city. With refinery construction, metal finishing, transport, and support, 18,000 civilians and 4,000 military personnel called it home. To the northeast another 9,000 oil drillers and pipeline workers with protection labored to provide the oil. Only Washington D.C., and presently reinforced Pittsburgh were home to larger Coalition populations.

In waging modern warfare armies shoot from a variety of guns or rocket launchers, coordinate components of their forces, consume ammunition and spare parts, etc... But they run on oil. During World War II British and American planes dropped 2.7 million tons of bombs on Germany. But the ball bearing, ship building, steel and other production would recover and keep the war going. But when oil production and transport became a key target, the army collapsed. Later conflicts followed the same form. Cut off the oil, and sophisticated armies grind to a halt. Hooker and Lee were both enlightened to this, and planned an attack for just after midnight, July 5.

At 9:30 P.M., as chance would have it, Coalition workers began a fireworks display at the north end of town. This was where Hooker's main body had assembled. Fearful that their cover was about to be blown, he ordered the attack quickened. At 9:45 P.M. a mass of 5,600 men struck directly at the Coalition spectators. Taken completely by surprise, the scene was one of total chaos. As this force pushed through stampeding spectators, a second force of almost 2,500 struck from the south.

The military force quickly responded to both groups. In the south they were successful. But up north the conglomeration of attackers mixed with fleeing Coalition workers rendered any weapon superiority as useless. The ground was becoming littered with bodies. The two assaults were totally successful in their mission, though, regardless of casualties.

As the Coalition military confronted the two flanks, they left their center exposed. Hooker sent another 600 armed with his grenades, rocket launchers and plastic explosives in. Cutting through the woods to the west of the refinery complex they rapidly hit their targets. Some stopped to destroy construction equipment, machinery, and refinery materials. Others headed directly for the refinery complex. For 15 minutes they had total free reign before a company of defenders could challenge them.

Pittsburgh was immediately notified, and by 10:00 P.M. aircraft were already taking off, bound for Franklin. The transport with the dignitary celebration party was put on a holding pattern and forced to circle until the whole attack force departed. As it did, it neared one of Hooker's small diversionary forces, now near Penn Hills, about eight miles east of the city. The force responded with its entire arsenal of missile launchers. One clipped the right wing of the transport, hitting one of its engines. Before anyone could don a parachute, the plane spiraled into the east bank of the Allegheny. There were no survivors.

By 11:15 P.M. Hooker's forces had retreated from Franklin to his base camp west of Rocky Grove. They left behind 611 dead and 487 wounded, who were subsequently executed. The Coalition had lost 1,635 dead, mostly civilian, and a refinery, with critical equipment, now in shambles.

Clinton immediately approved a search and destroy policy, to annihilate all surviving attackers. Lyberte ordered the Coalition persuers to disregard civil rights and treat them as convicted war criminals. Hooker's main body was relentlessly persued. Fighting into his camp, the force under General

Preston Hibbing pressed a relentless counterattack. They killed another 1,503 of Hooker's force, including over 1,000 wounded, with a loss of only 98 of their own. Several of the dead were surgeons, orderlies, and a woman nurse, one of a dozen who attended to the needs of the wounded.

In 1861, a clerk in the Patent Office named Clara Barton had left her job to minister to the troops in the field. At Bull Run (Manassas), she became an American Florence Nightengale, dispensing bandages aiding the wounded, and giving kind words. In a host of other battles she aided, at times with kind words, at other times in surgery. At Antietam rebel artillery threatened the field hospital. While others scampered for cover, she stayed in her place, earning the nickname "Angel of the Battlefield."

Knowing that she would be needed again, she and a few other nurses went with Hooker to Franklin. But this time her heroine spirit kept her in the surgical tent too long. Coalition bullets killed her and the surgeon she was assisting. Had she survived, she would one day have founded the American Red Cross. Unfortunately, in 1863 she had chosen the wrong side.

In Pittsburgh, Gerald (Geraldean) Corona still feared an attack on the city. At just before midnight the commander countermanded all other orders and called the aircraft back to Pittsburgh. Without air support, General Hibbing abandoned his offensive against Hooker. With this reprieve, Hooker led his survivors to the west, towards Cocranton. There, just before dawn, he was joined by General George "Pap" Thomas and over 2,400 men.

Thomas was a native Virginian, but when war came at had remained loyal to the Union. He had made a name for himself at Murfreesboro. After an early loss Roscrans had asked him his opinion on continuing the battle or retreating. Thomas was said to reply "I know of no better place to die than here." His fortitude contributed to a great, but costly victory. When the Coalition had invaded, he had been cut off from Roscrans, and when the latter was captured, he went into hiding before heading north to Ohio. On June 29 he had heard of armies forming in Pennsylvania, so with his growing band he headed east. Now with Hooker and a total of about 8,000, they considered their next move.

At just before midnight another attack got underway in Virginia. With all available air power, General "Hawk" Taylor ordered General Livonia-Baldwin to attack Stonewall Jackson across the Pamonkey. The Battleship Missouri, under Admiral Marcus Gladbrook had been furnished a list of coordinates for his attention. But when his second in command, Elroy

Phillips saw that the list included civilian and historic cites, he balked. When Gladbrook ordered him to step down he refused. A mutiny ensued, and erupting into bloodshed, resulted in a great explosion that sunk the ship. Almost 3,000 lives on board, including Gladbrook and Phillips, perished.

Livonia-Baldwin pressed the assault without the Missouri, forcing Jackson to retreat. At a little after midnight Jackson was hit. As he transferred command to Early he asked what time it was. He was told that it was almost 12:30 A.M., Sunday, July 5. Jackson said, "It is well, I have always wanted to die on the Lord's Day." Early bade his friend farewell and pulled his forces to the northeast, saving almost 7,000, of which over 1,000 were Coalition deserters.

Desertion and open revolt in Coalition ranks was becoming pandemic. While the rebels seemed more than willing to die for their archaic beliefs, the Coalition was now fighting the mentality that nothing was worth dying for. This frustrated and bewildered leadership. There were so many things, values, ideals to die for, civil rights issues, prosperity, advancement. Yet those who had the most to lose were giving up in mass to those who had the least to lose. With Clinton's approval, Lyberte ordered all deserters to be shot on sight.

Late that evening, July 4, General Grant also began an offensive movement of his forces. With an eye on the Black Hills gold fields he headed north. He invited the few Sioux he encountered to join him in his objective. Most consented, they now trusted Grant to redeem them from the Coalition.

When news of the double disaster in Pennsylvania hit the nation, the shock waves, in the minds of many, soon turned to rage. In justifiable fury there were increasing calls for righteous retribution. If the Coalition could not fulfill its upright mission in rewriting a shameful and perverted history, it would guarantee that those responsible would be made to regret it.

One of the benefits of humanism is the absence of moral absolutes. There is no set in stone set of values or rules. All depend upon the superior wisdom of man, and his (or her) ability to apply ethics as the situation dictated. Coalition beliefs had shifted, and now most were ready to take whatever steps necessary to assure their survival and mission fulfillment.

Clinton called a special meeting with department heads. He proposed a temporary suspension of the Constitution. A policy of limited terror was far superior to melt down. To do otherwise ran the risk of events spinning beyond anyone's control, and a savage barbarism to take over.

Martial law was declared in Washington, and soon would apply to all Coalition bases. All radio and T.V. communications were now monitored and subject to censorship. When Dan Rather attempted to communicate outside his normal channels to tap his information sources, he was discovered and cut off. A very uneasy, and now unstable army corporal, Carmi Streator, was assigned to keep track of him. He protested her presence and attempted to slip away from her. In a rage over his distain for the new rules, she ordered him to halt. When he refused, she shot him dead.

When Mary Berry arrived in Nashville she immediately went to work. She found a group of ex-slaves at dawn holding a religious service on the edge of town. When she identified herself, one of them known as "Preacher Joe" answered her. As she began to defend her mission he cut her off. "You can'ts lift us up by keepen us on no plantation." She protested that she was there to bring equal rights, prosperity, and justice. He answered, "No ya ain't. You's here to keep us slaves to someone elses money and power, and we's nevah gonna be free that way." As she walked away a rebel sharpshooter locked her in his sights from a nearby field and pulled the trigger. Her body was taken back to Washington.

Les Lyberte found his role as head of the Homeland Security Administration becoming more prominent by the hour. Increasingly he was bypassing Clinton in his actions and his council. He began to form a strong tie with Overall Force Commander Craig Walden in Washington. And with his star rising, becoming head of the Coalition was not something he was not pondering. Civilian leadership, either through the executive or judiciary had failed. The joint leadership meeting almost resulted in total anarchy. He, with Walden could provide firm direction and still save the mission.

Early Sunday morning, July 5, 1863, he ordered a policy of abduction and assassination of American leadership. As they were emerging from the cracks like weeds after a rain now would be the time to act, while they were still relatively small. Those already in detention would also be eliminated. Then it hit him. All detainees would be taken to San Francisco, New Orleans, and Hampton. Facilities would be immediately be employed to terminate them all. That would prevent escape or their ability to build leadership networks. And it would free up Coalition resources. At 4:30 A.M. he issued the order to begin transport of the now 200,000 detainees. Clinton was not informed.

He also gave orders to every base commander to shoot all prisoners of war. Only in circumstances where valuable information could be garnered were they to be taken at all. Then he issued Directive Number 66. Beginning with Baltimore, all major cities would be destroyed rather than allow them to be used as bases for insurgency. Again, Clinton was not informed of policy.

In Detroit, Col. Lilly Penbrook had Walt Whitman, William Sumner, John Fiske, and Asa Gray brought from Ann Arbor and placed in the detention center. She was unsure about obeying the coming orders to send them to Hampton. Always loyal to her orders, she knew what was happening was not right, and she was not sure she could be a part of it. But Clinton was still President, and she trusted his judgment.

CHAPTER 18

At 6:00 A.M., Sunday, July 5, Bill Clinton ordered Tom Daschle released from custody and brought to him at the Executive Mansion. At the detention center, Captain Adrian Sandusky attempted to turn them away. He was on orders to prepare transporting the prisoners, and he would not allow any releases for any reason. He was asked on whose orders. He replied Lybertie's. When Clinton's messengers pulled rank, Sandusky had them held at gun point.

Two hours later, concerned about the delay and lack of contact, Clinton called General Walden, Washington and overall force commander. Walden told Clinton that he would have a response within an hour. His response puzzled Clinton. But Clinton was in the dark as to what was happening.

Walden had come to the same understanding as Lyberte. The only way to save their mission and their skins was to destroy enough of America to bring the nation to a broken destitution. As friends, they took the suspension of the Constitution one step further, together. Lyberte would become Chief Executor, Walden, military Commander in Chief.

At 9:00 A.M. Clinton watched as Lyberte and Walden arrived together. At least 600 armed troops, with armor and chopper cover surrounded the building. Clinton could not but feel a sense of danger. As Lyberte and Walden approached, they were escorted by Green Berets and Delta Force members. The White House of 1863 was not equipped with escape routes like the modern one was. All Clinton could do was hope things were not as they appeared.

In conjunction with Lyberte's plans, Walden had already ordered all available bombing and air attack units in the area to coordinate a strike on Baltimore. The city was condemned to incineration, and the siege on Ft. McHenry would be lifted. It was set to begin at the same time they met with Clinton 9:05 A.M.

As they came to the door of the White House, the President's guard ordered their escort to remain outside. Walden contradicted the order, and the first Delta men proceeded to enter. The White House guard opened fire, but were quickly overwhelmed. Storming in, they quickly killed or disarmed the rest of the guard. At 9:10 A.M., five minutes later, Lyberte and Walden faced Clinton in his office.

They proceeded to inform him of the new Coalition standards. He could either join them or resign and give them free reign. Clinton tried to negotiate with them. He also asked what legal theory they had used to justify their actions. They responded "Yours, Mr. President". Dumbfounded, Clinton asked how they came to that conclusion.

Walden ran through a list of Clinton's presidential policies, from unauthorized use of FBI documents to court martialing American military personnel in Bosnia for failure to pledge allegiance to the United Nations. Clinton's whole presidency was a challenge to the old order of fixed standards and rules of government. His legacy was his bold leadership into the uncharted waters of existentialism in government, truth and law was what he said it was. Now they were taking his "truth" just a couple of steps further.

As Clinton tried to argue Lyberte cut him off. "A great leader" he said "once said that political power grows out of a barrel of a gun." And right now, like Mao in 1949 China, Lyberte and Walden had all the guns. And as they spoke, the first attack on the incorrigible elements of America was scheduled to have begun. The fate of America now hung on Coalition power. No foreign power would befriend them, 19th century Americans hated them. The world would have to be brought to fear before they could be converted. Then the new world order could rise up from the ashes of the old.

As Clinton attempted to appeal to the Delta guard, Lyberte pulled out a pistol and shot him dead. Nearly 18 other judicial and executive leaders were shot throughout Washington at about the same time. Judge Elizabeth Patterson-Roberta was able to escape a death plot against her, however, and flee. But as leader after leader fell and America plunged into a post constitutional era Lyberte was heard to quote from French philosopher and sociologist August Comte. Prior to his death in 1857 he had envisioned the necessity of an all powerful state to keep mankind from destroying itself. While some argued he meant this for Napoleon III, it was now fulfilled by the educated new age.

In Baltimore, a people was continuing a liberty celebration that had begun the night before. From their churches the singing could be heard throughout the city. At 8:57 A.M., the first helicopters of the coordinated air assault appeared east of Essex and heading west towards Baltimore. The mission plan was to have 200 acres of the city center in flames. The helicopter gun ships were then to strafe for any hostile fire or survivors. Air Force General Homer Spenard was in command. The attack was to begin at 9:10 A.M. with others to follow within the hour on five other cities, Boston, St. Louis, Los Angeles, Indianapolis and Chicago.

As Spenard's force began to close in on Baltimore the chopper's beating caught almost everyone's attention. A sense of foreboding came over the city. Many fell to their knees in their pews and began fervent prayer. Others came out of their churches linked hands and prayed or sang. Several looked to the sky. At the Baltimore Cathedral, the oldest Catholic Cathedral in America the parishioners were singing. The words "From wars alarms, and deadly pestilence, be thy strong arm, our ever sure defense..." echoed from the building. This was to be the beginning point of the attack.

Outside, a small child, holding a daisy, looked into the sky. One old pilot remembered a TV commercial from his childhood. In 1964, in Lyndon Johnson's reelection campaign he had ran an ad showing a child with a daisy. An atomic bomb was detonated as the caption "Its just another weapon..." was displayed. Its effects were devastating to Barry Goldwater's political campaign.

Many in modern history still remembered the Cold War. Even more were familiar with the break up of the Soviet Empire. The opening up and tearing down of the Berlin Wall and other events. There were those who had argued that Christians played a critical role. Romania was often cited as an example.

In December of 1989 the Nicolae Ceausescu government was in trouble. The people were starving for freedom, for reform, and literally for food. Things were so bad that Ceausescu began to realize the depths of malnutrition and misery of the people and considered stepping down.

Public demonstrations in Timisoara on December 16-17 protested the exile of the Rev. Laszlo and the state of misery. Tanks filled the streets. By the 20th, 50,000 assembled in spite of the army presence. Throughout Romania, 161 people had died by the 22nd. General Vagile Milea refused to order soldiers to fire on the demonstrators, and was executed. On that day,

December 22, orders were given to end the demonstrations, regardless of the human cost.

In Bucharest, the soldiers again began to fire on the praying and singing masses. People fell, young and old. At that point, it was said that one old woman told the soldiers that they were killing their mothers, sisters, and daughters. The army broke, the massacre ended, and Ceausescu fell. With the blood of 1,104 of her people Romania had bought her liberty.

As the pilots came to the Basilica, several saw the child as well. When the old pilot, Whitmore Hana was to have given the order for his squadron to begin the attack, he instead ordered them to abort the mission. His squadron aborted. Subsequent waves refused to fire, and the air waves filled with group commanders ordering them to fire or face court martial. Spenard cut them off. He ordered the craft to attack only military targets. After strafing and bombing rebel positions around Ft. McHenry they returned to base. Lyberte and Walden ordered Spenard executed.

The other strikes of that morning and afternoon fared little better. Several did not even get off the ground. General Emery-Mills sought confirmation from Clinton, not yet aware that he was no longer alive. She did not order her planes off the ground to attack St. Louis. General Rupert in San Francisco took the same route and did not attack Los Angeles. In Bridgeport, the attack on Boston was aborted, General Anderson refused to obey the order.

Aircraft took off from Ft. Smith redirected to St. Louis, instead of Indianapolis but the command was not totally obeyed. Aircraft limited their attacks to factories, river transport and railroads. Only the aircraft from Pittsburgh carried out their mission, a 1:00 P.M. attack on Chicago.

Chicago was a city of rutty, often dirt streets, and buildings packed like sardines. Historically, Chicago was to have been torched by a massive fire on October 8, 1871. With inadequate fire control and a logistical mayhem, an area of three square miles was destroyed. One third of the population, or 100,000 were made homeless, 250 died, and 18,000 buildings ceased to exist.

Now, eight years earlier, Coalition planes arrived at the mouth of the Chicago River. On packing plants, ship yards, factories and businesses they rained their fire. Forming two semicircles, one north along the Milwaukee River, the other almost to the Kinnackinnic River, they rejoined over Lake

Michigan. They left behind two firestorms in the city built on an old swamp. A fire department adequate to meet even a small emergency did not exist. No Civil Defense plan existed either. All Chicago had was the heroic courage of her people to help stem the panic and dispair.

People fled to the lakefront to escape the inferno. There, over 80,000 trapped residents huddled together and prayed. Within sight were nearly three dozen transport vessels that had been seized by the Coalition. They could have rescued thousands, but made no move. North of the Chicago River the heat was so intense that nearly 20,000 trapped people died. In total, death claimed over 30,000 inhabitants.

When reports of the attack on Chicago reached New York, now General Nelson Lund took the news in person to some celebrity detainees. He mocked Rev. Morgan Dix and Mayor George Opdyhe asking "where was your God when Chicago perished?" Dix replied "He wasn't in your planes dropping bombs." Lund walked out in a rage.

Walden and Lyberte were quickly making plans for more raids. They also were pondering on how to replace several insubordinate commanders. The news of the mutiny put them in a position of having to retake command of several bases.

The transport of the detainees from New England to New York was completed by 10:30 A.M. as the last convoy arrived from Connecticut. But elsewhere results were not as good. In Detroit, Col. Lilly Penbrook refused to obey the order. Despite news blackouts, censorship, and carefully worded news releases, rumors were leaking out. From Memphis, reports of a massacre of over 500 prisoners had gotten out. In reality, only 36 had died in an attempted prison break. But throughout the nation a score of base commanders had heard, and refused to send their detainees to the collection points. They were joined in opposition by many of the civil rights and special interest groups, especially as news of Clinton's death filtered out that afternoon.

Walden ordered an immediate replacement for Penbrook in Detroit, Colonel Jamul Fresno from Annapolis. He was due to arrive at 3:00 P.M. But Penbrook learned of this. Having heard of the execution of Spenard, she believed that would be her fate as well.

Rumors of plans to destroy Detroit also were rife. With the city leaders all in detention or under house arrest the civilian population was virtually helpless. Any such attack would leave thousands dead. She did not want that on her head. Meeting with her subordinates, she found them in consensus with her. As they met, a crowd of Detroit residents had come together to petition her for the safety of their city and release of the prisoners.

In other communities, such assemblies would be fired upon. But Penbrook ordered that unarmed citizens would not be fired upon. She hoped to redeem the past and not destroy it. As Fresno's chopper neared the city the crowd began to circle the makeshift runway. When the chopper landed they linked hands in an unbroken ring. Again, Penbrook refused to order her forces to fire.

Fresno, however had no such scruples. If the past refused to be rewritten, it must be erased. The chopper opened fire killing and wounding more than 30 unarmed men, women, and children. As his men walked over the bodies, he ordered Penbrook to clear the runway for other craft to land.

From the detention center several of the prisoners were able to watch. Asa Gray viewed from the window and relayed events to his friends. Fiske commented on the hopeless situation. "If there is a God" he pledged, and if we survive, I'll abandon Darwin and dedicate my life to Jesus." Sumner agreed, and Gray, in desperation and disillusionment cried out for God to save them.

Penbrook could face her own death for treason. But she could not face the death of thousands of unarmed people. She ordered her troops to disobey Fresno's orders. One of Fresno's men shot her he and demanded obedience to his orders. Instead, chaos took over. In the ensuing melee, Coalition against Coalition, Fresno and his force was wiped out. A helicopter and a transport were shot down, and the rest returned to base in Washington. Of the 372 Coalition personnel in Detroit. 149 were dead and the rest defected. Prisoners were released. And true to their word, Fiske and Sumner got religion.

In Bridgeport, General Anderson refused to relinquish his command. This base was critical to the Coalition and it could ill afford to lose it. But the besieged Anderson realized that death was virtually inevitable. He would not go down without a fight, but he could not rely on his base to support his decision against such overwhelming odds. He needed some allies.

Sometimes history hinges on armies, sometimes on single men or women. Jeffrey "Spike" Bernalillo was captain over 186 Air Force personnel. He was Hispanic, but his family had a long military tradition. Rallying anyone who would listen he cried out "My great-great grandfather fought with Roosevelt in Cuba, my great grandfather with Pershing in World War I. My grandfather served in the Pacific in World War II. Some of your ancestors have fought for our nation. We are Americans, it is time to defend our country." Almost the whole base rallied, including all the nearly 800 Hispanics. As Coalition loyalist forces began to arrive, they were driven back with considerable loss of life.

With his base behind him, Anderson then ordered all bases in New England and New York to resist orders from Washington. Buffalo, Portland, and Burlington all sided with Anderson. But A.T.F. head Brandi Syntax was in New York, keeping the base loyal. She ordered the immediate processing of the nearly 39,000 detainees now in the city to be sent to Hampton.

At 2:30 P.M. cargo space was available to haul the first 8,300 of them. Included in this first installment were Elizabeth Stanton, Susan Anthony, Stowe, and other women's leaders. So also was Rev. Dix, Mayor Opdyke, and George Templeton Strong. As the planes were being loaded, Syntax had a visitor, ex-Governor Horatio Seymour.

As a Peace Democrat or "Copper Head", Seymour had been a great source of discomfort for Lincoln. When earlier that year Lincoln had sought to arrest Ohio Congressman and fellow "Copperhead" Vallandigham, Seymour was instrumental in aiding him. Had history continued, he would have helped Vallandigham escape to Canada as well. When the Coalition, with Democrat leadership, came to America, he had at first offered his aid. But finding too great of a gap between his beliefs and those of the Coalition, he withdrew from the public arena. Now, as a crisis loomed ominously, he saw an opportunity for a legacy of his own.

In negotiations with Syntax, he offered his support in bringing stability to New York and New England. With his immense popularity in New York City itself, he had much to offer. And the reality of rebel armies forming all around the city was common knowledge. He would use his influence to negotiate peace. In return, he asked for the release of the detainees into his, and federal hands.

But Syntax was a bureaucrat, not a diplomat. Her orders were clear, to cripple American resistance, and that meant leadership as well. She had not risen through the ranks to agency leadership by thinking or rationalizing, but by obeying. Seymour was leadership. He was arrested and put on the first plane bound for Hampton.

With his air units still intact, Anderson decided to move against New York City. At 3:20 P.M. his fighters began to arrive over the city. The first transports with 1,700 prisoners had already taken off for Hampton, with Seymour, Stanton, and the other leaders. The fighters tried to force them to land, but to no avail. But others led an assault on Coalition headquarters on Manhattan Island. Bernalillo had volunteered to be in the first wave.

In the Bronx, Syntax and Lund had hoped their very limited antiaircraft capabilities could halt any attack from the east or north. Several in the ground crews were natives of 21st century New York City, and one traced ancestry to Seymour. Fearing a blood bath and a destruction of their city, they revolted. The missile launchers never fired.

Within minutes, Bernalillo had established a solid base in the city and others began to pour in. Lund ordered his units to retreat to the naval base in the Hudson Bay. His forces had been unable to destroy any of the city in their retreat, but they did set explosives around the detention center in Central Park. Bernalillo and 31 of his fellow Hispanics worked, frantically to disarm them. Before they were able to complete the job, one charge detonated killing him and half his men. But the sacrifice saved all but 88 of the prisoners. Several survivors, including Samuel Chase, Edwin Stanton, and William Seward (Lincoln's Secretaries of Treasury, War, and State) heard one of the dying men speaking Spanish. At first they thought Mexico had sent the men that saved their lives. And in the case of 17 of them they were right. The three resolved to repay a debt of gratitude to the Mexican people.

For Lund and Syntax, their only real option was to flee to the assorted ships in the harbor. But three of the Coalition vessels, two destroyers and a frigate refused to take boarders. When efforts were made to compel them, they opened fire on the fleeing Coalitioners. Many of the survivors of a once 13,000 sized force began to board maritime and Union vessels in the harbor, and by 4:30 many had begun to leave the harbor area.

Anderson's forces did not interfere as over the next hour the entire force departed. When asked why not, he replied that he wanted them far enough out to prevent their return. At 4:55 he struck, and within moments every vessel in the convoy was sunk. Fewer than 300 survivors made it to shore. Both Lund and Syntax perished.

For England and Europe, the deadline for their ultimatum had passed without Coalition response. Efforts to raise a response through the Vatican were unsuccessful. But it was apparent that something was going terribly wrong for the Coalition. Lord Evergreen (Palmerston) at 3:00 P.M. sent a note to whoever was in charge that at midnight a state of war would exist between England and Europe against the Coalition. Again he received no reply.

In America, turmoil now reigned. At Bonneville, Emery-Mills was a classic case all in herself. At first she had believed Clinton had given the order to attack. Believing him incapable of such an order, she sought verification. But out of her deep affection for the man she did not want to disappoint or disobey his orders. She had planes readied for a confirmation that never came. Her aircraft waited on the runway until 1:00 P.M. (Washington Time). Ordering them to stand down she promptly changed her mind to order an attack on Washington to save Clinton. She believed he was still alive at that time. But before they got off the ground he was confirmed dead. She aborted the mission, but left them lined up on the runway just in case.

In New Orleans and Pittsburgh, aircraft were hastily and improperly rearmed and refueled for attacks on Bonneville and San Francisco. Several were lost in flight due to mechanical failures. With the new Coalition policy, their crews did not have a high survival rate when captured.

The force that made it to Bonneville met with great success. An overzealous attack squad set most of the aircraft on the runway ablaze. The invasion force quickly retook the base and found a number of personnel still loyal. Emery-Mills career, and life, were ended. But, in the process of recapture, the aviation fuel depot was destroyed, grounding all air units.

Over California the force from New Orleans was repulsed. With ranks seriously diminished, the survivors returned to New Orleans. An open revolt was in process there as well, and they barely kept the base in Coalition hands, strafing and bombing their own people. Losses on the ground were heavy and the air base rendered barely functional.

Memphis, Nashville, and Jacksonville declared strict neutrality. General Cody Newcastle from Jacksonville took overall command of these bases. A spirit of apprehension had taken hold of Coalition leaders nationwide. By 4:30 P.M. only a handful of bases were still loyal, almost all in the

Pennsylvania to Virginia corridor. Over 90,000 Coalition members had perished in the infighting, and only about 155,000 were still loyal. Vulnerable Comstock and Black Hills bases were searching for protection from wherever it could be found.

By midnight the Black Hills mines were in Grant's hands. Loyal naval units had only Seattle, Hampton, and for now, New Orleans to moor at.

At Hampton, 1,700 prisoners from New York joined 21,500 others brought in from the south. Among them was Hannibal Hamlin and William Lloyd Garrison. Both had made peace with their God and were ready to accept whatever lot fell upon them. But the former vice president vowed to Garrison that if he survived he would honor the famous abolitionist with two Constitutional Amendments. One would forbid slavery, the other would recognize Christianity as the sanctioned religion of America.

The area around Hampton and Newport had been sealed off due to the growing dangers. Civilians were forced to leave their homes and most of their possessions. The same was true for Washington. In Bonneville, new base commander, General Chipley no sooner took power than he also sealed off the base area. But he took one more step as well. He offered amnesty to all Coalition defectors. The Mormon community also approached him seeking terms of harmony.

In Washington, Patterson-Roberta (assumed dead by Lyberte) came out of hiding. Producing a forged release document, she was able to rescue Daschle before he was taken to Hampton. With her "Charles VII" she could not accept that all was lost. If she could address the nation, she believed, the scattered Coalition would rally to his side.

At 5:00 P.M., he was able to make a nationwide appeal. His first order was for amnesty for all Coalition deserters, and all 19th century detainees except felons. Bonneville and other bases were elated, and nationwide almost 200,000 Coalition personnel began, as best possible, to reestablish contact with Washington.

But Lyberte and Walden were not about to let power slip from their hands. At 5:40 they were able to isolate Daschle's and Patterson-Roberta's location. Ordering this surrender, they refused. A flame thrower then filled their room with fire. Joan of Arc again was martyred, but this time her king was also martyred with her.

In Hampton "Hawk" Taylor was ordered to begin the "final solution" of the detainee problem. One final appeal was made to the Women's Rights leaders to accept Coalition beliefs. Both Emily S. List and Connie Dumm (NOW and P.P.C.) were on hand to make one last plea. Stowe replied "What standards? In the name of your rights you have taken them away from everyone." Anthony also responded "Our goal is to elevate all that is good and noble in womanhood, yours is to desecrate it". In righteous disgust List retorted, "You are not of us" and ordered them sent to be executed.

But as they were being led off, the voice of Daschle came over the radio. The guards let them go, and began to empty the cells of the thousands of others. General Taylor urgently contacted Washington to see who was in control and what policies were in effect. Before he could obtain an answer most of the detainees had been released, and Gov. Seymour had taken responsibility to get Lincoln's men (Hamlin, Newton, Smith and others) to safety and the rest to cover. Orders to restore the directive of death were ignored, and the base turned into a war zone. In a paranoid frenzy of blood letting fewer than 1,000 loyalists escaped towards Washington on two warships. Behind, they left 32 other Coalition naval vessels, some aircraft, and a base full of weapons and supplies.

Hamlin, at 6:30 P.M., declared "Today, Sunday, July 5, is our second Day of Independence ... On this day, a new birth of liberty was won, and under God, the government of the people, by the people, and for the people, shall not perish from the earth." This victory was won over a people seven score and four years from the future.

From Washington, Lyberte and Walden were giving orders to bases and armies that no longer existed. As deserters made contact, whenever possible, they had them destroyed, adding heavily to the Coalition genocide of the day. Memphis was attacked at 7:00 P.M., General Douglas Prescott responded with all force at his (and Jacksonville's) disposal. A short time later Nashville was next in line.

The new reality of the situation was sinking in even in Lyberte's and Walden's closest advisors. New Orleans refused to respond to orders to attack or destroy any deserters. With the power melt down everyone was now trying to cut deals with everyone else. But Lyberte was not willing to give up. He had taken a taste of leadership, and he had liked what he tasted. He would not now willingly give it up.

But he was not alone. News hit the nation of Hamlin's return to his vice presidency, and according to the Constitution, in line for the presidency. Burnside threw his lot behind Hamlin. But Fremont also had enjoyed his taste of power. He now courted Lee, Hooker, and others to prop up his regime. He also was reaching out to disenfranchised Coalition groups, Trisean of FDA, and Durte of Agriculture among them.

Attorney General Ida B. Derapp sought to establish a power base of her own. Several special interest groups began to line up behind her. Other agencies and generals moved to establish power bases. It was as if a dozen politicians were stumping the primaries for delegates. But no one held much power, except Lyberte. And he still held 100,000 soldiers and loyal civilians.

At 7:00 P.M. he employed his security and monitoring capabilities to isolate almost all his local opponents. His agents simultaneously eliminated every cabinet or agency position except Treasury head Preston Cash and Sam Unella of Health. Along with them over 15,000 others perished. All remaining Coalition blocs began to line up behind Fremont.

But Fremont's base was far from secure. James Seddon, head of Fremont's army deferred to Lee. Lee in return, had been in contact with both Grant (now in South Dakota) and Hamlin. In a move to unify power and save the nation he officially reconciled the south with the north in the now emerging new republic. Also acknowledging Hamlin's constitutional claim to office, he offered his army to his command. Hamlin made Lee commander of all armies in the east, and Grant in the west.

The generals Halleck, Buell, and southerner Bragg immediately responded by giving their support to Fremont. In exchange he gave each a third of the nation to command with Bragg receiving the south. But Anderson placed his command under Hamlin, seriously damaging Fremont's credibility.

The final blow came from Europe. Fremont had claimed European support as the ultimatum had specifically named him as recognized leader. But Clavendish, as authorized spokesman for the Crown and Lord Evergreen responded with the phrase "or elected government". Hamlin was elected in 1860 and fulfilled that obligation. At 8:30 P.M., July 5, 1863 Taney swore him in as the nation's 17th president. America celebrated its new birth of freedom.

Seven Score and Four

Anderson was able to secure command of what was left of Hampton, and the aircraft carriers, Forrestall and Enterprise. Both were out to sea and of little value at the moment. But Walden and Lyberte still had the Constellation and a significant air force at Washington and Pittsburgh. Only with now a slightly larger air force Anderson was able to strike first.

As death and destruction rained on Lyberte it was apparent that his sanity was in doubt. He ordered a foolish strike against New York and Richmond by the Constellation, leaving the ship virtually defenseless. Anderson was able to sink her and the vessels with General Taylor and the surviving Hampton loyalists.

Hearing his ravings, Yorklyn in Pittsburgh ordered her forces to ignore orders from Washington. Corona went to church, confessed his sin and renounced his sex transplant. He found forgiveness and acceptance. The Coalition force surrendered to the city leaders. As they did so, Lyberte issued orders for a nuclear strike...

General Walden, realizing Lyberte's state tried to reason with him while at the same time hold control over a shrinking power base. Lyberte accused him of treason and shot him dead himself. With the bombs of Anderson's planes vibrating around him, he named Ann Junction of the ACLU as his successor, and Seattle the new Coalition capitol. She surrendered hours later while demanding humane treatment. But with the Carriers Coral Sea and Midway, Seattle held out alone, defiantly.

He dictated one final entry into the Coalition log, "We do not die, but only sleep. In due time we shall return, wiser and stronger than before. America, and the world do not yet understand, but a future world will revere us as martyrs. And when we arise anew we shall again take our stand against the dark evils of Christianity. And this time, we will prevail." At 12:15 A.M., July 6, 1863 a single revolver shot rang from the Capitol Building. Lyberte dropped the gun to the floor as he slumped over, dead.

For America, and the world, the repercussions and reflections would go on for many years. But history books would record that a great war was fought in America the result of it was an affirmation of two truths. One, all men were indeed created equal. And two there can be no future without God. America had paid dearly in blood to ratify both truths, and reconsecrated herself to the heritage of liberty.

Printed in the United States
26645LVS00003B/271-315